Praise for the N

NATUR

"For Robson, world-building is a literary device like ..., ...seful for exposing buried fears and desires to the light of day, no matter how strange the sun." —*New York Times Book Review*

"A thought-provoking SF stand-alone . . . Fans of the sweeping, politically and psychologically aware space opera of Iain M. Banks and Ken MacLeod will be intrigued by Robson's setting and the new slant she takes on universal questions." —*Publishers Weekly*

"What distinguishes *Natural History*, then, as with the other best examples of New Space Opera, is not that it reinvents the essentials of the form, but that it infuses those tropes with a political resonance and moral complexity, introduces major characters who can at once be deeply flawed and touching, and draws on genuinely provocative physics theory in place of the old hyperspace and FTL jargon. . . . The novel lives in its brilliant details and its often beautifully crafted language." —*Locus*

"[Robson's] strongest novel yet, reminiscent of Moorcock, Banks, M. John Harrison and MacLeod, and should assure her position as being one of the most exciting genre writers at this present time . . . Her characters are closely portrayed and wonderfully believable, yet she never takes an easy route. She is able to defy the expectations of the reader and to carefully dissect the standard assumptions of the reader. Lyrical and full of a sense of wonder, this is the highlight of the year."
—*SFRevu*

"With a clean, powerful narrative drive and a cosmological sensibility, [Robson's] clarity of vision now demonstrates itself as her major asset, making her one of the very best of the new British SF writers."
—*Guardian*

"Interesting characters and a nice weave of plot threads; the background involves everything from Solar politics and the ethics of genetic engineering to trans-dimensional travel in line with current theoretical physics, and the properties of Stuff. Slim volume, deep ideas." —*San Diego Union-Tribune*

"A bold mix of space opera, evolutionary growth and string theory . . . *Natural History* grows in wonder and interest as Robson builds her story of a post-human world." —*Denver Post*

"[Robson] has really hit her stride here. It's space opera for adults, with all the imponderables, shades of grey and equivocal responses that implies." —thealienonline.net

MAPPA MUNDI

"Once in a great while you stumble upon a book that gets a firm grip on your imagination and just will not let go. Even when you are out—driving, eating in a restaurant, carrying on a conversation—you're thinking about that book, anxious to get back to find out what happens next. Enter into that restrictive list, *Mappa Mundi*."

—sfsite.com

"British literary sci-fi has a new star . . . ambitious, assured and visionary." —*SFX* magazine (Five stars out of five)

"Justina is a prodigious talent. . . . This is a gripping, often fairly bleak SF thriller that sustains pace and tension throughout. . . ."

—*Dreamwatch*

"*Mappa Mundi* . . . is a thought-provoking and intriguing work that confirms Robson's place as a major player in the current pool of British SF talent." —*SFRevu*

"This is cracking stuff, a helter-skelter of speculative science and transcendent SF. . . ." —*Vector*

SILVER SCREEN

"Idiosyncratic and unpredictable, *Silver Screen* is a well-told, compelling story tackling big ideas. Justina Robson's writing is an intriguing example of how and why science fiction is no longer merely generic but relevant to our scientific present. She manages to integrate the alarmingly futuristic with a firm grasp of the history of ideas—a novelist of real vision."

—Zadie Smith, bestselling author of *White Teeth*

"With *Silver Screen*, Justina Robson has found the perfect blend of excitement and thought-provoking concepts which lifts this novel far above the ordinary. Ideas and future trends are pitched with determined realism, doing what science fiction is supposed to do, and leave you thinking with considerable anxiety about the way we're heading."

—Peter T. Hamilton, author of *Pandora's Star*

Living
Next Door
to the God
of Love

Justina Robson

BANTAM BOOKS

LIVING NEXT DOOR TO THE GOD OF LOVE
A Bantam Spectra Book / April 2006

Published by Bantam Dell
A Division of Random House, Inc.
New York, New York

Book design by Virginia Norey

LIBRARY OF CONGRESS CATALOGUING-IN-PUBLICATION DATA
Robson Justina.
Living next door to the god of love / Justina Robson.
p.   cm.—(A Bantam spectra book)
ISBN-13: 978-0-553-58742-5
ISBN-10: 0-553-58742-0 (trade pbk.)
I. Title
PR6118.O28L585 2006
823'.92—dc22   2005056271

Printed in the United States of America
Published simultaneously in Canada

www.bantamdell.com

BVG   10 9 8 7 6 5 4 3 2 1

For Freda Warrington
Now, or never.

Acknowledgements

Thank you for editorial advice: Peter Lavery, Colin Murray, John Parker, Juliet Ulman. Where I took it I think it improved matters. Where I didn't take it, it's not your fault . . . ☺

Thanks for feedback to the readers of earlier and present versions: Stephanie Burgis, Tricia Sullivan, Peter F. Hamilton, Freda Warrington, Adam Roberts, Jack Womack and the Not So Quarterly Writers' Group of Brum.

For conversations that proved very useful, thanks to: Stephanie Burgis, Tamar Yellin, M. John Harrison, John Powell, the TTA Discussion Board group, Freda Warrington, Jenny Taylor, Becky Yarrow, Liz Fennell, Patrick Samphire, China Miéville, Tamsin Constable, Christopher Priest and Simon Kavanagh.

Thanks to Alicia Rasley at Alicia Rasley's Writers' Corner on the Internet. Her turborevision tips were very handy.

For handy hints on physics and for sending me interesting things about atmospheres, thanks to Jonas Wissting.

Thank you for supporting me through the many hours this took: Richard Fennell, Daniel Fennell, Ruth Robson, Eileen Thomas, Stephanie and Patrick Samphire, Freda and Gill Tavner.

Thank you a thousand times to Swedish fandom, especially the organizers of ConFuse and all at Science Fiction Bokhandeln in Stockholm for inviting me over to meet you: I had a wonderful, wonderful time. This book is partly for you all.

Have you ever wondered what it is like to be someone else?

Suppose there was an instant, a split second, in which you knew
what it was like for them. Completely.
You'd be them in that instant.
Everything would change.
You couldn't shut them out, edit, ignore what doesn't suit you,
Leaving it
Behind the skull's censor and the tongue's lies.

Now watch the face they gave you,
In the mirror of their eyes.

PART ONE

Metropolis, Earth, Sankhara

0/ Jalaeka: Metropolis

There's a kind of hush all over the world tonight: the sound of lovers in love. The rosy fug of it is so overpowering that I can't hear the special kind of silence I'm listening for; the one that will tell me I'm about to die.

It's long past midnight. From my premium vantage point on the top of the Syndicated DC Building I can see the whole of Manhattan before me, stretching north towards Central Park. Hoboken's bricktown lies over the water to my left, the brownstone weight of Brooklyn to my right, a rain-washed splendour of light and concrete. Its electrified pizzazz fades very suddenly into the murky gaslights and pillared mansions of Gotham. Gotham, seeded by trees in permanent winter coats of ice, shrouded eternally in mist seeping from the ground, ruled by wolves.

Staten Island simply does not exist. The rotting piles of an enormous, abandoned shipyard stand in its place, every stanchion and plank half as big again, in its way, as any human structure. I can smell the pitch on their vast timbers. The copper has long since oxidized to green on the signs that tell of ferry journeys to the Euphrates, the Tigris, the Congo, the Styx. No ship has ever moored there. They say that ghosts come and go over the water from its silent terminals, so in this world at least one charm is missing.

If charms ever had such power I'd be chanting charms like a machine gun spits bullets.

Behind me the wind blows fitfully from Gotham's worm-riddled Germanic spires. It smells of incense and twisted passions.

I like to visit but I couldn't live there, although some of my best friends do. It's popular with everyone young enough to play with death.

Two witches pass high over me on the way to Fifth Avenue. I can hear them chattering excitedly about some new restaurant down there. The wind abates after they've gone, as if someone flicked the switch on a fan. I'm glad it's stopped, it was making my flesh crawl.

I can't see anybody I'm looking for but I can feel them moving through the hidden walls of this world, searching for me. They're very close: one breath out of place and they'll taste my shadow, come swirling around the edge of the hydrogen atoms and sink their neutrino teeth right into me. My flesh is still crawling. So, not the wind—maybe they're actually under my skin.

I wish someone would hurry up and commit some felonies out here. Breaking and entry, robbery with violence, gang fights, pimps beating on their girls or boys—I'm not fussy, any of the standard moves would do. Anything to create a diversion.

A Batmobile cruises along Avenue of the Kryptonites. It's one of the early models, all white-wall tyres and fins. There's no rush for him: he's obeying the traffic signals and his jets aren't lit. I wonder where he's going to that he couldn't go as a Bruce Wayne. Maybe he's off to that bar the witches wanted to get into, where the good guys and the bad guys drink together, roll their sleeves and complain about the price of Active Spandex.

I've drunk with them plenty of times. We all get pleasant jaw ache recounting how many years you can go on getting beat up day after day before you have to retire and go home to Earth to watch your rocket boots gather dust. Of course I was lying to fit in, but that's not the point. Ennui is the fashion for heroes. Every fantasy loses its lustre in the end and nodding sagely about it is the consolation prize. Glory and approval are for neophytes, for whom every bar goes quiet and faces turn away. Old boys and girls are beyond that. They want something bigger, deeper, without knowing what it is. They want to taste immortality and feel its cold fingers close around their hearts, but the hearts themselves don't want to know.

I don't drink in those bars anymore. Whiskey isn't my drink and besides, they made me cry all night. Come to think of it, I really have listened to too much country-fusion since I've been here.

Ten million people live here and over 20 percent are heroes. They have to pay triple whack to get anyone to be a civil servant, and the service industry has created more millionaires than the stock market.

Two blocks over I can hear one of the Daredevils fighting some drugs gang. I tune in. He's being assisted by a Nomad, who seems more at home here than he ever was in his comic book. They're both tough guys. Very noble. I like their ideals, but we haven't got much time for each other. Eastside nobility are all trad. They don't trust those of us who were created from mongrel imaginations or primal source mythology. I'm supposed to despise them in turn as either old fogies or Johnny-come-latelys, depending on who they are, but I'd rather just watch them have their fun. I like to imagine that I belong, that we're all on the same side, whatever that is.

The drugs gang they've come to tackle are a bunch of Stuffie patsies moonlighting from their day jobs to provide a large enough criminal element to keep everyone happy. Nobody in Metropolis actually needs drugs for their highs. They've got the Engine.

It's almost 1:00 A.M. The traffic lights on Seventh and Kryptonites are changing red to green and back again, slashing the wet streets with liquid colour. As a Humvee of Nordic gods crosses the intersection, the signals all light up at once and Odin laughs, drunk as a skunk. He bellows a word and every lightbulb explodes in a great pop of sparks, showering the divine with plastic particles as they hoot and holler. Thor swings his hammer wildly and all the glass flies out of Tiffany's front windows. The gods swerve by, reach in for an armful of diamond trinkets and then burn rubber all the way to Central Park. I watch them briefly, then follow a Spiderman as he slings his way casually over to the rooftop gardens on the Time building for a meeting with some Maryjane. She's going to break off with him again because she's being blackmailed by a Joker who doesn't mind a bit of cross-world devilry. I just can't watch that. I can't bear to feel that lurch in his heart. It's so painful it makes me feel sick and the vertigo will pitch me into a fall.

Instead I make a desperate mental lunge and latch on to Vicky Vale #24 as she's building up the nerve to go into Arkham Asylum. She has a nice car, a Buick eight. And she's easy on the eye. She has augmented sensorimotor skills and, to help her nerves, she keeps on mentally building and rebuilding her Bulgari watch, using a bunch of imaginary tools small enough for leprechauns. The MekTek that's made her such a sharp little martial arts model has overwired her cortex, and she can never stay cool. She knows she's going to fumble her lines, and then looking like Veronica Lake isn't going to be enough to stop people from laughing slyly at her. She fears that more than a bullet.

I cut a few of the bad neural connections in her head. She stops what she's doing and looks down, trying to visualize those nonexistent cogs in her hand: the little diamonds she imagines on the watch mechanism are just like the diamonds Odin's wearing on his fist. She feels better, doesn't know why, only better. She thinks she might be okay. She says, "Is someone there?"

I have a little starburst of a heart with an arrow through it that I can use as a kind of calling card on these occasions. It came free with the body and the powers but it's so cheap and nasty I wouldn't soil her with it. I let her *feel* my presence, touch her. Her smile is as beautiful as a new day and more than I deserve.

She casts her eyes to the skies and prays to some god in thanks. I don't mind.

My kindness towards her relied on a lot of 7-dimensional trickery however, and it draws my pursuers directly to me. Helping Vicky was bound to have that effect though, I wasn't just making nice. I wish they'd hurry—the waiting is the worst part, so they say. Anyway, hard to class it as a kindness, more like a selfish interference. I'm sparing *myself* the pain of her suffering.

Plus, as long as I look at Vicky I don't have to see the fifty thousand human beings in my immediate area, their electromagnetic aural patterns, the shifting flows of their blood and hormones, the nonstop growth and change and juicy, potent bubbling foam of life's primordial forces pulsing through every last one of their cells in all its multi-molecular, transconscious glory. All that irrelevant shite is tasering my acuity.

The people, the Unity *agents* I'm interested in, don't have biocellular energy matrices. Within the 7-D they're less than shadow—empty vessels, owl silent and venom quick. They'll only assume shape and mass when they have to. But I'm forced to listen to romance and all that kiss-me-deadly drama, because it goes with the job and the material universe and the 4-D I'm hiding out in. I'm locked into it, just like Vicky here is locked into her chosen role as a plucky journalist with a weakness for men in armoured rubber. Unlike Vicky, I never wanted to surrender to the inner conflicts of my personality in full Technicolor, but in the 4-D of Metropolis there's no choice: you don the cape or you're out.

I'm trying to listen to the rain that washes the darkness where the Tiffany windows used to be. I can hear it trickling over the black casing on the broken traffic lights, two hundred metres down. I can hear it running off my night-black, frictionless and shiny polymer skin. Freak Heroes, as we're charmingly known, don't do costumes—physiology is enough.

Hero may be the wrong term.

My hunters are so close in the 7-D that I know for sure I'm sharing space with one of them, that they're moving through me in that tricky way they have of sneaking through matter. If I try to find out for sure, that's the end, because I'll have to look into the 7 and that would give it all away. Pretend I don't have any Seven-senses for this moment, and they might miss me. It's hard though, when they're inside. The itch is driving me crazy.

I stare around, desperate for distraction. To my left the slightly taller tower of Marvels Inc. shelters me from the prevailing wind. Multiple bomb holes have laced it uninhabitable from the twentieth floor upwards. It only stays up out of bloody-mindedness. Some of the holes go through into other universes, and I'm watching those carefully. Unity controls them all.

From the busy skies over Central Park a figure detaches and arrows in on me directly. She's got feathered wings and they work without mechanical support, so it takes her a while as she carefully dodges the big gusts coming in off the sea. She goes higher to get some vantage point on the way, and I can feel her gaze on my back like sunshine. Ardent glances are always hot. Hateful ones too. Temperature is a measure of how much energy a thing holds. She holds one hell of a lot.

She comes in to land beside me on my chilly ledge. The warmth, the smell and the white feathers are a dead giveaway, even though I recognized her immediately, and can't help the rush of gratitude and pleasure at seeing her. She comes to the edge and squats beside me, her wing-tips tickling me intentionally.

I'm immediately swept away into the heavenly blue of her gaze. She possesses an actively radiant goodness I've only ever come across in a very few heroes, and only once in a regular human being. You can't get away with all that grungy Han Solo shit in Tribeca, where she's from. It's an aspirational neighbour-hood. Right now her considerable glamour is all directed at me, and I can tell she's here hoping for more than a friendly hello.

Angel #5 only measures six-foot-seven including the halo. Next to her I feel colossal and automatically protective. I can hear the divine vibrations of her chakra system whirling, fu-elling that halo with the power to bring out the best in anybody she wants to charm. She's the only one of the Angels who isn't a moronically righteous son of a bitch, and if I weren't on watch for my life I'd sweep her off the building and take her out of this miserable spot and somewhere beautiful with no questions asked. I should tell her they're gunning for me and that therefore she's in mortal danger, but her halo power is too strong for my conscience. It lets me believe I am good, and then my sudden overconfidence makes me believe I can save her.

I curl my tail around her waist and tickle her in a private place with the tip. She licks the rain off my triceps. Because I'm frictionless, she can only feel me via pressure, and so she applies quite a lot of it. I can feel every taste-bud on her virtuous tongue, and so for her I make myself taste of honey, sweeter than wine.

"Hello Eros," she says, bathing me in her dizzying perfume of pure grace. There's nothing about her that isn't sinless, even her lust.

"Angel, you have to go." I grip her more tightly. I can feel Angel #5's love all over me, all inside me. Even if it weren't a casting rule of the Metropolis Universe Engine that I personally cannot act against any loving intent, it would be impossible to throw that adoration off, and nothing in me wants to do it. I want to stay here, inside her, forever.

The gnatlike itching at the edge of my awareness goes quiet.

Fuck, why now?

Out of pure fear I tear my face away from her regard and look around. Disoriented, my mind fishes the undertow of the world. In that instant I'm aware of all the billions of people who ever had the misfortune to come into contact with Unity. It and I are related, and I can hear their lost voices in its swirling depths. They rise and crash to nothing like waves on an endless shore.

If I want to have them, all their memories are mine, all their knowledge, all their hopes and dreams. Two-billion-plus species. Eighty-plus-thousand star systems. Eighty-plus teratonnes of knowledge and experience, tears, passions, joys and deaths. I can have it free, gratis and for *nada*—if I only let go and drop into Unity, if I let it eat me up. I will become one of those waves then. There may be moments when I return to myself. But if you do the maths, you can see how unlikely that is, and for how long it will last. Unity has no linear time, no awareness like a human one. It is the soft welcoming embrace of everness.

Just feeling the possibility is so hypnotically, mindfuckingly enticing I feel myself beginning to topple in. I'm tired of running and tired of the whole damn thing where I fight to stay free and it keeps on coming. It would be so easy . . .

Angel #5 collects a tear from my eye on the tip of her finger, and the spell breaks with her touch. I'm so grateful I kiss her, because it's the next thing I want to do, and if there has to be a last thing I do then I can't think of anything better than that.

She tugs my long hair playfully. She isn't dumb enough to let me look through her eyes in a direct stare, like I let her do to me for the first time just now, although I can see all her intentions even without doing that. I see what's in people's hearts clearer than I see my own night-black hand in front of my face.

"You don't want me to go," she says in her educated Southern accent, staring right into my soul. Uh-oh. My need to be close to her has let her get too close for her own good. She starts to realize that I haven't always been entirely straight with her. She sees, without understanding what it is that she's seeing, that I am not human but that I am not a Unity creation either. She starts to form a question and her delicate eyebrows begin to frown.

I wish she could be seeing something better. Looking at the inside of my soul must be akin to watching slasher horror—so it feels to me, anyway.

"You have to go!" I finally find my guts as her halo becomes diffuse with confusion, and I try to wrestle her bodily off the parapet. It's a no-contest and she goes easily, absorbing my energy. She falls a few metres and rises again with her arms folded definitively beneath her breasts, gold strands of ambrosial fragrance twisting off her like smoke. She hovers in front of me and fans me with a breeze that smells of Estée Lauder's Beautiful Springtime and a hint of the burned flesh of sinners in hell. Angel #5 fights Wing Tsun style and she accessorizes with a razor-sharp sense of irony.

I am utterly frozen with adoration. And . . .

"What's the matter?" she demands. When I don't answer she tries to compel me to reply by directing the interrogative beam of her halo at me, but I'm out beyond its reach.

The Unity agent within my space just noticed Angel #5 talking to nobody, making love to nobody, on this slaughterhouse roof. As have several other heroes currently out hoping for trouble.

Something strong, slender, like a thorn, tries to hook onto the inside of me. It searches for an opening through which it can transform me and remake my substance into ordinary Stuff.

The human heroes become wary, disgusted, intrigued and afraid, as they see my form flicker like a candleflame. They have no trouble identifying me once they know where to look. Even through all the Forging and the MekTek, humans are a bipolar gender species, and twelve-foot-tall naked hermaphrodites with demon tails mostly give them the heebie-jeebies. Some of them try and claim their whole costume and identity good/bad thing isn't linked to their sex lives but they're lying out their ass.

As Unity attempts to drag me into 7-space unsuccessfully and I try to think of any way to save Angel #5, one of the Silver Surfers floats past, idly leaning around the buildings. He's a MegaCity man but he's very keen on Angel #5—you rarely see him far from her. He whistles at her and she blesses him. He does a backflip with ecstasy and I look away.

Unity cannot eat me. I knew this before. That's how I knew there had to be another game on tonight—a poker hand of persuasion that will almost certainly suck Angel into its trouble. I still can't see the strategy though: what the hell is it going to do? Something very bad.

I try to disconnect its hold on me where it surrounds me in complete 11-dimensional stickiness, but the fucker is really tricky. Every transform in 7-space that I use to repel it takes too much time. It's faster on the draw than I am. It fights Wing Tsun style too, and when I break its grip it just gets a new one.

I suspected that this time it might try to finish me off. We've done the dance of all seven veils and there was no nice bedroom routine at the end of any of those, so now all that remains, if it's serious, is to go for the knockout in some way that doesn't involve eating me.

And then, at last, it shows me the gun.

There's a new wall around Metropolis through which I can't see, hear, feel, taste or touch anything on any level. The pinnacles of the Bates Motel range are winking out of my sight in the far distance and I can tell that the darkness falling over them isn't light being taken away—it's everything being taken away. Laughing and crying and joyful and hurting people are falling off my barometer by the hundred thousand and it's like I'm going emotionally blind. The Metropolis Engine is *undoing* the world.

I didn't think Unity would go this far, but obviously I'm wrong. This universe and everything in it will soon be over. In the time it takes my slow brain to figure this out the giant harbour is consumed by nothingness. A final shadow drapes Gotham. A curtain drifts gently across the top of the park, silent and blank.

I wrap the end of my tail around Angel #5's ankle, preparing to fling her, but I don't know where I can send her to. There really is nowhere, because their plan is simply to close Metropolis altogether, to end this 4-D, and me with it. If I stay fully 4-D I am dead; and if I try to go through the 7-D I can easily be smashed in the colossal gravitational tides that this destruction is creating. Desperation makes me hesitate. I think I can save myself through a complete 11-D shift, but she can't come with me. Well she can, but only through the same mechanism that I've fought against all my life, through the same mechanism by which Unity has become what it's become.

I can save her, if I eat her.

People who are eaten do not come back the same, if they

come back at all, and I'm not sure that ever happens. There's no time to think it through. I wish I could explain it to her, but all I can do is love her with all my heart.

"Eros?" Angel's cross with my stupid behaviour now, but ready to be friendly. She zaps my tail with a Purity charge, but, thanks to the literal rules of combat here, I don't have to let her go because I don't mean to hurt her.

That doesn't make it painless however. Her energy bolt seeks out the deaths on my conscience and burns me for all of them. I hiss at the horrible sensation but tighten my hold on her and snatch her back to me for one last instant.

Her face darkens with suspicion and she cries out angrily. Her blue eyes try to read my intentions, but I'm watching that wall of silence whip around both of us, watching the stupid glory of this place vanishing as time catches up with it and knots itself to an end. To her credit I can feel the shift in her emotion fix itself on steely determination as Angel #5 gets a bearing on what's going down.

My Vicky Vale is already the history of a world that will have no histories.

All of my friends, except Angel here, are dead. There are no more Angels.

I fling her through one of the holes in the Marvel building, one that leads to another world, maybe. I have no idea. It could simply be a hole with nothing behind it except a singularity and nothing in front of it but my bad decision, but there's not enough time to find out.

As she flies away from me at close to the speed of sound Angel opens her arms and her heart towards me. A sphere of white light emerges from the centre of her chest, so bright I have to close my eyes. The light hits me in the solar plexus. All Angel's power and dreams, the love and the anger she feels for me for not explaining why this is happening to her, bury themselves in my heart.

I spread my wings and fold myself inside them, into a new universe.

1/FRANCINE

" 'S'not like Ashley is even that nice a guy," Sula said, tipping the last of her Slingshot into her mouth and swallowing thoughtfully with only a slight wince. "I mean, he went out with Miki on all those not-really-cheating dates during your open-relationship phase."

"It was allowed," I said, looking at my empty glass. I had drunk three cocktails and was feeling pleasantly venomous with regard to Ashley; also brave, also sloshy.

"Don' defend him," Sula admonished me in a single slur. She signalled for another drink with a flourish of her perfectly manicured hand. (Oh the endless hours of preening we did and the money we spent just to keep up, not even winning, only staying in the game.)

She added without grammar, "Spent five bloody months doing that. Where it got you? Nothing."

"Nowhere," I agreed with drunk logic. I'd planned to tell her about several other men I'd had take an interest in me. I always planned to, but never got around to it, as if there was going to be a future time in which she wouldn't be surprised to find that her quiet and studious best mate had an alter ego whose agenda was a hundred times more out of control than she let on. Popular, cheerful, happy Sula was the defender and social saviour of quirky, geeky, quiet Francine, who'd rather hole up with an interface than face people all the time, head-on. Those were our professions at school, our stock-in-trade outside. But anyway, Ashley was an asshole, I had to admit it, although I hated to admit it because of the time and energy already wasted in being in love with him for so long and taking all the:

You could make more of yourself; and the
Why don't you dress more like Su; and the
I can't stand it when you start arguing; and the
Don' talk about the generation of Forged Class Orders and

other smart stuff in front of my parents, okay? They don't like
weird people; and especially the
  You look better when you smile.

"There comes a point when you stay because you've invested too heavily to face buying yourself out. You have to pay yourself back, with interest, and you pay everyone you know, in the currency of their dismay at your deceptions . . . And then, the gambling . . ."

"Francine!" Su shook me by the shoulder. "You're talking to yourself."

"I know," I said crossly, because I hadn't realized I was doing it. A jolt of fear at my own behaviour ricocheted off the inside of my sternum and it was so alarming that I giggled. Always the girls with the inappropriate laughs . . .

"Here, have a cocktail." Sula pushed another glass at me as the waiter came over and delivered two of the pretty yellow and orange drinks to our table. "God this'll finish my allowance. Never mind. I'll tell some sob story to Dad when he gets back from Ingeborg or whatever he's doing and that'll sort it out." She batted big eyelashes at me, grinning, and I watched the lights sparkle off her eye glitter with the cold beauty of frost. Sula twisted all men around her fingers, dazzled them with the flash of her inconstant eyes, the strange flicker of her attention that gave her commonplace engineered beauty an indefinable eroticism. I longed to have her power.

"I was seeing Roni Vance in secret and two days ago he came on to me and we had sex at school in the games lock-up," I said. It came out sounding a lot flatter and nastier than I intended. I didn't recognize my own voice.

In the mini-movie of me giving this speech I had been a lot more amusing. But now I've got the voice of the tougher and more real me who's been living inside Francine recently. She's my disappointed half, the part who wanted to feel warmth, see colour, hear the world as if it was an instrument she could play. She went out with her sign turned to say Open, had no door policy and . . . well, that Francine's not so nice now.

"Va-va Vance?" Sula gave him his classroom nickname. He was the sports teacher at our school, and by the way he dressed you could see he considered himself quite the hunk. He was good-looking, but around girls he had the careful attentiveness of a pit viper.

I'd thought . . . I don't know what I thought to be honest. There wasn't much thinking. Using him was like test-driving a disappointing sports car. It goes for sure, fast—and that's when you realize that not only haven't you got anywhere to go in it, there aren't even any roads out of town.

"He Va-va-vooms through it like a train," I said in a sudden need to explain, excuse, get free of the horrible gaze we were sharing that told me (contrary to my expectations) that Sula was *appalled*. She should be laughing. I want to make her laugh. I want to stop her staring at me as though I spat on god. I want to fabricate a joke, but the truth will do as it happens. "Va-va . . . and then he's like giving me all this *dross* about his girlfriend getting on his case while he wipes himself off on one of the basketball bibs." I took half my drink in one go. "It's the one at the bottom of the red pile, so don't be point guard next week."

"Frannie?" Sula said softly, her shock evident by the paling of her face.

She's not angry with me because she thinks I'm bad. She's distraught because she can see that . . . (and suddenly I can see that) . . . I'm hurt. Really hurt. I did it to myself and I don't know why.

I want to vomit on her lap but I don't. I pick up my Slingshot with easy grace and look at the shine on my chromed nails. I list a few of the boys in the senior year and a bunch of names she's never heard of, all men old enough to be one of our fathers. Well, if we had any idea who my father actually was. It's hard to say and, after the chromosomal tracking and filtering is all done does it really matter who's what? I have thirty fathers, all their strengths, none of their digressive mutations . . . and one mother, who spent all her student years designing me over and over on the page decades before I was born.

I tell her about the men's various styles, their habits, their ways, all of which involve dumping me in one way or another. I have a worldly air that is supposed to be sophisticated but somehow, although it is on other people, it's not on me. I tell her about Dix Clarke, the small-time LeedsGuide show host who picked me up last Tuesday with a lot of lines about how he liked intelligent girls and dropped me off at my house with a packet of candy and a thumbprint on my Abacand that gets me half price of whatever shit they're promoting this week, all in return for a hand job.

"Be glad they only show him from the waist up," I said, admiring my cool, my stony delivery of a nice line. It's bullshit. He was nothing out of the ordinary as far as I can remember, which isn't far, but I need to hate him—that sad, lonely, wretched, awful man who wanted me to cuddle him after. "He took my number. Didn't call. I call that rude."

"Frannie," Su was quieter now. She put her drink down. "Are you serious?" But she doesn't need the answer. Francine is always serious about whatever it is. "Are you okay?"

"You know what Darren calls me?" Darren is my mother's boyfriend. He lives with us, and has done for five years. He's big in the design of disposable tableware for spaceflight catering; ergonomic handles, nutritionally enhanced plastics, all that. "Hive Spawn. Because I'm like those Forged, to him. The ones that think and live inside machines. He has a thing about insects too, which makes *that* all the nicer. Allergic to bee-stings. You should see him when one comes in the house." I flip and flap my hands, dodge the imaginary bee, squeal like a kid and laugh. I want to die.

"Frannie."

"What?"

"You're scaring me." Su isn't drinking.

"Don't worry," I assure her. "I'm probably just acting out some desperate need for love. Not to mention issues at home; dingbat ex-model mother losing her looks and getting old, devious stepfather bent on social climbing into the stratospheric heights of county politics. Nobody who understands me. You could do me as a project in Psych in ten minutes." My self-pity made me nauseous.

"Here," Sula said sharply, taking two fluorescent tubes of Hydro out of her bag. She cracked the tops and handed me one as she tipped her head back and sucked the liquid out of hers. With a cough she flicked the empty tube onto the floor under the table, not even glancing to see if anybody noticed. She paused and closed her eyes as the soft drug brought on its temporary calming, alcohol-neutralizing glow.

"Do you hate me?" I knocked back my tube, tasting the sharp lime flavour, feeling the almost instant rush fade into a dreamy sense of princess-wellness in about two seconds.

"Of course not." Sula hesitated, then took a tissue out of her bag and wiped her eyes with it carefully, under the mascara line, blotting the moisture. She checked the white paper for smudges before she put it away. "But holy shit, Annie, you know how to drop the bloody bombshell. I'm the Slut With Problems. Me. Not you. You're the smart homework girl. You're the all-A girl who was going to do something extraordinary one day long after I was some big sassy momma eating brown rice and bringing up a thousand kids nobody else could be bothered to have . . . fuck!"

I can't stand looking at her face anymore. I get up, full of determination, and make for the Ladies. Inside the light is too bright and the tiles are too shiny. I lock myself into one of the cubicles, put the seat lid down, sit and open my bag. I've thought of this day a long time. Kind of surprised it's today.

I put the pathetic little first-aid numbing patch on the back of my left hand and trigger it. It probably won't go deep enough, but it's all that was in the medicine cabinet.

I yank a load of tissue out of the dispenser and spread that under my left hand, and some within easy reach of my right, balanced on the top of the paper-holder to keep it clean. I know if I think about this at all I won't do it. Four Slingshots is about enough to get there, not too many to make me shaky, and the

Hydro has taken off the worst of the motor-neuron interference from the alcohol. I've practiced with a piece of card dozens of times; hundreds of times with a stylus. A designer's knife is lot like that.

With my index finger I trace the outline of the Tab chip in the back of my hand and use an eye pencil to mark the corners. I overdo the pressure on the first pass and feel the blade snick into and drag the stupid chip, cutting its surface so that my vision instantly fogs up with red warnings from NorthNet, advising me that I may be experiencing technical difficulties with my Tabacand, telling me to get some advice on how to fix it and would I like to know about special offers on replacement models? I get NorthNet itself talking to me a second later. It speaks with the voice of an angel, Michael or Raphael, always gentle, as if it cared. And I used to confide in it, as if it cared.

"Francine? What are you doing?"

Leaving you, you stupid AI.

Oh god it hurts.

I look around the warning notices at what I'm doing, but it doesn't help much because everything is lost in a huge upwelling of blood. I put the blade down with a hand that can't stop shaking, pick up the first swab set and wipe the loose skin to the side, blotting the ooze at the same time; an action which is ten times more agonizing. Blinking away tears, I pick up my eyebrow tweezers, get a hold of the slippery fish scale of a chip and rip it out of my hand.

There's a black moment. I open my eyes and gasp with pain so awful that I pass out for a second or two. I'm dimly aware of my head hitting the wall on the way down and briefly I really do see stars. I thought that was just a saying.

I wake up on the tiles, my hand a hot, burning fury. The surgical patch that cost me two months' allowance is lying on the floor with me—I can see it on the white tile, yellow and flesh-coloured, face-down. I'm glad I didn't strip the backing off before because I could have ruined it. Now I grab it and peel it. I flip the skin flaps back into place over the wound and slap the patch on. Immediately the pain lessens to a bearable degree and I get up.

Everything is covered in smears of blood and the more I wipe it up with the cheap tissues the more it spreads around.

The chip itself, the Tab, which has connected me to North-Net and LeedsGuide and all the pearl-strung AIs of the Solarverse since I was six years old, is a square of gold, floppy at the edges and carrying the residue of my nerves, damaged as they are. I still have the skullware in my head naturally, but I won't be getting that out. And it won't work without the Tab. Well, people get it to work in spy films by using devious bodily infiltration robotics, but I don't think that's what the Police do here and I can't.

I feel very clear, very pure, suddenly weightless. The silence . . . hard to describe it. I didn't know the world was so empty. When I look at things the knowledge about them that used to sit behind my mind isn't there. The world has become meaningless, open wide, nothing to tell me where to go, what I can do, what I can't. If I think about this anymore, I'll become too scared to go on.

I take off my shoe and smash the Tab with the heel. It cracks and flattens on the white tile, becoming a pink and gold mess. I pick it up in another bit of tissue and flush it all away, then get out the can of NanoMom I brought with me for the purpose and clean up the cubicle. Maybe it's forensically good enough to cover my tracks and maybe it isn't, but I won't be here long enough to find out. I clean the can and my fingers and stuff the tissue and can into the bin. In my bag are my toiletries and the few bits of tradable stuff I could lift from home. At the last minute, I change my heels for running shoes.

My hand no longer hurts, it simply fizzes with the patch's work. I feel drunk and giddy on one level, but the queen of truant cool, who has been waiting a lifetime in the wings, takes her cue inside me. Out of the door, out of the toilets, along the club wall at a normal pace. I pretend to be Sula.

I'm smiling. It's impossible not to. I think I could fly.

Sula doesn't even see me as I circle around the back of her. Then I'm in the street, walking fast, like I've somewhere important to be, and for the first time I can remember there are no words or pictures superimposed on my vision, no voice in my head to tell me where I am. I glance left and right and no information appears. I look up, look down—nobody calls and I can't hear anything except the drizzle and the wash of water in the street as cars pass.

I start to run, don't mean to, just have to, and beneath every light and sign I say silently *sorry, sorry, sorry* to the Guide AIs, and to all my friends who can no longer hear me. Talking to the dead. But I'm the one who died.

As I pass the closed shop windows the holopeople in the adverts running on the glass stop their promotions and turn to watch me. They move into close shot and crane their necks to see me go. The ProHair lady with her mermaid curls waves uncertainly at me and I know it's really NorthNet, forsaken, looking through her useless eyes of light. I skip sideways and point myself at the street eyes above the storefronts and I wave as I skip, both arms overhead like I'm signalling aircraft or leading a cheer. *Good-bye. I said I was going. I wrote it in my diary to you, NNet, and you know, and you're going to let me go . . . I know.*

The dapper young man who puts his perfectly tailored suit jacket on a thousand times a day in the display window of Tinker Tailor, and a thousand unseen times in the night, leaves it hanging on the back of his chair and blows me a kiss.

I turn into a no-holo, eyeless street—St. Paul's—and slow down under the lights, barely recognizing anything without its overtype of map data. I make myself walk because I've got all the time in the world now that nobody and nothing knows where I am, or what, or who.

I need an out-of-state taxicab now. Sympathetic cabbies hang at certain locations—vendor pads where they park up to take a rest. If there are any of them willing to take an illegal passenger, they'll leave their doors unlocked. It's half an hour before most of the club-goers will be heading home, so there should be some cabs nearby.

I find the coffee bar on St. Paul's easily enough, and the taxi rank. Some of the cars are parked in bright light. They have their warning flashes bright on their flanks—*out of service, do not attempt entry*. They shock to stun.

In the darker areas outside the streetlights most of the taxis are similar. *No*, they say in Technicolor that even the un-Tabbed can read. NO. In fact, there's only one that displays nothing and has no driver. My heart sinks as I see its registration plates and billboard; it's an out-world taxi and it's from the Stuff Universe called Dindsenchas.

Dind is a historical Sidebar, devoted to all things Celtic, "the premier destination of the true Briton." Dind shops are full of hand-beaten gold and rough textiles, stinky cheeses and soil-caked old vegetables, pottery figurines of tough pre-domesticated pigs and bags of strange dried herbs. I don't want to go there and live by farming the land and riding around on a horse like a peasant of old, which is what I will be. Or worse.

But you have to be prepared to go anywhere to get out of range of your home Guide and away from obvious trails. North-Net wouldn't stand in the way of a police pickup if they found me, no matter how deep we were down with each other.

There are two officers standing at the coffee-house door-way, chatting. One of them is a Tek, all armour plate and rocket packs. I walk past. That's it. I can't go past again or they'll suspect. But I can't face Dindsenchas. My mother is into all that Faerie and Celt stuff. She collects figurines and has her runes cast once a week. It would be like getting stuck in our living room forever.

I keep walking. Crap. Now what am I going to do? Hang and hope the cops move? Sod's Law says they won't. I dawdle as much as I can without looking like I don't know what I'm doing.

To my right in a narrow alley the minor streetlights flicker suddenly, as though they were lanterns blown in a sudden gust of wind: signals. I automatically look that way. One of the lights winks again. There, half on the pavement and half off, is a taxi.

The sound of a car on the main street seems too loud and acute suddenly, the swish of its tyres on the wet road hissing like it's trying to call me back from a dangerous mis-step. The taxi's plate says Sankhara.

Sankhara is as frightening as Dindsenchas is boring. It's a High Interaction Universe, although I can't remember much more about it than that. Sankhara is quite a long way out from here—a hundred miles overland to the Gateway, plus who knows how many light-years after that? I have no idea what it's really like, but I remember watching a documentary about it once with Mom's boyfriend, Darren. He turned it off after five minutes, saying, "Bloody lunatics. What do they want to go and live there for? Asking for it. Alien shit. Cuh."

So it'll do.

The car is dark. I tap the lid of the trunk on its sensor strip and it opens. I glance back towards the coffee shop and see two shadows approaching along the pavement. One is bulky and tall—Tek. I drop into the trunk and close the lid. It shuts silently then an interior light comes on, a tiny glow.

"This taxi's next destination is Actaeon Parkway, Sankhara," the taxi AI told me in precise English with a strange accent. "If you, illegal person of no means, do not wish to enter Sankhara, please exit now. Journey time will be fifty-one minutes and fifty-eight seconds. This message and your travel have been sponsored by the Free Agents of Infinite Time. Please remember, and give generously."

The light dimmed and went out. I had to put my hand over my mouth to stop myself laughing. It had never occurred to me that the refugee underground was a commercial enterprise. Who in Solaverse were the Free Agents of Infinite Time?

I didn't laugh long. Rain beat on the lid. It was very quiet. The car was well looked after. Its tough nylon fabrics were hard and scratchy and hot, but not dirty. After a while I got used to being curled up and found a way of resting my head on my arm.

When the journey finally started I ignored the pang in my chest where I took the bullet of Sula's hurt, and concentrated on the soft, floaty suspension rocking me. I fell asleep soon after I tried to count the junctions we stopped at on the M62 motorway, picking up cars in our snaking landtrain. And that was it. Really pretty easy, for leaving life behind; disappointing that nothing came after me, that instantly I missed none of the things that had filled my waking days before this moment.

2/JALAEKA

The Infinite Strand—that straight stretch of shore-line between Desolation and Unforgettable Beach—was always marked with wreckage. Most of it was of the usual kind, pots and boxes, barrels and crates of wood and leather broken by the ferocity of the offshore currents and vomited onto the edge of civilization like so much bad food. Occasionally a metal con-tainer came intact and sank into the soft sucking mud of the shallow bay, but it wasn't this that interested me.

I was watching a Stuffie. Most of Sankhara was populated by Stuffies of one sort or another. The 4-D fabric of the world was built of Stuff, everything, every person and animal, except for the immigrating humans who had come here from the Sol uni-verse. But this one was unusual. Stuffies of Sankhara and the other Sidebars were isolated from Unity. Locked into the ordi-nary constraints of 4-D living like the humans. Architecture and geography insensible. Vegetable awareness barely a shim-mer. Animal senses no wider than their doppelgänger range permitted. And other beings, magical or otherwise, all shut away from Unity into the lockbox of linear time and single-minded awareness. Not him though. He was like me, a little. He could see Stuff. He knew what he was made of and like me he could trawl the awareness of the human race, tracking their thoughts like a hunter on the trail of easy prey.

As I watched him do what I'd sworn off forever, I was struck with longing so fierce it hurt like a knife blade under the ribs.

I'd first noticed him purely by accident as I sat overlooking the early-morning ocean. He had come along the beach, combing the tideline with slowed footsteps and a bowed head, dredging the sleep of the human booty who lived in tents at the strand's end. I saw the humans changing, stirring in their unquiet dreams as the images and thoughts darted out of their heads; shoals into his net. And I knew him then for what he was, a part of the Sankhara Engine itself.

He was strong and young, light and agile as only creatures of his race could be, but more than usually alert. Once he had pulled himself carefully onto the hard, cold steel frame of the container he had coveted he sat down and looked about him for signs of sea snakes, the Ootoo, whose beautiful voices could sing him to sleep before he had a chance to run away.

There was one not far away, its silvery and tourmaline scales shining in the gentle morning sunlight, but the tide was out and it was in danger of beaching itself if it came for him, so he turned his back to it and placed his hands down on the heavy hinges of the container's sky-facing door.

Confident he would not notice me, I walked to the edge of the high cliff and jumped down into a deep tidal pool, soaking up its fatal impact energy and using it to warm me as I swam out towards him through the cold currents. I drifted there and watched, transfixed by the sight of another Stuff anomaly—the only one I had ever known before being that Paladin of Unity, Theodore, killer of my friends, destroyer of worlds.

Cool, grey water furled and foamed around a metre below the elf but he didn't mind water, nor beasts, nor anything much that would have worried a human beachcomber. From the tips of his long, pointed ears to the soles of his enchanted boots he manifested restlessness, anxiety and determination. I watched him immerse his attention into the locks, the substance of the metal container itself. He persuaded certain strong bonds to change their strength and shape . . . he asked it to become brittle, to wither and become fine like ashes. Because he had the Engine's mandate and some of Stuff's immeasurable powers granted to him, the steel obeyed him. It snatched oxygen from the air, crumbled under his fingers like dry biscuit and fell into the sea where it stained the water brown and red.

The elf slid away from his post and back into the shallow water, treading it at a safe distance as he heated the seawater inside the container enough to create a sufficient pressure differential to fling the door open in a single blast of steam. Concentrating so hard was exhausting, and climbing up the side and into the hot container must have been unpleasant but he went to it with nervy grace. I swam closer, ignoring the Ootoo, which, after a brief attempt at serenading me, followed a more interesting vibration into deeper water.

He had found sugar, but not the kind that sweetened tea. This kind of sugar was deadly material and the trade in it within the precincts of the city was ferocious and lucrative. Candygirls could ingest it and convert it into alchemical drugs. They could manufacture almost any biochemical compound from it, and many with the pseudo-magical properties that made Sankhara the playground for the daring and suicidal. Candygirl sweets were almost guaranteed to contain enough Stuff interactions to send any Solar human over the side into Translation, the cells and molecules of their bodies slowly converting over time into Stuff itself, until they had painlessly bled away into its alien continuum. They were highly prized in spite of, and because of, this danger. I couldn't understand what this Engine sprite wanted with it though . . . his obsessive stuffing of the packs into his bag, risking his life, was fascinating. I thought I would follow him.

Then the weight of his body and the continued refilling by the sea through the container's various loose joints told on its position. The pile of slippery packages shifted under him as the whole container tipped a few degrees and, with a tug of one particularly large wave, settled much more deeply into the velvety soft silts beneath it. He stuffed two more packs into his bag and clipped it shut, leaped up to catch the rim of the doorway with his fingers, and missed.

He landed unluckily and packets slid from under him, making him twist his knee and stumble into the lowest corner. The sea boomed against the side of the container and the liquid mud took another gulp. The top of the container where it leant lowest slid below the waterline and a thick torrent of hungry ocean seethed eagerly down on top of his head. He was strong but hardly invulnerable, able but mortal. Maybe the Engine would remake him, I thought, if he died here. Maybe not. Stuff wasn't known for restoration.

The elf braced himself against the container wall and waited for the water to fill up the empty space but the uneven angle was increasing rapidly as the weight tipped the heavy box over onto its side.

The Ootoo, attracted by the vibrations and the curious sounds of the container's fall, returned from deep water. I heard his angry prayer to the Engine, trying to summon its occasional mercy.

He asked for a gift of Banishing, begged it to consume the Ootoo, let him escape the humiliation of ending this way. He begged for intercession, debased himself, promised his slavery . . . eternally, but the Engine did not turn for him. He began to drown.

The problem of a Stuffverse is that I can't do anything to it, like I could to normal matter, not without summoning the attention of Theo's ever-vigilant pack of hounds.

The Ootoo's song had sent the elf to sleep. Water filled his lungs.

By any sensible margin I should let him drown.

I shockwaved the Ootoo into unconsciousness—it was no more able to resist a precision pressure wave than any other living creature—then dove past it. I swam forward to the elf's floating body, grabbed the tough fabric of his tunic and pulled him rapidly up to the surface, where I towed him towards the beach.

In the shallows I was able to get my footing on soft sand instead of muddy fines. Using the basic first aid of my long years in worlds where medicine was unknown, I turned him on his stomach and pumped his lungs out, trying not to crack his ribs. He vomited, coughed and lay panting there for a minute. I watched him get to his hands and knees, then sit back on his heels.

He turned to look at me and his glance, ready to be grateful, became the long stare of the unbeliever. At first surprise, then incredulity, then a strange, canny smile crossed his features. His emerald eyes narrowed slightly and even a child could have seen that he was thinking fast. I found a ridiculous grin on my face.

"Wha—" he began but got no further, his mouth hanging open as he tried so hard to see what I was made of.

"I know," I said, deliberately misinterpreting his confusion. "This hero shit is really addictive. Sorry. I should already have run away, but I missed my cue."

"What *are* you?"

I put my hand out to him. He looked at it for a moment, then took it and pulled himself to his feet. "Jalaeka."

"Damien," he said.

I cracked up laughing.

"What?"

"Nothing."

"It could have been worse!" he objected, a grin stretching across his agile face and making it wicked. He started to laugh too. "Steve . . . Bobby . . ."

"Damien the elf!" I repeated, catching my breath and biting my lips to try and stop.

"It's not that funny."

"No. Okay."

"You don't even have a proper name . . ." he said. "Or a . . .. what did you say you were?"

"I didn't," I said. "Shall we go and dry out, get a drink?"

"You're buying," he said with a shrug. His eyes glowed, literally, as a natural streak of roguish bravado emerged. "Where's my pack, then?"

I picked it off the sand and held it out to him. He took it, briefly inspected the contents, and slung it onto his shoulder. His glance as he looked back left me in no doubt that I had met with his approval—more than that. "Been here long?"

A pang of hunger ran through me. "Ten days."

"Ahhh!" His smile this time stretched almost to his ears. "That explains it."

"Explains what?"

He looked me up and down, slowly. "I'll show you after . . ." He made a drinking gesture and beckoned, coughing and spitting a final bit of seawater. "Come on."

 # 3/FRANCINE

Two months later . . .

It was raining salt water again. I could taste it when I licked it from the back of my hand. It fell on me gently from a grey sky that was soft, like a blanket placed over your face to hide you, but you can see light through it. There wasn't any breeze, even off the sea. Ludo, the leader of our happy band of moronic dreamers, said this morning that we were in a depression and laughed about it, like the old joke hasn't worn thin on him yet. Maybe after a billion repeats it gets funny again.

I kept going along the length of the boardwalk, handing out leaflets. They were going soggy, and the few people who passed me were all turned in on themselves because of the weather. After another fifteen minutes had crawled by, and nobody showed any signs of interest in the Love Foundation (and it would have been pretty difficult for them, because I wasn't exactly the enthusiastic convert), I took myself out to the end of the pier and leant out over the ornate iron railings. The tide was in.

Lonely, depressed, unfulfilled? the violet papers said hopefully.

I let them go and they separated out as they fell, like giant leaves, down and down onto the surface of the waves. Hey—it's a purple autumn this year in the kingdoms of the socially dead . . .

The sea refused to take them away.

I figured that for fair: after all, the sea in Sankhara wasn't unfulfilled. It was too full of sacred whales, oceangoing dragons, spellbinding Ootoo, pirate treasure, lockers of the ancient dead, tribes of merpeople and Forged research submarine bases for that. And it was already too salty to care about the rain anyway. At least the fish would enjoy eating the Foundation's words. The Foundation got them printed on premium biodegradable rice paper, vitamin-enriched, so that if any of them *were* to end up in the trash (heaven forfend), then they'd be food for the wildlife.

Best place for them, I thought—shit to shit.

I ran back down the pier and turned onto the weathered grey boardwalk that stretched the length of the beachfront. Katy, my team leader, was back up by Buddy's Surf Shack with her psychedelic rainbow umbrella, promising self-worth and unconditional acceptance to the unwary. She was nice in a prole sort of way, and I didn't like not liking her because it seemed really unfair.

I hunched deeper in my borrowed raincoat and tried to look smaller so I could pass her unnoticed.

"Ssst, you there! Pasty-faced Earth girl!" The sharp, clear voice hissed out from between two of the sheds that served on good days as market stalls for the fishermen. Today they were just wet cubes of wood panelling with a tall, dark figure crouched theatrically between them, beckoning to me with a long, pale hand, his coat sleeve dripping. From beneath the brim of a ridiculous pale cream cowboy hat I saw his long, agile mouth grinning at me, teeth white.

"Damien!" I jumped in beside him, glancing around to be sure that Katy hadn't noticed the move. I looked up into his face with its high, sculptured cheekbones, its long and slanting eyes that glowed with faint greenish light. "I haven't seen you since forever." (Four weeks is forever here.)

I stood back and made to look at his outfit, too pleased to be angry with him, though I should be, the way he picked me up and dropped me on this crew of fools. He was wearing a detective's trench coat besides the cowboy hat hiding his ears. "What's with the disguise? You look a right . . ."

"Look, my hat does *this*!" He overrode me, as usual, tipping his head forward and catching me with a stream of cold, stinging water from the hat brim. Then, moment over and forgotten, he jumped forward and picked me up and kissed my cheek and put me down all in one swift action. "I came to say I was sorry sorry so very sorry for leaving you with these awful lost-dog people but I had money problems and, look . . . tell me you're not a convert, tell me everything in fact, every single . . . shall we get the hell out of here? I can get us drinks and oh, I knew there was a good reason to see you, my pretty angel of the sands. I got you a job."

I was surprised, thrilled. "You what?"

"Well it's a really dull job, really bad but there's nothing you can do except that kind of thing and . . ."

I pushed the brim of his hat back—it fell off onto the walk— and kissed him on his still-talking mouth. "Thank you! Gods, Damien, I'm so . . . you don't know how grateful I am . . . You know when I didn't see you for all that time . . ."

He blushed, bent and turned in a big, graceful move to recover the hat, the long, long tips of his pointed ears turning pink as he stood up. The beads and bone voodoun charms braided through his long brown hair tinkled as he replaced the hat.

I couldn't prevent myself insisting. "Why are you in disguise?"

"I owe some people a bit of cash," he said. "Never mind that. Why are you . . ."

"Because I have to or they'll make me go through that bloody praying and chanting boot camp everything-is-solved-with-love mindscrew again," I hissed at him. "You *didn't come back.*"

His face was a picture of regret. "I'm here. I'm here, sweetie, now, here I am. Come on, I can hear your madwoman there getting closer. Come with me and drink free tea. I'll show you where your job is and everything. I know it took a long time, I know that, but . . ." He took hold of my hand and put it with his into the pocket of his coat. Water ran down from his cuff onto our fingers. Then he glanced at me with his elongated eyes wide and as cheeky as no elf should ever be. "I was in a bit of trouble, actually. Had to hide and keep my ears to the ground and it's all very very boring, honey. But the thing is you're all right and I'm all right and it is all my fault that you are living with the biggest dickhead to fall down the pipe in ten years, did you know that? I guess you knew that, right? Has he tried to fiddle with you yet? I always thought that must be his thing but I heard it was more complicated . . ."

"Shut up," I told him, too happy at seeing him again to get as angry as he deserved. I knew what trouble meant for him. He'd probably been in the criminal world's equivalent of prison, or trying to keep up three lives at once, and he probably deserved it. "Tea. You promised."

"I am a creature of my word, for you at any rate," he said, looking very conspicuously around the side of the fish-stall that hid us from Katy's sight-line. "Coast is clear. Madam, this way."

I looked past him at Katy. She was so intent on talking to some uncomfortable wet person, and so blinkered by the snorkel hood of her coat, that we slipped past her easily. All the surfy hardcases were hanging out at Buddy's, including a few I knew from begging off them in the past, so I made Damien keep going fast until we were well beyond them, although I guessed they were more interested in bitching about the lack of waves and the weather than they were in recognizing me. Homeless starving girls not so cool.

We turned in towards the city proper at the tram stop called Engine House and walked into town.

"So, tell me your life," Damien said. "Come on. We'd only got through the early years last time, and tell me what you're going to do with this money I'm going to give you just as soon as I have it." His slim, cool fingers tightened fractionally around mine inside the pocket.

He was hugely unreliable, a born liar. Talking to him was far too easy.

Whoffy lines . . . mist . . . memories unpacking . . . here we are in my past . . .

I told him about Sula, leaving out the night I left her, and about my home. I said that it'd been almost eight months since I left, and it was possible that my mom would have forgiven me for running away.

It was even possible that, in a fit of despair after I went, she finally realized that Darren is someone who only has pretensions of behaving nicely because he wants to be liked, so that he can get what he wants out of people, and not because he actually likes them. But I doubt it.

My mother prefers to think that everyone is basically honest, and of course she wants to believe that Darren's feelings for her are genuine, and not preprocessed feelings he has to stop and talk about like a psychologist so that he gets them right. If she had to recognize they were as manufactured as plastic, then she'd have to realize that Darren is using her. So, in order to save herself from being miserable, she chooses a lie.

So, I guess that even if I was to go back, and we had a reconciliation (unlikely), things wouldn't last for five minutes, whether Darren was there or not. I can't stand not living in the real inside of me. I try to tell the truth as much as I know it, even though it makes people quite uncomfortable because it's either too much, not enough, the wrong thing to be feeling or the wrong time to say it.

Normal people don't blurt out the workings of their true selves and I can see why. It's very frightening to have to believe what other people say about what they think and feel because you don't know what's *really* going on in their heads. And, because you know that they are lying to themselves about it (and even if they wanted to be brutally honest it would be hard, because everybody has so many fears and doubts and needs and wants and, between all those different inner proddings, they find it difficult to know which way is up, let alone whether or not *you* might be a genuine friend or whatever), this makes them untrustworthy.

And because *they* suspect that they themselves are unreliable witnesses, living in the post-psychology age where everyone knows they're making themselves up, they know that everyone else is too, like it or not, and so they have to dance through it all with various calculated kinds of lying just to get from A to B. And it's all very tiring so you want to scream.

But I don't want to get from A to B. I think it's more interesting if you could go sideways from A, along some kind of A-line, and get to F, or even Z.

Of course there's a danger in lying. From the minute you start you never know who you are anymore.

The day before I left home we were in the kitchen when I informed Darren that he hated me because I was standing in between him and what he wanted—my mother to support him emotionally and financially—and I told him I fully expected him to try to get rid of me. He was going about it a really clever way too, I said, and he even probably believed that he had Mum's best interests at heart, so it wasn't necessarily evil—unless evil is like a flea riding up on top of the guard dog of wanton ignorance.

Darren had rolled his eyes and said, "Can you just listen to her? That's not right. Not normal to talk like that. Fleas and dogs. It's silly not to have her sent for an assessment at least, Dawn. Come on, if it was straightforward autism, or something with an obvious label like schizophrenia, you'd be straight off to the clinic with her. It's not like there can't be a reason for it. You know what I'm talking about, don't you? The lab report on her genome always said there was a chance that things had gone a bit wrong in the mix when there was that protest which cut the power. And if there's a reason, there can be a fix. It's nothing to be ashamed of."

Oooh. Power failure. Lab. Genome. Be still my beating geek heart.

He had all the lingo, I thought as I sat at the top of the stairs, biting my nails, praying that she wouldn't go along with all that crap.

"*If* it was autism, she wouldn't have it," my mother said angrily. "They'd have filtered it out right from the start. Let it alone, will you? She's just sensitive and more intelligent than most people, which is exactly the way she's supposed to be. Top of the class, remember? Gifted. Scholarships all the way. Sponsorships. Guaranteed. Anyway, don't you remember being a teenager yourself? Pretentious gloom and self-righteous idealism go with the job."

I came down from the landing on the heels of that ringing endorsement. "Darren wants me to go so he can persuade you that you need him around and can't do anything without him, when really it's the other way around and he can't do anything on his own." I wished she didn't have to feel all the anxious worry that she always felt about me (feels about me, I suppose) even though I'd told her not to.

"Don't talk in that silly way." Darren tugged at his hair and raised his voice as he turned towards me. "For god's sake, HS," (he always shortened it when my mom was around), "can't you find something an ordinary thirteen-year-old girl could be interested in, like boys or clothes or whatever?"

"I'm *fourteen*." I stuck my tongue out at him and left the room (kitchen) because if I stayed there, I thought I might have to stab him with whatever sharp implement was nearest (fork). But later, as I sat and pretended to immerse in a soapverse, I could hear him talking her round.

I do speak in a peculiar way, I realized that: too many words, in badly organized orders. But I think that way, and it was the only way I'd found that stopped words from changing what I meant into an approximation. But it wasn't always very clear even then, because conveying meaning is tricky. And finding it in the first place is even harder.

Of course, I was bound to hate Darren for the same reasons he hated me, so we were even.

No, I'm not going back yet, but I wish I could because I'm very cold and hungry here, and not only outside but inside, which is much worse. Damien knew it. It's why he was holding my hand and why I wanted him to.

There's nobody like me here either, even though I thought maybe the Engine might have constructed a few. And nobody in the Love Foundation has any more real patience than Darren either, although they really try their hardest to put a good face on it. They've all come to the end of something in themselves, and this front is their despair, trying to write them a letter.

Whoffy lines . . . mist . . . memories all told.

I thought silently about the day I found Damien, when we had a fight about who got to dig through a trash can first and I saw that he was trustworthy, at least for me, for now, and when there was nothing in the can either of us wanted he gave me a credit. Every day after that he came by the boardwalk and found me and gave me another credit and we sat under the 'walk drinking soda and we talked, neither of us having anyone else to whom we could tell anything like the truth.

Then one day he didn't come. The days became a week and

the week finished me as effortlessly as a finger knocking over a domino because I had no idea where he'd gone, until today. Now I explained to Damien's ever-ready ears that the price for meals and a roof over your head ran to sitting in meditation and lectures three hours a day, communal bathrooms, domestic chores, always telling them where you are and spending two days a week going out recruiting with them. And without them I'd be dead by now.

"Sorry," Damien said quietly. "I couldn't make it. I didn't mean to leave you." He looked genuinely pained.

"No big," I said, shrugging awkwardly in the lie. "Where are we going?"

"Can't go in the Massif today," he said, leading me past its huge gateways, their arches like the entrances to the palaces of ancient kings, guarding a few of the inroads into the biggest structure in Sankhara. "But I'm good in Aelf 1, the old home-town. Reputationo intacto. Okay?"

"Are we going to your flat?" I asked hopefully, wanting a rest.

"No, darling. I'm . . . sort of in between flats at the moment actually."

We soon came to the front of Aelf 1, the great tower of glass—more like a minor city in itself, along with its partner, the living giant tree that is Aelf 2.

Damien led me inside beneath the blue and green lintel of the Water Element Arch. Here the sea-coloured glass of old shores had been liquefied and extruded into curling, watery shapes at three times the normal scale until they reared up the huge face of the building to unite with the other Elemental Force Supports: Air, Earth, Metal and Fire. Then they shot up two hundred metres towards the sky, where they all ended in a big spun-sugar orgy of abstract decoration just beneath the clouds.

Out of habit we unlocked fingers and both took a run up, joining with a couple of kids who were also running and skid-ding along the preternaturally slippery floor. All boot soles slide here, even the ones charmed to stick like glue to anything short of thin air. We braced our feet and shot along like snowboarders.

From far beneath us—the glass goes about as far down as it does up—the frozen expressions of mythical beasts glared up at us silently as we surfed across the world's biggest paperweight. We jumped clear at the end, onto the marbled surface of the atrium proper.

Here, where the centre of the tower was completely hollow and open to a tiny dot of sky, I took a walk past the ubiquitous coffee franchise and checked out what people had left on the tables, just out of habit. Damien caught my sleeve and pulled me away. "Not today, Cinders," he said, pulling me with him to the slick service and slicker underwater theme decor of Ran's Kitchen. "Today we pay."

"You pay."

" 'S'what I said."

He bought me tea and a fiendishly expensive dish which he claimed incorporated every possible vitamin and goodness a body could want. I ate it, trying not to gulp or look desperate. Elf food was better than Foundation food. He smiled hopefully at me, playing with his hat, his ears twitching as he told me about this job—cleaning—and how great it was going to be and how it was like, really good money for that kind of thing and at the coolest place in town. Then, when the flight of red cardinals came down, scattering like sparrows to the corners of the atrium to announce the hour at noon, he muttered something about having to go.

"Now I know where you are I can see you more often, babe," he said, batting his eyelashes in a way that would have been coy if it wasn't on him.

I felt sick, and not just because of the food half-chewed sitting in my stomach. I didn't know how to ask him, to beg him in fact, not to leave me alone again.

He got up. "So, don't forget you start the day after tomorrow. You gotta show up or I'm gonna get it. It was hard to slot you in there. Not that . . . well, show up, okay?"

"I will, I will." I nodded vehemently, knowing it could be my way out of the Foundation. "I'll be great at it. I'll be there."

He jammed the cowboy hat down as low as it would go. "Do I look stupid?"

"Yeah." I touched his coat, just to feel something that belonged to someone I knew close to me.

"Good." He stuck his hand out and ruffled my hair. "Life, volume, colour, baby," he whispered to me, grinning. "Life, volume, colour." And then, with a wet flick of his coat-tails, he was gone.

I stuck around at Ran's as long as I could until the waitress pointedly came to wipe my table for the third time. The usual collection of minor Stuffie celebrities were all hanging out at the fountains in the atrium, showing off and shopping. I passed them, feeling 6 billion years old in my faded anorak, invisible, unreal.

The busy central streets of the Aelf broke up into a jumble of lesser zones behind the SankhaGuide Massif; another structure of awe-inspiring stupid size. I leant against the rock-face of the Massif to get warm—it always holds heat, even in winter—and pretended I was reading the map cut into it, showing all the city districts. Within the rock the obscure technical gubbins of the SankhaGuide AI itself hid, administering the Sidebar and everyone's life in it with the cheerful good grace that Solargov likes to see in all its slaves. I had a soft spot for SankhaGuide though, because it chose not to notice me at all. Maybe it was friends with NorthNet?

I made my way back to the Foundation's squatted apartments in Temple slowly, kept my eyes on the pavement, hands in pockets, prayed not to be noticed by anything dangerous, though the main streets were usually perfectly safe from predators, even for single pedestrians. When I got there I lay on my bunk and flung the cover over my head. My peace lasted about thirty seconds.

"Do you want to come and join in with the afternoon prayer?" It was Ludo, the leader of the group. His voice was rich and warm, though there was this hint of stupid-teenager-you-don't-know-what's-good-for-you about it that always made me want to cut his throat.

"Go away," I said.

I could hear him thinking before he decided to play Mom. "Did Katy send you back here?"

"No." Obviously.

"It's not safe for you to be out on your own, young lady."

I could tell by the tone of his voice that he wouldn't take no for an answer. Saving people required their suffering and I wasn't going to get away with it. I put the blanket back so I could look into his face.

Ludo believed in his heart that he was the great benefactor and kindness to all, because he knew the right way to live and could show others how to do it; what made him happy would make them happy. Clickety click. He was ruled by Should and Ought and the moral package that came as a freebie when he bought them wholesale.

I got up thinking that in a few days I'd be able to put his self-satisfied face out of my world forever. I concentrated on the fact that I had a job.

I pretended to be Damien, from whom I understood how to tack on a big, shit-eating smile to my words in the knowledge that if I didn't, worse would follow. "I'd love to join in."

4/Jalaeka

Locked into my new human 4-D, I spent some time exploring and discovered the strange compact that the true humans of Solar Earth had made with Unity.

Were they the first humans? I used to think I came from a world like Earth, with a natural population that was unique to its surface, evolving by the normal means. Now I have no such confidence. Unbound by time and space, Unity's only restrictions are voluntarily imposed. And does it matter who came first, or how they were made?

This distinction was the heart of Earth's dilemmas when they found Unity, thirty years ago. Then their new chimeric races, the Forged, went out of the system and into the tiny universe. And now, like me, some of them suspect with unshakeable paranoia that they are only an experiment in a long line of experiments, running in a laboratory as wide as the fabric of linear time can hold.

The truth or otherwise of this is unimportant, since it is beyond analysis.

I should have left Damien alone. Fishing the Engine's fisher—hah! I should have stayed silent and hidden in the ways I learned in other lives, where no special tricks are required, only the desire to be ignored.

We got drunk together. He kissed me and I kissed him by the rolling surf. I was starving.

Then he took me through the city to the strange districts of the past, through Moorlands and Hoolerton, where council housing estates of brick and mortar, bleak grey concrete and weed-strewn paving were home to gangs of feral children who could barely speak. Along one very ordinary lane, the lengthy and twisting Crisscross Street, we took the paths and ginnels of forgotten childhoods that were never ours and emerged beneath the dark span of an industrial railway bridge. The street beyond seemed to go on forever.

"Watch this," he said, and took one more step.

He vanished.

I stepped forward after him and passed through into a universe completely contained within the Sankhara envelope—a bubble of space and time walled off by a dimensional division so thin it was as intangible as grace.

We stood on a huge road, beneath dark overshadowing trees towering more than fifty metres high. From a greyish-white sky snow was falling, and the wind was like a whetted knife against our skins.

"All new, this," Damien said, shivering and holding himself in a hug for warmth. "Appeared a few weeks ago. Manufactured on a special order I thought, but I could never see how, or why. Never picked that dream up from anyone's head. How long did you say you'd been here?"

"Thirty days."

"Welcome, mate," he said, his teeth chattering. "This is you."

Standing in the empty halls of the house he showed me, I remembered every damn thing I wanted to forget and, inside, I burned.

5/GREG

It was raining hard outside. The sound of water flooding over the leaky guttering sill wasn't enough to drown out my girlfriend. I glanced up from my book. "Pardon?"

". . . we should split up."

"Huh?" I heard her the first time. I just preferred reading the Last Throes column off *SankhaDaily,* instead of listening to someone I used to love doing a bad impression of it.

Oh, listen to me. I'm turning into an asshole. Have turned actually. When did that happen? I'm as disappointed as she is.

"For gods' sakes Greg, haven't you been listening to a bloody word? I said that tonight obviously proves we should go our separate ways," Katy repeated. "You aren't interested in the Foundation or what I've got to say about it. You never gave it a chance. I know you think I'm crazy and frankly I don't care. When you're here you're not even here. You don't live life anymore, you're too busy making a fucking documentary about it!"

"Break up. Finish with each other. End it. Divorce," I said. The words popped in fits and starts. If I wrote me into my documentary I'd have a narrator voice over and call this bit of exposition a glossolalic constipation.

Hmm. Words like *glossolalic* are making a bid for freedom. It's worse than I imagined. I'm not an asshole. I'm the whole arse.

Katy packed at a more effective languor, in stoic silence, appraising each one of our objects and picking the ones she'd decided were her due. She wrapped them in her clothes, carefully, stowing them in her holdalls like she was wrapping artefacts for a museum. "I take it from your vivid lack of shock that you agree?"

What could I say? The bit of me prepared to fight on the side of Our Relationship seemed to have fallen asleep or been lost. I could not compete with the religious, absolute inanity of a con doctrine like universal love.

A huge, completely enervating calm came over me. "Yes. No. Wait. It shouldn't be like this."

I stopped talking aloud and let the words run on to myself: *I don't want to remember you this way. I want to say good-bye to the enthusiastic English major who was doing Sankhara for the sake of somewhere to put on the CV that looked just a bit braver than most of the rest. She was honest, and you—you're a different kind of honest, have in fact raised honesty up the flagpole and laid down flat before it and put your face in the sand. The Foundation has given you permission to become the painful honesty that doesn't know when to shut the fuck up.*

I was so angry that I couldn't say anything. I'd ruin even this awful moment and make it into a farce.

Katy walked around and took her bag to the door. She was heading for the Love Foundation's score of apartments in the Temple District of Absalom, where the statues of divinity talk on cue; platitudes to the wind. I've recorded all of them and conducted exit polls on 98 percent of their devoted servants too.

She gave me a smile like giving out a bribe. "It's like you've gone away. I don't know who you are. You hate everything. You're so cynical and sceptical you won't give anything a chance. All because Gaiasol won't listen to your paranoia about Stuff after Metropolis vanished." She paused and when she spoke again her voice was quieter. "I feel sorry for you. I really do. You used to like Sankhara. Don't you remember when it was different? Every day was an adventure."

My chest and the front of my shoulders felt very tight. I was sorry. She was right. Sankhara was paradise two years ago, when I first came here and set out my stall at the university, researching the Engine and its methods, hoping to understand the psychological substrata that made up the modern human mind . . . I thought Stuff would be the perfect toolkit: Sankhara was my laboratory, where all human imaginings (and most of them were pretty ordinary) walked the street. And then Metropolis vanished and I saw us for what we were here—only the mice in the maze, being given the runaround for tidbits.

"Say something." Katy glared at me. Anything I said now about the Love Foundation being only a sop to the spirits of needy people, and probably a pyramid scheme run by exploitative humans for profit; this would only send her into a fit. But even if everyone in the thing was a true believer, then they were mad.

I wanted her to be gone, not to go.

Katy wasn't cross for once, only perplexed. "This is it, isn't it? This is your whole response. Nothing. I wish I knew what went on in your head, maybe then I'd have a chance to say something that would get through." She took a deep, harrowed breath and let it out. "I'm going then. You can come over anytime, you know."

It's a bad day when your love leaves you for better loves she gets out of a handbook and the empty words of a grifter. But I hadn't got better. I hadn't got anything to make a counter-offer with.

Katy picked up her bags again, taking a last lingering look around. She paused. "I wonder if you could come round later. There's someone I'd like you to meet."

"We're not all great talkers," I found myself saying to her as the door opened for her. "That's all."

Katy nodded gently at me. Tears, refused by my eyes, ran down my nose.

"What time?" I asked.

"After dinner. Eight or nine."

"Okay." It was the last thing I wanted to do but I owed her. I couldn't imagine there was any member of the Foundation I wanted to meet.

Why say yes? *You moron, Greg.*

The Love Foundation was a cult of curiously unitarian twist. It didn't adhere to any particular religion, didn't care if you were atheist, didn't mind what you were in fact, as long as you were devoted in some fundamental way to recognizing all human beings as identical in their inner being. *Inner* here meant when all personality and other temporary encumbrances had been stripped off—*taking it back to the real,* as they said.

The Foundation believed in a kind of soulless essentialism that everyone could express in any way they liked, although it was always spoken of as the Great Quest—for Love of course. Any kind of love would do, but they weren't big on vice, so you'd be disappointed if you went in hoping for lots of free sex and drugs. They intended each person to find love from other Foundation members in the form of a noncritical acceptance. Devotional time was mandatory and group-related. There was a load of New Agey angles that were old long before I was born, and a lot of talk about a psychic heritage leading back through principal figures of the past—name one and they'd fit them into the pantheon. They were friendly like that.

There was a further piece of good that the Foundation did for Katy—it liberated her from a lifelong dependence on her family and its corporate wealth. Finally, she got to stop being the poor little rich girl from Texas and started being Katy Pawlak, defender of the weak and unloved.

In spite of the fact it was a load of idealistic, cloth-brained recidivist claptrap, it wasn't a bad bargain, I thought. It certainly beat being Dr. Greg Saxton, Topographer of Sankhara, lecturer in Unity Studies. Not worth putting on a headstone, that.

I was interrupted from self-pity by a flash from my Tab. I saw Damien's green leaf icon blink and cued the chat channel, voice only.

"Got something to show you," he said. "Very peculiar. You'll love it. Got time?"

"How much do you want?" I asked, some little inquisitive bit of me perking up already.

"Fifty solid honour points with SankhaGuide."

That was a huge price. I hesitated. "After I see it."

"Twenty before, thirty after. You'll want to give me more."

Honour point trading was illegal, resting as it did on the Guide's assessment of your Global Civilian Worth. It didn't surprise me that Damien needed them. I would have to give him my points, and take a price hike on all my government purchases until I could restore them through publication or extra classes. But Damien was the only reliable source of genuinely interesting anomalies in the entire Sidebar, and he knew it. "Where shall I meet you?"

"Crisscross Street," he said. "Hoolerton end. By the park gates. Be here in twenty minutes."

I met him in the late-afternoon light on the corner. Litter blew around us and stray, sniffy dogs trotted past, one eye on us and one on the lookout for trouble. Most of the population here was Stuffie and I had extensively surveyed it the summer before, thinking I knew every alley and permutation reasonably well.

Damien, always mobile, was more restless than ever. His strides ate the ground at such a rate I had to run one step in ten to keep up with him as we passed the rows of identical terraced houses, their pretty-flowered gardens, their concreted driveways. "Where are we going? There's nothing down here until you reach the moors and that's miles away . . ." I protested.

"Set your recorder to maximum resolution and width," he warned me. "You'll need full capture."

He slowed down only when we neared the railway arches. Their dark, almost black bricks were marked with the illegible graffiti of dead and artificial languages: Greek, Latin, Sanskrit, Coptic, Klingon, Quenya, Sindarin, English and Cobol. Sankha-Guide would do instant translations, but I liked their obscurity, and had never asked what they meant. I was too worried they would say something like *Dave Is a Wanker,* or be a pretentious quote from Shakespeare: after years of analyzing people's fantasies you got a nose for that kind of thing. Damien had once brought a red paint stick and corrected a line in Sindarin with an angry swipe. I still didn't ask . . .

Under the archway the temperature dropped like a stone and I was shivering and gasping before I drew two breaths. I took a temp check and was watching the level when I noticed how the light had changed. I glanced up and saw Damien looking knowingly at me from hooded eyes, his face brimful of anticipation, waiting for my reaction.

"It's very . . ." I began, glancing beyond him. Where the street should have been lying straight before me I saw a road crossing in front of me like a huge bar of stone. To either side and above me the bricks of the arch had become rotting wood, filmed with green mosses and dripping icy water onto us both. It was a tough, barbaric structure . . . I looked back. There was no sign of bricks or streets, only a graveyard behind me and the ruins of a cathedral fallen into green grassy humps among broken tombs. We were standing in a lych-gate, where the coffins stop . . .

Flares of recording data scrolled in my vision as I cued full sensory capture. The temperature was the least of it. Snow and thin ice sheened everything, every blade of the vivid grass. And around and above us the trees—I had never seen such monstrous upgrowths of vegetable rioting, gnarled and twisted, but as lofty as spires. Their leaves were so dark green as to be almost black.

The glade where we stood, backed by the graves, was a small

pool of ex-civilization in a very large boreal forest, dotted here and there by the sword slices of vast spruce and cypress. These lined the road on either side, glowering over it with a primeval covetousness, restrained only by huge grey stone walls of granite blocks higher than a man. I could hardly think, I was so busy looking at it.

I heard Damien laughing softly. "Do you know what this is, Dr. Saxton?" he asked me, huddling with his back to the bitter slice of the wind that tore gleefully in towards us from the funnel of the road.

"A new landscape. A change . . ."

"No. You are farther from Sankhara than you have ever been right now," he said, enjoying my discomfort as I stared at him.

"What?"

"This is another universe. As far from the Sidebar as the Solar Envelope. But inside Sankhara . . . a bubble in the fishbowl. Do you understand?"

I couldn't get it. Why would the Engine make such a thing? "Why not just part of Sankhara?"

"Why indeed," he said and I could tell that he had an idea he wasn't prepared to share yet. "It has been here since Metropolis was destroyed."

I stared openly at him, my mouth agape. "Exactly?"

"Give or take a few minutes. And I didn't even find it myself until yesterday," he said. "Then I found the records of its spawning in the Engine logfiles . . . no warning, no clue. It is a secret of the Engine. Such things are . . ." He shrugged.

"Rare?" I guessed.

"Not possible," he said. "I know everything the Engine makes. I give it everything it gets . . . but I didn't give it this." He bit his nails compulsively and I saw the ragged fear that ran him.

In silence I gave him his fifty honour points, touching the back of my hand to his where our Tabs lay beneath the skin. "Have you looked any farther?" I nodded out beyond our tiny shelter.

"Yes," he said. "But I won't go in there now." He shrugged

awkwardly to show that he didn't enjoy being afraid. "The master is not at home, and it seems that when that happens then the wildlife gets very, very aggro. We wouldn't make it to the house."

"There's a house?" I couldn't see anything but the dour gloom of the road.

"Palace, actually. Big. Massive. Lovely things. But ooh, very sharp nasty things all waiting long before you get there." He made a pouncing action with his hands. "So, I'll take you, with permission. Which I've yet to get. Though I will. I will. When he's here. If he comes back."

"Who is this 'master'?" I asked him, observing his clear discomfort.

"Hard to say."

"You must know," I objected. "All Stuff things . . ."

"He isn't Stuff. Well, he's like it, but different. Come on. Let's go."

I stared at him, the cold forgotten. "Different?"

"As in not the same. Similar. Probably. Can't actually tell. Let's go."

"No way," I said, hardly able to believe him. "We have to see more than this, right now."

"You can if you like," Damien said, "but give me your money and points because you won't be needing them much longer." He held out his long-fingered hand, palm up. I saw that his arm was bandaged from wrist to elbow. Blue-green elfin blood leaked to the surface of it. He raised his eyebrows at me, daring me.

"What do you mean you'll get permission?" I said.

He dropped his hand. "Not sure exactly. I'll know when things stop attacking me the moment I step through the gate."

"Do we need . . . ?" I racked my brains. "Offerings?"

He shook his head. "None that you'd understand. Just wait. I'll figure it out."

"How big is it? Whose is it?"

"His. Don't know. At least as big as Sank, probably. Maybe bigger. Hidden from You Know What . . ." He wouldn't even say the name Unity.

My mind went blank. There was no such thing as a thing that hid from Unity. Especially when it was made out of Unity . . . like everything in Sankhara.

Damien shrugged. "More things in heaven and earth?" He grinned at me.

No matter what I said or offered, he refused to be drawn anymore. He left me standing there alone in the freezing rain and ran off with his newly honoured status intact.

It was then that I realized the depth of silence around me, above and below the ordinary noises of the world. There was no Guide here. There was nothing. No connection. Every frequency polled only cosmic activity. Not one wavelength of any kind of broadcast at all. Nothing.

I stepped back nervously and was back on Crisscross Street, its late-afternoon gleam a sudden withering heat against my face. SankhaGuide started running diagnostics to ferret out the glitch that had caused my temporary absence from its awareness. I told it I had no idea what had happened. It rumbled unhappily and asked me not to cut it off without warning in the future.

In my room at home I replayed the recording of those few minutes in the hidden world. I started to put together some plans for going back and only stopped when my alarm chimed to tell me I had promised to go out.

I went to the Foundation at eight o'clock, leaving my efforts to understand Damien's claims at home. Katy answered my knock and let me in.

The first room was a mess of coats, boots and rucksacks like an explosion in a luggage depot—a pitiful collection that was dwarfed by the anteroom's graceful proportions and beautiful eau-de-nil washed walls. There was a weaving pathway left among the rubble. Katy led me along it, through a meeting room where groups were seated on the floor and on cushions, talking fifteen to the dozen. They all ignored me apart from the odd curious glance. They knew me and I knew them and we didn't have much to say to one another. Some of the easier ones gave me a smile, one or two not even forced.

I looked past them out of the tiered square panes of the Georgian windows. It was raining in a real summer downpour.

Ludo held court in the next chamber—we passed through, our feet sounding unnaturally loud on the hardwood floor, interrupting his speech about the sound genetic basis for kindness. The last four rooms we skirted were all living areas. Camp beds were lined up as though it was an army barracks, with two shin lengths between them. People lay or sat and read on them. Some played quiet games. One girl I saw in the last room, in the corner. She stood out like a ray of sunlight coming through heavy curtains.

With the strange recognition you get when you see yourself outdone by the next latest model I saw that she was one or two generations younger than I was. Even Pure Line Unevolved like myself—ordinary humans who have never had the dubious benefit of gengineering in their line—counted in generations these days. We lived a long time, but she was still in her teens, I thought, whereas I wouldn't see thirty-five again and some more years after that as well.

She was definitely Genie—a heavily engineered but ordinary model human, not Forged. There was an odd familiarity about the way she was made—athletic and good-looking. But this attractive mediocrity was totally at odds with the way she held herself. I couldn't put my finger on it until we were almost up to her, then I managed to find the perfect word when the lamplight caught her hair as she moved her head back and forth, playing with the zip of her parka by running her chin across it, opening the collar, then catching the zip tongue with her teeth and dragging it back up again.

She *burned*.

She was playing with one of the Love Foundation's lilac card decks, her head with its careful screen of amber-coloured hair bent over her hands where she held a fan of them, the suits pointing outward so that the backs, each with its own homily or remedy on it, faced her. She was picking them out with her free hand at random. After she read she would let her eyes roll upwards until only the white showed, then she'd say quietly, "Crap," and flick the card with a snappy wrist action so that it spun and flew like a Frisbee across to the bunk opposite. She had good aim. All but two cards were on the bed.

"Francine," Katy said with a ring of authority I could tell she enjoyed. "I've brought a friend of mine to meet you."

Friend. That's nice.

Francine looked up at me with the most curious stare I'd ever been subjected to. It took me in, chewed me up and tasted me through in about half a second or less, and I was surprised to see her smile. All the sharp, canny calculation of the first instant melted into a completely charming softness in the second. She liked me.

Such instants are all it takes to move from one universe to another. I was so goddamned gratified I couldn't bring myself to wonder why. Her toughness and intensity had been attractive, but her sudden acceptance was devastating. It must all be because I felt so raw from the day's previous agonizing, I thought, as I stepped forward with my meet-the-nice-Professor smile on, my hand out.

"This is Greg." Katy introduced me. "He's a teacher at the University. He lives here while he's documenting the Sidebar."

Francine's large grey eyes ate me up as if Katy had said I were water and Francine was the desert.

"Greg, this is Francine. She's joined us from the Beach Community. One of the underground people a little down on her luck and been here quite a while now. I thought she might help you out if you can fit her in to your Cataloguing Programme. She's very academic, very bright, and she wants to know more about the 'Bar. I said you were just the person."

Ah, now I get it. I am going to help Katy's next big project, to wit, Francine from the Beach Community.

Francine lifted her head, chin bright red from all the zip tugging, and held the card deck out to me. "Pick one."

I saw that her nails were all bitten down. She was thin and her skin was almost translucent with the telltale sign of malnutrition fed for a long time only on water. Her expression was impish.

I took the five of clubs. She nodded at me, indicating the legend on the back.

Katy watched with her arms folded, a smile on her face, not as patronizing as it might have been. I read, "The search for love should be approached with rational organization and determination. An ordered mind brings a quiet heart."

"Well?" Francine said. She glanced at Katy, a challenging gaze that Katy herself was probably immune to. I'd always liked her thick skin.

Katy looked at me, one eyebrow raised. I really walked into this one, I thought. I glanced at Francine and guessed she wanted to see if I was going to tell her what I thought or fob her off with what I thought she should hear.

"Speaking as the freshly rationalized, it's difficult to make a judgement on that one." I offered the card back to her.

Francine took it and nodded. "Crap," she said and flicked it onto the distant bed without looking. She bent the remainder of the deck in her hand between her fingers and thumb and sprayed them all out, over the foot of her bed and on the carpet, flicking the last one away from her.

Katy didn't twitch a hair. "Would you like something to drink, tea maybe?"

"Yes," I said.

"Okay," Francine said. "Do I have to make it?"

"No, I'll get it." Katy gave us a meaningful look as she walked away, meaning we should Talk with a capital T.

Francine seemed to catch my thoughts. "We should all be praying to the Engine for plumbing in this freaking place, instead of compassionate and undifferentiated kindness."

"It doesn't respond to prayers," I said reflexively. The Engine built Sankhara at our bidding, allegedly, but it doesn't do requests of the kind that Francine was thinking about.

"Well duh. Anyone on the beach can tell you that."

"Is this better than the beach?"

"It has a roof and there's food," she said. "On the other hand, there's Ludo and Miss Tolerance and everyone here is an idiot or too nice for their own good, or both. They're all hopeless. It's good they stick together, they need each other." She drew her knees up to her chest and hugged them. "Katy left you to come here. She left you for this. That must sting."

I was so taken aback that she knew and thinking about how she knew and what that meant that I struggled for a few seconds, all my surprise and dismay clearly showing. "You could say."

"You seem okay to me."

"Thanks."

"So, what's the deal with you?" She glanced up and around at the room we were in. Her eyes were bright and they moved fast before sticking on me with the same abject hunger I'd noticed before. It was deeply unnerving.

"I document Sankhara, for study purposes. Try to mine it for recognizable story fragments, anomalies, new mutations on old themes . . ." I explained it to her as briefly as I could. I had never been so unsettled as I felt talking to her. It reduced me to the level of speech she seemed to prefer: excessively casual, a little bit coy.

"It's okay," she said when I'd finished, ducking her head back to her zip. She spoke around the metal tongue as she held on to it with her teeth again, very quietly. "To ask questions, to want to know things. That's okay." She was speaking to herself.

Katy returned.

Francine sat up and took one steaming mug from Katy with great care.

I was glad for the distraction when I took mine.

"So what have you guys been talking about?" Katy asked.

Francine and I shared a glance and I felt a curious, charming thrill as we decided we didn't want to say. "Francine's going to be coming round helping me," I said, not even knowing I was going to until the words came airily out, as though it was a well-crafted plan. "From tomorrow she'll be my assistant and we're going to enrol her in some courses." I finished and risked looking at Francine, trying to imply by my gaze—*well, this is what you wanted, isn't it?*

"I got a job today," Francine said, apropos of nothing apparently, switching her gaze to Katy, her eyes widening into the look of innocence.

"Paid employment?" Katy repeated. "You mean within the criminal fraternity as an unprotected illegal, do you?"

"Have to start somewhere," Francine said, giving me a hard stare and a sweet smile that told me she'd be even with me for dropping her into so much scheduled responsibility. "Greg said he could put a word in for me and get me something safer if it didn't work out."

"Did he?" Katy didn't bother hiding her surprise and scorn. "Well, you amaze me. I didn't know he knew the first thing about the underground. But of course, he knows so much about everything."

"He was only being nice," Francine said, giving Katy an innocent look. "You shouldn't be a bitch about it, especially since you just dumped him. How is that feeling his pain? More like adding to it."

Katy and I both stared at her.

"I'm just saying." Francine shrugged and turned away from us to stare through the steam coming out of her cup. Her face had a strong, classically beautiful catalogue profile. Francine did not have grandeur; however, she had sadness and uncomfortable vulnerability. I had that intuition that comes out of nowhere with the conviction of perfect knowledge—she would come with me to Damien's strange bubble. She was the key to understanding it.

6/FRANCINE

I was supposed to be working, but there wasn't much to do so I faced the grim reality of having to think about the state I'd got myself into. *Think, Francine, think about the cash that will get you out of the Foundation forever . . . money, money, money. . . .*

First though I admired all the makeup on the dressing tables as I flicked my duster over it. They didn't spare any money here, they bought the best, most expensive stuff. And all the best brushes, real animal hair. Everything was a mess, pots upturned (I righted them), brushes scattered (I washed and replaced them), powder everywhere (get that with the static-charge cloth).

I didn't like the people who used these rooms. They never noticed me except to complain that I was late, shouldn't I have gone by now? And they didn't like to look at me because I reminded them of some who-knew-what that made them twitchy. I looked at them sometimes and my failure to be ambitious in the way that they were cut like a dull knife.

I could see time clicking by on the wall clock.

It is reported by schoolbooks that time isn't a thing that goes, only a state of relationships changing in space, the movement of 3-dimensional objects through the fourth dimension. Today it went slithering by, shedding the seconds like skins, and I watched it going. I wondered when Marion, the cleaning commando, would come into the dressing rooms, thinking I should be nearly finished. I tried to care.

I tidied things up, wiped them down, put them back, pretending that I was the salesgirl on the big counter at Aelf 1's huge wandering trade show, the Embargo, where they still employ actual staff. It was difficult though, because I didn't look like a shop girl and thinking about it made me think about SankhaGuide waving to me through the masseuse in the window. Good-bye. Instead, I pretended that I worked here and that Marion, transformed into the agent of criminal and corporate evil, was going to come and drag me off to have sex with a rich guy for money because I was a rare and fragile Unevolved beauty and worth a lot of money.

Correction. My degradation is worth money.

How this pretty-woman thing got to be a romantic prospect is tough on the imagination. Maybe the point is that I will be saved from a terrible fate, but it clearly already happened to me, so that might not be it. Okay, I'll be saved from the continuance of a terrible fate.

I'm poor. I have only my looks. I'm a sort of Cinderella, and the john will be a handsome charmer, a roisterer in town on business who's used to the high life and is looking for something out of the ordinary to stimulate his dulled appetites. There'll be some slightly implausible scenes where he falls in love with me because I'm so special and sweet-hearted (aha, I'm beginning to get how it's romantic, although this is really worse crap than the Foundation manages to come up with), then I'd leave him and take his cash. He'd be really sad I was gone and try to find me, but not because of the money, because he was in love with me.

Again, the romance comes in on the no-ball.

Anyway, I couldn't leave him permanently if he really was sorry, because I don't like to make people sorry. I'd probably go back to him and spend years being miserably married in a gilded cage, making the stupid schmuck's life hell.

But before *that* charming story can unfold into being there's still today, and the next hour, and the waiting . . . as I'm always waiting, longing for an event out of the ordinary in which my ordinariness is transformed. In that moment all life's meaning would be revealed to me and be accompanied by a happiness like none I've ever known, and this happiness would last forever. But I know the way that stories go—first there's the sordid beginning to live through, and that's now.

I don't care about the middles or the ends anyway. Middles: things are beyond the initial high, exciting possibilities are stifled by too much knowledge and so are starting to fade.

As for the end, who needs it?

As I clean the shelves and tidy the varnishes, snorting, cynical Francine tells me what the reality of my fantasy would be like in cold terms (she remembers Va-va-vance only too well).

The sex would be like some other bodily function that can be disgusting: blowing a nose and finding blood-filled snot pouring out of it all unexpectedly; passing a bowel movement when you have bad piles, or violently explosive diarrhoea full of chilli; bursting an abscess in a shock of pain and seeing strangely congealed matter fly out of your living body—as disgusting as a dead dog three days old. Probably.

It wouldn't be worse, she promised me. To be worse than that it would require I care, and I wouldn't care about it because I was Hardened and Smart.

Of course I *did* care, both real and unreal Francine because sex is the place where the insides are stripped bare, whether you like it or not, and yours and theirs get mixed up, whether you like that or not, and whatever it does to you it does without your permission and makes you different, even if you don't think it does. And oh, what if you held nothing back and then ...? Then I think you fall in love whether you like it or not.

Ugh, I don't want to think about that. Most people here do it like it was breathing, with about as much care and attention, I'm sure of it. And that's a big disappointment too.

However, I have to pretend that I don't care in my game with myself, which is two pretences in one. The double barrel of pretences is half the fun of course, and I like the idea of being lots of contradictory things at once. I imagined having the kind of willpower that overcomes all squeamishness and all biology. I imagined steely determination and backbone, like someone in a Jane Austen book. I dreamed that I could be that good, that cool, that strong in my ideas that the body doesn't matter. I'd be the kind of person who proves that Heaven and Hell are real places, necessary real consequences of a morally fibrous world. My mere existence asserts it absolutely: I mean, I make it real because I act as though it is, which is how most real invisible things are made.

Giddy with the sudden sense of a gilt-edged future, I imagined myself as a great Diva, walking out with my head held high. Actually, scrub that. Romance like that is for the biggest idiots in creation. It's a kind of superlie—a real whopper that involves seeing the entire world in a way that's all about you. In reality the people who work here sell their bodies with the ease of shrugging off coats from their backs. Everything about life that bothers me has never crossed their minds. They're either beyond giving a toss because they're too junked, or above it because they're already too rich, or have realized their UltraMe, or because they're stoked on romance inside and have to carry on in spite of all the evidence life flings in their faces or else they'll collapse.

Even though I hate all that, I sometimes think I'd accept it as an alternative to the stupid moralizing high ground I seem to have stranded myself on. Oh shit.

Anything but to have to get through the next second in my own body, as myself.

It was ten past six. *Clean, Francine, you silly cow. Don't let Damien down.*

I glanced over the long room, assessing what I still had to do. Along the great white length of the dressing tables, half-hidden by the costume racks and heaps of rubbish, I could see a bare back. Vertebrae humped up from the bronze skin like a monster surfacing. The humps were moving very slightly back and forth, so at least they weren't dead (cleaning trolley bins not big enough for dead people). I was glad they were asleep, because that meant I didn't have to talk to them.

As I went up to them I imagined that I might steal enough cash from them to get out of this place and out of Katy and Ludo's long, considerate reach. They might have recently been given considerable gifts by some grateful millionaire who's rediscovered their libido. That wasn't so uncommon. I prayed for it as I stood on tiptoe and peered over clothes rails laden with three centuries of fashion, and forgot money.

A young man, straight out of the catalogue of sexually un-threatening transvestites, was slumped comatose over the counter-top. He had long, straight black hair like the mane on those fancy Dutch black horses, and an athlete's body—they all do. His arms were splayed out among a load of empty soft drinks cans, his head facing me so that his cheek was flattened and mouth open. He was asleep and drooling slightly.

A gold-sequinned evening dress was fitted to him like a sec-ond skin. He was a real work of art, the heart of a sacred mys-tery, Shiva and Shakti reunited, beauty personified. It was the kind of thing that was so beyond me in every way I felt quite free in my staring. I thought I was immune to this . . . you see a lot of it in Genies and Stuffies, but there was a weirdness to this one. He looked as if he'd been born that way.

Whoever he was he slept like a princess, his tongue protrud-ing slightly, an unlikely pink against the crimson glitter of blood-and-diamonds lipstick. The effect was only mildly spoiled by a long red scratch across his forehead. The emptiness of his aban-doned face filled me with tenderness and jealousy.

I cleaned around him briskly, hoping he'd wake up, and also that he wouldn't. I sorted the clothing that needed to be sent away for repairs and threw the destroyed garments into the rubbish. I picked up hair and gum and gum wrappers, discarded pep-patches, and TempTek that had become hard and crinkly when it died, just like the skin it mimicked when it hauled in all that fat, plumped out all those voids, sagged, wobbled, perked and defied logic to present bosoms and cocks at peer-less angles.

I inspected the refrigerators and replaced used stocks of drinks and snacks. I ate the leftover bits of snacks from dis-carded bags, the last quarter inch of drinks out of cups, but they only made me feel hungrier. I looked at him but he hadn't seen me stealing.

I used plastic tongs to collect the self-adhesive clothing that wasn't disposable, and put it all in a sealed plastic container for decontamination. I took an air sample, and samples from all surfaces, to test them for viruses, bacteria, macrophages and alien proteins in the Trolley Testbox. I downloaded the data to the office on the top floor where they care—or not. I sprayed the sinks and showers with Nano-Fresh ("Cleans at the flick of a switch!") and swept the floors old-fashioned style with a push mop. I cued the self-polishing mirrors to dump their waste into the dry sluice, and pumped the sluice into the trolley's bin.

I licked the vinegar taste of cleaning spray off my hand, hoping that it might clean out my intestines a bit and do me some good, and thought for a second or two of the seafront because it reminded me of fish and chips. Then only the princess was left, his feet still strapped into their six-inch stiletto sandals beneath the chair.

I sat down next to him and wished I had something strong to take. I laid my head on the table-top just like his, put my arms in the position of his, opened my mouth and slackened my tongue to see what it felt like. I wondered what his name was and what he was doing here, and had been doing before he got here, and why he hadn't gone home. The position we were in told me nothing, except that he must be more concussed than asleep because my cheekbone was already getting sore against the hard surface.

I stared at him resentfully, hating my own feelings because they were ugly.

He looked all right now: transvestite pussycat, he looked all pretty and nice. But as soon as he woke up, he'd change.

Nobody was the way they ought to be below the surface, especially people like him. He ought to be lovely if you only went on looks; a true friend, a wonderful lover, a great-spirited advocate of everything light, a fighter with attitude and a wicked sense of humour, a hero who didn't swagger and annoy the shit out of everyone with the burden of being good. He should be as empathic as god would be if anybody generous-hearted had made god up.

There're many people I'd seen like this princess: all miracle surface. No surgery or treatment proves too extreme to serve their vanity (check my mother out), and their desire to enslave everyone. All have been bastards. Even I'm a bastard.

I stared at him and wished he was the real deal. Shame on him if he wasn't. Shame on me because *I* wasn't, because I can imagine it but not *be* it. Why the hell is that?

I looked at his perfect lips, thought of my own predictable face with dislike, and wondered if he had sex, and what with and for whom, and if he liked it or only pretended to and meanwhile had some stupid behind-the-scenes thing going where he was only doing it to finance a career in Solar journalism or a degree in one or other tedious legal subject that came with a whole package of fabulous futures. Perhaps he was only touring misery and I'd be some special stop on it, not a tart, not a heart.

His eyes opened as I was staring at them.

A thousand locked doors swung wide.

I stood up without knowing what I was doing except that I was very frightened, and just an instant before I had been in a state I couldn't name, where every part of me was seen and called uniquely beautiful.

The sound of the music systems being tested upstairs brought me round. I picked up the floor brush and quickly pretended to be cleaning.

The princess slowly peeled his face away from the table. He put one hand over his chest for a moment and rubbed it back and forth, frowning, looking like he'd misplaced something. He swallowed and clearly didn't care for the taste of his own tongue.

I swept the same two metres of floor again. I felt this unaccountable kind of energy in my bones, as though my body itself was laughing and wanted to dance. After another second or two the princess looked at himself in the mirror and scowled, peering into his own eyes for a long time, carefully, cautiously. He touched his cheeks and chin tentatively. Then he glanced sideways at me, then back at himself. He took a few breaths, then drew himself up to his full height with a single gesture, like a conductor lifting their baton for the first bar of a mammoth opera.

I tried to drink him in as much as possible, so I'd always remember and always be able to see him in my mind's eye. Right now, before he ruined it all. He held out his right hand imperiously towards me. The nails were half a finger long, crusted with false jewels and unknown substances. He raised one eyebrow in a perfect arch and batted his fake eyelashes, inviting me to share the joke with him because beneath the pretence he was smiling a slightly shy, delighted smile.

"Cadenza Fortitude," he murmured gently, just like a real queen, abruptly shifting gender in some undefinable yet exact manner. "A pleasure, Francine."

I glanced down at my bright orange tabard and the name tag on it. Suddenly I noticed the mottled skin of my chilly hand on the handle of the broom, my bitten nails. I couldn't look back, couldn't believe I'd been about to smile that smile of recognition, the way I'd smiled at Damien days ago, as if I knew this guy and he was special to me from a long time ago and had returned from a long journey, as if he was the one.

God, he had to be a Stuffie, of course. Some new one I'd never seen before.

I said, "Piss off, will you. You're in my way. I want to get home by seven."

Cadenza Fortitude grinned, dropped her hand and got up. She was well over six feet tall in the high-heeled shoes. She rolled her eyes in their smoky black sockets and sighed in an exaggerated way at my rudeness and stupidity, smile undaunted, actually charmed as though I was playing along. Her sigh became a giggle, which she stifled with the back of the same hand.

Every pretty thing I'd ever seen I forgot about.

I said, struggling to keep hold on reality, "You can't have a shower. I just cleaned them."

"Really?" Cadenza examined herself more closely in the mirror and dabbed the scratch on her forehead, examining her fingertip for blood. "Christ." For a moment she looked as though she was going to collapse and I took a half step forward but she corrected herself with a jerk and I leaped back, flushed and hot and angry with myself.

Well, that was that. "Really." I finished wiping the table and stuffed all the cleaning gear rapidly back onto the trolley.

Now I wished Marion would hurry up. I bit my nails, but they were long gone. I bit the skin on my thumb instead, really hard so that it hurt, feeling fresh compulsiveness wash across me—the need to be somewhere else, doing something else. I tried reverting back to sensitive Francine instead of bolshy Francine, but no dice.

"Stop that!" Cadenza turned, reached across and yanked my hand out of my mouth with a finesse worthy of a prima ballerina.

I jerked backwards, almost spitting. I hadn't been prepared for her to touch me. Nobody's touched me in ten months, except for Damien's hand holding. Nobody.

I saw that she was cross with me because I'd been hurting myself. My hand burned where she'd touched me. In her eyes the thousand doors, open.

Her expression softened and became gentle. She drew my hand to her mouth and kissed it. I pulled free and folded my arms. I was so hot, I didn't know where to look.

"You can wash your hands, all right?" I snapped. "But I'm not doing those bathrooms again."

Suddenly she took one stride forward and stood towering over me. I looked up and bit my lower lip until it was painful because I wanted to touch her so badly.

She gave me a death-ray stare that quite clearly said *Well, if you're going to play stupid I am too,* held up her hands and snapped off her long fake fingernails, one after the other. She dropped each one individually into the trolley trash, as though she were dealing out tokens to minions. Then she stepped out of the ludicrous shoes, shrugged off the dress and kicked it under the table.

Looking directly into my eyes, the person who'd been underneath Cadenza all along thumb-keyed the tags on his corset and cast it aside. He was so close that if I leant forward even one degree I would have touched him.

I wanted to cry because he was so lovely and I wished I were too. I braced, waiting for the hit to happen to me, when it would all change, this haze destroyed to prove my earlier, uglier fantasy to be the brutal truth.

His expression softened and became serious as he looked at me with such concern that I had to look away. "Frannie?"

I stared furiously at my hideous, dirty tabard, then I looked up at him again, ready to kill him if I had to.

He bent down to look into one of my eyes, then the other, with a play-acting scientist's serious scowl.

I stared at the centre of his bare chest, waxed smooth, all glittery. I didn't know what to do.

"Uh-huh." He turned, crossed the room, went into one of the showers and rubbed himself against the walls, covering himself in the part-foam part-slime of the Nano-Fresh. He didn't bother to pull the curtain. "Flick the switch."

I just stared at him. How could anyone just clean themselves off with industrial nanocyte compounds meant for scrubbing toilets?

"The remote. The remote for the cleaning stuff," he repeated with tangible irritation.

I pressed the button on the trolley. The greasy cleaner suddenly became droplets on his skin. The droplets ran into each other and scurried quickly downwards, attracted by gravity and their software imperatives to gather in the drains ready for collection. They took with them everything that wasn't attached. I was still puzzling about how he'd managed to keep the top layers of his skin as he came out of the cubicle. He rifled through several lockers, and emptied each one until he located a set of worn denims and bike boots, which I was sure weren't his own.

He dressed and looked at himself in one of the mirrors again, shaking his head with a look of rueful resignation I couldn't begin to understand. His expression became guarded for a second, then transformed into the smooth flat planes of determination, at the same time gaining in acuity like light being focused through a lens. His chin dropped a fraction as he turned back towards me and started to walk purposefully towards the exit. Within two strides his walk had assumed a monumental inertia so great I felt myself borne backwards on its invisible pressure wave and I had to take a step back. As he passed me he reached through this tidal front and caught hold of my hand. He twisted the broom out of my hand, tossed it, and tugged me along at his side, sliding his fingers in between mine with the easy confidence of the oldest friend I might have had in the world. He glanced at me and blushed very faintly. His smile was wicked. "Come on, don't stand there with your mouth like that or a tram'll drive into it."

I thought of a lot to say: that Marion was about to arrive, that I had a lot to do, that he was only going to make fun of me, that I needed to get another shift sorted out or I wasn't going to manage the rent on a new apartment, that he should go fuck himself.

"Look at the state of you." He shook his head. We were still walking.

"I'm fine," I said.

He was still holding my hand. We had passed the door. The street came rushing in at me, all twilight and shadows, the smell of the onshore wind as it freshened, the hot spicy odours of frying food at the delicatessens on the Forum, where people had started to order dinner, the busyness of commuters quickening their pace towards home, the hum of traffic crowding the roads, bicycle bells and rickshaw horns blurts of sparkle and glare, the clatter of a knight's horse and his heavy armour as he turned off the main street and onto the green strip of parkway that started just beside us at the Circle's edge, the flaring torches of Aelf 2 making every shade leap and dance, elemental fires tearing free to run up its massive trunk and gather with others among the leaves and gutters at the levels of the first roofs so the whole building was dripping upwards with light. Night was falling in Sankhara. Far away on Floating Mountain the deep, earth-toned boom of the monks' ghost-calling horns sounded the sun down from the sky.

He held my hand. We were the best of friends. This was a fact, like it was a fact that water flowed and fire was hot.

"This can't be real," I said, mostly to myself, in case I'd fallen asleep and was right now lying on a park bench somewhere else.

"I say that all the time," he replied. A sadness passed through him but it was gone before I could see it properly. He looked down at me, quiet now that we had left the building, all inertia balanced on the point of my attention. "Where should we go?"

There were more than a thousand doors. Their count was beyond number.

I led him into one of the small cafés that litter the roads around Pythagoras's Circle and the Forum. I sat in the window beside the radiant heater and ordered a hot chocolate with a double cream top. That was stupid because I was sacked by now—Damien was going to be really mad. I suddenly realized I was still wearing my tabard, quickly took it off and pushed it down the side of the seat.

I watched people just walk up off the street and stare in the windows at him. They were drawn from a distance and seemed surprised to find themselves looking in, puzzled as though they had forgotten the reason they were there until they saw him properly, at which time they relaxed quite profoundly so that bags on their shoulders slid off and cases in their hands dropped to the pavement. They stood around as if they were in a museum looking at a fabulous and inexplicable thing, an idol from an unknown continent. They smiled, expressions dreamy and distant, content.

I would have been afraid, if I hadn't known why they were doing it.

Jalaeka noticed them and gave a funny kind of shrug. They drifted away almost immediately, picking themselves up with their belongings, and it didn't happen again, but the noise in the café slowly increased all the time we were there, voices becoming more animated and volatile, laughter suddenly bursting out with greater frequency, happy sounds erupting spontaneously, conversations rippling with affection that was as tangible as a tide rolling in.

I nudged his knee with mine and he smiled at me, and we grinned and started laughing because it was funny to be secret friends like this, with nobody knowing what just happened or how we met. It was funny to feel no fear.

"Why?" I asked him, from the new calm inside my head. I knew his name without knowing how I knew it. "How?"

"You saw what I ought to have been," he told me.

"What kind of crazy answer is that?"

He dipped his finger into the cream on the top of my drink and wiped it with careful precision onto the tip of my nose. Then he grinned and leant across the table and kissed it off.

7/RITA

"That is such a beautiful coat," said the Earth woman as we both looked into the clear plastic display cabinet at the full-length voluptuousness of silver fox, its inner white hairs glazed over by the fine blue-grey outer pelt, so that their thick fullness seemed deeper, their downy inner hair purer than the pearls cascading from the neck of the headless display model that wore them. "Can I try it?"

"Of course," I said and thumb-keyed the case at its lock. I smiled in spite of my aching feet and my longing to go home at the end of a day that had been average in every possible way. As I passed her I saw that her shoes were a good copy of a designer I knew, and her bag was last season's. She twitched the bag out of my way apologetically and gave me a nervous, hopeful smile. I stepped inside the case and lifted the fur down, laying it carefully across my arms to keep it placid while I carried it to the full-length mirrors.

The customer trotted after me and put her own coat down over her bag on one of the courtesy chairs. She brushed and groomed herself with darting pats of her hands across her blouse and the top of her trousers as I approached her. I held out the coat and she slid her arms into the satin linings before I settled it on her shoulders. I smoothed the upper pelts gently with flat hands and she gave a nervous giggle as she felt the barely sentient response of the coat moving of its own accord around her, discovering her shape and smell. It was all but asleep, fortunately.

I told her all about the care and maintenance of such living coats—things she would never need to know—for I was sick of the alarmed reactions and squeals and occasional nasty scenes that followed these moments of guilty customer fantasy when the coat was wakeful and they would catch sight of its eyes watching them, or feel its feet burrow about against them, searching blindly for another foot to hold on to and grasp in comforting security. Calming the coat after it had been flung off was a lengthy business, involving a lot of grooming. As a bonus however, this shop floor in the Embargo was so expensive that few people came here, and if they did, they only wanted to browse and shake their heads at the stupid things that rich people were prepared to pay for.

My customer admired herself, turning this way a little, then that way, and I purposely stepped out of her range of vision so that she could enjoy her stolen moments alone. I was pointlessly adjusting the lapel of an ordinary, vat-grown rabbit jacket when a trace of a vibration—the tread of a distant leviathan or the first erotic quiver of a significant earthquake—ran through me. I put my hand out and held the coat rail, my other hand to my heart, because that was where it had come from.

I saw the other woman's feet turning, stepping, beneath the mirrors' lower edge; neat and careful, turning her ankle this way, that way. Across the floor I looked for my colleagues and saw them going about their business as though nothing had happened, checking and rehanging items, brushing and cleaning, making things ready for the change to the night staff.

It came again.

God, no, I thought. *It can't be. It can't be now. Haven't I done enough for you on Earth—all those businessmen and scientists, all that lying and stealing? Your sleeper, then your spy. Years and years. Leave me alone! You promised that was the end!*

A fine membrane below my sternum broke and from the gap came flying an immaterial gossamer net that spread out and rippled across the simple space and time of my own moment and around all the corners of that moment, into the hidden sevensheet, giving me a vertigo so extreme that I lost my balance and fell. Clutching at anything, I dragged the coats over me in a wave of soft, heavy deadness.

I lay on the carpet, drowning in darkness, my senses opened up in ways I'd never wanted to experience again, the whole of Sankhara screaming into my brain as it rose from beneath me; the fundamental ocean, the dust come to claim its payment for my existence. Unity's agent looked through my eyes, my ears, my body as I struggled to cry out for help. At the edge of vision, far out, I saw a shimmer of the sevensheet that wasn't part of us, nor the Stuffie collective, nor the fabrications of the Sidebar or any other structure in the known. I saw, I heard, I felt movement that wasn't me: Us. I tried to snatch it, but it was gone in the storm of presence . . .

Then came the voice I'd never wanted to hear again. Theodore.

Get up, he said, *get up . . . !* and his voice was changing as it came, rising from the infinite depth of Unity like a shark barrelling to the surface of the sea: jaws. Within the instant I was his puppet, my thoughts and my actions lost to his.

I flung the coats aside and got to my feet, staggering on my high heels for a moment as the woman in the silver fox bent down to help me up, saying, "Oh, are you all right?"

I pushed her aside and started to run. Spikes of pain, the legacy of the day's standing around, drilled through the balls of my feet as I flung my hands out to brace myself against displays that were in my way, specifically designed as they were to prevent anyone leaving with products unseen in a straight dash. In my wake millions of credits' worth of jewellery and clothing went tumbling, and customers and colleagues alike stood still as statues, their mouths hanging agape or with indrawn breaths ready to call out, raising their hands to stop me from metres and tens of metres away.

I wanted to stop. These were not my hands. They were not my feet.

I made the fire escape and ran down it, jumping two and three steps at a time, which hurt so that I gasped and my pencil skirt seam tore with the force of my running. I slid and fell at the penultimate flight, going over on my ankle, lungs heaving, the sound of my own blood singing in my ears, my own heartbeat like a jackhammer in my temples. I got up and ran on, out the exits and into the streets, where I turned without a second thought into the great Forum and across it, scattering early-evening shoppers, running through the ground-level jets of the Aelf 1 fountains as though they weren't there. I ran as I could never have run without hell inside me, following the look of a vague alien shape, that form that defied my sight.

On the far side of the Forum a café window stood in the torchlight of one of Aelf 1's massive structural legs, lit within by a variety of candles and gaslights. It was packed, and I had to step over bags and children and push my way to get to the front, where I could look in. I found myself with my hands against the glass. Voices surrounded me. Someone smiled at me and pointed and I saw my reflection in the glass for an instant, a madwoman, soaked to the skin, hair in rats' tails. I tried to walk away but went inside. I shoved my way between chair backs and tables, losing a shoe, sloughing off the other one as I reached the empty table by the window. I sat down in one of the empty seats. It was still warm.

Here, said Theo in my head—Theo who made me and whom I never wanted back. His voice was calm and thoughtful as he receded from me, the sort of voice that would have been comfortable walking in the park, speaking of genteel affairs as it meandered into the distance. *It's gone now, but it was here. You'll find it, Rita. You'll find it for me. You and I, we'll do it together.*

I sat alone at the table, dripping, gulping air, shaking compulsively with a violence I couldn't stop, even when I held the table with both my hands. When Theo abandoned me there I tried looking on my own for the thing he had pursued and lost. But without him I was only human. My feet were agony. Before me lay an empty cup, dried frothed milk and chocolate on its sides clinging in patterns like clouds.

8/Jalaeka

Francine and I were sitting on the tailgate of the Hoolerton tram, feet hanging a few inches above the road, ignoring the patient AI voice telling us calmly that we should ride safely inside. The broad avenue with its central reservation of grass and tall palms unspooled beneath us, pushing the huge triple fortress of the Massif and the Aelf away until they became a single three-pronged spire of light against the pitch-black perfection of the night sky, stars blotted out by the fairy dust glow that shone off every roof and shallow plane in the city so that every building from the greatest to the most humble was limned in a pale golden shimmer like ancient glory. Then we turned, following the line of the Purbright river towards the docks, and everything but the triple spire was lost to sight, hidden by the close brick walls of the warehouses and yards, their sides peeling with the eczema of old bill posters proclaiming legendary DJs, obscure political agendas and the return of the Justified Ancients of Muu Muu. From beyond the broken bottles that topped their ramparts came the sound and flare of forges working, metal being hammered and cut and moulded and melted. A heavy chemical flux lay on the air, fighting with the odour of fish and a dank smell rising from the gutters.

Her hand in mine.

"So what were you doing last night?" Francine asked.

"Obliterating myself."

"Why?"

I shrugged, slightly embarrassed. Why does anyone?

I glanced at her. She was watching the street and being careful not to stare at me. I longed not to be the pathetic old veteran who stares with a doggy, washed-up gaze that sees shrapnel ripping into everything he looks at. But I know Theo and I know myself, and so I am that guy.

She leant against me with a very slight exaggeration of her position at my side and I leant back much more strongly, accepting her invitation. Sick and tired, because she let me be, I rested my head on her shoulder and let her support me. She wasn't confident enough to put her arm around me, though I wished she would. After a moment I felt her hand stroking my hair where it fell across the back of my shoulders, so lightly that if I'd been human I might not have noticed.

Farther on, as Hoolerton proper began, the brickworks broke into smaller units, the factories becoming shops and houses, clustered close in ranks of terraces like ordered troops. We passed two concrete tower blocks and I wanted to tell Francine that I used to know people who lived in places like this and had even seen them and been inside their homes less than a decade before in my time, but that was ancient history to her. Nonetheless I watched the ugly towers' pattern of window lights with a horrible affection, and then their punch card faces bent away from us and drifted away to the left behind the mountainous bulk of a stone mill, all its windows bricked up across five storeys of machinework floors. Above its gates the name Lazarus Works was carved into the archstones, but beneath them more bricks blocked the entrance. It became the side of a canyon, while on the right a municipal park stretched out in damp, recently rain-drenched dark, the swings and slides in its deserted playground moving silently, gently, as though they'd been left only minutes ago.

I tightened my hold on Francine's hand. "Get ready. Jump!"

We ran ourselves to a standstill at the corner of the street where an all-night store and a pub, cast in the Tudorbethan mould, glowed brightly with light and the promise of civilization. A sign swung outside the pub's Herculean-scaled black and white slice of old England—the Pig and Piper. The air even smelled like Earth's Western urban nineteen eighties; car exhaust, stale beer, burgers, cigarettes.

I led her through the maze Damien had shown me: along several narrow ginnels, muddy underfoot and thick with nettles. They were in white flower and their herbal scent was sickly sweet as we brushed through them, hands high to avoid getting stung. It was still hours until Engine Time.

"Where are we?" she asked.

"Crisscross Street," I said, as we emerged onto it. If there was a more ordinary place in Sankhara, I couldn't think of it.

"These are houses?"

"Yes."

"Monsters here?"

"Only yourself."

She laughed and everything became light to me.

"Stop."

"What?"

I took off my jacket and gave it to her.

"I'm fine," she said.

"Put it on."

She hesitated, but then slid her arms into it. It was too big for her, but the man's cologne on it smelled better now that she wore it. I took her hand back and led her under the railway arch. As soon as we were through she gasped with the cold and surprise and pressed against my side. I put my arm around her shoulders.

"This is where you live?" she asked after she had taken a moment to look around. She swallowed and her face was ashen. "When you said we could go to your place I . . ."

"Not out here!" I smiled at her. "Come on."

She turned to look back through the lych-gate's suppurating arch. "But where . . . ?"

"It's there. Less than a moment away. All still there. I promise."

Her face showed all her doubt, and the moment she discarded it.

She was dwarfed by the trees rearing huge and black over us, their boughs stirring restlessly in a strong wind. She clutched the jacket close around her with her free hand, the other hand holding mine tightly, and walked over the rough faces of the black granite slabs that paved the road as if she was walking on glass. An icy gleam sparkled on puddles of recent rain shivering in twin grooves where the wheels of great carriages were supposed to run. She looked at these lines in both directions. Their silver ran out to our right for miles, but to our left sank almost immediately into an overgrown penumbra where the walls had been brought down by fallen titans, their rotting bodies stretched out and blocking the way. She was careful not to tread near them.

I led her a short distance, right, to the other side of the road, where the wall dropped to a quarter of its former height and was topped with black iron railings, each the width of a forearm and the height of two tall men. They were bent into soft wavy shapes that coiled around each other as though they were snakes crawling up the vertical face of the air. Halfway along their span a great pair of gates were set between raw megaliths of the same material.

Francine halted of her own accord and stared at the gates. They were almost unrecognizable as gates; had suffered a terrible and catastrophic assault at some time in the past, their bars frozen so that they looked like a 3-dimensional drawing of a missile strike wake. Their anguish spoke volumes about the force used against them, though not one that had struggled to gain entrance to the Park they guarded—they had been devastated by something that wanted to get out.

I followed Francine in picking my way through them, my feet splashing in rusty water where one had worn a shallow quarter-circle depression in the paving.

Beyond the rails and gates a broad gravel expanse swept directly to the central door in a colossal and beautifully proportioned palace, almost a perfect copy of its Earthly Baroque antecedent, Rastrelli's Winter Palace. In the light of the full moon overhead its white columns, window-frames, apexes and statuary glowed with a ghostly radiance, the stucco between them a flat grey that made them seem to float in thin air, as though there were no walls. It must have been more than a couple of hundred metres wide. Of its three storeys, all the windows were black except for one I had lit earlier in the day. I could see the hint of that room's flamboyant, wildly coloured wallpaper.

"Is this . . . it?" she whispered.

"The light," I said.

"Oh."

Wings crossed the moon, vast wings of taut skin that let the light show their veins and cartilage and the long body between them, diamond-headed.

"Is this . . . yours. Is it yours?"

"So I'm told."

Francine turned and looked at me, her mouth twitched up at the corners. She reached into her pocket, dug around and handed me a piece of flimsy paper. I glanced at her questioningly, saw her nervousness and concern, and then obediently read it.

Do you thirst for more than an ordinary life?

It was lilac paper, with pink hearts.

*Despite your job and family, is there something missing, deep
     inside?*
*Do you ever wonder what the point of life is now that you can
     be young, beautiful, wealthy, educated and long-lived?*
*Do you feel that science and technology have discovered all
     there is to know?*
*Do you find no pleasure in wealth and in possessions
     anymore?*
*If you think there's more than meets the eye, come to a
     meeting where your local Guide shows the symbol of the
     heart.*

I looked down into her hopeful face. "You think I need
help?"

She took the paper from my hand and screwed it up, letting
it fall on the ground, where it blew away. We were close to one
another in a way that seems to come up by accident, until you
notice it and the pull of one hand to another—my hand to her
cheek, her hands to my waist, her legs to my legs, my face to her
face, her mouth to mine—takes on its own magnetism, slow
enough to taste and soft enough to slide down through like new
snow; but I fell harder than that as her body pressed against me.
Her lips were cold and tasted of the freezing air. She treated me
so carefully, she broke me.

"Why are you crying?" she asked when she finally drew back.
The moonlight made her face white, her eyes and mouth blue
bruises like watercolour splashes.

"I should be on my knees," I said.

She shook her head. "Show me inside."

We walked up the left-hand curve of the outer staircase to
reach the palace door, a single piece of oak, studded with iron

and carved with deep recesses in Celtic knots that no Russian palace ever boasted. Set within the door was a smaller door, which opened to the touch of my hand.

"Things live out there," I said self-consciously, locking it after us by the same act of will. My voice echoed and revealed the size of the hall in which we stood even more effectively than the gleaming electric light that came on to her touch. "Wolves, tigers, bears . . . other things."

I barely noticed the splendour of the place this time; there were some marble stairs, white, and a carpet in bloody red and statues in niches and pillars that dripped gilded decoration, balustrades like entire ski slopes, pillars of blue stone, and great archways that led into darkened galleries and halls receding beyond sight, all that kind of thing. I glanced at the roof because Francine gave it a fearful look as she walked up the first flight of steps. She stood on the landing beside the tortured figure of Laocoön wrapped in snakes and stared at it.

"Huey Cobras," I said, staring at the meticulously rendered details of a mural depicting helicopter gunships over a burning jungle of gruesome orange and grey. The light from the pendant crystal chandeliers gave it a flat, decomposing look.

"You what?"

"It's from an old film about a war. It changes now and again."

Vietnam. *Apocalypse Now.* You wouldn't know it. You were born hundreds of years too late. Last time I saw that film was in the house of somebody I thought I would be with forever.

The place didn't echo, didn't mutter. It was as quiet as a tomb. I listened to her fill it up. I took her to my room, smaller than the rest, its lamps lit to show its hot red/pink brocade walls, damask curtains, impossible, vast bed. The fire in the hearth burned on logs that would last the night, big enough to roast an ox on. It was hot in there. I moved some of my books, worried in case they were going to catch fire where I'd left them piled on the rugs so close to the heat.

"You live here? Sleep . . ." she looked at the untouched plains of the bed, "here?"

"I don't need sleep," I admitted.

"But you might like it," she said. "It's nice. To get away, for a while, sometimes. I like it." She took off my jacket, then her coat and came closer. I sat down on the floor to let her do what she liked and when she sat near me, lay down on my side, looking into the flames. After a while I rolled onto my back and caught her looking at me. She was biting her nails and snatched them away from her mouth instantly, pushing her hands into her pockets.

"Touch me," I said. "Please."

PART TWO

Earth

9/ Valkyrie

Valkyrie was standing in the Field Stores warehouse, strip-checking an Eberstark Volsungshammer sniper rifle when GovGuide intruded on her peace and quiet by playing the first four notes of Beethoven's Fifth. She finished gazing through the long barrel she held and adjusted the sensitivity of her vision to normal before allowing the Guide to deliver its alarm report. She'd hoped for at least another day of silence, but Guide Alarms overrode her compassionate leave.

The message wasn't even voice-delivered. It was flagged with Solargov security codes and in plain text:

> MetroGuide offlined—Metropolis Gateway shut down—all contact lost—emergency quarantine procedures enforced Earthside—GovNet awaits official instruction.

As Valkyrie read she felt only a momentary rise of interest. Ah Apocalypse. She wanted to go back to the smooth simplicity of the gun and feel its interlocking pieces moving together in her hands until the thing was whole and could be put back beside its fifty brothers on the rack. A second message followed in a bright flash of intimate urgency protocols. They overrode her normal function and flooded her sluggish endocrine system with artificial enthusiasm.

My office: now.

Valkyrie placed the gun barrel down onto the workbench in front of her and laid her oilcloth over its unfinished business. She turned and strode the length of the warehouse, passing its racks of firearms, missile launchers, gas grenades and sonic devices in quick time. As she passed she saw herself dimly reflected for an instant in each of the burnished dark metal curves of the weapons, a dull yellow blur of android motion. Her armoured boots made dull thuds on the concrete. She turned, taking a short-cut to the emergency exit through the medical section, and narrowed her vision to a tunnelled shape so that she didn't have to look at the beautiful white and green ranks of field dressings and surgical patches. She'd seen enough of them to last a lifetime.

The emergency door opened for her as she reached it; closed and locked itself after her. The pavement was relatively deserted near the armoury. There was nobody by the yard gates but a pair of engineers taking a rest in the late-morning sunshine to see her step away from the building, open her wings, ignite her rockets and take to the sky.

As she ascended into the aerial lanes over London she saw thousands of others dropping out of the sky—small craft and individuals, Forged flying forms and the small robot drones of the Guide systems, all of them ordered to land to clear the air for the emergency and governmental services. They fell smoothly and gracefully, like a swarm of locusts seen from far off. Valkyrie, connected to GovNet, was able to make a beeline across the miles to Unity House, where her boss worked, and where the alien entity maintained its ambassador.

Valkyrie flew as fast as she could. Insects smashed against her visor. Beneath her the city visibly quavered as the information shock of MetroGuide's disappearance spread from node to node. People turned to one another with bewildered faces and Valkyrie imagined that she heard a collective intake of breath. They were all thinking what she had first thought—this could be no more than a temporary fault of some kind. But when she set her feet onto the roof and exchanged credentials with the building's security guards she lost her reasonable doubts. Their faces were ashy and bleary as though they had been woken from a bad dream. Their expressions prompted her to renew her contacts with the newswires and networks she'd cut herself off from. Every one was error-clogged with excessive traffic.

Valkyrie began to accelerate. Earthside staffers moved aside to let her through, both there and in the lift and in the lower corridors, flattening themselves against the walls as Valkyrie moved in an uncomfortable crouch with her arms jammed against her sides. Eight feet of bulky, metal-clad aerial Forged moving fast in a confined space had that kind of effect generally, but today Valkyrie saw the regular staff let her pass without their standard expressions of mild annoyance that field agents should come in making a mess of their beautiful, serene existence. Instead they seemed almost glad to see her. So it must be very bad.

She went straight in to her boss's rooms and joined the queue of agents waiting for attention. When her turn came the under-secretary seemed so flustered, she gave her name to him with formal politeness. "Light Angel Valkyrie Skuld, tactical intelligence support."

He glanced up and smiled for a fleeting instant. "Hi, Valkyrie," he said. "You can go on past this lot. Go right to the desk. She's waiting for you."

"Jensen." She said his name to him as thanks, and turned to excuse-me and pardon her way through the outer offices.

The doors to the Queen's inner sanctum opened for her, but not quickly enough. She caught one of her shoulder guards on the doorframe and tore a long splinter of the beautiful polished hardwood free. The rip and crack of it was ignored, despite the room's near silence. Nobody took any notice as she picked up the broken wood and screwed it up into a ball in the palm of her hand. Inexplicably she found herself holding back tears. She flicked the splinters into the closest trash can.

Valkyrie had occasionally had cause to regret her low level of AI systems compared with other Forged and Tek personnel, but as she stood and watched her boss now, she felt no regret at all.

The Micro Ticktock Hive Belshazzar was holding a perfectly adequate conversation with her principal secretary, who was also in the room with her, and four other simultaneous discussions which Valkyrie could see logged on the wall where a projected layout of all her current communications was permanently on show. She was talking to the Guide AIs of two other Sidebar Universes as well as with the out-world AIs, Mode and Myanfactor, who hosted the entire Solar Virtual Community and the Forged Dreamstate of Uluru and with the Solargov Emergency Actions Unit. She was also conducting over two thousand other more minor discussions, the subject of which repeated across the board endlessly—Metropolis Sidebar.

The volatile smell of kerosene made Valkyrie look down automatically, running an internal check. One of her fuel lines was leaky. A fine film of pungent discharge was creeping, translucent, down her bronze leg, evaporating, hazing the air. She took a patch of trouble-gum out of her chest compartment and did her best to seal it temporarily. Belshazzar glanced at her with the briefest flicker of acknowledgement as Valkyrie leant over to the desk and whisked a couple of paper tissues out of the pretty floral pack beside the coffee-pot and its discarded cups.

Valkyrie rubbed at the kerosene and was glad she didn't have billions of sisters calling on her attention. Every second they blurted and babbled their news into the Hive Queen's waking mind; those scattered sisters who spied upon and tinkered in the innards of machines across the entire Solar System. Witnessing so much cognitive power held in the form of an ordinary human woman with no outward sign of Forging (though every inward one) was, at best, awe-inspiring. Usually Valkyrie found it intimidating, and today it was simply beyond her.

She used the solvent and tissues to rub a few crusty insect bodies off the polish of her arms although it was a feeble effort and the tissues soon disintegrated.

Belshazzar shut down one conversation and took the opportunity to smile warmly at Valkyrie. "Skuld, a moment please and

I'll be with you." Her words came via short-range radio because her mouth was still issuing instructions for the day's reschedul-ing to the secretary.

Valkyrie gave a tight smile and moved left to place the wad of tissue in the bin with the piece of doorway. No one except Belshazzar had called her by her personal name since Elinor had died. She felt the absence of her old partner on her right side; a commonplace emptiness that did not lessen as the days passed. Elinor would have laughed at the fuel line and the door incident. They would both be smiling now, if she were here. Valkyrie's face set like stone.

"Tell them the truth, then," Belshazzar was saying angrily. "Tell them we have no idea."

At that, with the suddenness of lightning, everyone seemed to wrap their business to a conclusion. Within seconds the room was deserted except for Valkyrie and Belshazzar. The wall, hith-erto streaming with information in a waterfall of complaints and demands, shut down silently and became nothing but a wall.

Belshazzar, middle-aged and dusky, her cropped black hair half-silvered—pushed back her chair and stood up. She lifted her chin to take in Valkyrie, and her dark eyes brimmed with a mixture of determination and anger. The cessation of the wall's coverage was a sign that they might speak freely, cut off from contact with the outside world for a time. It gave Valkyrie a mo-mentary sensation of intimacy and trust which unclamped the stern discipline keeping her jaw shut.

"It's gone for good?" Valkyrie asked.

Belshazzar beckoned with one hand for Valkyrie to follow her, and spoke as she walked. "Theodore has an explanation. I want you to hear it."

Valkyrie didn't move. She glanced involuntarily at the doors behind Belshazzar, far off across metres of pale government carpet, and framed by detection technology as powerful as that used at any of the Sidebar Universe Port Authorities for the de-tection of Stuff particle contamination.

"What's the matter?" Belshazzar asked, turning back towards her when Valkyrie did not come.

Valkyrie knew that time was of the essence but it was easy for Belshazzar. She talked to—the thing—every day. It must seem normal, Valkyrie thought, as though it was just another man, but to her Theodore, Unity's ambassador, was nothing of the kind. There was a dream-sim of Unity in Uluru. Everyone's minds were run together in one undifferentiated soup, not even parallel, but volatile. Valkyrie detested it. Things emerged from it that . . . she didn't even have the mental tools to think about it or the words to express it. And that was only a bunch of human minds.

"I don't want to . . . that is . . . I don't think I can . . . I mean, I don't want to see . . ." Valkyrie had never knowingly come across anything of Unity, not even a piece of Stuff in a lab. She'd hoped that she would never have to reveal her opinions about it publicly. She wished it had never been found.

"Skuld." The Hive Queen saw what was wrong and spoke quietly, though there was nobody to overhear them. "He's *bound* to be human, just like the rest of us. It's like talking to anybody else. Form determines. Experience and perception follow as the night the day."

"He'll hear what I'm thinking," Valkyrie said. She didn't want to say that she was too low in the hierarchy, that Belshazzar was making some mistake, surely, in taking someone like her into The Presence. She longed for an adequate excuse.

Belshazzar shrugged. "I doubt he'll bother. I used to assume that about him myself, but if he does pick my brain, then he doesn't use his knowledge to any advantage I can make out." She beckoned again, with quick, practical fingers that clearly would have liked to snap with impatience. "You can stomach this. I wouldn't have called you in for the assignment otherwise. The long and the short of it is that you're the only agent I consider capable enough to send on this particular mission. You've got the field time, you've got the right kind of mind—frankly, you lack imagination, which is essential—and you're strong. I need you to be my eyes and ears *and* big stick when you go in on this joint action with Earth Security. Their field agents won't last five seconds if things get out of hand. Too clever and too jumpy for it, and I want someone who doesn't get easily distracted doing my business. You've got nothing else to do. You're the one."

Valkyrie knew she'd been expertly railroaded. How could she show her cowardice after a peculiar accolade like that? She took a deep breath, brought her chin down and circled the elegant desk, giving it a wide berth so she didn't damage it.

"Good." Belshazzar took Valkyrie to the double doors of the ambassador's office and preceded her inside. Valkyrie had to duck to get through.

Theodore was sitting in an executive lounge seat in the otherwise empty room and he didn't get up as they entered, although he did give Belshazzar a deep nod of acknowledgment. Superficially he looked like an ordinary human, Valkyrie saw: his body was the Apollo type, that tall and tanned and handsome look, with its yellow hair and its agile, athletic strength. But he hadn't personalized it one jot from what Valkyrie knew to be the baseline stereotype as defined in Ryanson & Sinha's *DNA Boilerplates for Fashion and Design*, it was simply copied from that Genie catalogue. As he continued to sit motionlessly in his easy chair and stare into the distance he gave off all the charismatic charm of a plastic mannequin.

Valkyrie could hear Belshazzar's frustration with Theodore as she introduced them to each other, voice taut as a high wire. Theo didn't spare Valkyrie a glance. He looked at Belshazzar with amber eyes whose expression was quite detached.

"Metropolis has gone," he said, as though continuing a preexisting conversation that was taxing his patience. He placed his hands together in front of him in what might have been a sign of *namaste*, signalling peace in deference to Belshazzar, or showing that he had nothing more to add, or both, or neither. "Everyone who lived in it has been Translated."

He made this latter statement so gently that Valkyrie found

herself floating in a dissociated clarity of mind, as if she weren't really there at all.

She wondered if worlds fell this way all the time. Not with a bang but a whisper. No, not even a whisper. With no sound at all.

She knew what *Translated* meant. It meant made into Unity, assimilated into that being, like Corvax and Isol and Zephyr Duquesne had been, the first humans to interact with Unity; like people were today, if they became infected with Stuff—through trafficking with it unwisely, occasionally voluntarily. But those who wanted to cross over could never have amounted to *millions* of individuals, not without warning, or asking, or . . . any reason at all.

Valkyrie tried to imagine the scale of it, and failed. To her mind, Translation simply meant death. If it had been done, then he, Theo, must have done it, because he and Unity were one thing. She stared at him, feeling as though he had literally blown her insides away, her shock was so great. He had consumed an entire world, and he spoke of it so lightly.

It seemed to be an age later that he added, in the same executioner's *sotto voce,* "We regret the loss of continuity for all the families involved. *Deeply* regret."

Belshazzar didn't wait for him to give her his attention, and Valkyrie was glad of that. "Before we're ready to accept your condolences, I think that we would all like to know why you chose to destroy a perfectly functional and fully populated Sidebar. One point eight million people's next of kin aren't going to be comforted by the idea of their loved ones spending eternity at one with something they can't see or touch."

Theo sighed, performed an elaborate motion of his shoulders and crossed his legs. He looked pleased, Valkyrie thought.

"Yes, in spite of thousands of years of empty religious promises of exactly that. It's quite perverse, I do agree. Whereas what I'm saying to you is that nothing has been lost." He tipped his head a degree to one side with the missed timing of someone who's been exhaustively coached, though Valkyrie fancied he deliberately got it wrong. "Nobody has died. They are all *within,* every life perfectly recorded, every experience distributed. Fascinating people, all of them. I am glad to have come into the sphere of their influence."

Valkyrie's jaw dropped as she realized the sense of what he was saying. The people of Metropolis were now part of Theodore's undertow. He wasn't apologizing. He was thanking them for a donation.

"Your *reason*," Belshazzar insisted, allowing this gross insult to pass. "Twenty-five years of nothing. No trouble in any Sidebar, even the most complex. Hardly any accidents. Single figure Translations, pretty much all voluntary, no transgressions on either part. Now this."

Valkyrie curled both her hands into fists involuntarily and her metallized skin creaked. Theodore looked up at her for the first time, although he didn't lift his chin to do so. She saw that he felt no obligation to offer a reason, and that there was nothing anybody could do about it if he never gave one. Belshazzar's twenty-five years of rule-abiding cohabitation with Unity in the Sidebar Universes had simply provided Solargov Security with reasons to believe in the wisdom of the choice they had made when they agreed to the construction of the Sidebars in the first place. The quarantine had been so good, the idea so bold, the future so very bright. The infinite research laboratory . . . an infinite amount of space and time . . . worlds . . . no hitches, not compared to the ages of adventure long past.

They had nothing on Theo, on *it*, and they never would. And even if they had hard evidence of any infringements, it wouldn't matter because there was nothing to be done. Unity was unassailable. Valkyrie admired Belshazzar's cool in the circumstances—Valkyrie wanted to kill him. She let him know this as she stared at him, more angry than wise.

"I tell you only to warn you of potential further disruption. There is a splinter cell," he said finally, grudgingly, dismissing Valkyrie by returning his gaze to Belshazzar.

"A what?" Belshazzar said. Valkyrie didn't think she'd heard it right.

Theo shrugged. "Well now, how shall I put it? Unity is an extremely large entity, not unlike a complete biosphere or planet, say. It is a dynamic, living system, with its own pressure points, highs, lows—all kinds of energy exchanges. Consider it as a liquid. Droplets of Unity can become separated from the whole during stormy conditions. They can be scattered across any of the dimensional surfaces, or all of them. Usually we reabsorb such losses very quickly. They are mostly nonfunctional matter, Stuff that assumes the form of quartz, the type that your Voyager Lonestar Isol discovered on her way to Barnard's Star thirty years ago."

" 'Mostly nonfunctional,' " Belshazzar said, "hides a multitude."

Theo made a minute, concessionary nod that managed to convey an absolute lack of concession.

"How can you have a splinter of Unity?" Valkyrie asked suddenly. Her voice sounded harsh to her own ears. "How can there be *more* than one of it?"

" 'Unity' is a human word with limited associations," Theodore said slowly, measuring her stupidity. "When splinters break away from the whole and become 4-dimensional material they usually remain attached to the sevensheet of Unity fabric, even though they are separated in the material 4-verse. But on very rare occasions they may become separated across all eleven faces of the continuum. When this happens each piece becomes instantly self-complete. There is nothing that one part of Unity has in ability that the other lacks. The difference lies in the quantity of information accessible to each one. Unity is memory in fluid dynamic potential, living information. Both instantiations of Unity can survive and pursue separated evolutions distinct from one another. However, such events have always ended with a reunion of the two parts. Essentially, although they were separated, they were functionally identical. Once they meet again, they instantly merge. It is in their interests to do so, as they are then maximally potential. The Metropolis Sidebar was the foam on a wave of Unity that has returned to the sea. It is no loss. Only change. The assimilation of the human individuals there has increased the Unity potential for creative acts. They are becoming. Not gone."

Valkyrie imagined droplets of mercury sliding on a piece of glass and uniting to form a single pool. "From the way you said it I thought it was more like trouble than just some bad weather event. Doesn't seem to warrant the extinction of an entire world."

Theo yawned. "And sometimes splinters are created when a particular weather system is pushed out deliberately, because its inclusion would cause potentially fatal destabilization to the whole. Unity's structure is vastly complex, certain modalities that have high individuation potentials are—unsympathetic, at times." He gave Valkyrie a glance that considered her insufficient to a better explanation and she felt herself duly patronized. "Isol—or should I say the human beings that were Translated—had an effect rather like that of a very large and heavy rock being dropped into still water. All conscious structures new to Unity do. There was a splash. Some of the splash remains detached, weak and human in nature, and we are in the process of recovering it. Think of it as fallout."

"Fallout?" Valkyrie repeated, forgetting herself. "We were a rock in your pond and now the fact that you're committing genocide is fallout? It's our fault?!"

"This thing is loose in Solar space?" Belshazzar asked softly, but precisely, ignoring Valkyrie's outburst.

"A conscious splinter is somewhere inside the Solar Primary or 'Bar worlds," Theo said, letting his fingers slide through one another to form a double fist. "Through consciously adaptive contact with humans it has become somebody, probably human, almost certainly in fact."

"Like the Stuff constructs in Sidebars?" Valkyrie asked.

"No," Belshazzar said. She turned to Valkyrie with a cold and unpleasant smile that Valkyrie read as a kind of victory. "He doesn't mean that. Stuff constructs aren't what *he* is. Stuffies are made and operated by Unity, human in all but name and fundamental matter, able to be swallowed up at an instant's notice into the tide and flow of Unity. They're made of it, but they're not part of its conscious flow until the moment of their return. They have no access to it nor it to them. *This* is a human-made being, not under Unity control, separate: an individual. It's just like Unity, as powerful as Unity, but it's not Unity. It's not even a different kind of *you*, Theo. It's not an agent that allows Unity to think in human terms. It's . . . its own thing. That *is* what you mean, isn't it?"

He inclined his head by an infinitesimal fraction.

Belshazzar pressed him. "And you can't retrieve it?"

"Primary contact has proven—difficult, this time."

"Primary contact?" Valkyrie asked. "Is there some chain of contacts?"

"Your mind is locked into meaningless hierarchies," Theodore told her as an aside, and said to Belshazzar, "It cannot be reassimilated by normal means." He let his hands fall into his lap.

"Why not?" Belshazzar asked.

He shrugged again. "We don't know. It seems to have undergone a critical state change in its interaction with the seven-sheet. I cannot say, because I cannot replicate the transforms."

"You don't know," Belshazzar repeated in a calm, even tone. "You say it has evolved? Does it—supersede you?"

Theo had become even more still. Valkyrie wasn't sure he was breathing. He was suddenly all comfortable and loose, like someone had cut his strings. He smiled vaguely and spun the chair with his foot so that he faced them completely. He sat forward and became disturbingly affable although the skin around his eyes never changed its smooth, doll-like quality.

"Not yet. If you'll allow me to finish—this splinter came to Metropolis only relatively recently. Unity operations that require energy transforms across all 11-D maintain stability because there is only one operator. But with two such operators, each not knowing what the other is doing or plans to do, there is a virtual certainty that energy transactions across the 11-D will cause a fatal instability and destroy the conditions that permit the existence of all expanded 4-D space-times, including your own. The splinter is a conscious operator, like myself, capable of destroying all expanded 4-space, whether it intends to or not. Being much less than Unity, the chances are that its calculations are less refined and the probability is high that what has happened to Metropolis is what will happen to all the universes you know, if this situation continues."

"So your killing all of them was what—a lesson?" Valkyrie demanded.

"Since we have been unable to reclaim the splinter by the usual means, it was our effort to destroy it, in order to avoid catastrophic potentials." Theodore met her gaze again and did not blink, or drop it. His smile was bright and its contempt withering, and Valkyrie quickly looked away. Her heart thundered in her ears and her face heated.

"Which has failed," Belshazzar said.

Theodore sat back and recrossed his legs, putting one ankle up onto his knee and flicking some imaginary lint from the pressed line of his trousers. "Yes. Temporarily. But whatever its intention, it has come here and I believe it is inside the Sankhara 'Bar. It is completely inactive across the sevenface, so I cannot track it. But it will do something eventually—it always does." He looked utterly confident.

"So, what? Is this your demand for evacuation?" Belshazzar asked him.

"No, we will make no more futile efforts to destroy it. All the human worlds are safe, unless the splinter itself destroys them, either deliberately or by accident. It is massively ignorant of its capacities, so there is a reasonable chance of that."

"And why are you telling us this?" Belshazzar asked.

"To let you know." Theodore got up and walked over to the windows. He looked out and down into the streets. "We will continue to operate and pursue our course of action in Sankhara and across all other 4-dimensional expansions necessary to ensure the splinter's destruction or assimilation, and we regret . . ."

"Thank you. I believe you said that already."

"You doubt my sincerity."

"I don't doubt it. I just know what it's worth." Belshazzar got up too, and indicated to Valkyrie that the audience was over. Valkyrie didn't blame her when she allowed herself one parting shot. "I wonder if Tom Corvax or Zephyr Duquesne would tell a different story, if you *let* them return."

"But they are always here," Theodore said of the first humans to translate into Unity, as though vaguely surprised anyone could have thought they weren't present. "Informing me." He looked over his shoulder, and shrugged, and vanished.

There was no crack of inrushing air to fill the vacuum of his position. He had become air, Valkyrie thought, as she felt a breath of it push past her face and hands. It smelled of stale dry-cleaning solution, acrid and poisonous.

"But they're *not* you." Belshazzar closed the door behind herself and Valkyrie, shutting them back in her office again. The doorframe sensors remained silent above them. Valkyrie wished the parting shot had not sounded so ineffectual.

When they had moved away from the doors the Hive Queen turned to Valkyrie and spoke quickly and calmly. "I want you to catch up and review everything we know about Unity. Give yourself a thorough grounding. Then I want you to go to Sankhara and find this splinter he's so angry with. Find out anything you can. Officially you're to be the strong arm of the Solargov Security Agent out there, Bob Clovitz. But that will only be your cover story. I want you to pursue your own investigation and report to me directly, as well as doing whatever you have to do for Clovitz, when and if he makes contact with you. The Departments are divided on this one. He probably has an agenda to terminate the splinter though he won't let you in on it."

"But Sankhara is a high-interaction world," Valkyrie said, halting briefly between words. She stuttered slightly, trying to find good reasons for her fear that weren't to do with terror of Unity. The last thing she wanted, especially after today, was to go closer to it. "Among so many strange things this—thing—is going to be hard to find, impossible maybe."

"But me no buts. I need you to discover if anything Theo said is close to the truth. I don't expect you to even approach the splinter if you do find it. I'm looking to verify his claim, that's all. If Theo is right, we need to be careful around it. Don't do anything to piss it off. We might need it. If it is human, then it can have a conversation, and that means there may be a solution to this that does not involve Unity running wild across us. Perhaps it will free us from Unity, understand?" The Hive Queen's bearing had become stiff, bristling with suppressed emotion.

Valkyrie hesitated. "Did you know anyone in Metropolis, Ma'am?"

"Yes." Belshazzar was already turning her attention to another emissary arriving as Valkyrie left. "Many people."

The emissary was the Solargov Deputy President Tekgenesis Atahualpa, or rather his everyday avatar, as projected by the office system. His actual body was on Mars. Valkyrie watched the large olive baboon stalk around the furniture with his tail high and huge teeth bared.

"Where is that fucker, Theodore?" he bellowed. The door closed before Valkyrie could hear Belshazzar's reply.

Moving more slowly now with the burden of the task weighing her down, Valkyrie loaded all the available data on Unity at high-speed compression during the stop-start journey the public elevator took in its descent to the ground floor. At least it gave her another excuse not to have to look people in the eye. Too many of them wanted to show her sympathy about Elinor. As the facts slumped wearily into the spaces allotted them in her unconscious mind, like tired commuters finding a seat on a train, she slowed the absorption rate to consciously read one academic paper that got her attention for a second:

"It is generally supposed that Translation entails the complete cessation of normal consciousness so that the Translated person becomes effectively nothing more than a memory form, in the same way that Forged and Tek-adjusted individuals may have prints of their final neural patterns taken just prior to death and maintained within AI networks. But this is a mistake."

Valkyrie frowned. Elinor existed as a memory print within Uluru, a very damaged one, and Valkyrie was interested by anything pertaining to them, in case there was hope of restoration. AI loading was like a photograph. It could not render dynamical, realistic change. AI revenants had never been successfully rendered viable, yet. The Elinor stored in Uluru was not alive. She was a simulation.

"AI network prints are static snapshots which may be mined for information. Within Unity however, [information source classified] the Translated individual remains alive, in the sense that they are able to continue the natural processes of consciousness. While these processes also involve constant change there is no cessation of self-awareness; the individual lives on. AI prints, on the other hand, are simply photographs of personality made to move and speak in the illusion of life, without the continued experience of the dead person."

Valkyrie shuddered and scanned into the appendices, where she read that those who had been Translated were not, as Theo insisted, actually dead. Not dead, as such. They had simply become the same thing as Unity itself. Their physical bodies were gone from 4-D, although they might be made again, supposing there was a need. What could that be? She needed Elinor. Would that be enough?

It did not say what that need might be, nor whose. Perhaps wanting to be back was not an option or was not allowed—the text didn't say anything about whether people who were Unity could give effect to their will as they used to. Being Theo didn't seem to Valkyrie to be the ultimate in corporeal self-expression for anyone, least of all the millions beneath him. And the incorporeality had to be one hell of a change, she thought. The Corvax Declaration stated that the Translated were in a state of superposition, being both themselves and alive and conscious, but also unified with all other conscious beings within Unity. It was such a grand statement, but try as she might she could not imagine the reality. Would it be like being an entire committee? That seemed absurd.

"Well whoop-de-do," Valkyrie said, surprising several other people sharing the lift with her. She shrugged and pointed at her right ear, to suggest she had mistakenly spoken aloud during another kind of conversation and they nodded, all guilty of the same thing from time to time.

She still considered Theo a mass murderer, and superpositions beyond time were not cutting it as a defence. As they paused at the second floor to take on more anxious-faced workers, Valkyrie linked up with the all-AI network, Teragate, to see what the cold word was on Metropolis. Teragate was where all the Solar AIs talked. It typically excluded all non–machine users, but Valkyrie had done it a couple of favours in the human world and it would sometimes give her a snippet of information.

SankhaGuide allowed her to access its civilian tracking data, highlighting two specific instances of lost contact inside the city. It gave her minimal legal information on the two individuals concerned, one Stuffie, one Unevolved, known to each other. Valkyrie looked at the human name: Dr. Gregory Saxton. He researched Unity Engine activity. Valkyrie knew nothing about Engines, except that they were what kept the Sidebars going.

Valkyrie grabbed that fact and hung on to it as her starting point. The lift paused on first, couldn't take any more people on, and passed down to the ground. Valkyrie was last out. She pretended that she was not dawdling, not putting off the inevitable journey, the move forward into a world without Elinor.

Sankhara the city was notionally sited over Blackpool, on Lancashire's coast where the west of England met the Irish Sea. The Gateway into its Sidebar was located on a slip road leading off the M62 west of the Manchester Vast. Valkyrie bought tickets for a high-speed air link to the north as she walked towards St. James's Park in the weak sunshine of a London spring. She wanted to go back to the arsenal and lose herself in the minutiae of cleaning and repairing inanimate things where she felt, if not good, then safe. Instead she sent a message to the Master-At-Arms, informing him that her leave had been unexpectedly terminated.

The shrine of Uluru Metatron in this park was one of over thirty such places in the city, but it was Valkyrie's favourite. It looked like a huge silver sphere, balanced delicately on the top of the grass as though it was lighter than a soap bubble and could take off at any second. Only a Forged human being would have the knowledge or the senses to detect where the ever-shifting doorways were. They were open portals behind convincing illusions of mirrored surfaces. Valkyrie watched her own reflection stride towards her until the moment she stepped through their light-built lies and into the Zen-quiet of the interior.

Inside the sphere lay a plain space, rather dark, with seats of varying sizes and types lining the walls. Standing areas were equipped with simple handrails and locator clamps. This sort of shrine offered security and safety for complete immersion in the Forged's virtual universe, Uluru, and this one in particular was big enough that visitors need not feel obliged to greet one another. Valkyrie chose to stand and set her hand on a free bar, locking her exoskeleton in position so that she could use all her processing capacity to render the virtual world. There was an instant of vertigo as her inputs switched over from her physical body to digital signal, and then there was a different reality all about her.

The Skuld in this place was a grubby urchin child with ragged trousers and tangled hair. Freed from the bulk and limits of her armoured life as a Light Angel, Valkyrie wandered with artless curiosity among the familiar landmarks of her youth. She reverently ran her fingertips along the worn aluminium fuselage of Tom Corvax's silver aeroplane as she passed its resting place. It was long abandoned: grass and daisies grew thickly around its wheels, and its tail was almost buried in the side of the hill. Valkyrie, and many other Forged, liked to stroke it and had incorporated it into their personal experience of Uluru much as they might hang a reproduction painting on their wall at home. To touch it was to touch a legend.

Metatron, the avatar of the twin AI systems who ran Uluru, showed his face in a reflection on the plane's wing as she explored her favourite bulky line of handmade rivets.

"Hallo, Valkyrie, can I get you anyone?"

She thought she should do business first. "Is there anybody here who has personal experiences of Unity or of the Independence Occupation of Origin, Unity's homeworld?"

"I will ask." The face dimmed to indicate the departure of Metatron's attention but brightened again almost immediately. There was never long to wait. "One comes who would speak anonymously." Metatron inclined his noble, seraphic head and winked out of existence, job done.

Valkyrie looked around her and presently saw a black butterfly with red eye marks on the wings slowly fluttering towards her. It landed on the plane close by her hand, then expanded into an attractive golden gryphon and stretched out along the warm metal, tail tip twitching. Where most people broadcast on the emotional attunement bands in Uluru, this one gave off only the merest hint of itself, the bare minimum for politeness' sake: a distant friendliness.

"What's your interest?" it asked. It had a voice that was rich and musical, the kind of voice that would have been good for reading ghost stories late at night.

She showed her Security ID. "Official," she said. "What's your experience?"

"Unofficial," it said. "I am a . . . researcher."

"I'm—"

"I know who you are, and where you're going, and what for," the gryphon said, eyes almost closed as it looked askance. "I advise against it."

Valkyrie was instantly suspicious—she was used to the machinations of the various agencies, their shifting agendas and their knowledge of one another's business; it was routine, though she didn't like to be so easily bested. She assumed this was someone from another team like hers, possibly Solar Securitat, though it reminded her of something or someone else. She was nagged by memories that stubbornly refused to materialize. "But . . ."

"Unity is unstable," the gryphon said, one of its claws gouging a scratch across the metal wing of the plane as it flexed one of its eagle forefeet. "And things have got personal with it. If you must go, don't get involved. But that's rather like saying don't go at all. So don't go." At the same time it emphasized its honesty over the affinity link.

Valkyrie backed off quickly—the weight of the gryphon's conviction was so strong it threatened to overwhelm her receptors. She believed it before she had time to object. At the same time the peculiar emotions she could taste on the line between them unsettled her; they were so strong and powerfully felt, but they were complex and sophisticated—they verged on being a kind of thinking all of their own, a kind of superintuition.

It was rare to find someone capable of experiencing certainty as powerfully as this gryphon did. Her curiosity burned her terribly, but in Uluru you got what you got and asked no questions. It was the law, and permanent excommunication was the penalty for attempting to access beyond what was offered. Valkyrie had to take the gryphon's statements at face value. "I have to go. Can't you give me some advice that's more useful? Anything? Because gnostic predictions aren't enough to make me stop."

"No, that's all I can think of," the gryphon said absently. "But I'd still appreciate it if you stayed out of things when you got there."

"That would be easier if I had any idea who you were, or if you were as truthful as you seem."

"So it would." The gryphon yawned, curling its pointed pink tongue. "If you go, then you will certainly meet me there, and I will certainly have to stand in your way, should you choose to interfere. I must tell you that I will do so until one or other of us is ended." It returned to being a butterfly and meandered off over the fuselage.

Valkyrie sighed, reached down near her bare foot, pulled up a daisy and twirled it. She pulled off the petals, counting,

"I'll see her, I'll see her not . . ."

It ended on "not." Probably for the best—AI prints degrade with visiting. She left the yellow daisy centre there on the silver wing, for Metatron, and opened her real eyes into the chilly shadow of the shrine.

Two Arboraforms, Park Attendants, were sitting out their break there, leaning against one another, lost in Uluru. Skuld wondered who could already be involved from the human world with a situation like this one in Sankhara. How could they know so much?

The only answer she could think of was one she didn't like at all—they knew what they knew well before Metropolis was destroyed, either because they knew Theodore, or they knew the splinter.

Valkyrie didn't bother going back home. There was nothing there she wanted. She made her way to the air terminus and caught the speed link, leaving it when they were high over the three cloud decks that blanketed Manchester in rain. She turned northwest and began her descent towards the Sankhara Gateway.

10/FRANCINE

I woke up and didn't have a clue where I was for about ten seconds. The pink ceiling, white borders, dripping patterns of leaves and forests, the luxury . . . I had no idea. And then, I did.

I rolled over and saw the fire was down to hot white ash, with a few red embers glowing here and there. I was alone, and I ached from lying on the floor. The carpet was thick but I'd slept so deeply I had hardly moved. The room was bigger than I remembered and now that the curtains were drawn back it was lit by brilliant sunshine coming through huge windows. The deep pomegranate colour was so intense it almost hurt my brain.

I got up slowly, rubbing my sore shoulder, realizing I was still wearing my old clothes and the anorak I borrowed from Katy the day before. Above the fireplace was a mirror which I was just tall enough to see myself in. I looked appalling.

I didn't remember exactly how I fell asleep. I did remember that he asked me to touch him, but he just lay there. He looked sad. I put my hand on his shoulder and he relaxed, kept looking at the fire. He put his hand on mine. A glowing heat ran over me. I lay down behind him, I put my arm around him. He held my hand against his chest. I felt his heart beat. That's the last thing I remember.

But . . . where was he? Was it all a trick? Oh, now suddenly I thought of the Stuffies and all the rumours of what lay beyond the city confines . . . the rebirth of the oldest stories, the primeval lords of the universe, demons, beasts and all the lying, conjuring magical creatures of ages never. I started to look for the door, realizing then that I had no idea where I was, and neither did anyone else I knew.

I listened. It was quiet. I tiptoed to the door and opened it cautiously, slowly, and almost jumped back. There was a white pedestal in front of me, bearing a huge hand-tied bunch of baby pink roses. A note, propped against them, said, in perfectly scripted handwriting, Not This Way. Their scent was delicate and beautiful, nothing heady. I touched one and it was real.

The hall beyond was silent and empty. I turned back, peering closely around the furniture, glancing out of the windows. Everything was peaceful. Hope and terror fought for control of me. I walked to the other door, on the left of the fireplace. It wasn't quite shut and swung open easily onto a dressing room or drawing room of some kind, ivory and gold. White petals were scattered at my feet in a trail that led across its dark hardwood floor and richly coloured rugs. It wound gently in a curve to another door, passing lengthy, luxurious sofas and tables covered with books and papers . . . huge amounts. I glanced at them, taking a few tentative steps: they were mostly novels and histories, biographies and old bound collections of comic strips.

Beyond any ability to stop, I followed the white roses.

They led into a white marble bathroom, across the floor, over a stack of perfectly folded white towels, over a chair with a set of clean clothing on it, over a pair of silk slippers, over a white mat and over the edge of a tubful of water where they lay scattered among bubbles that covered the whole surface. Steam rising had wilted them, but they were still fresh.

"Hello?" I whispered and turned to see the door close softly at my back. The lock was on my side. I stood there in my horrible old clothes and realized I smelled of barracks living and cleaning compounds. I hadn't had a bathroom to myself in months—only quick showers snatched in the few allotted minutes of privacy allowed by the Foundation's schedule.

I didn't believe this was for me. Or if it was, the prelude to something . . .

Beside the bath was a stand holding a broad glass dish of toiletries. All the best, labels I'd never even seen before, not for real. The bath itself smelled heavenly. I went back and locked the door. The grip turned easily in my hands. I tested it. Solid.

It took me a long time to work up the courage to get in the bath. I put my clothes as close to it as I could. I had to work very hard at my fears. My heart was thudding so fast, so full of hope and excitement that there wasn't room for much else. I wanted it to be for me.

Of course, all this stuff was for idiots. If Damien were here, he'd tell me all about it in an instant.

The water covered me to my chin and I stayed in until it got cold. After I got out I thought about getting back into my clothes . . . but put the new ones on. What good would a few bits of old cloth do me against . . . things? And the new ones were beautiful but plain, a white shirt, tough blue outdoor trousers, socks, shoes. Even the underwear was the right size, white, plain. No sacrificial robes or frills and fusses.

I opened the door and found an entirely new trail of peach-coloured rose petals. They led through another door and out onto a balcony with the most incredible view; it ran across formal gardens, down a huge grassy avenue, broad parks and forest, miles of forests rising to white-capped mountains beyond. The sky blazed and the sun shone, making the cool air pleasant, but I only noticed these things tangentially. He was leaning against the balcony rail, watching me, the petals leading all the way to his feet. He still had a rose stem in his hand and was dropping the last of the flower head onto the ground. As I met his glance he grinned and tossed it over his shoulder, biting his lip as though I'd caught him doing something naughty.

"Damn, I thought I'd be quicker than that," he said. "Water not too hot? Should I have led you to your chair instead? I used to know about this. It's been a long time."

I followed the trail to its end. At close range he was so intoxicating I actually got dizzy and had to put out my hand. It came in contact with his shoulder. He glanced down at it and I felt him breathe in sharply. I whispered, "Are you going to eat me?"

"Only if you ask nicely," he said, looked into my eyes and winked at me. "Ah, who am I kidding? If you ask at all. But I'm like the vampires that way. I only do requests. So, be careful what you do with your mouth." His expression became unmistakably lustful but friendly at the same time. His gaze dropped to my lips and lingered there and his own lips parted slightly.

I felt my face turn as hot as the sun.

He looked back up, smiled and took hold of my shoulders, turned me around and sat me down at the table. "Eat something. You must be starving. I didn't even feed you yesterday."

I looked blankly at all the food laid out before me, champagne on ice, orange juice, sushi, fruit, bread, pastry . . . there was nothing left out. Flowers and branches covered in fresh berries tumbled in skeins of excess through it all, almost too much, but not quite. I didn't feel the slightest hunger. My stomach was locked with excitement. I looked at him as he sat down close to me. He pulled a cherry off one of the branches, reached across and put it against my mouth. I took it and his fingers just brushed my lips. I bit it and the hot, sweet explosion of juice was a shock but then suddenly his mouth was on mine in a kiss that sealed it in.

He leant back and smiled at me. "Bet you can't spit over the railing from here."

I chewed carefully around the pit and lined it up with my tongue, took a breath and . . .

"Wrong again," he said and shrugged as the pit vanished over the drop. He laughed self-consciously and held his hand out. "Want to see the rest of the place?"

"No," I said. I didn't think I could take any more strangeness. I wanted to stay there, potentially forever.

"Okay." I knew nothing about him. It didn't matter. All my sense screamed at me that being here was a complete mistake, only a moron could fall for this stuff, and at the same time I was happy and every time he did anything it was just the right thing, for me, at that moment. I fell out of love with sense. I watched him move and sometimes even listened to what he was saying. I didn't notice myself eating, and he didn't much, but somehow the table's feast diminished and the sun swung around and it grew too cool to stay outside.

I told him my story.

He told me what he was. He explained how he hid. He said he couldn't prove any of it.

"You're a Stuffie." I shrugged. "I'm a Genie. Who cares?"

"You do," he said with a discomforting direct gaze.

I shrugged. "Don't."

"You identified yourself as a thing. You care about it. A lot. You hate it. You're furious about it."

"And you're not?"

"Oh, I am. Angry enough to flatten a city and then some . . . Never pretended otherwise." He shrugged. "But at least I get to have an opponent I can point at—Unity, and Theo. For all the good it does. You, you're mad and you can't even bring yourself to identify who with."

"I'm not. I can. I'm not angry."

"Liar, liar," he said quietly.

"All right then, I am angry and I do really . . . dislike . . . Darren, my mother's partner. He's . . ."

"N-uh uh. You're not mad with him. The only way to stop is to face up to the real person you're mad at."

"Oh, so it's my fault . . ."

"Nope. You've circled it, but you're not calling it."

"Well, if you know so much, you call it."

"Who made you without asking?"

"My mother loves me."

"Never said she didn't. Where IS she by the way?"

"She's back at home in . . . what has that got to do with it?"

"You ran because you were frightened about how angry you were with her. You didn't know what to do about it and it was starting to leak out."

"That's stupid."

"No. That's actually quite self-sacrificing and noble and only a little bit stupid."

I glared at him and got up. Unable to find a way to contradict him, I marched back into the building, through the hot pink room and the pedestal with the roses on it and the note . . . and into the hallway, and along towards the stairs and then I stopped, only then realizing the real size of the place I was in. The corridors ran for miles, the doors . . . I couldn't count them. I caught my breath and ran down the stairs, only then realizing that of course I'd left Katy's wretched anorak back in the bathroom and it was probably freezing outside because it was cold in here.

I ran down the steps, not wanting to go, but having to, now that I'd made the move, and came to the door. I opened it, ducked through and screamed.

At the top of the outer staircase a creature like a leathery, emaciated gryphon, bigger than a draught horse, was sitting on its hindquarters. At my appearance it turned its ugly, bony head with leisurely interest and stared at me from huge yellow cat's eyes. It opened a long mouth, beaky at the edges but still full of teeth and gaped, like birds do in the heat. Its voice was almost incomprehensible, lost in guttural snarls, but I thought it said, "Greetings."

Jalaeka appeared and put his arm around me. I tried not to be glad and comforted. "This is Hyperion," he said. "I was going to introduce you more formally, but . . . Hyperion, this is Francine."

"Hello," I said. "Are . . . are you . . . ?"

"He is Forged," Jalaeka said. "Human."

"Oh. Oh right. Sorry," I began apologizing to him; it was such bad manners to not even recognize your own species and I didn't want him thinking I was Separatist.

"Glun-ah nratah!"

"He says it doesn't matter. He'd talk to you properly, but you seem to have no Tab," Jalaeka translated.

The gryphon, Hyperion, was wearing rudimentary scale and leather clothing, and decorations and jewellery—bone amulets and various beaded bindings and piercings shone dully. His large, wolfish ears turned constantly, listening to the forests that crowded this side of the Palace closely, encroaching on the garden.

"Does he . . . how do you know each other?" I asked, trying to figure out what Hyperion had been Forged for exactly. They all had a purpose, since they were abominably expensive to create.

"Hyperion found this place first. He is a mystic hunter."

"Uh serghnant uh zhe gutt," Hyperion growled.

". . . a servant of the god . . ."

". . . eeyagh ghorse . . ."

". . . the higher force . . ."

"I didn't even know they made Forged for . . . that . . ." I said, looking at the claws on Hyperion's forefeet, which were much more like hands than I had realized. His joints were unusual and as I watched he got up from his resting position and became suddenly bipedal.

"The Pangeneses made him, not the Authority," Jalaeka said. "He says there are lots of them, unregistered Forged, created at the whim of the father-mothers. He doesn't mind telling you, because you are like him, he says."

"What? How?"

The huge creature stretched like a cat, long arms wider than the two of us could have stretched together. As he yawned I saw all the way down his long purple mouth. He had teeth on his tongue.

"Wanderer," Jalaeka said, eyes looking vaguely up and across as he listened to Hyperion inwardly. "Searcher. Ranger. Hunter. Made by the many hands of Tupac and Mougiddo to go beyond the veil. He says. The veil of illusion . . . the inner veil." He glanced down at me and shrugged. "Don't look at me. He thinks I'm a god."

Hyperion barked, sounding exactly like a big dog. It was a laugh. "Hghlugh!" Love.

"He tells me that's what I am. And he was made to find me. So he knows what he's talking about. And now he's going into the wild, so he can tell me more about who I am. Nice. Saves me the bother of analysis."

I thought of Greg suddenly, and what he would make of all this. If it were true. Hyperion walked down the stairs in a few steps, careful on his huge hind paws. He vanished into the tree-line a hundred metres away. When I had watched him go I looked up at Jalaeka. "And are you?"

"The god of love? No. But I lived next door to him once."

"Where?"

"Metropolis."

"You were there?"

He nodded and looked down at the floor.

"I thought nobody got out." I'd heard all the stories, read all the newsies.

"Just me." He looked at me, as guiltily as I'd ever seen anyone look. Hunter and hunted, he'd said about Unity. "It would have been better for you if you'd never met me, never changed me. But now you have." He was almost talking to himself.

I didn't know how to tell him that, even though it blew my

mind, it didn't matter. "You know, I should take Katy's anorak back when I go and fetch my stuff. Would you mind coming with me? I don't really want to go there on my own. She'll try to make me stay."

"Fetch your stuff?"

"So I can bring it here, now I'm living with you."

He looked at me, full of objections and all the other complicated, alien things rushing through his mind. His smile was shy. "Yes, of course I'll come."

I held my hand out to him, unable to suppress a shiver. "Freezing out here."

"Of course it is," he said, taking my hand and looping my arm around his waist. "What was your favourite story when you were little?"

"My . . . um . . . 'The Snow Queen,' " I said, watching my breath mist in front of me as we turned into the building's icy shadow. "But that couldn't . . ."

"It's our nature to be changed by dreams," he said. "And I definitely didn't get this from my last girlfriend."

A spark of jealousy struck me hard. "Oh. What did you get from her?"

"Still not sure," he said and unconsciously put his free hand to his chest, as though shutting something in.

11/Greg

I left the University at eight-thirty, about three hours later than I wanted to, too late to meet up with Francine, who mailed me a lunchtime note to say she had been studying for pre-entry exams all day. I worried about her travelling home on her own as I delayed even longer to pick up food at the stores in the Low Massif. Katy said she hadn't been home the last night, but I didn't worry too much—I worried more than that . . . only Francine hadn't been forthcoming about herself during our few days of getting to know one another and I hardly had the skill or the position to badger her for what was really going on. She worked hard all day on the days I saw her, a perfect student. Now she was gone and in order to catch up with her, I would have to go back to the Foundation's loathsome apartments— since she was illegal I couldn't register her for student accommodation.

Meanwhile my upper left vision was full of transparent, scrolling updates on the conversations of my colleagues as I kept up with their discussions on various topics but mostly today's closure of Sankhara. During the time it took me to leave the office and do the shopping I got a lot of requests on my recent papers, some of them from TV research AIs surfing for background material they could use to fill out the hyperlinks on their permitted fifty-word byline, which was going to explain, very quietly, that Sankhara was no longer issuing visas of any kind and that all nonresidential permits were, as of this evening, revoked. We were under quarantine.

I wondered if it was because of Damien's undiscovered space. I hadn't reported it. I didn't want anyone there before I had a chance to record it all. Even though he had led me there, it felt like it was mine, but anyone could stumble over it at any time. I wanted to take Damien and Francine there to help me get it done straightaway, even if I had to pay Damien a year's salary. I called Katy to tell her I was coming.

"Good," she said. "I need to talk to you on a very important matter. That appalling Stuffie you waste your money on is here too. We're having an open night. Can't you get rid of him? He puts people off. And Francine . . ."

"I'll be there in ten minutes," I said and cut the line, glad that Damien was already present, as it would speed things up.

When I got there Katy was outside the Foundation apartments, lying in wait for me.

"There you are," she said, brushing a loose strand of hair back behind her ear with the same gesture I'd been watching for three years and never noticed until now that she used it as punctuation to give her an extra second to think of what she ought to say. "How are you?"

"Knackered, hungry, longing to talk about my inadequacies and get home before Engine Time."

She glanced down. "I'm sorry you're hurt but this is not about you."

"Yeah, well, I'm sorry too." Stinging riposte, Greg. Well done.

Katy pushed her hands into her trouser pockets, tipped her head back and took a deep breath before fixing me with a firm stare, chin dropping to an angle of stern temperance. "It's Francine," she said and abruptly lost her sangfroid at the same instant I lost mine.

"You and Ludo should stay out of other people's lives . . ." was my starting line.

"Now look, I know what you're going to say . . ." was hers.

I finished, ". . . leave her, and me, alone."

She finished, ". . . some really strange guy in there with her."

"And what do you want me to do about it? You have fifty-odd assorted strange guys in there with you on a regular basis. Maybe she found a friend who hadn't decided to sacrifice all personal loyalties in order to spread the joy of harmony around at anorexic levels."

"He's not one of us."

"Thank heaven for that, then." I stepped around her, wondering what she was so bothered about and determined to find out.

"Greg." She caught my arm, her voice low in tone and volume. "I'm really worried about her. I know perfectly well how different she is. I'm not stupid. But she's also a teenage girl with no Tab, and completely vulnerable, yes, to people like me who mean her well and to others who might not, so I'm saying, trying to say—you're closer to her now. I accept that no matter how inappropriate I think it is, but whatever, she's been okay so far, I know she's working, she's started studying. It's all very positive. But the underlying issues that brought her here and made her rip the Tab out of her hand haven't gone away. For gods' sake, I just want to ask you to look out for her, okay? And we're here, if you need us."

"So, you're not standing here implicitly blaming me for being too late to walk her home and directly causing her to pick up with someone you haven't managed to vet?"

She let go of my sleeve. "You're doing that yourself."

Music started thumping out from the central room. I heard Ludo's voice exhorting someone to try the Foundation out, just for a week, just for one week, and see if it didn't make a difference. Straggling ones and twos of people wandered in and out past us. "Where is she?"

"In the kitchen."

The Foundation kitchen was a huge, well-built community cooking centre, warm, tiled and by far the only usable room in the entire place. It was packed with members old and new, every seat taken and most of the standing room too. The long table was covered in plastic drinks cups and a dull roar of talk rebounded from all the shiny surfaces. I recognized a few faces, Unevolved and Genies, people with names like Slooky and Punch, Drifter, Bushwhack and Pippin, great collectives of lost characters in search of a story. I almost didn't recognize Francine, only because she was standing next to Damien, who cut an exceptional figure in his forest green leathers, his every pocket and strap bristling with offensive-looking items, mostly weapons, and his face bearing its customary sardonic smile.

She was wearing beautiful clothes and talking with an animation I'd never seen her use before. Her face was alight with passion as she spoke with Bobsybob, a Stuffie drifter who looked rather like a young sea captain down on his luck. I made my way over to them.

It was only as I reached them and went through the Hi and Hellos that I noticed Damien grinning at me even more annoyingly than usual. "Hey, mate," he said.

"What?"

"Damien!" Francine kicked his ankle and in doing so knocked over a ripped and battered old backpack at her feet which was half-full. She bent down to straighten it out of the way and I noticed for the first time that a man was sitting behind her on the work-top, his legs hanging down on either side of her. I was too surprised at not seeing him before to say anything as she stood up, leant to the side and said, "Greg, this is Jalaeka."

He stretched out his hand to me. "Nice to meet you."

I felt Katy move up beside me, elbowing her way around the crush. She nudged me in the ribs. I realized this was the Man In Question. He looked so ordinary I couldn't understand what on earth was giving her a problem. His smile was warm and friendly, his handshake confident and his style of dress blissfully normal. Damien's leer notwithstanding, I didn't get the joke. I glanced at her and gave a micro shrug at which point I saw her staring at him with an expression that suggested something quite other than disapproval.

"So, Jalaeka," Katy said in her breezy voice, the one that suggested everything was interesting, "tell us about yourself. Francine seems to have really attached to you so very quickly."

Nine million points to you, Katy Pawluk, I thought, groaning inwardly and waiting for Francine to explode. Francine's eyebrows did go up, but with pity. Behind her, the unremarkable Jalaeka put his arms around her, his knees on either side of her hips, and rested his chin on top of her head.

"I was made as the people's champion on a pre-industrial world coming under the sway of a ruthless Unity-driven empire. After my capture and enslavement I became a Companion to the wealthy classes and learned the arts of seduction. I fled my position after several years, having become the favourite of the Empress's son—a dubious position, too prone to assassination for my liking. To make my escape I had to betray one lover and tear my friend from his quiet life of peace. In the wild forests beyond civilization I learned I was not human. I did not manage to learn how my nature worked in time to save my friend from death by pneumonia and starvation. I fell into despair and went up a mountain to die . . ." He paused and smoothed down a stray piece of Francine's hair with one hand.

"At that point I began to dream of time and space and to understand the motions of the stars and the particles of matter but I still did not understand how to alter their paths.

"I was found by someone who owed me a death. She was a mercenary fighter and had a thousand ways to kill me, none of which worked. We fought to exhaustion and fell in love. We became pirates, by sea and land. We flung ourselves headlong at the world. During one of our many temporary partings—we fought a lot, did I say that?—I was trapped by a sorceress and held to ransom for my powers. The sorceress wanted me to open a portal into another world. I could not do it, and I would have fallen there if my ordinary love had not found me and lain down upon my tomb and dreamed that she would give me a path out into another world.

"I was always vulnerable to dreams of those who loved me. When I awoke I was on Solar Earth, it was 1987, and I knew how to change the fabric of creation. And then some more *stuff* happened"—he held out one hand with fingers spread and waggled it to indicate glossing over a lot—"and I came here and Francine found me. And now here I am in your kitchen, until she decides it's time to leave." He kissed the top of Francine's head protectively and glanced at Katy. It was a glance of fierce warning and at the sight of it I lost my eye-rolling contempt for his story and began to have serious doubt that maybe Katy was right to be worried.

Damien looked smug.

"Don't worry," Jalaeka said. "My days of carnage, treachery, murder and rape are long over."

"Why, what happened?" Damien asked him, giving him a look that I found distastefully worshipful.

"I saw the light," came the deadpan reply and, thrown away at the end of it like a tossed piece of trash, "going out all over."

"You were never like that," Francine said, squeezing his knee, as if they'd known each other for months and she had all the evidence that he was only being modest, or self-deprecating.

Their familiarity and physical comfort was alarming if nothing else. They looked as if they belonged together.

"Depends on who was looking at it," he said and glanced at me.

"No it doesn't," she said. "You never did any of those things on purpose."

"I did," he said. "That's the pity of it."

"Circumstances," she said.

He gazed at me and I felt myself minutely examined, as if at the bottom of a microscope. It took half a second, maybe less. Then he relaxed and I really saw him.

"I think you should stay here . . ." Katy was saying as I moved past her and grabbed Damien's arm, dragging him forcibly towards the hall.

"Hey . . ." he objected but didn't really fight me. He was light and easy to move. The door to the bathroom opened as we passed it and I ignored the queue and hauled him in with me, slamming the door shut.

"Dr. Saxton, I didn't know you felt that way about me . . ."

"Cut it out. *What* is that?"

"That?" he said, shaking his long hair out with a strangely soft expression on his face, as if he'd just left a lover's bed. "That is a god. Or as good as it gets. That is another Unity in action, in person. Behold. The master of your new domain."

I stood a long time, fixed to the spot by my thoughts. "You," I said finally, wagging my finger at him. "You put this together somehow . . . you . . . did you put her in his way?"

Damien was past me in a flash, to the door, his hand opening it effortlessly. "We all do what we have to in order to survive," he hissed at me. "And to get the opportunity of a lifetime, which this is for you. He's right there. Self-aware. *Mucho* mojo. In love with our Francine. And he talks, baby. He TALKS." He whisked out.

A girl came in. "Oh," she said, seeing me. "Are you done in here?"

"Yeah," I said, standing there.

She waited. "Do you mind?"

"No."

"Out . . . ?"

"Oh." I went out.

That night Francine left the Foundation and moved in with her new boyfriend. After a couple of days I followed, invited by Jalaeka to take up any room I wanted, free to wander and to have Francine's help in taking down all the documentary evidence I could wish for. I liked to think that the biggest reason for my going was to look out for Francine, because I didn't trust either Jalaeka or Damien, but I'm not sure it was.

In a pocket of quiet on my first night there, when the wind died down for a few moments, I heard Francine's voice through the wall—their apartments and mine were side by side. They were thick walls and there wasn't much leak, but when it came through the rising and falling tones were distinct. I heard her laugh. She sounded so happy.

Weeks later, we sat in my apartment, a dinner eaten, drinks long finished, the preambles of his getting to know my business in Sankhara and the Park and with Francine all done with. It was late—Engine Time—and the attics above us were filled with skittery sound, like dry windblown leaves on an autumn day, or the hundred feet of an unkindness of ravens, made from the dust by the Engine's sculpting fingers.

Jalaeka sat with his legs curled under him on my modern sofa, Francine lying with her head in his lap, asleep. Outside, the wind that had spent the best part of a fortnight seething restlessly through the taiga had died down to breezy murmurs, leaving cloudless skies, and the Palace was quiet, except for the attics.

"I can't prove it," he said in reply to my questioning him through his claim as to how he had got here. He spoke following a minute of silence and my minute of silence followed in train, as minutes had been following and lengthening our conversation since it started hours before.

Francine, who had been an active participant, had long since tired of both sides, but her sleeping presence—if she was really asleep—reminded me to watch my words. She'd turned to Jalaeka with all the convert's zeal she so loathed in Katy and I didn't want to do anything to upset the now-delicate balance that existed between the three of us. I turned my empty glass in my hand and watched the final drop of scotch in it run to nothing against its wall. "That's a great story."

"It's a pathetic story," he said, dismissing its colossal central claims—about Metropolis, and himself—with what I was learning to see as a peculiar pragmatics born of despair. He looked into my fireplace where the logs had burned themselves down to embers and glowed alternately red and pink in gentle movements of the air towards the flue. The room was pleasantly warm and the atmosphere docile.

He'd said a lot of very interesting things, wild claims about being hunted down by Unity, through its human agent, Theo. He'd said that Theo, "who Unity thinks it is when it's human," ate Metropolis—an assertion anyone could have read as speculation in a hundred net magazines and the answer I had most dreaded.

I asked if he might repeat such behaviour and he said, "Theodore never does the same thing twice. Metropolis was a calculated risk, it failed. Next time . . ." but he hadn't finished that statement. His dark minotaur eyes looked at me, hard and calculating for an instant, and he drew and let out a breath in a very measured way but didn't finish.

"Unity . . ." I said, turning my glass over but the drop had evaporated, "is powerful beyond comprehension. It closes and expands space-time, it processes matter as easily as thinking." I was trying to imagine what such an entity might be interested in, concerning either Jalaeka or Theodore, and I wasn't having a lot of luck, although for all that I had witnessed and recorded across the years this approach to discovery seemed perfectly in tune with all of its previous strategies, for many of them were beyond my ability to fathom. Perhaps there was no underlying grand plan. Jalaeka seemed to want to say there wasn't. But could such a being arise purely by accident on the churn of chance?

"Dull, isn't it?" Jalaeka looked down at Francine with a tenderness that made a pang of envy shoot under my sternum. I took it that he meant such omnipotence was dull, and it seemed like it must be for the wielder, and that he included himself. If he really did have comparable power, then he was certainly long bored by it.

"So, how exactly did you escape from Metropolis again?"

He gestured vaguely with his free hand, conducting his own lines as he spoke in a mild singsong that affectionately mocked my doubts. "I created a temporary universe, connected it to this one, as the Park connects to Sankhara, walked across, here I am, closed it after me." He was already laughing at himself as he finished talking.

I nodded. "Why come to another Unity world? One so chock-full of Stuffies and interference?"

He fixed me with an amused, tired, long-suffering look and his fingertips stroked Francine's shoulder, back and forth, back and forth. "Do you know of any other kind?"

Hyperion, the Forged shaman, met me on the steps as I was leaving for the University, Francine and Jalaeka still asleep on my furniture, buried to the nose beneath a soft heap of down comforter. The air had a cold bite to it on this sunless side of the building and the formal gardens before the railings shimmered with a sparkling rime of frost. I locked the small access door behind me and was carefully negotiating the icy stone steps with my eyes to the ground when the sound of feet on gravel made me look up sharply and almost slip.

Hyperion had sneaked up on me. He was a Salmagundi—the Forged term for "salad." He referred to himself as a Greenjack when asked his class, but this returned no data on any Guide check I was able to perform. He rose up to his impressive grizzly-bear bipedal height as I noticed him, so that he could offer me his hand to shake. The many bone, metal and wood charms that he wore in necklaces, braces and piercings tinkled and clattered as he moved. He was wearing his skin coat—the hides of a wolf and a deer sewn roughly together, though it couldn't have provided any warmth. He spoke via Tablink. "Dr. Saxton. I was waiting to see you."

I descended to the height of three steps from the ground and shook his hand. It was like grasping a cluster of metal bars. "How are you keeping?"

"The forest grows apace," he said. He rarely made any statements about himself, always deferring to the landscapes and creatures he lived with, because they were what he was made of, in his mind, and so their welfare was always the matter of his concern. "The Engine has extended it east and west to cover even the moorland beyond the first hills. If you look to the south you will see it creep up the mountains until the air and soil are too thin even for enchanted trees." Steam from his breath gouted from his mouth and long, narrow nostrils.

"You want to speak to me?"

"I had a vision," he informed me.

Hyperion was a scholar of Unity and his studies were of the direct kind, among its creations. He had become, over the last fifteen years, a kind of legend in his own right among the Stuffies of Sankhara. Rarely seen and greatly venerated, he was a kind of spiritual leader, though he wasn't interested in any kind of ministry and his insights were "the results of simple observation and meditation, no more," in his own words. His rituals and fetishes were the necessary accoutrements of his work, building as they did great psychological architectures of mastery over himself and his knowledge. He was mystical, and he was utterly rational. We met in the Park, its first two explorers, and had become colleagues and friends in a distant, cordial fashion.

"It was not a prophecy," Hyperion continued, dropping slowly to all fours with the hydraulic grace of a machine so that his head and mine might be at less unequal heights. He began to pace with me towards the gates. "It was a revelation. Unity was the greatest of all oceans and I was a fish within it. Through the crashing of waves on distant shores it sang Ariel's song to me, through the growing trees that were made from the wind—do you know this song, Dr. Saxton?"

I was pleased to quote it to him:

> *Full fathom five thy father lies:*
> *Of his bones are coral made:*
> *Those are pearls that were his eyes:*
> *Nothing of him that doth fade*
> *But doth suffer a sea-change*
> *Into something rich and strange.*

"That is the song," Hyperion said. "Though I fancy Unity must have heard it long ago, when Isol first encountered it. She carried it with her and must have known it well. It is a space-farer's favourite, though they often change the words—a crime for which they ought to drown in vacuum. I heard this song and then, yesterday, I came across a new structure down in the Temple District where they say the Engine most likes to listen to the minds of the prayerful, though you and I both know that cannot be." His yellow, goat-pupilled eyes swivelled to me with a wink. "The temple of Apollo has been levelled. Upon it stands a cathedral, on one side beautiful and ornate, on the other side raw and crudely carved. It is still under construction. SankhaGuide has not yet enabled reporting, since its origins defy analysis. I wonder if you would care to meet me there sometime."

We had reached the frozen agony of the gates and he stopped there, showing no inclination to leave the Park yet. Between the pale trunks of the trees behind him and to his right I saw the grey forms of timber wolves slipping back into shadow and inside my coat pocket my hand tightened around the pepper spray canister I carried. "I will," I said.

"Until then," he agreed and without another glance or word turned to jog off into the trees at exactly the point where the wolves had been watching us a second before. His bounding, elastic gait covered the distance in seconds and I ducked through the holes and into the road. Verkhoyansk Boulevard's empty grandeur was too big for me. I was glad when I could enter the warm, balmy, filthy air of Hoolerton and Sankhara proper.

After I filed all my research and caught up with my work, I met Hyperion as he'd offered. The cathedral was as he said but the Engine had formed it in a state of construction and there was nothing to indicate that it was also related to Jalaeka. I looked at Hyperion's discovery and Jalaeka's appearance as two sides of an equation. The numbers didn't look right to me but I thought of it too often for my liking, and when I factored in the timing of the day Jalaeka met Francine and looked again at the cathedral's half-built exaltation I didn't like it at all.

12/FRANCINE

I lay under the comforter, completely covered by it; the bed and the room both felt dangerously large to me and also, Greg had come by to offer us both coffee in a gesture that was as touching as it was interfering, and I was hiding. I felt unspeakably embarrassed to be caught like this, alongside Jalaeka, who was genuinely asleep, or doing a better job of faking it than I was. We were both naked, last night's laughter having given way to lengthy petting and the very thought of Greg even knowing about it made me blush from head to foot. That made me even hotter and I listened, longing for his quiet effort to be gone and to see a look on his face that wasn't condemning.

I wanted to see him later, to hand in my work, to study, to sit and plan our expedition into the vast expanses of untracked Palace grounds. I wanted everything to stay normal between us but I was nagged by this annoying conviction that he would disapprove and be displeased with me, but he wouldn't be able to show it and so it would just sit there like a half-visible snarling gargoyle between us.

Jalaeka's foot slid back and stopped when it touched mine.

Greg moved with deliberate efforts to be quiet that drove me crazy. He put the drinks on the floor close to me, then went out and I heard the apartment door close with a click.

Why should I be guilty? I hated that I felt it. I didn't even understand who was being crossed.

I flung back a half metre of covers as soon as the door had closed and took a deep breath of the cold air. Jalaeka, perfectly content as long as he was in physical contact, didn't move. The smell of the coffee cut through the air to me and I was suddenly awake and hungry. I sat up and reached for one of the cups.

Jalaeka rolled over as I slid away from him and murmured without opening his eyes, "Where are you going?"

"Drink," I said. He reduced me to monosyllables. Glancing at him now, I felt myself flood with the kind of desire so physical and immediate that it threatened to burn me alive if I didn't do something about it, right now. I took a deep breath and held on to the coffee. Much as I wanted to do something about it, I was scared to.

I tasted the coffee and didn't want it.

Jalaeka moaned softly, a pining noise. I wriggled back down beside him and we turned to face one another. He let one eye open a fraction.

"God, it's blue in here," he muttered and closed it again. He stroked the side of my face with his hand, unerringly light and sensitive, tracing my features as though he was blind. "That's better. Now I only see you."

"Those things you said last night, were they true?" I asked him, looking at his exposed head, neck and shoulders with the distinct pleasure of gazing over a full box of chocolates, trying to decide what to have first.

"My life story? All factually accurate. Short on detail. Mmn." The last hum was slightly discomforted.

"Tell me?" I brushed some of his thick hair away from his face and neck where it lay in a heavy tangle. I bent over him and put my mouth against the exposed skin just below his ear. It was very warm and smooth under my tongue, deliciously forbidden and at the same time completely mine. I felt that I could do anything I wanted and he'd never turn to me with the cold face that lets you know you've gone too far and fallen off the invisible pedestal you never knew that you were on.

"Nnuh," he said, rubbing his head deeper into the pillow and moving it so that I could get to more of him. "If I do, you might stop."

"Why?"

He rolled onto his back, arms flung relaxed to either side. I ran my tongue along the curve of his collarbone and kissed the hollow of his throat at the end of it.

"I haven't always been yours."

I placed small, quick kisses up his neck, around to his jaw, across his forehead. "Haven't you?"

He glanced at me, eyes open. "I don't think so." Genuine confusion shone there. "I'm secondhand. Well, more like sixth hand . . ."

"That's not bothering me. But something bothers you. All last night there was something you didn't say to me." I lay down, pulling the covers to me, shy to be seen because he was unearthly beautiful and I wasn't.

"Tell me."

"I'm worried that Theo will find you and kill you." He rolled back to face me, on his side, putting his hands under his head. "It was careless and stupid of me to let you in. But I wasn't paying attention and I opened my eyes and there you were and then . . . it was already too late."

Of course he had told me what he was, and who Theo was . . . but I still couldn't really believe it. "You could stop him. Why not? You're equals."

"At the speed he can move I can't stop him. I could only . . . pre-empt him . . ." He became thoughtful suddenly. "There is one thing . . ."

"What?" I tickled his chin with the ends of his own hair. "Don't you ever shave? No stubble."

"Androgyne tendencies," he said. "Assimilation. Translation. You into me. But I never did that. I don't know what happens. I don't want to be you. I don't want you to be me. But in the past I could have done it and I didn't."

He was serious. He turned his face away from me to hide a sudden expression of grief. I left off tickling him and laid my head on his shoulder. I felt his arms slide around me and hold me close, as though we were meant to fit together, two halves of one nut.

I considered it. Leaving aside the complete terror of such a suggestion I said, "But isn't that a 7-D move?"

"Yes. It would reveal me instantly. And possibly annihilate you."

"And you?"

"Don't know. I can't think of a way to separate you out. I just have no idea how it works at all." His voice was bleak now. "It's everything I hated about Unity in the first place. Only Theo knows, and he isn't telling. Why should he? He wants me to go back to the great one. I don't believe him when he says it won't finish me. He has no ethic, only a mission. But I could do that, if he threatened you."

"Assimilate me?"

"No. Let him take me back. And I will. If it comes to that. Don't worry." He squeezed me and rubbed my shoulders as if I were cold.

"No," I said. "Don't you dare."

"It's all I can do," he said. "If he finds you. When."

"No. I forbid you."

"Francine, don't . . ."

"Do the other thing instead."

"Please . . ." He started trembling suddenly. "You don't know what you're asking. It's not a human thing. I can't explain it."

"If those are the choices . . ."

"You don't understand the choices!" His hands were hurting my arms.

"I could," I said quietly. "If you let me. Do it."

"No," he said, in a voice very much like his earlier moan. "Then where will the difference be between me and it? No."

"I'm not afraid of you." I meant it. I felt nothing for him except passion, lust, love, trust.

"Yeah, but you ought to be," he said. He took a deep breath and became still as he let it out. His grip softened. "That's the trouble. You don't understand, and I can't explain. This thrall you feel for me, even that's a product of what I've become. Isn't that dangerous enough for you?"

"I'm a Sankhara girl," I said. "I got used to that kind of thing. It's why I came here."

He laughed and relaxed and rolled over onto me and for a second the sharp gaze of a master calculator was on his face, but then it disappeared into a mischievous grin. He took my hands and put them on the pillow above my head, pinning them down with one hand. I tried to pull free but he was strong enough that I couldn't budge them a millimetre. The feel of his naked body on mine and his hold sent a hot electric thrill through me that shorted out my thoughts. My body, left to react without a mind in charge of it, bucked and tingled as he deftly pushed one of his legs between mine, then the other. He held my gaze with his infinitely dark one and with his free hand turned my face to one side so that the arm holding my hands could stretch out against my neck without pressing against it. Then he slid downwards and began to kiss and lick my breasts.

I lost track. I became desire and pleasure under his mouth.

"I want to be myself with you," he said.

The words took a long time making meaning in my head. "Why, who else is there?" I asked from my delirium.

When he released my unresisting hands and kissed his way down my body I lost track of what pieces belonged to me and what to him. I forgot myself. Everything ran into a single centre of pleasure on the axis of his hands and mouth. I died. There was only bliss.

When he got up to go to work he leant over me where I lay on the floor and kissed me with the breath from his nostrils. "Don't go anywhere until I get back." I thought I was awake, but maybe I was sleeping.

His voice echoed through me, all the dissipated parts of me that had flowed like water around the rooms, carrying away my arms and legs to different locations where they must have been left, because I couldn't find them. I wanted to tell him it was a ludicrous command, since I wouldn't be going anywhere, but I had misplaced my mouth.

Eventually, in spite of my longing to stay dissolved, I put myself back together and find I fit better than ever into my skin. Perhaps it's metaphorical, but it feels as though it's true. I'm not entirely sure. My mind is floating halfway between the physical and the imaginary.

"You look more like me," I say, as I inspect the results in the bathroom mirror. "And what happened to your hair?"

I don't know what happened to my hair. It was always amber, which is a posh way of saying it was dark dishwater blond going slightly red. Now it has bright platinum streaks and, underneath and behind my ears, thick black bands like the gaps in Saturn's rings.

I found my hair lying on top of the green leather-bound edition of Grimms' *Fairy Tales*, I seem to recall. Now I wonder if I made a mistake and picked up some other girl's hair. But even if it is the wrong hair, it's grown into my head now. I bring forward a black piece and look at it. This is Jalaeka's hair, I realize, finer than mine. Well, it beats a hickey any day.

I pull it and wonder if it's hurting on his head now.

After I bathe and dress I decide to make reparations. I go through to Greg's kitchen and cook a late dinner. When he comes in he looks surprised to be greeted by a plate of spaghetti Bolognese, but not that surprised, because it's one of only three dishes that I know.

"You're looking well," he said, tired and accepting of any kind thing at this stage of the night, even a kiss on the cheek from a truant student. "Did you do something to your hair?"

We share a pleasant evening. I help him to make up his records on the Palace and we plan out our joint assault on those remaining rooms of the ground floor that are still undocumented. He gives me the prospectus for next year's applicants at the University and explains what kind of things I need to compose in order to fulfil the daunting demands it makes: Outline Your Interest in Unity Studies ("My boyfriend is an alien" will not do apparently), Give a Brief Summary of Your Recent Achievements (I have cooked edible food, I have held down a cleaning job, I have agreed with Dr. Saxton's theory that the taiga is a representation of the conditions of the generation of early human consciousness and also exists as a metaphor for the tangled nature of the unconscious mind and the incoherent aspects of self-generation, I have learned how to give a blow job—none of these will do either, apart from the cleaning).

I go back to mine in time to sweep out the fireplace and set on more logs. I then prepare to disassemble myself on the rug, which will be the only warm spot in the room until later. I keep my arms and hands attached so I can turn the pages of the books as I read.

13/VALKYRIE: SANKHARA

Valkyrie stood up on the top of the SankhaGuide Massif and looked down across Greater Sankhara and the lands beyond it. In her hand she held several paper flyers which had been foisted on her by individuals down in the streets, before she took to the skies. She opened her fingers and watched them flutter away into the wind: a pink one with lilac hearts on it, from the Love Foundation, promising to heal Sankhara through healing her inner loneliness; a blue one with a pentagram on it offering Wiccan retreats at "the extent of the known world," including a guided meditation into the depths of "our common soul"; a green and grubby one proclaiming the imminent arrival of the Justified Ancients of Muu Muu and exhorting her to preserve Sankhara's pure human encounter with chaos by not keeping a dream diary.

SankhaGuide itself didn't say anything except that leaflet day was on Satyrday and strictly limited to the beachfront and the Temple District. Temple lay to her right, complete with its new cathedral, which she had gone to inspect that morning. It was gothic and black and almost entirely dwarfed by both the huge rocky bulk of SankhaGuide Massif and the twisting, half-alive towers of the Aelf, in whose shadow it stood at this time of the afternoon.

The sky was auburn with a coming storm. The wind had risen from the east and the sea was almost black as the sun went down. In the last, long and clear light, the shadows and light-sprites of the Aelf towers moved independently of the trees, stone and glass that cast them. Valkyrie looked at them with a sceptic's fascination. They made shapes that vaguely reminded her of animals, like a hand-shadow play, but no animals she cared to see for real. They shimmered between the two high points of the towers and TacMassif's radio spike, clustering around the most exclusive of all the city's districts, Kodiak Aerial.

Light shone through the old cable cars that were suspended on the wire there, and through their lenses it became the eyes of a beast that stared back at Valkyrie. Few people could live there, but Valkyrie was one of them. She opened her wings and jetted across to the car that had recently become her one-room house. At the last minute she folded her arms across her chest and furled her wings to drop vertically in through the roof doorway and land on the mat below. The car swung and rattled gently.

Valkyrie made a tea for herself and reviewed all the articles and news that SankhaGuide had been able to find for her concerning Theodore and his past on Earth. There was precious little, and it amounted to nothing new. She doubted that any useful information would come out of the public domain, though she had higher hopes of finding some by the more usual spying methods. She checked the time, finished the drink and sat down in the darkness, looking at the city light up beneath her. Closing her eyes she allowed herself to detach from that world and make the connection inside to the Forged dream net.

In Uluru the avatar Metatron rose from the parkland grass, green, his wings leafy. He walked with her past the silver acroplane, and prompted her, "Can I get you anyone?"

"I want to see Elinor."

Metatron paused and half turned towards her. "I thought we had agreed there would be no more visits. You want to save her."

"I need to see her."

"The data that comprises the last full build of Elinor is unstable," Metatron reminded her like a lecturing father. "The more often you interact with the routine, the worse it is going to get. It is already over fifty percent decayed."

"It's not like I'm killing her or anything," Valkyrie said sharply to him, against the jolt of pain in her own heart.

Metatron sighed. "The price . . ."

"I'll pay anything." She watched the avatar consider her offer.

"Very Faustian," he said. "Fortunately, although I archive Forged neural prints, I am not a collector. You will have to pay for the copying error damage. The Dead Archive doesn't run on charity and you can't afford what it would cost to keep multiple copies. Come on, Valkyrie, it would do you good to leave her as a treasured memory and meet the living, don't you think?"

Valkyrie felt her insides harden to the strength of armour. "Just bring her here."

Metatron returned a moment later and with him came a ghostly figure, another Light Angel Valkyrie. Where Skuld's armour was golden this one wore silver and blue and its wings were the feathered kind, not the aerofoils that Skuld bore. Valkyrie felt herself tip over into joy as she recognized her friend's dear face, very different from her own, as it smiled at her.

Valkyrie changed instantly into Little Girl Skuld in her tartan dress. Elinor switched to avatar shape, a gangling child in blue jeans and a green hoodie, ever the more tomboyish of the two. Her black pigtails stuck out at uneven heights because they were so recklessly made. But where Skuld's colours were strong and definite, Elinor was a pale wash of nearly nothing. Her expressions had no transitions—they flickered from smile to sombre.

"Elly?" Skuld said and ran forward. Her hands almost caught Elinor's hands, but the dead woman was too insubstantial, even in Uluru. It was like touching spider silk.

"Skuld," Elinor said dreamily. "I've been a long time."

"I need to ask you some questions," Valkyrie said gently. "Can you hear me?"

"Far away," Elinor said. Her face switched to a smile. "I died. I remember. But that was just now. Are you dead?"

"No." Valkyrie forced herself not to waste time, since every interaction counted. "Elly, you once did a job that involved Theodore, do you remember?"

"The Unity Agent," Elinor said. "Is he here too?"

"No."

"Good. I didn't like him."

"Me neither. Listen, do you remember what that job was about?"

"Belshazzar thought Theo was running other agents on

Earth." Elinor stared around her, dreamily. "Is this the park? Is that the aeroplane? Is that you, Skuld? I can't see you."

"And was he? Honey, look at me, was he?" Valkyrie stared into Elinor's misty eyes. She could see entire blocks of pixels all identical in there, simple flat zones of emptiness.

"I think so," Elinor said. "Is that you, Skuld? I can't see you very well."

"It's me. It's me, honey. Now just one more thing. Did you get any proof? Do you know who they are?"

"Can't tell," Elinor whispered. "Don't know. I thought I saw one but then, I forgot it. Bel said he did something to our minds. Can't be seen, won't be seen. Deep hiding. A woman in a talking coat. She . . ." The whole of Elinor's small body winked out of existence, returned, failed again.

"Elly!" Valkyrie cried out.

Metatron appeared at her right side. "That archive has reached the limit of my capacity to run it. If you try to speak with her again, you will destroy her. And your account is empty."

Valkyrie jerked her arm out of his grip, returning to her Earthly actual form of the armoured flying woman, her true self. "I can see that. Get me out of here."

"As you wish."

Alone in her cable car home Valkyrie hugged her knees to her chest and let the wind rock her back and forth, back and forth. She would not cry.

A short while later, after the moon had risen, a knock came at the door.

Crossly she unfolded and thumped the access panel controls. The roof hatch opened, shut, then the side door slid back. An Elf was standing there. An actual Elf from the Aelf, Valkyrie decided after a few moments of incomprehension. A Stuffie.

He was quite tall and willowy, dressed in forest colours, with brown hair that was part braided and part not. He stood on the narrow platform before her door without any concern for the serious open drop behind him and said brightly, "Hi. I couldn't help noticing that you're new, and I thought you might be interested in some of the latest magical protection from the worst of Sankhara's nasty night-time haunts. Although"—he stood back and openly stared her up and down before giving her a grin— "I can see you're the kind of woman who doesn't need that kind of help most of the time."

His expression was so cheeky and so infectious that Valkyrie found herself beginning to smile. She had an idea. "Come in," she said. "And show me what you've got."

His grin deepened. He skipped across the threshold and took his bag off, dropping it on the floor. "Junk," he said of it, peering around him with unbridled curiosity. "Gee it's so, I don't know, so stark in here. You from Earth recently?"

"Good guess."

"I don't guess," he said. "I know." He shivered. "I could get you some nice rugs, good fabrics, great curtains. It's really—it's like standing in an old, creaky, freezing cable car with no furnishings and no heat. Prison camp chic. But maybe you want it to stay that way? Are you punishing yourself for something, cause I can find you a good priest, or is it a secret religious fetish? Is that a real gun?"

"Yes." Valkyrie picked up her sidearm and showed him how it attached, took it off and put it away carefully.

"And rocket packs and wings. That is so cool!" He was almost beside himself with excitement. "Seriously. I know where the cheapest fuel is and I can get you upgrade packs and I can even get ammo for that skull-popper . . ."

"I'm the Light Angel Valkyrie Skuld," Valkyrie said quietly, holding out her armoured hand.

"Damien." He took her offered shake and ran his other hand over the metal armour on her forearm and her gun ports.

Valkyrie read his biosigns, his hand-prints and his vocal range and identified him. An Engine adept. Usually they were much less conspicuous characters. But this was useful . . . "You're very forward," she said, squeezing harder.

He let go with alacrity but showed no signs of dismay. "People say that. So, what's new on Earth then? What made you come here to the Aerial to get all self-hatey? Who's in that picture? It's not you. Is that your sister?" He turned rapidly to catch Valkyrie's reaction.

"No," she said and took the small photograph of Elinor out of his hands, replacing it beside her sleeping roll. "Now answer me a question. What would it cost me for you to come here every evening and tell me all about what you saw in the daytime around these very interesting shops and salesmen you must know?"

"Data? News? Gossip?" He was almost beside himself. "That's what I do best. Easy rates. Let's start with, say, fifty credits."

"Oh come on, you'll just make it up for that. Twenty."

"I wouldn't do that. Forty-five, and I promise I won't invent a thing."

"Twenty-five, and you make sure to pay attention to certain things more than others."

"Forty, and I won't tell anyone you're a spy."

"Thirty, and I won't dump your cold, dead, bullet-riddled body in the sea."

"Cool. Thirty it is. Can I start now or would tomorrow be better? Do you have peppermint tea? I so love that." He gazed at her with clear, green eyes, then glanced up at her ceiling. "Nice horse bone charms. I guess the landlady left them for you. She's a real good friend of mine. I'll give you three credit points for them."

Valkyrie handed him a cup of her tea.

"Redbush," he said, sniffing it and taking a sip. "Good. Have you ever been to Africa? I wish I could go there."

"About your thirty credits," Valkyrie said. "Will that be in kind?"

"Oh no, I'm strictly legit." He showed her the back of his left hand, where his Tab lay under his skin, and he opened the same hand and showed her the smooth silver lines of an Abacand Direct connection. He was better wired than most government ops.

Valkyrie picked up his account codes and paid him from the

department slush fund. "Now," she said, sitting down. "Tell me everything new over the last couple of weeks."

"Since Metropolis got axed by that loser, you mean," Damien said, collapsing into a cross-legged bundle of energy and exquisite prettiness on top of her sleeping roll. "What the hell was that all about? Anyway . . ."

Damien told Valkyrie about the Cathedral of Cadenza Piacere, which she had already seen, although she didn't know it was sacred to Stuffies and Damien himself wasn't sure. He said that the truth of it was still being revealed. He was massively overexcited because the Engine had never built anything for a Stuffie before. That was a change that permitted reflexivity . . . he prattled on with terms she didn't understand. And then he said there was some rumour about a club downtown—"Some new guy there, or maybe it's a woman, I'm not sure. You want me to check that personally? It's really expensive and I'd need new clothes, plus hair, plus bribery money and the rest. Say, a couple of hundred credits would do it."

"I'll think about it," Valkyrie said. She felt wearied by his garrulous diversions. "Come back tomorrow and ask me again."

"Okay!" He sprang up and swept his bag onto his shoulder, flicking her horse bone charms with his fingers as he passed. "See you same time. Don't get up, I can let myself out." He thumped the control panel, much as she had done, and vanished into the night leaving a trace of woody forest smell behind him.

A smooth, soft quiet replaced him. Valkyrie watched him walk nonchalantly across the long support wire that linked Kodiak with Aelf 2 and closed her eyes.

A few days later, still uncertain about the wisdom of giving a confidence guy like Damien a big chunk of money, she sat drinking espresso in the fan-vaulted splendour of Aelf 1's public foyer and saw an unusual Forged come to the counter of the refreshments stand and order tea. He was a Salmagundi, and presented the appearance of a human who was halfway into changing into another animal: furred, whiskered, doe-eyed and with Anubis's black-tipped jackal's ears. He had a tail banded with golden Tek, and he glanced at her as he collected his drink, then held out a paper flyer to her, casually. Clearly it wasn't something he was selling.

Valkyrie took it—harmless rice paper—and saw that it was for one of the clubs on Pythagoras's Circle.

"I heard you broke something and were looking for the pieces," he said, smiling and revealing his long, sharp teeth. "Bob Clovitz," he said, holding out his paw—or his hand. "Solar Security. We bite what you discover. I've been here ever since Metropolis. Saw you the other day, figured you were the one Queen B's sent to help. This is my whole angle, by the way: one crappy bit of paper and some underground bullshit about the grace of god. I thought we might succeed better together." He showed her his badge via the Uluru comms band, and she verified it.

"Valkyrie Skuld," she said. "I haven't got anything to donate— except that I came across a patch of sky that I couldn't cross the other day."

"You think there's a hidden pocket? Wouldn't be the first time you get worlds within worlds in one of these Sidebars."

"It's what I think too," she agreed, "and I've been looking for the entrance. It's not in the air and not to the north. I'm thinking it must be somewhere in Hoolerton."

"Ah, Hoolerton, paradise of industrial-world fantasy, highly romantic in a squalid way, neighbourly with the Hinterland. Could be. Not many people like it there." He nodded and seemed well satisfied. "I'll search the interiors, ask the inhabitants. You do the streets. We're best suited that way." He glanced up at her. "No offence."

"None taken."

"Another?"

"I can stand another."

"Good." He gave another toothy grin and sat down beside her.

14/GREG

A couple of weeks later the seasons in Sankhara had turned to an idyllic summer of long days, warm nights and higher sea temperatures, drawing everyone towards the miles of gold and white sand that marked the city shoreline from the mouth of the Purbright to the far rocky headlands of Suski-ashokton. Late afternoon on Thorsday found me with Jalaeka sitting with our backs to the shadow of the boardwalk a half klick from Engine House.

We were discussing the nature of reality and Unity's position in it. It was the one place we really disagreed. He said we didn't. But we did, because deep down I didn't believe he was anything more than another Stuffie. But that wasn't why he was losing his temper with me. That was because I would not give up my conviction that there was a reality which was singular, verifiable and fundamental. The real world operated according to scientific laws that were discoverable. It did not, except through the intervention of Unity in the case of the Sidebars, react in any way to what the inhabitants thought about it. Whether I could discover this reality and its workings or not, it was there. And the same thing is true of individuals. Whatever story they make up about who they are, they are what they are what they are.

Jalaeka was talking crossly. He did not see that it was possible to call any version of reality, or oneself, the Real Thing. "Why can't you give up this bloody notion that there is an underlying capital T Truth superior to the one you made up?"

"It's the touchstone of my faith in science," I said.

"You believe that if you can only find it then all your problems will go away," Jalaeka said. "Unity talks about the Mystery, you know, when Theo decides to talk about why it made all these worlds for you to play in. He says that's why it made me. At first I used to think it was true—that if it assimilated all things that they'd somehow sum up to an Answer. But later, after

I changed and saw how hungry it always was, I realized that Unity isn't *searching* for the Mystery through these 'Bars and all the rest of it, Greg, like you're searching for human nature. It's trying to *create* it. It knows all about fundamental reality, and the answer to why life exists and what it means and what it's worth is not in there."

The sea had made his long hair into salty dreadlocks. He brushed them out of his face and flicked a piece of seaweed at me. He snorted. "So now it's sifting through meaning. Unity eats the things that matter, always. It rips them apart to see what it is they've got that's so good."

We were both hot and getting hotter in our wetsuits as the sun came around the corner of Buddy's Surf Shack and started to bake us. The sea was warm, but not that warm. Sankhara was a northern latitude.

Jalaeka snorted and drew circles in the sand with his bare heels. I became uncomfortably aware, as I often did, of his proximity and of my curiosity about what it would be like to touch him. He flirted with me continuously, even this argument was a kind of flirtation, and I couldn't help overhearing occasional times when he and Francine were making love. I thought she had a burning quality, now it was incandescent.

Suddenly he gave up on me. Abrupt withdrawals were common with him after he'd presented his case. He got up and picked up his skimboard, turned and started walking back towards the waves. I added the gist of his conversation to my Abacand's file, placing it alongside a recording I made of him yesterday, which I didn't need to play back to remember.

He'd said, very uneasily, "I should leave Francine. I should go. But then again, can't run forever. Greg, I think I made a big mistake."

"What mistake?" I'd asked.

"Getting lost. Finding you," he said and went quiet again.

"Talk to me," I'd suggested, but he wouldn't.

I watched his easy run down the gentle slope of beach where the water sucked back slowly and reflected the sky like mirrors.

He threw the board and jumped on it. His effortless skim into the whitewater of an inrushing breaker was the sort of poetry in motion you only get when you're relaxed, when you don't care one way or the other, you're just boarding. He let the water take him out a short way, turned in the wave's death and slid back onto the sand. At the end he stepped off and flicked the board up with a simple motion of one foot, catching it single-handed. He walked back up onto the hard, dark line just beyond the reach of the white foam, stepping over shells and stranded jellyfish.

I envied him, and I didn't. I wanted to be like him with all his ease and charm, but I didn't, not with all that hid behind the breakwater of his silences. I listened like he said I should, inside, and heard, without believing that I heard, the soft, rich click and almost-silent roll of tick following tock downtime.

I made a note about it.

I recalled that he'd once said that Francine *made* him, that he belonged to her. He'd said it with a serious expression, as a literal truth. These occasional statements worried me deeply, and other things about him worried me more and kept me awake nights writing imaginary reports to Solargov Intelligence; for instance his claim that there was no such thing as an Engine, only a belief in them, whose power would vanish like smoke the moment it stopped being a complete conviction. He said that the Engines weren't made by Unity at all, and the entire edifice of the Sidebars was a myth Theo planted in our minds, and which we sustained effortlessly when no Unity power could have made it without us.

Nobody would buy that. I kept it out of my reports.

Jalaeka skimmed another wave in his absent way. I stood up, too hot to stay put another minute, and walked out into the sea, then back again when I saw through the clear, shallow bay to where the pale bank of the sand tumbled slowly to a shelf's edge and fell towards deep water: sinuous, finny shapes were gliding there. Some of them were black and some were silvered, some long and winding like animated hawsers: Ootoos. Some were emerald green, red as jasper or sapphire blue and they were attached to human torsos: mermaids, tritons.

Jalaeka jogged back to me as I walked back up the beach and laid his arm across my shoulders. "I've annoyed you," he said sadly, freed me and slapped me in a flamboyant blow that didn't hurt. "Stupid me. Let's get a drink."

We left our boards under the wooden walkway in a shadow, relying on luck to preserve them from thieves. He swung himself up onto the walk and through the railings. I climbed carefully over to where he waited for me, too self-conscious so that I wasn't able to copy him in any way. I stood with my back to him as we showered off the worst of the seawater at the main entrance to the sands. He bought me a coke at Buddy's and we sat on the shack's worn benches, resting our feet on the rail where the Shack faced the south shore. Pleasant, vapid and energetic pop tunes played in the background—his favourite. The sea wind blew gently in our faces, making them saltier and more clingy and sticky than ever.

"Why do you carry on working at that club?" I asked him, feeling that I could ask anything for a while, as though a tide of largesse had swung in between us and I could state what had been on my mind unsaid for a long time. Work was a bit of a euphemism. After arriving in Sankhara, Damien had got him a job in The Italian Well, a nightspot which left no imagination unplundered in its efforts to offer unlimited pleasures. A miniature town of unbridled hedonism and sensual excess, it was known throughout the 'Bars for its dangers and delights: he had fitted in perfectly and was soon top of the payroll. I had only a vague notion of what he did, but for some time rumours had circulated that illegal Translatory procedures were available there and who better to administer that kind of thing than someone who claimed to be a second Unity?

I had long since figured out he was one of several variations on the Love God theme. For Francine's sake I had hoped he would be less second rate.

"What do you do there, exactly?" I added.

He leant back in his chair and rubbed sand off the side of his foot onto the worn wooden upright next to it. "Come with me tonight and find out. Don't worry about the cost. You can write it off, call it research."

"Are you being a condescending wanker by any chance?"

His dark eyes flicked sideways and fixed on mine. His look was canny. "You think it makes me a bad boyfriend. A cheat."

"That crossed my mind." He had been perfectly accurate. "Francine might put up with it but I'm sure she doesn't like it."

"*You* don't like it," he said with quiet precision, and his candour and my transparency felt lethal.

"Francine deserves better than that."

"Ouch," he said, perfectly relaxed, utterly unconcerned.

"It makes me angry that you treat it all so casually."

"It? I treat *it* casually? The sacred dance of true intimacy, one of the great roads to self-knowledge, the path of which I am master . . . *I* treat it like the rest of you, like a bodily function, like a whore?" The lightness of his sarcasm was withering.

"I'm not moralizing about whatever you do. I don't care what you do. I'm worried that Francine will end up being badly hurt by you." Master? What new flight of ego was this?

"Me too. But it won't be because I do strangers for cash." He let the last of his breath go in a sigh that was exasperated with itself. Then he leant forward and undid the neck flap on his 'suit, pulled the zip down his back and shucked it from his torso. He let it hang round his waist as he sat back and took another drink.

I watched the sun going down, the high delta shapes of Forged Gliders mingling with the twin arrows of seagull wings over the ocean, their shape and colour echoing the white sails of the day's boats heading for the marina. He bought more drinks. We got a pack of cards from the bar and played gin. More people came into the bar. I watched him acknowledge their interest and pass on it, with care, with some kind of grace that left them unhurt so that they didn't feel bad for looking and noticing him or for him not wanting to notice them. I paused and wrote some notes about it.

Jalaeka watched me—he was always patient for this kind of task, which distracted me often—and then asked, "Can I write something?"

"Okay." I passed him my Abacand. He wrote on the screen, the tip of his long index finger making rapid symbols, occasionally pausing, then dashing on again just when I thought he must have finished. It took a while. I shuffled the cards and went back to the endless game of picking Stuffies from real people, watching the more colourful characters walk by on the pier; a mermaid pulling herself out of the sea onto dry sand where her tail became long, bronzed legs. A friend on the shore gave her a towel and they walked to the shower stand. A few minutes later both women stood at the bar in long white cotton dresses, mermaid barefoot, her girlfriend in sandals.

They noticed Jalaeka in an instant, disregarded me immediately, and after a few mutual nudges the mermaid came across and sat beside him. She gave me a polite smile, friendly and interested to know who I was, then she said, "Eros?"

"Just a minute," Jalaeka said, writing faster.

Why would she call him that?

The mermaid gave me another once-over. She had a hungry look underneath her poise and prettiness, and I felt myself assessed as something more akin to dinner than date.

"Here," Jalaeka folded my Abacand into a small cube and handed it back.

I looked at the file briefly, then back up towards him. The Mermaid was saying something about *darshan,* a word I'd heard recently somewhere but couldn't place where.

"What did you call him?" I asked her, interrupting them both.

"It's a nickname, like 'wanker,' only more so," Jalaeka said in a quick dismissive snap, before she could open her full and glossy lips over her pointed teeth.

She looked at him more thoughtfully now. "Sorry," she said under her breath. She nodded and got up and gave me an apologetic glance and a tiny nod, suddenly respectful and not at all planning to do me the least harm.

As she left the restless unease that had made him talk me into coming out 'boarding in the first place washed through him again. He reached across and took the cards from beside my elbow, began practicing flicking them into a fan like a street conjuror.

I tried to read what he'd put and I couldn't. It was all in maths. "What is this?"

"Gift aid," he said. He smiled, leant across the space between us over the bench and kissed me on the lips. He waited just long enough to see if I was going to respond but I was too surprised. He sat back and returned to flicking the cards into a smooth semicircle and back again as though nothing had happened.

I stared into space, about to ask him what . . . but then not able to. Instead I asked my Abacand what the maths meant. It told me it was an 11-dimensional transform with unusual torsional constraints which made it unique in M-theoretical supersymmetrical analysis. "It's a way of bending 4-D," it said, rendering unto English that which was ill-suited to it. "If you could get at it from the back, as it were. Haven't seen one of them before. Can I use it to trade through Teragate? I bet it's worth a fortune."

Proof, that's what it was.

"Nah, it was a present," I said, and Jalaeka glanced at me and winked.

I made the excuse of going to change out of my wetsuit and sent a surreptitious message asking my ultimate boss, Belshazzar, if she knew the connection between Eros and Metropolis: the mermaid's name and his claims of history. She replied almost immediately, before I'd even got out of the shower and towelled dry, and the Abacand transmitted her voice silently through my Tab into my head.

"There is no record of that name on the Metropolis Roll

of Heros nor the Roll of Antiheroes or on any listing of registered Villains, Criminals, and Wild Cards. But there is an entry. MetroGuide wasn't limited to official populations of Stuffies or humans, it counted bodies, and it made entries for those who didn't write their own. Like all the Guides, it had a collector's passion for records.

> "Eros. Designation: Love, Son of Night, the first darkness before all things. Creator of worlds. 'Whoever judges not Eros to be a mighty god is either stupid or, having no experience of good things, knows not of the god who is the mightiest power to men.' Status: active. Allegiance: not applicable. Advisory: for legal reasons no advice can be offered for this entry.

"A full and comprehensive standard disclaimer follows with which I will not bore you. May I ask as to your interest?"

"Just something I heard," I said, pulling my street clothes back on as fast as I could.

"Stay in touch," she ended the call.

Back at the beachfront I watched Jalaeka get bored with the cards and staring to the horizon over the water, though he made no move to go. I guessed he was waiting for me to come to some decision.

Eros was the primary meta-fict in certain branches of narrative studies; desire itself viewed as the ultimate creative and destructive impulse, the thing that turned Unity on in the first place. Eros had no entry in MetroGuide's categories because he was a god and, I would have bet anything, the only such listing. It was widely assumed that Theo, having all of Unity's capacities, was akin to a god, but nobody talked about him in public like that. Nobody wanted to admit certain basic and grisly truths to themselves or anyone else, especially in Sankhara.

No wonder Belshazzar was personally involved in seeking silence on this one, even if it was no more than a misunderstanding of some kind. I began to wonder if my impulsive enquiry to

her was really so intelligent after all, and to doubt my immediate trust in her claim to sympathize with my suspicion about
the Sankhara Engine, our AI and the allegedly missing light. In
my confused state, angry with Katy, tired of being overlooked,
I'd swallowed her every word with great relief. But what else
would she have said if I had just given her worthwhile evidence
and she wanted me to continue? Nothing. She wouldn't alert
me to it.

Jalaeka turned his head towards me. "So, are you coming?"

I had to know the truth, no matter how awful it was going to be. God or not. Transform or not. Truth or dare. "Yeah.
Let's go."

15/JALAEKA

As I'm waiting for his answer to my question about going to the club I'm within one breath of telling him my entire
story. I ought to tell him. I should give him the opportunity to
opt out now, but I know that if I try to explain everything, he'll
almost certainly not believe me, and it still won't make any difference to the outcome.

I imagine that I am telling him, and even in the privacy of
my own head it has a nasty, self-regarding desperation:

"I was thinking about running away, leaving. I thought it
would be honest, because it would rule you and Francine out of
the equation. Theo's tried to eat me and he's tried to kill me, but
it looks like we're an even match on every single front. The only
way left to him is to force a submission and the only leverage
that exists is you and Francine.

"None of this would matter much and I wouldn't burden
you with it or spend time getting to know you in the hope that
you could help me out, if it wasn't for the fact that he's close to
finding me because it's just not that hard to do. He finds me, he
finds you, he finds Francine." Fuck.

Then Greg would say something like, "You must have known this right from the start." He'd be right and I'd be the stupid bastard I am, thinking I can hide when I can't.

So I don't tell him anything, just like every other time the opportunity came up, ever since we first talked and I tried to tell the truth. I can't tell him the truth because he's too clever and I like him too much, even though I know I'm going to regret it if I don't. I know Damien put us together too, though I don't know why. I think Damien knows a lot more than he's letting on and, him being the Engine's minion, I don't like that.

"Yeah, let's go," Greg said finally, resigned to testing me one more time.

I put my hand out and stopped him with a touch on his arm. "Wait a minute, sit back down, I've got something to tell you." And I did, everything on my mind.

16/GREG

When Jalaeka was done talking, the sun had gone down and a crescent moon shone across the bay. Sand midges and mosquitoes hurled themselves towards the lights and were annihilated by the Zap geckos perched in the rafters below Buddy's imported banana-leaf roof. I listened to a few more of them get ingested as the impact of what he had said soaked into me. There were two of him in my mind now, one a person and one a thing. I couldn't put them both together.

"You've got to be joking," I said though I knew he wasn't. He nodded.

Below and in front of us on the high, dry sand the early-evening calypso band lit up a fire and settled around it, starting to play. The twinkle of fire at the beach head, where the pitiful scatter of homeless huddled under the lee of the cliffs, glinted far off in the corner of my right eye: Francine's old home. The wash and draw of low tide sounded as a fuzzy, continual backdrop, the beats of its slow retreat almost regular, yet impossible to anticipate. "Theo . . . and you. Two. In the end, that's my choice? You're saying I don't get to escape? Unity . . . but it has always left us alone."

He got up. "I'm going to change. Then we should go meet Francine. After that, you can tell me if you think I should take the fall for you."

He greeted about fifteen people on the way to the locker room, some with words, others with handslaps in various surfing codes or simple nods. Everyone, particularly the Stuffies, seemed to know him. I saw Damien among them. He spoke quickly to Jalaeka, who rested a hand on his shoulder in passing.

I went up to the bar and bought Damien a drink. "Don't see you here very often."

"You know what they say about elves and the sea," he said, twitching one ear towards me as he accepted the drink.

"No."

"Well, something to do with seagulls anyway," he said. "Never could stand them myself. How's the darling girl? I heard she quit my fabulous introduction to the world of entrepreneurial high jinks."

"She gave up the job?"

"After three days." He pretended surprise at my ignorance. "Said she was going to spend more time on your fool of a project scanning the Palace bubble, Anadyr Park. She told me you thought it was a metastructure built from non-Guide mind-fucking. Apparently the idea excites her as much as I can see it does you, so much so she asked me to look into getting her a Tab again. I don't suppose you have an official line on that, Dr. Saxton? The mind-fucking I mean." He glanced quickly at me and I could tell he was enjoying his superior knowledge and the fact that he was letting me know I wasn't the only friend Francine had around the place.

I decided to humour him. "I'll tell you what, I'll tell you something and you tell me . . ."

"I already told you plenty."

I pointed at his drink and he rolled his eyes at me in an oh-please way but shrugged at the same time because he was already well satisfied with baiting me. "Tell you what?"

"Something about Jalaeka. What's got you so manipulative, Damien? Here you are, making eyes at him, pushing me off Francine, always you everywhere I look. What gives?"

He gazed into the distances of the spirits optics thoughtfully as though he was considering his next point, but his ears flattened against his head and his fluid body language became stiff and unforgiving. "I'm gonna pass on that one. Stakes too high this time, baby. Some of us are superstitious about that kind of thing."

"Why? He's only another one of you."

"You you you," Damien repeated, contemptuous. He turned to me. "You Stuffies. You things. Toys."

"Ah come on, stop it with the racist accusations, you know that's not what I meant."

"It's what you *said*." His narrow, long eyes were incredibly green. "And I always take that as a token of what's meant. But since you asked me so very nicely"—he pushed his nearly full glass away from him with his fingertips—"and since you have been so good to Francine, I will give you a piece of information. Whatever you think you've found in Anadyr Park, you should go and see the completed cathedral in Temple District."

"You're the second person to mention it."

"Then I must be right and you're overdue."

Jalaeka came back, carrying his wetsuit in one hand. He dropped it on the floor, paused behind Damien and put his hands over the elf's eyes.

"The Count of Monte Cristo," Damien said with bland rapidity. "Zorro. Luka Frikazik. Conan the Barbarian. Space Leader Zero. Death. Multiple Beast Tribe Boy. Thunder Road. Buffy the Vampire Slayer. Reyku Queen of Ancients. Pippi Longstocking. Oh, I give up."

"And you said you'd know me anywhere." Jalaeka dropped his hands and picked the 'suit up. He put his free arm around

Damien's neck and pulled their heads together, turning to whisper something into the elf's ear with a jackal-like grin, fierce and canny. Damien grinned. His arm went around Jalaeka's waist, hand slid into the back pocket of his jeans. They both looked up at me at the same instant, and separated. Are they . . . ? I thought, mind flinching somehow at the conclusion—lovers. Damien's look to me was distinctly sly, but Jalaeka was blithe as he picked up my bag.

"Come on," he said. "We'll be late."

"See you there," Damien said to me, turning back to the bar.

Outside Jalaeka took a slip of paper out of his back pocket and read the name on the fold. "It's for Francine." He didn't open it up.

I was so busy watching him that I stumbled and almost tripped over a woman coming the other way as we turned the corner around the Shack and onto the dimly lit stretch of walk that led to the tram stop at Engine House.

"Sorry." I reached out automatically, but she was already apologizing to me. Her fur coat was soft as it brushed past me but I could have sworn I heard it snarl.

17/Rita

I stumbled with my heel caught in one of the gaps between the boards. As I was falling time slowed right down so that my fall took minutes rather than moments. My recovery was lent a treacly elegance and importance that was quite out of keeping with its reality. I tried to run.

"I'm . . ." I began saying to someone I had nearly knocked over, but Theo rose close to the surface of me, his senses painfully accelerating my human normal until I felt as though the whole of me had been stretched into a thin skin, drum tight, close to splitting. My vision became acute, my hearing impeccable. ". . . sorry . . ."

Then ordinary speeds and processes resumed, as though nothing had happened. Theo was gone and I was already past the man I'd touched. I caught up with myself, heart pounding, hardly able to think straight at all, praying that Theo wouldn't come back—look, I was doing what he told me to, wasn't I?

I saw the target from the street as I approached—the Shack sides were open to the warm night air and its colourful lights shone out cleanly, surrounded by only a few other open stores. I walked up to the bar and asked for the strongest thing I could think of. I had no idea how I was going to achieve what I was supposed to. The obvious thing had crossed my mind but now that I was beside him it was instantly clear to me that he wasn't into women. I sat down and took my coat off, laying it carefully on my lap. Its noses sniffed the air, searching out the hormonal markers of potential hostility and, when they found none, became calm.

"Nasty coat," said the Elf.

"Thank you." The bartender—Buddy I supposed—came and refilled my glass. I risked a glance sideways. "I heard . . . that is, I heard that you knew something about the *darshan*. Am I saying it right? I don't even know if it's a real word." I wanted to get it all over with as fast as possible, I couldn't even think of a way of lying about how I knew anything in the first place—because Theo told me.

"Then how do you know that you want to know about it?" he asked smoothly.

"I lost my friend," I said. "And someone at work said they'd heard of this thing, downtown, that there was one of us who was different. They said you hung around here and I've been here a lot of times looking for you." I spoke tonelessly and the despair on my face was real enough as I begged him to give me some clue, any clue at all, so that I could keep Theo at arm's length and retain just a fraction of control.

"It's nothing to me." He glanced up left, looking at his own internally displayed Tabtime. "I don't own it."

"Where should I go? Who should I ask?" I grabbed his hand

compulsively, scared of touching him in case I felt Theo there as well, because he could be in any of us and here testing me. I was also scared of him generally. I didn't know the elf and this dealing with the underground world of Sankhara was well outside my experience.

I offered him money on my Tab and he picked up the contact transaction: two hundred credits passed between us and he didn't even blink. I gripped my refilled glass with both hands, staring at the amber liquid inside it. If I drank it, I was sure I would be sick. I had no idea what Theo wanted, only that I must find out about this *darshan*. I had to locate the giver. I had to get it from them.

The elf was watching me closely, though an outsider would never have thought so from his demeanour, which had become casually disconnected from me, his face angled slightly away, as though he was observing the room over my shoulder. "You're very beautiful,"—he was only taking a note of it. "Are you going to drink that?"

I gave a minute shake of my head. What if he didn't tell me? Then what would I do? Theo would come back and I wouldn't know anything. I longed to ask why Theo didn't simply read this one's head like he read mine and take what he wanted to know, but I daren't because I had no idea what Theo could hear, even my innermost thoughts maybe, as I treacherously thought them. No doubt. No doubt. I thought he enjoyed my predicament, that was why. He liked to watch me running, and I was nothing to him, and he liked that too.

"I could help you maybe, if you could tell me the truth," the Elf said. He gently pressed his hand over the back of mine and opened the financial transaction ports again. The money hung suspended between us in nowhere. "I trade information, prefer it to money. I like stories."

I jerked aside in a panic and knocked the glass over. The money jumped back to him. I found myself standing up, the coat in my arms suddenly alive and hissing, made fierce by my fear. "This isn't me," I said. "I work in the Embargo. I don't care about any of this." I backed up a step and hit the woman behind me, almost knocking her off her stool. She turned in anger.

"Hey . . ." she snarled at me and my coat snarled at her. She laughed. "That's a cool coat." She put her hand out fearlessly, silvered with scales on its back, and stroked the fox-furs. They redoubled their efforts to bite, though it didn't put her off. She let one of the little heads fix its jaws on the pearlescent talon of her right index finger and played tug of war with it, smiling softly. "If the elf doesn't help you, follow me when I leave here."

"Take my arm," the elf said, at my shoulder suddenly, and I had to because otherwise I would have fallen down with shock at the speed and silence of his move. He steered us both out of the bar and down the steps that led past the dripping shower stalls onto the beach. Soon we were beyond the reach of all the voices, except those of the calypso singer and the sea.

"That is one desperate mermaid," he said lightly, releasing his hold on me bit by bit.

I leant on him to take off my shoes and held them on the same side as the coat. We walked a few hundred metres and stopped when I decided to. The slope of the beach was shallow and the water distant. There was a moon and its light brought out the hidden runes in his skin so that he seemed to be aglow with secret writing—at least he hadn't lied about the stories. I saw traces of them running into him like tendrils of vapour, from everywhere, from all the real humans in the area. I was glad I was no magical creation. It looked weird.

"Do you ever hear it?" I asked him, calmer now that we were alone, though I had to whisper. *It* meant Unity. All Stuffies knew that.

"I thought I did the other day, actually," he said in a conversational tone. "But it was gone before I was sure. Could have been the Engine doing something—you know how that is."

I nodded, eager for any sense of companionship. I did know what he meant. All Stuffies were always subject to the Engine, though as one who had assumed herself to be simply filler I'd never expected to be important to the humans who lived here. Filler was filler, a sketch and nothing else, even filler that was purpose-made for Unity to take head trips in. I didn't understand why it didn't trip everywhere, in every vehicle. But I wasn't Unity, so what did I know?

He held my arm a moment longer in sympathy and I held on to him, as if by holding one another we could preserve ourselves from Unity's rewriting and all the other subtle erosions that came from beneath. He squeezed harder.

"You're a partial," he said. It was clear in his voice and the sudden upward movement of his head that he'd only just figured this out.

"I don't want to be."

He took a deep breath and let it out in an unhappy sigh. "Shit." He was afraid of me now, but he still didn't let go of my arm. "I can't feel anything. Are you reading me?"

"No," I said, sniffing back tears. "He—it's not here now. I don't think so. I don't know . . . you never fucking know, do you?"

"I do," he said. "I can usually see it . . . I would help you, but there's a reason . . ." He detached himself from me, taking my hand away from him and gently placing it back at my side.

I watched him do it, unable to stop him. "Please don't go."

"I have to." He began to back away from me. "I'm sorry. If you can—I can't tell you why but—if you can, don't pursue this thing. Let it go. It's important. If you meant what you said about wanting to be free." By the time he said the last words he was in the shadow of the boardwalk, and when he stopped speaking he had simply merged with the night. I saw a trace of movement against the tall pillars of the supports running under the pier, then I knew myself completely alone.

I looked up at the stars, the constellations whose names I didn't know. "I hate you," I whispered to them and, when nothing happened, I screamed, "I hate you! I hate you!"

There was no answer.

18/Valkyrie: Sankhara

The operation took a lot of time to show any fruit. Valkyrie had walked most of Dogwood and Hoolerton several times over before she decided it was time to spread her search pattern farther afield, and take into account the transitional areas between Hoolerton's uneasy border with the Hinterland and its steady meandering into the uninhabited slag-heaps of the Ablates, where wild grasses and rotten shale rolled in orange and black hillsides until they met the banks of the Purbright and fed their iron-loaded springwaters into its dark rush.

She flew to the top of Moorland Towers, one of a twin pair of concrete blocks whose tired apartments stared out towards the sea on one side and at Dogwood on the other. A few streets away, near the bulbous shape of the gasometer that marked the beginning of the Hinterland, there was a public house, the Pig and Piper. It sat among streets of brick-built terrace housing, its faux Tudor timberwork exterior masking a Herculean-scaled interior, panelled in dark oak with Vicwardian stained-glass booths and tiles all around. Valkyrie found it both hideous and comforting. All her work had been wasted to its left—revealing nothing; now she looked over the right side.

Most of the space within the walls of the Hinterland was taken up by the steelworks industry and her eye was drawn for a moment by the flash and fire inside one of the huge black sheds, but she made herself concentrate on the long lanes that ran westwards. The brick terraces of tiny houses there gave way quickly to stone terraces of wider and more pleasant aspects. There was a vast stone mill, Lazarus Works, which she understood to be mostly empty. It had a massive tower of its own, concealing a chimney-stack at its heart. This was taller than Moorland Towers and, on a whim, she jetted across to it and cautiously landed upon the stone of the viewing platform near the top.

Many buildings in Sankhara were unstable, and she didn't know the story of the Works or what pocket of the deep human memory it had sprung from, so she kept her senses tuned for any disturbance. The flagstones beneath her bronze boots were sturdy, enormous and well made. They were the summit of a long, steep climb by ramp, which wound around the inner core of the tower and was broad enough to have driven a coach and six up. Wind blasted down the throat of the chimney, and things far distant in the mill clanged and rang in reply.

Valkyrie saw that some of the tangled streets that wound throughout Hoolerton actually had narrow, overgrown paths running among them, between buildings and across bits of land that ran wild. One track along these snickelways looked particularly well used. It stretched from a narrow lane running beside the pub into the long tedium of Crisscross Street.

Promising herself a return visit to the Works later, or at least a good gloat over its story in SankhaGuide, Valkyrie stepped over the broad balcony rail and opened her wings to glide down into Crisscross Street. It was early morning and no being was about except for a single wiry-haired mongrel dog who trotted nimbly away from her. It made the length of the street as far as the spot where the way was crossed by a low railway bridge of black brick, the road beneath closed to normal traffic by iron bollards. There it paused and sniffed, and its ears drooped with a dispirited kind of unease. Instead of carrying on through the tunnel to the street on the other side, it shook itself vigorously, turned and made off along the footpath that followed the railway line.

Valkyrie hurried to the same place and looked carefully at the bridge. Triptrap Bridge was not too far from here—the only means of crossing the Purbright at this end of town—and the troll and the toll were notoriously cranky to deal with, but this did not look like a troll bridge, and it wasn't in a part of Sankhara that had many leanings towards that kind of thing. She was more worried about its collapsing on her than about magical guardians springing forth to challenge her. But when she put her hand on it and scanned the structure she couldn't detect anything wrong with it. The shade underneath it was a few degrees colder than she would have expected, but she could see through to the sunny street on the far side. With an eye out for attackers lurking, she walked through.

There was no warning or sensation to mark the join of two realities, but with one step she crossed over from the mildness of Sankhara's early summer to a startling brightness, the sun at a low angle, the air cool and dry. Instead of the bricks of Crisscross she was looking at vast slabs of marble in her path, all perfectly laid. To her right ran a high stone wall, and across the road to her left she found herself facing a low wall topped with huge and ornate black iron railings.

Beyond these lay extended formal gardens of a magnificence only matched by the building they surrounded. Vast, Baroque, to Valkyrie's eyes incredibly bold in decoration and majesty, it stretched its beautiful lines of pale stone Corinthian columns and capitals for over half a kilometre. Between the stone pillars and window-frames colour-washed stucco stood out in shades of eau-de-nil, powder blue and rose red. Wild, snow-capped mountains were just visible through gaps in the forests that clustered thickly to either side of the Park boundaries and ran on behind it into the distance.

SankhaGuide's Image Search found what she was looking at, although it meant little to her compared with the sheer impact of standing there in that sudden cold, all alone in a huge land. Valkyrie was so astonished that she stood still there for many minutes, wondering why the Engine had built this copy of Catherine the Great's Winter Palace, and why it had chosen to hide it down an alley in the cheapest end of town.

But at least, she thought gleefully, I have something to tell Bob and Belshazzar.

*   *   *

She ran a check on the building's inhabitants, but the Guide went a little tricky on her and stated that nobody was registered there, as the entire space was officially not part of Sankhara at all, and so lay outside its jurisdiction.

"Well, then, whose is it?" Valkyrie insisted. She didn't think that the gate left ajar and the footmarks on the paths were due to ghosts.

"I don't know," SankhaGuide said. "It's a relatively new structure."

Valkyrie felt a tingle of interest and excitement. "And all your unregistered citizens are in here, or in others like it."

"The University staff are mapping it. Would you like to contact them?"

"Oh." The glee at her discovery was somewhat spoiled, but she rallied. "Just give me the names. I'll do it myself."

She looked over the very short list of a single name: Dr. Greg Saxton. He was part of the department, and involved in the Isol Fragment research group, which ultimately came under Belshazzar's remit. Saxton was listed as having an apartment in the Montecathedral area. That would have to wait for another day, then.

Valkyrie followed the slushy footprints leading across the massive paving of the road and paused at the centre to look left and right. To her right the road carried on into the distance in a straight line. Close to the point where it vanished into the dark shadow of the encroaching forest, she could see the great park wall stop or turn. On her highest resolution she saw that it had in fact broken down and lay in ruins that were quickly swallowed up in evergreen creeper. Where they lay the road had also begun to decay. Tree roots buckled its perfect blocks and ice had cracked them into boulders. Saplings sprouted in the margins where the thinner paving slabs had vanished.

A pale flicker of movement caught her eye, inside the treeline on the park side of the road. She tracked it, her AI targeting systems automatically coming online, ready to deal help or death as directed by the surge of primitive fear the sight had caused. Old organizations of neurons within her that were still human and Unevolved had recognized the typical gait of the wolf. It was bigger than any wolf she would have thought to find in a Siberian forest though. Composite image enhancers rebuilt it in her mind's eye. It was huge. On its hind legs it would be taller than she was.

Valkyrie gazed reluctantly at the Palace, cast a single, uninterested glance to her left towards Sankhara Central and found herself not surprised to see the road run on into more glowering woodlands. A big tree had fallen from within the Park at some time in the past and its enormous, fungal-clad trunk blocked the way completely amid a pile of broken stones on either side.

She turned back to where she'd seen the wolf. The pale shape was still there and she felt herself observed. No sooner had the hairs on the back of her neck begun to prickle than she saw the half-hidden figure elongate rapidly and step out of cover.

She was right about the height. It was taller than she was and, like Bob, it was a curious mixture that was human and wolf, eagle and lion and horse and bear and something of the lizard too. She didn't know what it was, except strange. She took a backward step before she knew it.

The long ugly face stared at her from a slightly sideways angle. She saw it wore some kind of rough clothing and metal decorations on its face and hands. Its narrow, powerful limbs looked more suited to all-fours running, but it had no trouble standing like a man. It had a necklace of bone and stone charms among which were suspended a golden sun and an ankh, a cross and a Star of David, a crescent, a feather and an iron ring. Valkyrie had no doubt whatsoever that she was looking at another Forged.

She accessed her links to the outside world and requested a listing but *Who's What* simply replied—image not recognized, component features incongruent with current blueprint archive, refer?

—No, Valkyrie said and dumped the link as the being held up one hand to her, palm out, fingers closed in a clear gesture of warding before turning away. She thought of the golden gryphon and the butterfly. If the blueprint wasn't listed even for intelligence agents then this creature simply didn't exist. But she had no doubt that this was one of her cousins and that it had spoken to her in Uluru. It was too much of a coincidence to find it here. Without hesitation she ignited her jets and took off in pursuit as fast as she could.

The strange Forged dropped to all fours and melted into the forest, running. Valkyrie powered on through the icy cross-winds above the treetops and switched vision to heat-enhanced mode. Now she saw that whoever it was ran with real wolves, for they went leaping in yellow and green over the streams and rugged hills beneath the branches like a flowing mantle. The person themselves ran cool, almost at one with the ambient temperature, so that she could hardly see them. As she came directly overhead and looked down she could only tell where they were by the behaviour of the rest of the pack as they struggled to keep pace.

Valkyrie checked her speedo—35kph—that was very fast for such rough terrain. No way could any animal keep it up for long, and, even as she thought this she saw the weaker members of the group start to fall back and peel away. The band divided. Four strong runners turned back towards the Palace, while two kept to the line of a minor river, following the banks where she could sometimes pick them out in flashes of sunlit grass. It was then she realized she had been diverted by them, and in that instant of distraction had lost all idea of where her target had gone.

She dropped to earth like a stone and landed on the spot where the pack had broken up. The ground was soft and spongy and coated with a thick carpet of pine needles. Tracks were very hard to pick out but she found one clear mark. It was a wolf print, a pack print by its size, though it was peculiar. It had an extra pad mark, small and narrow, which looked a bit like the mark that might be made by a vestigial thumb.

When she straightened up she saw that something had been left behind for her hanging in the space between two trees. She strode up and snatched the little cloth bag down from the leather strands that suspended it. It was red. Valkyrie sniffed it, sensors on maximum, and discovered red ochre, iron, wolf hair and a cocktail of plant matter she couldn't immediately identify.

Surfing the intelligence net she found her answer soon enough. This was *gris-gris:* a voodoun charm.

Valkyrie turned the smelly thing over in her hands. On the bottom a picture was drawn neatly in narrow-line permanent marker. ☺ She knew what that was—you saw it all the time in the Temple area. It was an allusion to the first Stuff, which had manifested the same symbol when Corvax, the first human to look at a sample, had observed it.

Halfheartedly Valkyrie scanned the woodland and the surrounding cold hills but she found nothing, as she expected. She hung the *gris-gris* around her neck, counting it nothing whether it was meant to hex or charm her. She just wanted to keep it long enough to ask Damien some questions about it. As she returned to the Palace area, walking quietly among the trees, it bounced heavily against her breastplate.

She stayed in a chilly, uncomfortable hiding place beneath the overgrown rhododendrons just inside the gateway. As it began to grow dark a shambling figure appeared from the main doorway. It carried a storm lantern and in the bright light Valkyrie saw a most peculiar face, both pretty and grotesque at once, feminine but at the same time brutal and uncompromising in its look. This person wore khaki combat clothing, some white in the mixture so that it could easily trek around in the forests, Valkyrie supposed. Then again, it wore a pink silk sarong around its waist and a soft feathered boa around its neck. There was no connection to SankhaGuide for Valkyrie to use in search for this person's identity, but she knew well enough the look of MekTek—Unevolved humans who had undergone Forging after adulthood, into some new shape for their own reasons.

The figure set out for the iron gate. Valkyrie came out of hiding and showed herself, her palm up and glowing with the badge that identified her as a Solargov officer.

With a crunch of boots on ice they both stopped a metre apart.

"Who are you?" they both said at the same time.

Valkyrie identified herself.

"I'm Mandy," said the MekTek in a soft burr of low tones. "I'm the Keeper here. You aren't welcome, Officer Skuld, no matter what your mission. Be on your way."

"Not before I know your story," Valkyrie said. They were roughly equal in size, though Valkyrie packed more weight and armour. She was not intimidated although the other's face became grim and dark.

"I was a bishop's wife," came the unlikely reply in a measured tone. "But later, when we had fallen out, I became a man, and after a man I became Tek, to protect myself from the Church. Before this my name was Amanda Deneuve and now I am known as Mandy Before. I am the servant of the master here and no other. Love has treated me harshly, as I see it has treated you, if your face is anything to go by. Until the master found me I took out my rage on the world. Sankhara's graveyards are full of my disappointment. But after his light, I am a peaceful servant. Now I will have your story."

Amanda Deneuve—it was a well-known scandal . . . Valkyrie did not believe it but she could see immediately it must be true. The strange face could be shrunk backwards in delicacy and strength to the features of that missing society woman. Her picture had been in all the newscasts several years ago when she and some church money went missing; the bishop afloat face-down in the Purbright.

"I am a servant of the law," Valkyrie said.

Mandy Before lowered his lantern and spat on the ground. "Not here you're not," he said. "Hide if you like and spy yourself silly, but I am about to close the doors and light the lamps. If you attempt to interfere with the master, the servants of the lights will run to find you and you will not want to be caught. That goes double for the master's girl. Also, after dark, other things that are his less merciful selves will take to the air. They are not so charming as he is, even though they are mind of his mind. His baser instincts are less than kind." The huge figure shrugged, massive shoulders making the tiny feathers of the boa flutter and fluff in the icy air. With no more care for Valkyrie Mandy turned and continued on his walk to light the lamps that stood either side of the gate. Valkyrie watched him and he passed her by as if she were not there on his way back.

She returned to her hiding place as twilight came on. Presently another single figure came out of the main doors. It wore a long, heavy greatcoat of grey wool with a high collar and big leather riding boots but it moved very lightly for all that.

As it came level with her hiding place it slowed down and stopped. Valkyrie peered closer, her eyes expanded to their maximum to see if this was the Master spoken of, struggling to see by the weak light of the lamps. But if she was about to be rumbled then she was saved by a high-pitched shriek from the Palace doorway. The greatcoat turned as Valkyrie did, to see who was calling.

A girl with white-blond hair, who wore combat clothes and an unsuitably thin leather jacket, came running through the icy air, her feet in their oversize boots splashing through the muddy slush puddles that lay on the well-used parts of the gravel drive. "Wait for me! Changed my mind! Ha!"

The greatcoated figure held out the sides of its coat, and caught her up in them as she cannoned into it. "Hnuh! Ouch. You never dress properly."

"Sankhara is still warm," she objected. "I hate carrying coats. Greg's coming but he said go without him. Changed his mind too."

"Let's go then." But he made no move to undo the coat, which now contained both of them. Instead the girl inside it wriggled around to face forward and put her huge boot soles on top of the polished riding boots.

"You're so silly," she said and giggled as her companion started moving, doing the walking for both of them, much more easily than Valkyrie would have imagined. They moved like a heavy, clumsy robot.

Valkyrie watched the strange procedure as they went out through the gates. As they came into the lee of the forest wall the blond girl skipped out and jumped onto the pavement. She ran ahead and vanished neatly through the invisible hole into Crisscross Street. The man with her paused and looked back at Valkyrie for a second, then followed her. Valkyrie tried to regain an image capture of his face but found she hadn't got one. Whenever she tried to resolve her memory it insisted on remaining blurred and indistinct. He had no face. She couldn't even say with conviction whether or not he had hair or a hat.

She stood and walked to follow when a downrush of air startled her. Blades of darkness swept in from the starry sky and slashed at her head and shoulders. She felt no impact, staggered with surprise. The shadow talons of the invisible attacker passed straight through her armour and flesh. They did no damage to her body at all and she was recovering, her gun ready, when she felt sharp pain. The shadow touch had easily opened her most vulnerable, raw wound. Her heart ached so badly she thought it was stopping. With a roar of jets she made to escape. The dark hands that might be wings or only the shape of wings made by taloned fingers harried her all the way, their soft flutters laying open all the old scars of her past pain.

She stumbled through Sankhara in a state of shock. It took her an hour to return home and then she found a face she didn't particularly want to see, but she was glad to see someone and he gave her an idea.

Damien met her at her doorway, high in the starry sky, and

looked surprised when she flipped over two hundred honour points by way of a greeting.

"Got a job for you," she said. "Strictly a one-time offer. Here's the target." She sent the images she had taken of the people in the bubble envelope to his Tab.

"Nice juju," Damien replied, reaching out with one long-fingered hand to touch the *gris-gris*. "Where d'you get it? Looks like the real thing."

"It's yours if you do a good job."

"Nah, nah, I don't want that! More than my life's worth to take it off you. Are you crazy?" He stared at her with disbelief, then shook his head, hair whipping in the wind. "You Forged are all the same. No finer feelings for the real forces that slide under and take over. Trust me, you want to keep that. Hey, this image is no good. It could be anybody." He stared at it a second longer.

"You know who I'm interested in. I have a feeling you can find them without a picture."

"Yeah." Damien shrugged and turned a neat pirouette on his section of the high wire. "Mmn, a bit late for shopping on your schedule. I guess I can go like this."

"I guess you'll have to."

"But I get to keep any change."

"Don't get caught."

"Now you insult me," he said, turned, then came back delicately on his tiptoes. "Is there a special reason you aren't going yourself? Or the ratman friend of yours?"

"I'm not in the mood for parties," Valkyrie said. She backed into her cabin and shut the door. The *gris-gris* thumped on her chest. She took it off and hung it next to the horse bone charms. Then she sat down on her bedding mat with a glass of scotch and the files that Bob had handed her, loaded from the Well's internal network.

The club had paid out over a million credits in the last two months, all into the same unnamed account in the unattainable

mysteries of the Uluru banking service. It was split up in uneven amounts across nine separate entries. Next to every entry,
labelling the transaction, was the single word—*darshan*. She'd
looked that up long ago. It meant the grace of god, bestowed by
a glance.

Prior to these transactions there were other colossal payouts,
all unmarked, to the same destination account. It was the kind
of money that usually signalled criminal work, but the blatant
disclosure of it in the books and the fact that it had been legally
submitted for tax inspection puzzled Valkyrie mightily. The
first dated suspect transaction was a few days after the fall of
Metropolis.

But Bob had testimony, albeit from an unreliable source.
Bob's source inside the club said that it was some Stuffie deal,
and although it was peddled alongside the more usual sexual or
pharmaceutical experiences on offer it wasn't either of those
things. And they only sometimes paid. Sometimes, for reasons
nobody understood, it was free. Whatever it was, people came
out of it changed.

There was a file of anecdotal evidence on that, culled from
the most exclusive parts of the healthy/wealthy net groups.
They said it did your head in, a brainmelt of the highest order,
and that it was worth whatever it cost and that it lasted and
lasted and lasted. Personal ecstasy, salvation, rebirth . . .

No, Valkyrie didn't want to risk that. She folded Elinor's picture in her hand. "Where would you go then," she whispered to
it, "if I became content, and forgot about you?" And then again,
perhaps Elinor would be there, but Valkyrie could never afford
such a price and she didn't want to have to look at people who
got what she could never have.

The wind got up later in the night. The horse bone beads
tinkled against the *gris-gris*. Valkyrie, sleepless and heartsore,
looked up and saw the smiley face twirling around and around.
There were two wrinkles in the chin, which looked like another
pair of eyes when it was upside down. Happy sad, happy sad.

19/GREG

We met Francine at the Palace gates. She was carrying a bag with transmitter markers in it, the surveying type for long-term, wide-area data capture. The bag was almost empty and she looked flushed and was out of breath.

"Hey." Francine waved to us and I raised my hand briefly, Jalaeka jogging ahead of me. He caught Francine's hands and pushed his head through the bars to kiss her.

She glanced at me proudly. "The forest gets five metres closer every morning," she said. "I put out markers, you know, like you said you would but . . ."

"Never got round to it," I finished for her. "That's dangerous. I don't like the idea of you being out and about round here on your own."

"I've seen the wolves, they don't come near, if that's what's worrying you. And I don't just put out markers. I put out special things too, presents. Always gone in the morning."

That explained where my blue china cup had gone. "Oh well then, straight up to the attic for you as soon as we get in." The attic was a place neither of us was keen to explore and we'd made a running joke of putting it off.

She let go of my hand. "You first."

"I think *he* should go. If he's anything like he claims, he'll be quite safe."

Jalaeka opened the door and stood back to let Francine and me go through first. "I'll go while you two get changed. Give me the machines." He held his hand out for my Abacand and the bag of markers.

I gave it to him. "I'm not scared." I stepped over the lintel and waited for him in the hall. Mandy Before, the Palace keeper, had been around and lit the lamps. To our left and right the galleries glowed gently in their light, columns like orderly rows of ice soldiers, arches white and cold. I glanced up at the ceiling mural.

The helicopters and their sunset were gone. On a still river between jungle banks a small row-boat was floating in mid-stream, a thin rope trailing behind it. The boat was empty. Thick mist veiled everything around it. There were hints of faces under the water and in the shadows between the trees at the water's edge, but when I looked for them the illusion vanished. There was nothing there.

"Oh, that's much better," Francine said as she studied it.

"Was it like that when we left?" I asked Jalaeka.

"I don't know." He took a recording of it for me with my Abacand, as if he'd done it all his life. In one of those moments that seem to stand out in time I saw the black fall of his hair against the soft white and grey lines of the hall, the bronze line of his throat, his beautiful hands with the silver Abacand resting on them, and I saw how inhuman he was. He wasn't looking at a picture. He was looking at me; the intuition I had about it was too strong to resist. He was thinking. I remembered the calculations on my Abacand, the mathematics of existence. What was I in that? He was deciding somehow, and looking at that picture and . . . I lost it, as though my insight had evaporated.

As he turned to speak to me, he'd never looked less idealized, his expression one of slight surprise and great pain, the kind of expression that would come from the betrayal of an old friend or a knife in the back.

He was already hiding his expression as he turned to me but he wasn't fast enough. I wanted to touch him, examine him, interrogate him, demand to know what he was thinking. His pain was replaced by a strange, ancient weariness that made him look as though the gaslight itself was strong enough to white him out. Our gazes locked as he spoke lightly, "Murderer goes up the river to kill the old king in his den, kills him, becomes king, son replaces father, mothers become wives and sisters daughters . . . that what you're thinking?"

Did he read my mind? "Something like that." I sounded colder than I thought I would.

"Look, murdering son already got out of the boat." He

pointed at the image, at the boat and rope's wake, as caught on my Abacand's screen. "It's drifting back downstream." I felt his gaze as if it were a kiss on my face. The ghost of a smile moved his mouth. "Then again, maybe it's only a boat. Maybe whoever was in the boat forgot to tie it up, or they got taken by pirates."

"Maybe you're only some guy," I suggested.

"Maybe." He held my gaze and its challenge.

Francine had spent this time staring up at the ceiling but she looked back at both of us now. "Stop it. I already want to slam your heads together, and it's not even nine o'clock. Why are we changing clothes?"

"Going out," Jalaeka said with an easy shrug and a smile. "I promised Greg I'd do whatever filthy porno it is that I do for you both, so that he can pass final judgement and shop me to Solargov Security. You're my guests."

"And you were going to ask me when?" She put her hands on her hips in pretend anger.

"Francine—would you like to come out to the club to-night?"

She was so happy. I was such a fool.

20/JALAEKA

I didn't like the boat picture. I wanted to go back to Francine's apartment and watch her taking her clothes off, then watch her getting dressed. I wanted to brush her hair and put on her makeup for her, lose myself in all the trivial perfections of small moments in which there was nothing but love.

I went to the end of the gallery where apartments had surrendered a coffinated corner space to a simple, white-painted stair. I kept thinking about the things I'd tried to explain to Greg in the plainest words I knew, and how those words had built a wall between us that our sniping jokes didn't quite manage to vault. I knew that I needed him in the coming storm, and

I didn't like to speculate on the how and why of it. I knew it in my bones, in the angles of my superstructures across all seven hidden corners. I didn't like being at his mercy, though every time we came close to a moment of connection I knew he was someone who could imagine me a better way. He could make me stronger. But sometimes he wanted a friend and sometimes he wanted to finish me, and I was never sure which one was going to win. And I didn't like the boat picture.

At the top of the white staircase a narrow door with an iron ring handle opened onto a dim and shadowy world, floored by regular boards hammered in place by iron nails, lit by small, floor-level windows of plain glass set at regular intervals to left and right. Although it was dark outside the rest of the Palace, the windows here let in a sepulchral, sepia-toned light, just bright enough to illumine the empty spaces and the even scatter of dried brown leaves covering the floor. Their untouched carpet stretched from where I stood to a point that must have been an unlikely several kilometres away, all relationship to the Palace lost. At this false horizon the wooden floor was still a long way from meeting the roof, from which hung suspended an entire dead forest. A leaf fell from the canopy of a thick, faded red beech tree above me. I watched its fluttering descent through the motionless air, and listened to the tiny sound it made as it touched the floor.

I looked up to where it had come from. Bats hung in the topmost branches of a withered oak, its highest twigs a few metres above my head like rigid fingers stretching out in space to touch anything, touching nothing. The bats were sleeping with their wings wrapped around them, vibrating in space to the measure of their rapid heartbeats, their slight motion making the curled brown leaves shiver around them. Farther above me, beyond the bats, where the trees were rooted in sandy yellow earth, a road wound through the dells. I saw a tiny man on horseback riding there, dirt brown in an empire of dirt greys, the mane and tail of the horse and the hair of the man hanging down towards me. The sound of the horse's hooves was like the patter of mouse feet. Dust and sand filtered down in a shower where they'd passed and sparkled in the air.

I walked for about a hundred metres. Everything was very dusty, as though most of it had been stored up here for decades. After a short distance the leaves at my feet and on the trees changed. They were much older, most no more than skeletons. The ochre dust that lay thickly around each one was the dust it had crumbled to.

I crushed a few deliberately under the sole of my shoe and ground them into the planks of the floor.

Some distance beyond me a breath of air stirred some of the deadfall into a small circle, lifting the leaves up an inch or two, then letting them go. Their rustling was exactly the sound that the pages of a heavy book makes when someone riffles through it, not the sound of leaves at all. I saw other patches move and slither in the thick fall and the syrupy, leaden air stirred against my face. From the vanishing point ahead a figure arose, building itself rapidly out of branches, fleshing itself with the fallen leaves. A wicker golem, it came towards me slowly, though I soon realized that the apparent speed was an illusion caused by the distance. It was travelling fast, and in its wake the dead leaves and dust rose in a storm.

I glanced down at the picture of the boat shining in artificial light from the machine in my hand. I didn't feel afraid of whatever Unity's Engine had created here, though its creations were often worth being afraid of. I felt tired. I knew the boat. It had been my boat, once. I knew the old flaking rusty-coloured paint of its prow and the uneven action of the left rowlock and how it always felt like it was listing when it wasn't because the seats were warped. It currently rotted at the bottom of a river delta on a planet a very long way from this one, which was in turn a very long way from Sankhara's appropriated world and, from Earth, not even visible on a clear night or from a telescope stationed out at the system's edge.

I lost my patience with this dead inverted world—at that second something in me snapped—and I was done with hiding and done with waiting and—just done. I set down one of the markers, turned my back on the storm of leaves and whatever rode it, and walked back to the attic door. A tornado whipped into life behind me, roaring like a train. I closed the door on it.

For a moment I waited on the other side. An already-weak breath of air pushed some dust out between the door and the frame. Leaves battered and skittered against the panels, not even enough to shake the latch. A pathetic, lost scratching noise grated across the floorboards and up the other side of the door itself so that I seemed to feel a weak, trembling hunger scrabbling up the wood, scratching the paint with its fingernails. After a few seconds it stopped. It had no power beyond the dead wood and it would never get out without somebody else's fear to animate it. I pitied it for a split second.

I went into Greg's apartment without knocking and returned the Abacand. He was in the shower. I left it on his kitchen table and called out, "Nothing to worry over up there. Come next door, when you're ready."

Francine was in the middle of getting dressed. I fantasized that when I sealed the seams on her clothes and slid the boots onto her feet I was touching the people I loved in the world of the row-boat, even though the youngest of them was three hundred years lost in time and the others lost beyond reckoning altogether, whichever universe was on either side of the equals sign. I want to think that they live on in me, but that's not the kind of living on that counts. I want to see them again. I want to hold their hands like I hold hers. I want the first Francine, so that I can tell her she can have all of me, for nothing, for nothing.

"I didn't hear anything," Francine said. "What was up there?"

"Nothing." I crossed the room to her. She was wearing a silvery-grey top and leggings so tight they looked shrink-wrapped to fit, and over them a translucent dress whose seams looked like white line drawings of suggested outer clothes. Her transparent pink high heels sparkled with glitter. "Wish I were you."

She wrapped her arms around me, pressing her body against me, drugging me with it. "I want to be you," she whispered.

I kissed her vamp-red mouth. I got slightly lost in it, and when she pushed me gently away I was dizzy with the heady sensation that I could cross over.

21/Greg

Jalaeka dressed down, in filthy ripped jeans and a white T-shirt, the training shoes on his feet smeared with the ashy-grey soil and needle leaves of his last run out through the boreal forests of Anadyr Park. Always running, always dancing. He affected an air of happy nonchalance, but I remembered his face when he'd looked up at the boat as I watched him with Francine and the way they both changed in the other's presence: two poles, magnetism.

He noticed me watching him as we made the short journey out to Sankhara Central to the club but he didn't say anything until we were at the door, when he lost his patience. "Oh for hell's sake, stop staring at me, I've known you about a thousand years. Let's go analyze everything until it hurts."

"Damn," I said. "And there was I hoping for the fantasy vampire figure from the Love-Craft romance novel who was working here as a stripper in order to suck the life out of everyone's minds with his telepathic exchange system while they're in some kind of neurological love catatonia checking out his artificially pumped-up man-magic."

"That's somebody else's act. He's only in on Truesday. And am I the *only* person ever to come here who hates the cute Sankhara days of the week?" He took Francine's hand and led the way.

"I hate them," Francine said.

"Me too. Me first actually," I added as we passed through an ordinary door and onto a long, candlelit ramp. "I hated them long before you got here."

"Well, *I* hated them since they were made," Francine said over her shoulder in the blackness. "And even before."

"Okay," Jalaeka said. "As long as we all hate them, then everything's okay. I could never love someone who thought in their heart of hearts that Truesday was cute."

"Technically speaking it should be Marsday," I said. "If Wednesday became Wotansday and Thursday is Thorsday. But there's still no accounting for Satyrday."

"You could start a campaign, sign a petition," Jalaeka called back to me as we continued.

"You could get a real job." My bitching annoyed me, but I kept thinking that he was hiding far too much and expecting too much from us in return. I didn't have that much faith that the evening would be more than smoke and mirrors. I was ready to be disappointed.

The ramp pitched at a mild angle until we had dropped about one storey in height and then emerged into a large, cavernous space.

The club was every bit as depressing as I suspected, but architecturally interesting at least. Though topped with a reasonably sized building, the venue itself was sunk deep into the ground, as its name promised. A circular well roughly the diameter of a football pitch had been built of stone, with a solid wall outer skin and at its centre an inner skin of equally massive blocks bordering an open drop shaft some fifteen metres across. The inner wall was punctured at regular intervals with gothic arches, heavily barred against would-be suicides or acts of casual murder, which let in light from the middle well.

Between the two skins the club itself spread out in two broad helical ramps, one that led patrons down to the bottom, the other, beneath and above it, winding them back up to the top and the exits to the street. The gangway lay next to the inner wall, on our right, giving views across the great drop, while to the left pie-slice zones of ramp had been roughly divided into different areas with different themes and entertainment.

"This is hellish," I said, as our cheerful introductory pop

became the softly burbling jazz of an early-twentieth-century gentlemen's club, and suddenly there was wood panelling and cigar smoke everywhere.

"Nine turns of the screw," Jalaeka agreed.

"I thought you liked it here," Francine said, catching hold of the velvet rope, which marked the edge of the gangway and relative safety. She gazed around her with obvious excitement and pleasure and I felt every one of my years. She didn't seem to care that Jalaeka had agreed with me. He exuded a deep comfort as I watched him scan the almost empty spaces, the same kind of look that Hyperion's lead wolf occasionally wore on her face when she scented the air prior to hunting.

Ah Jalaeka, I thought, you're used to a lot more here than you'll ever let her know, at least you won't let her know it if I have anything to do with it. It was strange to me but curiously important that Francine's illusions in him not be ruined—at least, not ruined in a crass and insensitive way.

"It has the security of old familiar places, which I always mistake for comfort," Jalaeka said as I paused to look through one of the arches into the central well to see where the light was coming from. Its soft white gleam shone fiercely from a torrential fall of frozen water that had broken through from the wellhead and was crashing down to drown everything in a mighty flood. At first I assumed it was solid but then I saw that it was flowing in obedience to gravity, albeit incredibly slowly, a mighty stalactite.

"That's the hourglass," Jalaeka said, leaning out with me. "When it's filled the pool at the bottom and gone flat and dark, then it's closing time. They collect sunlight in it for three days out on the snow above the mountains of the moon."

"I thought that was a Slow Glass property."

"Moves fast, slow to release light. Sticky Glass."

"How many times have you explained that?"

He glanced at me, well aware of my hostility. "Never. Everyone always knew, except you."

I ignored him, though it was reassuring that he'd gone back

to baiting me. I felt him sigh heavily beside me, then he withdrew. Through the windows of the inner well I could see the plummeting depths of the nine-storey fall or look across, into other galleries and other fantasies. I saw flashes of all the things that had once been strange and had then become clichéd and then kitsch and then reinvented and cycled over so that they were all somewhere in that vicious circle: contortionist girls painted in rainbow colours twisted in knots, muscle men posing in some kind of dungeon, a huge screen playing close-ups of a man and woman kissing where occasionally the view flickered to show the interiors of their skulls, the bone and tongue and lips only, or sometimes only their faces melting into each other so the mouths were a continuous stream of muscle fascinated with its own movement.

We drifted down and down, through *Chocolate Floral,* with its background of pretty landscapes and naked people sporting in various outdoor locations of healthy aspect; hayfields, bluebell woods, torrential mountain streams; through *Funky Oriental* full of disco dancing extras from Chinese opera, and *Martial Law* and *Petrol Head (gayF and gayM and transexualgayF and transexualgayM* and *Transvestite* and *Celibate* and *Straight,* each in their citrus-labelled variants of extremis—there was no limit to the kind of people who liked tinkering with engines) and *Rubber Plantation* and *WarZone* and *Bunnyitis* and *Spacerobot* and *Miserable Tuesday Afternoon* and *Emergency Room* and *Ghetto* and *Haywain* and *Spooky Dookey* and *Normal.*

We got a drink and paused in *the Library* where a thin Unevolved girl in a tweed suit buttoned to the neck and heavy Bakelite-frame glasses came over and tapped me on the arm. "You're new." She wrinkled her nose and flickered her fake eyelashes behind their swimmingly enormous lenses. Her eyes were enlarged by the glass to the size of saucers. "Would you like to help me revise for my physics test?" She held out an Abacand in her narrow, anaemic hand. Actually she held it two inches to my left because she couldn't see much through the glasses.

Jalaeka and Francine were watching, trying not to laugh. I

took it and saw with a solid sense of disbelief that it was display-
ing a treatise on optical principles. Behind her several other
people were already seated between stacks, surreptitiously fumbling one another's knees below heavy wooden study tables lit
with green glass lamps. Books, pens, calculators and notepads
cascaded below their intently focused faces. Beyond them great
racks of volumes, decimal system markers lit in neon, stretched
far away into what was the illusion of a Borgesian infinity. There
was no music here. There was silence.

"Ah, leave him alone Lizabet, he's mine," Jalaeka said easily
and ruffled the hair on the top of my head like I was a schoolboy.

I burned with annoyance and handed back the Abacand.
Lizabet looked over her glasses at him. "What's the smallest positive integer that could be expressed as the sum of two cubes in
two different ways?"

"One thousand seven hundred and twenty-nine," he said
without blinking.

She smiled at me and Francine and put her hand over her
tweed chest. "Be still my beating heart. He always knows the answer. I'm gonna get him one day."

"What's the last even prime number?" he asked her.

"Oh you're just messing with me now." She batted her eyelashes at him. "Go and be bad somewhere else before I have you
thrown out for talking."

I made to get up, glad to be leaving, but Jalaeka held on to
my forearm and his grip was none too light.

I twisted my arm away. "What's the matter?"

"Don't make it obvious that you're looking," he said and indicated a tall and curving figure high up on a ladder in between
the stacks to our left. Francine looked cautiously and I waited,
then looked when she glanced back to him with a questioning
face.

The woman wore an even more severe tweed suit than Lizabet
had, her costume completed with seamed stockings, patent black
high heels with vicious winkle-picker tips and small, rimless
spectacles. Her suit bore cracked elbow patches of oxblood

leather and her dark hair was pulled back into an intricate bun at the nape of her neck, secured with a silver-tipped ebony spike. She was teetering on the top of the ladder's extent, reshelving some scrolls. Even from that distance I could see the scarlet of her lipstick, so intense was its colour, and the top of one stocking where her skirt rode up. Her waist was drawn in so small that her body had assumed a cartoonish shape.

She finished her ersatz task and climbed down with a lithe action, as though her corsets had liquidized her insides, smoothing the line of her skirt as she walked towards the Ladies'.

"Who's that?" I asked.

"That's what Unity's wearing tonight," he said. "That's Theo's partial in Sankhara."

"What?" I felt cold, jumpy. I thought it was another joke. The woman herself hadn't even noticed us.

"Are you . . . ?"

"No. Theo has a long history of seeding places with particular Stuffies who are all variants of himself. They live their lives, sometimes forever, and sometimes he comes back to do some work with them. Part of what he is, his function, if you like, exploring the frontiers of whatever species Unity is surfing at the time. That is his partial, here to find me and to find you, and she will, tonight."

"But," Francine started, sitting forward, her face a mask of anxieties, "I don't understand. Why now? How could it find you now?" She put her hands on his leg, high up, a confident, possessive contact.

"A woman I knew in Metropolis passed on a gift to me, this in fact—" Without warning he half turned towards me and placed his hand on the centre of my chest. I felt a sudden heat and saw the flesh and skin around his fingers light up red for a second and I saw, in my inward eye, myself, a long time ago, on Earth.

It was autumn and at my North American college all the trees were in their red and yellow livery as I walked along the street. I had a half-eaten ice-cream in one hand and I was walking towards my car. It was the end of my Ph.D. year and I'd just come out of my viva exam. My professor had offered me a fellowship on the spot and my head was ringing and utterly empty, the universe of possibilities that had suddenly opened up inside it expanding all there had been inside me to the limits of my awareness, leaving a space inside that was perfectly luminous.

The feeling returned wholesale with the memory, as these things do, but when the images and recollection faded the feeling remained as strongly as ever. I was buoyant on this resurrection and felt it settle, heard it die down to a residual harmonic like the afterglow of a great symphony in the first instant of silence, when all the music is present at once. It did not lessen. It did not fade.

Jalaeka watched me with care. "So, how was it for you?"

I couldn't speak. My suspicion of his motives hadn't gone, I still thought his taking up with Francine, relation with Damien and appearance here was all too weird, but he'd given me this great lift of heart. He decided to mistake my conflict for curiosity—I saw him make the deal with himself quite clearly.

"What's that?" Francine asked, looking into my face so very hopefully that I had to show her the good side of me.

"I'm only the conduit," Jalaeka said evenly. "It was her power. I don't know what you see and I don't feel anything. Only . . ." But he glanced down to his left guiltily and didn't finish. I stored that in my memory. He continued, "And that's what brought the partial here. Not because my doing that vibrates in the sevensheet, which it does a little—lots of Sankhara Stuffies have that kind of effect when they're apparently being magical—but because I traded it for cash here, because I gave it away for nothing here, before I even knew what I was doing, when I thought it was nothing more than a pat on the back, and rumour spreads, and here she is and it not far behind her."

"Greg, are you all right?" Francine changed seats to move beside me. I felt her hand on mine.

I turned towards her with what I hoped was a reassuring smile. "Never finer." I tried to say a billion things but they all escaped into the perfect, beautiful space inside my head. Jalaeka watched me closely.

One thing, I thought, one thing you haven't lied about anyway.

22/RITA

I asked the Librarian where I might find the host here who mended broken hearts. She sighed and took off her heavy glasses, wiping them on a lacy white cotton handkerchief which she drew from an inner pocket. "I'm afraid he's not working tonight, well, he is but it's a personal matter. So I can't refer. Is it for yourself?"

"Yes," I said and it was no difficulty. I was glad of the ridiculous corset. Its bones kept me upright and the pain kept me focused. I hadn't quite got used to gasping for breath. I had to measure it out. "But it's no matter if it isn't now. I wonder if you could tell me more, if I could make some appointment?"

"I'm afraid the price has gone up terribly since he started," she told me, replacing the glasses on her face. Her teeth were too big for her mouth. She flicked open her Abacand and showed me some numbers on its screen. "If you really have a hard time then there are ways . . ."

"I can pay," I said, putting the tip of my fingernail against the one with the most zeros after it. "What about tomorrow?"

"Why don't you come with me to the carrel and I'll fill you in?" she said, indicating a private reading room with a graceful extension of her arm.

"Thank you," I said and followed her. I had no sense of Theo at all, it was as though I went through these things for myself, only I had no reason to. I wanted to tear my own hair off, but I sat down demurely in the chair and let her give me the spiel and the endorsements by all the big names and the celebrity shit that went with it. *Darshan* they called it. I didn't know that word. She told me he had a rider in his contract that forbade any publicity of any kind. Days ago I would have been entranced. I paid her and I took a long look at the image of him she supplied.

A thought rose unbidden in my mind, in a voice not my own—*Don't you ever change?* And nasty words said themselves with my lips, "Does he fuck?"

"Sure."

My ribs and stomach ached suddenly as though I was laughing. I felt Theo sharpen to a point of pain inside my head.

I thanked her and made the appointment I would never keep.

My search didn't take long. They had said he liked to dance and they were right. I watched him for a while and I thought with jealousy of all the awful relationships I'd had for Theo's unknown reasons, and of the blessed solitude of my single-room apartment in the Aelf. I could see that that was why he danced too. For the peace.

He walked off the floor and directly across into the darkness near the Hub where I was standing, singling me out easily. There was no point in attempting to hide. I didn't know what he'd do. He came up to me without hesitation and, as though we were meeting in a friendly way, caught hold of my hand and kissed the inch of air beside my face. Sweat ran off him and his T-shirt clung to him. He smelled indescribably fine. He looked into my eyes, looking for Theo . . . and he saw only me in my wretched state.

"It'll be okay," he said.

I stared at him with furious jealousy. "Will it? Who's going to make it that way? You?" Beneath me a claw opened, a fin stirred. He might have stayed even so, with me having to endure his sympathy and Theo's voyeurism, but we were interrupted.

"Hey!" the tall Elf from the Surf Shack appeared from the darkness and clapped him on the shoulder. "You owe me a drink." He pulled hard on the splinter's arm and shot me a warning glance which made a pang of envy and resentment dart across my chest. *Not for the likes of you,* he was saying.

I stared back at him with my head high. A gang of revellers pushed their way between us and I let myself be dragged along with them into another place, farther down the ramp, where I made myself busy, so that I wouldn't have to see who else was with the splinter, or notice how much he was in love and how shockingly bad it had made his judgement.

All these things Theo enjoyed seeing. I wanted the splinter to win, so that Theo would die. I longed for it, daring Theo to drag me back to Unity for my wanton sins against him. It would have been a welcome relief.

He did not.

23/GREG

I drifted off for a while. Other things happened, some strange, some not. I surrendered to the need to get drunk in a pretty zone named *Ziggurats of Cinnamon,* where I matched Francine shot for shot, alternating mint tea and her favourite cranberry vodka as we sat on a heap of cushions in a private pasha's tent. Jalaeka went out dancing on his own to the racing Arabic music (she wouldn't, I couldn't). We lost track of him for a while and I wanted to go and find out what he was up to, but I stayed with Francine instead and enjoyed having her all to myself.

She talked nostalgically about a friend of hers from home called Sula, though she was careful not to let slip where she'd come from—I only knew that it must be Earth and somewhere in the Northern European zone. I would have guessed England and close to the mouth of the Sankhara Gateway but I couldn't be sure.

"You must miss her," I hazarded as we went into a tea phase. I filled her glass from the elegant bronze pot we had been left with.

She sipped it and gazed at the steam rising. "Su wouldn't like it here. She likes comfortable, predictable things."

"She might like to hear from you. You've got free calls all night courtesy of Jalaeka, and you don't have to reveal where you are." I narrowly avoided mentioning that she could call home. "You could write her a note."

The waiter, a man with a beautiful leopard-pattern skin, came and removed our four shot glasses, left clean and empty ones for us, and the bottle of vodka in a ceramic bucket of real ice.

Francine, doubtful about the prospect of calling, liked the idea of the note. She borrowed my Abacand and began to compose it, cross-legged on the floor. I lay back against my emperor's pile of silks and watched the people who had joined us in this low zone. The woman that Jalaeka had pointed out was nowhere to be seen, and, for the moment, neither was he. I Tab-accessed the Club network and asked SankhaGuide to find him for me. He was out of sight around the curve of the ramp, not far away. I didn't bother to get up. The spacey feeling in my head was too puissant. Then I saw Francine's friend Damien. He was hurrying down on the absolute inward edge of the Hub turn, his attention intent. He went around the curve. A minute or so later he came back towing Jalaeka by the arm and they both disappeared into the crush of dancers now packing the small arena in front of the staging area where hired professionals—like him I suppose—showed everyone what a lissome voluptuous gesture looked like when it was done properly.

Francine finished her message. "I sent it," she said, then glanced in the direction I was looking in. She saw what I saw—in the centre of the swaying mass of people Jalaeka and Damien all over each other, mouth to mouth, and their mouths alight as though they had a candle in between their teeth—a touch too exotically painful even for the likes of this place, I thought, feeling hot sparks of irritation and anger rush up and down across my shoulders.

"Oh," Francine said, slightly surprised.

"Don't you hate it?" I asked her, drink getting the better of my restraint.

"Hm? No." She grinned and reached for the vodka bottle. "Why would I? He's only doing what he did for you."

"He didn't do it like that."

"You're not a gay elf though, are you?"

"No." The more closely I observed her the more certain I was that she was getting a charge from watching the two of them together. I don't know why I should have been surprised by that. For all the shining prospect inside my mind, I was always finding these appalling moments of carping repression. I supposed that was proof that whatever he'd done to me, change me he hadn't.

Francine filled my glass and her own to overflowing, held mine out towards me. "Come on. You promised me."

"I've had enough."

"Don't be a dill." She pushed it at my hand insistently. I set my tea glass down and took it. There was a teasing look on her face I longed for and didn't care for at all. We drank them in one. I picked the tea glass up again and gave hers to her. She glanced nervously down at my Abacand where it lay on the low table.

I looked back towards the dance-floor and could only see unfamiliar faces and strange bodies moving in the dim lantern glow. Then, across the Well, through two of the central windows, I saw the woman Jalaeka had pointed out, sitting alone. The partial. I got up, not even sure what I was going to do.

"Where are you going?" Francine asked.

"Just to see someone. I won't be long. Pour me another drink," I said and went before I could change my mind. As I left I heard the Abacand chime to announce the arrival of a message.

Everyone seemed to be in my way. It took me a few minutes to reach the spot at the Well bottom where I'd glimpsed her face and I was worried the whole time that I'd get there and she'd have gone, but when I arrived she had only moved a small distance away and was sitting alone in a relaxed, blue-toned area filled with quiet, alpha-wave-enhancing music. Her eyes skipped restlessly through the people passing, and her icy expression didn't melt in the slightest as I stepped up to her. It would have entirely put me off if I hadn't been protected by my dutiful research intentions.

"Can I buy you a drink?" Not one of the best pickup lines in the world.

She looked me over but there was no flicker of recognition in her eyes or interest in her voice to prepare me for her words. "Aren't you with little Miss Blond IQ?"

I digested that for a second. "She's a friend of mine, that's all."

"Then go pay her some attention." She continued her inspection of the passers-by.

"I wondered if I might talk to you. I'm a researcher from . . ."

She didn't bother to look at me again, though her eyes narrowed as she spoke to me. "You you you. The best thing you can do is get back to her while you still can. My boyfriend doesn't like your boyfriend. Don't you know that by now?"

"Please, I don't even want to ask you about that, only about . . ."

Her brown eyes fixed me with the flattest, most dismissive look I'd ever received, one that indicated I was less interesting than secondhand chewing gum. "You don't know when somebody's doing you a favour. Go. Shoo." She waved her hands at me and flicked her fingertips. "Get lost."

On my return journey my ruined plans were even less clear. I thought I'd ask her to be interviewed, like the rest of the Stuffies. She was a special creation, she would have to know some special things that I could have got her to reveal, in time . . .

"You idiot!" Jalaeka appeared right in front of me and grabbed me by my shirt front. I'd never seen him angry before. His rage was electrifying. He hauled me bodily off the Hub and into the edge of the dance-floor where the crowd hid us from Francine's direct view. "What were you doing with her?"

I pulled away from him with a jerk. "Well, you said she'd find you and she hadn't found you yet, so I thought it was my last chance to ask her some questions about being a partial. I was working. That's all. She wouldn't even know . . ."

"Know what?" he hissed at me, face an inch from mine. "*Who* you are? What, is she fucking dumb, you think? Can't smell Francine on you? Can't smell me on you? Can't see this—" He rapped me hard on the chest with a flick of his knuckles, then did the same to my forehead. "Come on, Greg, what were you going to ask her? Whether or not I'm real?"

"How about whether or not you're a liar?"

"And what am I lying about? What have I ever lied to you about?"

"This. Here. This soft-porn show you're putting on for Francine and she thinks that's all it is, nicey nicey, hot stuff. But I don't think that's all there is to it. The *darshan* isn't it. You're acting out some game when you should tell her that . . ."

He cut me off. "That what? She knows all this. She *knows* it. I wouldn't be here if she didn't want me to be. I *couldn't* be. Go ask her." His dark eyes glittered, daring me.

"Or maybe I'll ask her what you did to her. You changed her. You know what I mean. You Translated her, didn't you?" I was only running on empty when I said this, because I had to find something to fling. His reaction stunned me.

A flicker of uncertainty ran through him. He stepped back involuntarily. His whole demeanour slumped.

"What the . . . Did you?" I slapped his shoulder, made a grab for his shirt, but it was stuck to him with sweat and I couldn't get hold of it. "Come here!"

He didn't back off any farther but he held his head back and away from me as I rounded on him. "What did you do to her? If you hurt her in any way, I'll . . ."

Then he looked down his nose at me, not just from his extra few inches of height but from a thousand dimensions of difference between us, in that second assuming all the power he never laid claim to and holding it over me. It froze me. "You'll what?"

His right eyebrow flicked upwards. He might as well have held a knife to my neck.

I shivered, walked backwards, slowly, shaking my head, eyes downcast, my hands held out, palm up. I turned when I was clear and made my way back to the tent.

"God, you've been ages. Where have you been?" Francine complained, then said with a smile, "Look, I got a note from Su. You were right. She was pleased to hear from me after all."

I sat down obediently to share the letter with her and tried to mask the fact that I was shaking from head to foot.

"Are you okay?" Francine asked. She held out a full shot glass. "Come on, you're one behind."

I didn't hesitate this time. I let her pour two more for me. "Francine. I don't know how to ask you this but . . . has Jalaeka ever hurt you?"

"No." She swallowed her dose of the liquor and squeezed her eyes shut for a moment. I hoped she was drunk enough that it didn't occur to her to ask or notice where my question came from but when she set her glass down she gave me a judicious glance. "Why?"

"Nothing. I think . . . I think you should try to get away from him, that's all." Oh, what fount of genius was that coming from? "He's not being entirely straight with you, I think. Something he said just now. Ask him if you won't believe me."

She frowned and stood up, by some strange magic I didn't understand more stable on her shoes than she had been when she was sober. "I will." Her glance was uncertain and not a little betrayed. I longed to take back what I'd said.

Through the tent doors I watched her go out into the dancers and find Damien there. She put her hands on his shoulders and they swayed to the beat, talking. Some of her gestures, quick and angry ones, came in my direction. While she was out Jalaeka came back, in a clean shirt. There was no trace of other-worldliness, godliness or anything else about him. He was as average as any Joe.

"I'm sorry." He sat down opposite me, where she'd sat. "That was unforgivable."

"I'm sorry too," I said, mostly meaning it, though I couldn't forget my fear of him that easily and didn't trust myself to say anything else.

"Fuck it all," he said conversationally, took the open vodka bottle out of the bucket and upended it into his mouth.

Francine came back with Damien and without another word being exchanged on our contentions we four sat down together. Damien and Francine played Go and Jalaeka and I watched. The leopard man came back with two more vodka bottles opened and a glass for the elf. They spoke to one another in whispers. Damien glanced at me with one of his inscrutable elfin smiles. Francine gave me an unmistakable glare. I nodded and bowed my head, guilty, guilty of spoiling it all, yes I was, and even so that lingering sensation of puissance went right on rolling inside my head in an endlessly confident caravan.

When I glanced back up I saw Francine had forgiven me. She picked up my Abacand from the table where it was lying in a pool of spilled tea and was about to hand it back to me but Jalaeka intercepted it. "I'll keep that for now." He put it in the back pocket of his jeans, the one without the tear across it. I didn't bother to contest it.

Much later Damien went off somewhere, and later still the three of us went back to the suite, an opulent, modern place, entirely soulless and forgettable. Francine went ahead but Jalaeka held me back in the narrow entrance hall, where it was so badly lit it was almost dark. He put himself in front of me, with his hands out onto the walls on either side. I halted clumsily and the door swished shut at my back.

He spoke with the careful but failing phrasing of the self-aware drunk. "I know you've got good reasons to dislike me, but what you've got to understand is that when I look at people, animals too sometimes, but really, okay, people . . . look, can I borrow your brain for a moment? I need to show you something."

"Won't that, you know, Translate me?" I slurred, trying to

think of a good reason to say no, although my curiosity was uppermost.

"No, no, no. I'll go through your Tab. Easy. Won't be like being me of course but good enough. What do you say? Go on. Indulge me. Just once."

"Can't you tell me?"

"If I tell you it'll all just sound drunk and you'll think it's the vodka."

"It is the vodka."

"Mmn, yes it is, all right. You're right. This is probably a very bad idea . . ."

"Go on then," I said, a thousand times more daring and witless than usual. I wanted to know, and the least kind part of me hoped it would be some kind of nail in the coffin of his mystique. "Should I sit down?"

"Nah," he said confidently. He abandoned his Samson posture on the walls and reached out for my left hand, pressing his thumb over the slim wafer of Tab beneath my skin. I felt a soft, tingling fuzz of electrical activity.

Noise. White distortion. Impossible geometry.

"Bloody useless technology," I heard him say. "Can't render the sevensheet. I'll fake it."

Space. And beneath it, around it, through it, the silent music of frequency and wavelength set up in massively complex harmonics; uncountable nodes, incomprehensible webs. Here and there focused knots of activity with ordered structures and patterns.

"Those are universal fourtime expansions," he said and without warning we dropped a level, into just one of those. "Sankhara."

This was no less intricate than before and there was much more information—blinding amounts of it—but now, although I could hear the harmonic reverberations of the sevensheet, I ceased to have any visual kind of representation of it.

Space. And scattered within it, glittering dust.

"Galaxies."

We fell again. The number of musical scales exploded, dominated by the relentless seething fury of the stars in their speeding dance as they whirled around the galactic nucleus. Disk stars and gas were so loud I couldn't stand to look at them. Halo stars sang in almost single notes by comparison—a relief.

We saw one star.

"Sankhara's star."

Within it were all the symphonics of earlier stages. Around it Sankhara's system revolved; the sinusoidal single tones of lone comets, the stately rhythm of the planets, the whispering chatter of rocks and dust. It had never occurred to me that Sankhara existed in a real astrological place. Somehow I had imagined that it ended at the limits of the city where the borders of the Engine's command were delineated. The agreements with Unity had always been that no Sidebar world would ever exceed a minor Earth nation in size, and no humans had ever been beyond the edge of the consensus zone. But it was real.

I saw the planet we were on, blue and green like Earth, a single moon in orbit. While the geology itself was as dazzling and vibrant as the rest of my vision there was another intensification here, located on the surface, almost like what I had been able to perceive had been doubled and the second pattern located here.

"Organic life."

"Whoa, wait . . ." but we were falling into it. Mercifully the dual scales cut themselves short as the secondary one increased dramatically in its volume and size. I looked on a moving structure that might have been a star, so intricate and lively were its patterns. But now I could see what it really was. It was the Sidebar Envelope. The border was clear in this kind of sound and vision, a peculiar shape and sound most like the colour blue. And inside the frenetic activity of the near-blinding light of the city, I could see the contrasting, uniquely peculiar forms of something which could only be . . .

"The Engine."

Tendrils stretched from it, melodies and lines, wrapping

themselves around and feeding up into various regions like bacteria or viral strains, mutating rapidly, changing the micro harmonics of structures small and large. It was working.

"Wait. Wait!" I was desperate to see it, desperate to try and get a grasp of my new ability to see and hear, but we were still falling.

I was now orbited by completely different songs to the stars, but no less intricate, I was surrounded by webs and networks, with brilliant nodes, each one of which was a perfect microcosm, but quite different from the nuclear kinetics of stellar combustion or the swirling electromagnetic storms of the galactic clusters. People.

Then I was looking at a single example, and it wasn't unlike a universe in and of itself. It was so very, extraordinarily complicated, much more so than even the universes we had seen. Every chord within it was in a delicate balance, constantly changing, a unique pattern that never repeated, was never duplicated anywhere, ever . . .

"That's you," I heard Jalaeka say and I was looking at the shadows of the hallway.

"Oh god . . . can we go back? I have to see that again. It was so . . ."

"Boring," he said. "It was very, very boring. Now, the thing is, with people, unlike with stars and universes and planetary cores of metallic hydrogen and any number of charming chemical reactions across the elevensheet, when you do something to them, they react to you. They don't just react like you knew they would by forming dimensional warps or mineral salts. They talk. They bitch. They moan. They sometimes long to call you a manipulative son of a bitch. They give you presents. They kiss you. They do strange physical things with you. Sometimes they kill you. But they're not boring. Look at you. When you're faced with that, the universe can go to hell."

Without warning he turned to me and kissed me, pressing me up against the wall for a second. At the same time he slid his hand down the inside of my forearm very gently and I felt him press my Abacand into my palm. He bent my fingers around it and then let go, placing both of his hands on my waist, neither pulling me into him or holding me away. There was a long, infinitely peculiar moment in which I found my mouth open, tongue against his, my body as soft and pliable as wax. I ran my hands down his back and felt him react instantly, conforming to my pressure with a delight that was tangible in his skin and breath; the most responsive person I'd ever touched.

I pushed him away with both hands against his chest. He was as light as air. "Don't."

I lay alone in one of the bedrooms with the door closed and tried to forget it. I was awake a long time and there were things I could have taken to sober me up and make me sleep but I didn't. Night turned to day. I got up shortly after seven and walked down into the Temple District to air my hangover.

I thought I should look at the cathedral that Hyperion had talked about and on the way there I saw the man himself, seated like an ugly grey dog at the foot of the eternally burning statue of Shiva Nataraja. The sun was bright but the air was unseasonably cool; he was warming himself in the statue's ruddy glow.

"Dr. Saxton," he growled as I came up to him, standing to meet me on all fours, his snake tail uncoiling. The look in his long yellow eyes was searching and suddenly he bent his forelegs and bowed to me, although it could have been the early part of a doglike stretch. "You are graced," Hyperion said, straightening. He seemed amused but because he had no smile it was difficult to tell.

"I was looking for the cathedral," I said, mustering as much dignity as possible around my headache. I actually felt reasonably sick. "Graced" was not the word.

"Look no further." The Salmagundi pointed to the massive structure of gothic extravagance in creamy yellow stone that had replaced the Apollo shrine. "We can sit down inside."

I scanned one of the pretty carvings of an antlered man on

the way in. The early sun caught him at an angle that caught the tiny facets of quartz and feldspar in his structure and made his whole form glow a deep, rich amber. He was made of Flappit Ashlar (SankhaGuide told me). The fact hit my alcohol-numbed brain, but it didn't get very far, though it did make me feel like vomiting for some reason. I passed on quickly.

The cathedral did not follow a cross pattern. It was pentagonal, with five transepts, one aligned to magnetic north, the others at their allotted points of the compass. We sat down in front of the enormous stained-glass window of the north transept. I realized that it wasn't a single sheet made by hand at all, but the face of a perfect crystal prism. Its structure had been manipulated so that the light that would have been ordinarily broken up into the full spectrum came through in specific wavelengths at specific points, creating a picture in pure light.

My stomach cramped painfully as I realized I was looking at an image of Francine in a white dress with a dark-haired woman in a red dress and red shoes lying across her lap, arms outflung, possibly dead in the style of a nineteenth-century pietà. Francine looked down, not up. Her body was arched in an attitude of horrified despair. She had a knife in her hand—a big one.

"It changes," Hyperion told me from where he sat on the floor beside my pew. "Every night something new appears. All the glass here changes. And during the hours of darkness the gargoyles climb down from the roof and refuse to let anyone in who is human or Forged. Extraordinary, isn't it?"

That was the word for it. I stared at it a long time. "Do you think Unity evolves?" I asked him.

"It lives," Hyperion said. "Therefore it must."

"What do you think that would look like?"

"Perhaps like a window in a cathedral, or a tree in the taiga or a sound where someone is there to hear it."

I half listened to his answer. I had no natural mysticism with which to respond, but as I was staring at the panels above us and unwillingly thinking the obvious—*Snow White, Rose*

Red—my hand found my Abacand in my pocket. I opened the file Jalaeka had given me. Hyperion settled down onto his chest and put his head on his forefeet in silent contemplation, and I began to read. I read until the sun had passed noon, then until the red colours shone so strongly at me with the effects of the afternoon sun that I couldn't carry on. I closed my eyes and rested my head on the pew in front of me, though I was only half-done.

My head ached. My chest felt tight, my back unbearably sore. I was no longer convinced that Jalaeka was a Stuffie fragment of Francine's, nor human—no certainly not—but not entirely alien either. At last his story persuaded me that I was foolish to be jealous of what I hadn't known.

Hyperion looked up at my change of position. "You are sober, Doctor."

"Ah, so that's what it is," I said to him, tempted to pat him as if he were a dog, but fortunately remembering not to.

"You are troubled."

"As usual." I didn't know how to tell Francine any of Jalaeka's history as I'd read it, or that I should. Everything had changed. I wanted to apologize to him. I had absolutely no idea what I would or could say. "I have to go home."

"I will walk with you, if I may."

"Please yourself." I turned back at the door and looked at the window again. It was clear to me that the window, and its changing fortunes, could only be about one thing—an event that had not yet taken place.

24/Rita

I picked up the heart-shaped lump of rose quartz at a shop in the Embargo where a tiny gnomelike woman, who looked half hedgehog if her whiskers were anything to go by, spent her days chiselling sculptures with her teeth. She sold a lot of quartz, as kitsch presents for Earth tourists. My bit was quite ordinary, until I wrapped Theo's hand around it and turned it into Stuff.

At the University I went to the Casual Classes office and enrolled in a ceramics group. My pass let me into the main buildings and Theo-in-my-hand opened the doors for me thereafter. I left the heart at the bottom of the dish on a desk where a lot of other quartz mementoes lay collecting dust. It was a tidy office. I had no idea who it belonged to and I didn't want to know, even when I was almost falling over all the evidence I needed. There were photographs on the wall but I didn't look at them.

I left everything else exactly as it was and went home.

All day the decorators come and go, the builder, the plasterer, the power technician, the designer worried about this and that in a raucous Earther accent that spits at me with all the vitriol of someone who despises professionals and longs to be doing the apartments of celebrities in Lalaland and other Sidebars of that kind. I make them drinks. I read fashion journals. I do my nails. I listen to Theo beneath me, talking at me, passing the time as he waits for Jalaeka to get to a point where Theo can make him suffer. His voice is like my own voice in my head, so similar sometimes that I'm not sure it isn't me, taking over when he stops, although he never stops. I drag the file across my nails.

Unity—from which I arose, to which I will return, in which I am buried as the arrow the target, and which is buried in me as the corpse the grave and the treasure hoard within its unbreachable chest.

He aspires to be human. Compared to that kind of pathetic ambition . . . ah no, they always say this, don't they? Those great villains of melodrama. And then someone will always speak up, some hero, and say that righteousness and kindness and compassion are universal and the greatest good that overcomes all. They won't even acknowledge that this is a fallacy invented by the weak, to enable them to mass together and become strong enough to conquer in blood like every other conqueror. They believe it's an actual sodding principle *of existence. We are living among beings who believe in universal justice, Rita. That's the level of what we're dealing with. Spatiotemporally bonded pond scum.*

We could leave now, you and I, we could let this system rot in its own entropy. The Mystery continues everywhere, in all places and at all moments. Why stick this out and call it important over any other waste of time?

Test. Test test test. Testing. One two three. He said I was a test that hadn't finished running yet.

Where are all the great thinkers that surge in the wave beneath me? Why can't they just give me a straight answer and be done with it? All that intellect, all those human hours embedded in the meat: they must know everything between them. But here we are. Here we are.

Do not let that Glaswegian pansy put the yellow wallpaper in the bedroom.

I'm no more than a servant. It's not for me to question why I'm still here. Maybe I've been alive too long, and it's destroyed the purity of my being, as dirt accretes on all things and entropy discomposes.

I didn't used to feel this way. I didn't feel much at all until he came that bloody day, a billion light-years from here, when I fought him to the ground and put my sword through his heart and left him for dead, thinking this was it, this was my time come. I waited for the second of bliss where I would be reclaimed along with him, back to the completion of Unity. And stood there.

And stood there.

And cut his fucking head off, and stood there . . .

A year of anguish followed: his body in the glass coffin, attended by the princess of the sea who dressed him in her clothes and tried to raise him like a necromancer, sacrificing chickens. I abandoned him there, before she annoyed him out of death. I had a lot to think on.

I think I have it out now. Stuff reacts to dreams. He did it by surfing for the right kind of mind, and he had the good fortune to be cast at the outset by someone who wanted a smart hero. Slight drawback with the doomed love angle on that one, but hell, worth the breaks. They were so needy, so dreamy, so desperate—like you, Rita, wanting eight place settings of the black lacquer dinnerware when you will never invite more than one person at a time to eat with you; because you dream of having that many friends. He was only made of Stuff. What can it do but acquiesce to people who pursue the Mystery with such passion? They all longed for it and they all made him. And when he found out that's how it worked, he went looking for dreamers with specific kinds of ideas and began to make himself, through them, into the figure of their desire.

And one of those devious little sods had the idea that he should be invulnerable. That's all it took. They decided that he was going to live no matter what, and the Stuff that he was made of, knowing that the greatest threat to him was Unity, changed. It altered the fundamental nature of what it was.

Hence Metropolis—let the physics do the dirty work, I thought; we wouldn't survive this kind of compression, so he won't either. Even if he sees it coming, there'll be nowhere to go. I had everything covered.

Elevenspace. I don't think you understand what it means to make more of it. There isn't anything outside it. All 4-D expansions abut on the same other seven. Elevenspace is the fabric of them all. Do you see where this is going? Every Sidebar is just a 4-D bubble, like every other universe, like a string of beads—all on the same string. The ones with which we live in comfort share our 7-D and they can get close to one another, even touch, but not cross. He made a new eleven. He made the stuff into which universes are born. He used it to drop next door, into Sankhara.

And now he's our enemy, because he has the potential to destroy us and outreach us, creating being so much harder than going with the thermodynamic flow. I have to assume he could snap us shut—no problem. But he's not of the same value as we are, Rita. He is one. He never consumed anyone or anything. He is unique and alone. We are multitude. To exterminate us would be to lose more raw information than he would come across in a billion years. And not information like those dead packets shooting back and forth on the nets the machines here bat around, but living things, people and parts of people, dreams and visions, the whole nine yards of life as it is lived, the entire Mystery. You, me, everyone.

He's got to go.

Theo shut up after a while. My initial horror had subsided now and was slumped comatose in the dull ache of his nagging whine. Despising him was better than fearing him. I was too tired of him to care anymore.

I made the designer go out and fetch me another set of curtain swatches, another crate of tile samples for the bathroom. I like terra-cotta, but I have this feeling that Theo is in the mood for black marble. I don't want to live in the hell of his bad loser–dom, and I sure as hell don't want to wash in it.

25/JALAEKA

Francine and Greg were working on the smaller rooms today, so they could be in any number of places. I went in through the main entrance and ran through the Military Gallery, between the portraits of great generals where the sunlight filtered down like spear shafts from the high skylights. I slowed down to pass the great doors at the end, and glanced left towards the cathedral.

In the real Palace, in St. Petersburg, I had seen the cathedral floored with beautiful marquetry, but in our Palace it was made of flowers and perfectly impossible to walk on without destroying. Many footprints of dead brown petals and crushed stalks testified to less careful visits, but it was still an incredible sight, and smell. The walls and columns were all covered in white lily petals, their decoration, sculptures and curlicues gilded not with gold but honey that dripped from their overhangs in slow time. The cathedral thrummed with a constant litany of bees.

Francine and Greg were not there.

I found them at last in the Bone Room. It manifested all the proportion and charm of the rest of the Palace, and all the skills that had gone into the manufacture of other marvels, such as the Malachite Room, but as it promised in its name, everything was made from bone; animal and human. A lot of human.

I heard Greg's voice first, saying, ". . . quite a bit of architectural humour in this pelvic archway. Look, all fashioned from . . . Jalaeka, hey, what do you think this is all about?"

Since the night at the club and the personal history I'd given him, he was both more respectful of me and less friendly. It hurt, but I couldn't blame him.

"War," I said, walking over the skulls and leg bones that had been cut to lie face upwards and end on, giving a strange surface of worn domes and gaps, like cobbles. Francine was sitting on the edge of one of the more robust chairs. She was fingering its arm with an amusing mixture of fascination and revulsion on her face. The radius and ulna of the chair were the same size as her own.

I pushed my face against her neck and nuzzled her, stealing that second to imagine myself making love to her. I wanted to, and it must have been obvious to Greg because he gave her a knowing look she didn't quite catch as she turned away from me. He waved at her, his shoulders lifting with tension. "Go on, Francie. I'll finish it."

"It's okay, I came to help you," I said.

"Look." Francine pulled me forward by my hand. "Look at this."

Beyond the arch they had been admiring lay a boudoirlike space, a secluded area just big enough for a small gathering. It had no windows and was intended to be candlelit. Francine picked up Greg's Abacand and used its light to illumine the walls as she drew me closer. It smelled odd here, mustiness unable to mask the sweetish stink of ongoing decay. She didn't seem to notice it as she ran her fingertips over the rougher bones. I saw that all of them bore score marks, some from edged weapons and some from teeth.

"I've seen this motif before, in the Aelf," she said, pointing out the design. "Greg says it's a symbol of the Valar. And this one is . . ."

"I know what it is," I said, glancing at the swastika.

"And these are linked in to fairy-tales." She showed me more of them. "And look here, between these knuckles." She put out her finger, ready to stick it into a gap, a keyhole. I grabbed her hand before she could complete the action, sweat breaking out across my back. "But no door."

There was a door, but I wasn't about to show it to her. I saw a lot more signs and symbols in there than I liked, some that weren't even of Earth. I didn't want Greg asking me about them. I didn't want to know about them myself, thinking that Hyperion was right when he said this place was mine, the Engine building old pieces of me into the solid world. That it reacted to me was the proof Greg didn't like to acknowledge, that I was not identical with Unity. Then I saw a scratch mark in the corner that made me go cold—the old symbol that used to be on my door, when I lived somewhere a very long way away from here.

"Francine," I said, to soften my own shock and to fix myself in place and time.

She glanced back to ensure that she was hidden from Greg, then kissed me.

"Not here," I said. "It's a very bad place for this."

"Are you afraid?" she taunted me, pleased with her boldness at even being in the room, in the alcove, delighted with finding the keyhole and in the mystery of the whole place.

"Very." When she stood back to go ahead of me I had the distinct feeling that the front of my body had adhered to her like thin tissue and was now tearing itself off. I had to follow her closely.

Greg glanced at me, a mixture of envy and resignation on his face. I rested my hand on his arm. "Let's go. You shouldn't spend too long in here. It's not only walls and floors."

He didn't meet my gaze but his voice was clipped. "Then what is it?"

"Everything here died by violence and in anger," I said.

"How would you know that?"

"All the marks. I was only guessing about the anger," I said. "I'd be angry, if it happened to me."

A long moment passed between the three of us, Greg making notes, Francine watching, biting her thumb, me with my mouth full of . . . "There are things in here that belong to me."

He glanced up at me, his face heavy with the suspended weight of all that lay unresolved between us. With Unity, and Theo. "What?"

I took him towards the back, where the door was, which I vowed he would never pass through, and showed him a panel. Made entirely of rib bones slotted together, it looked like narrow, wavy planking, stained brown. I touched three of them, two splintered, one shattered between them. "This is what happens when you get stabbed by a full-force blow dealt by a broad-bladed iron sword with a dull point. This is the first time someone tried to kill me."

He looked at it doubtfully and poked me in the ribs. "You seem okay."

I showed him the lyrical mark of the calligrapher who had devised a new character to represent my name. It had been scratched on a scapula and stained with black inks. "What does that say?"

His Abacand came up blank. He gazed stubbornly at me.

"That's my name. Why won't you let me save you?"

"I don't know what you mean."

"Gloves are off now. Theo knows. The longer you insist it's not going to happen the less chance I have. Come on. You know it's the only way."

Greg looked towards Francine but she had opened one of

the books he had given her—so many of them, history, novels, scientific scripts—and she read out of it, the vellum pages rustling under her fingertips:

"Unity: Machine-biological entity of unknown structure existing in 7-space . . . blah blah blah . . .

"Although 7-space is contiguous with 4-space it does not include a real time dimension. It does have imaginary time and other, pseudo-temporal membranes but these are not linear or expanded. This means that events in 7-space are not bound to time's arrow—the future is not dependent upon the present and the past is not indifferent to future events. All human notions of planning, intentionality and meaning pretty much fly out the window at this point." She looked up at him. "You wrote that. Last year."

Greg folded his arms across his chest. "I've written a lot of things. It's the way I think, by putting them down. It's not necessarily true."

She frowned in concentration and read on. "Unity in 7-space exists outside human perceptions of time. It cannot perform operations that depend on linear time; this includes ALL actions in 4-space, since they are all bound by RealTime. If it thinks or acts it must do these things in a 4-space structure inside 4-D. It is possible, and theoretically it must be certain (because we know that Unity does act and something must impel this action), that Unity must have an awareness within 7-space that is not temporal nor empty, but this cannot be perceived by any 4-D limited being (all humans)."

"Yes, all right. It needs a bit of work on this awareness thing," he said, clearly irritated.

I added quietly, "It uses everything and everyone it touches, as a matter of fact, though it isn't always conscious, even if they are." I watched Francine reading, thought that if I ate Francine I could see through her eyes, feel what she feels, know what she knows. I could be her. It's only a heartbeat away.

She moved uncomfortably under Greg's scrutiny and her

voice cracked a little. "Unity interacts with living 4-D conscious beings by becoming the stuff of their desires. It assimilates them piecemeal, becomes them, records them, consumes them. It is possible that Unity only has consciousness when it is involved with being somebody else."

Greg turned to me. "If the Engine made this, and this was you, then that isn't the same as what it supposedly does here in Sankhara. It was never permitted to drink memories or remake them. So Belshazzar insisted. I always thought it must do, though, but I could never find a direct link—one memory to equal one object. And you have two, right here in this room. But how do I know you didn't make them up? If you are truthful, then what the hell does a creature like you want with the two of us, here, now? And if you want us, then why don't you just take us? You don't even have to bother doing it bit by bit like Stuff does when it Translates people, waiting for them to lead it on by using it more and more. You could just do it now."

Francine folded the book closed. They gazed at me silently.

I shrugged. "It's like that old poet of Hyperion's, Ramprasad, said: *I want to taste sugar. I don't want to be sugar.* I don't know how or even *if* that kind of experience is possible to maintain as a Unity-type structure. If I eat Francine, what will we be? And if I eat you, what will we three be? And if I ate you without asking I'd be a fucking troll, Greg. Not your friend. So stop talking to me like you fell to Earth in the last shower."

The smell of decay was almost unbearable. "Can we please leave here?" I demanded, though I wouldn't have moved if they did not.

"I need to think about it," Greg said stiffly. He turned and walked out, head down. Francine waited.

"Me too," I said and moved across to her. She slid her arm around my waist as I reached her and leant into me as we left. I closed the door behind us—an ordinary Palace door, and, as my first truly unshielded act since I entered Sankhara, I fused it shut to the frame.

Greg was already halfway back to the corridor's end. Francine held me still where we stood. She slid her hands under my clothing.

"I trust you," she said.

"Not you I'm worried about," I replied. "Lower. Lower. There."

26/Greg

I considered Jalaeka's offer. I did nothing else, though I continued the motions of going in to work, checking my mail, making small talk with the other staff, holding seminars and tutorials, dishing out notes, having lunch with colleagues, writing papers and preparing a report for Belshazzar which, as time went on, I realized I had no intention of sending. Friends I'd been ignoring lately asked after me with concern. I replied to their posts and made myself accept coffee appointments with them, reassured them, though probably without a great deal of conviction. They assumed I was pining for Katy, and I let them.

I finished very late, working until my eyes were sore and no amount of uppers could help me make sense. After I had closed down my Guide links and was ready to leave I sat, thinking about his offer. One old acquaintance, Sheena Daley, a visiting professor from Dublin, stopped by to see me and we got talking about Translation as we shared a cup of tea.

"I don't know if it's true that you have to make the Stuff into a thing. Any kind of intention would probably do in a pinch. We get used to thinking of big dramas because of the way Isol picked up Stuff, because she had to have it or die, but some of the accidental cases I came across recently have been with people who were trying to use the Stuff for personal gain," Sheen said. "You know the kind of thing. More successful, better in business, better in bed, blah blah." She pulled the basket of quartz objects that sat on my desk towards her. They came almost routinely now as joke presents, mostly from grad students of mine.

Sheen looked through them and laughed. "I have my own selection. Yours are nicer I think. They must like you better. Ooh look. You have hearts. Six of them."

"Five," I said, taking the basket back from her and tipping them out onto the table. I put the rough stones and other shapes aside. She was right. Six hearts. Four rose ones and two grey-brown Cairngorm smokies.

"The smokies are my favourites," she said, picking those two up. "I always think of them as unrequited loves."

I held the four rose hearts. "I could have sworn I only had three."

"Maybe you have a secret admirer." She smiled at me and put the dark ones back.

"That'll be the day. I think this must be the first time I looked at them in a year, come to think of it." It unsettled me, but we were soon discussing a joint paper we planned to write about fiction and fairy-tale Stuffies of Sankhara and I forgot about it, as usual, wafted away on a whirlwind of ideas, the stones clicking gently in my hands as I turned them like worry beads, over and over.

Finally, "You look tired," Sheen said. "And it's time I went. Still living out in the middle of nowhere down Verkhoyansk way? We miss you in the old Montecathedral markets, you know."

"I'll be leaving soon," I said, thinking that would definitely be the case, one way or another. I put all the stones back in the basket, and went home.

The next day, the day I started to hear the gods, was a Wednesday. Fitting enough I suppose—I've never associated Wotan with fun. His wasn't the name that came first, but I consider it his fault. Odin. Whatever.

It was also the day of the Metropolis Report. It was issued from the Solargov Central Office and it stated rather flatly that Metropolis was officially Missing. All residents were presumed alive, but separated, possibly permanently, from Solar space. An hour after I received this whitewash I got a visit from a Forged agent, a Salmagundi called Bob Clovitz, who told me in no uncertain terms that the Securitat was watching me closely and would be much obliged if I said nothing, either about Metropolis itself, or about any suspicions I might be harbouring concerning Unity activities in other Sidebars, particularly Sankhara. His visit rattled me badly, so much so that I left work early, but it was nothing compared to what happened in the pub later in the afternoon.

The evening was wet and dreary for late summer, the sky overcast with the simmering unease of two major weather systems colliding. The moment of the first name was nothing special, qua moments. I was raising my glass and planning on ordering another. I was glad the place was busy and that hockey was on the TV; Sankhara Tigers vs. Blackpool Belles always guaranteed a lot of viewers, a lot of distraction and a good excuse to sit alone and not talk to anyone. I was brooding over Jalaeka's offer of Translation yet again, trying to separate my feelings about him from my feelings about the situation more widely and also from Francine, and I was having the usual success rate—zero.

The first name was unpronounceable: most of them are, I found later. It was hidden in the bony clack of pool balls striking one another as a Herculean smashed the cue ball into the pack. I heard the name of the god of all gods, and all the names of the gods counted in those few clicks; the balls became an abacus tallying divine power in an unknown base.

The clicks bypassed language. They spoke directly to me. It's hard to explain this but think of it the same way that a simple gesture, like a hand touching your hand, can convey all the comfort in the world. The clicks spoke like that, but they weren't comforting. They said: listen to this very special number, this integer of unknown magnitude. Here's everything you need to know about anything. Here is god, speaking to you, Greg. To you.

I tried to shake it off, but that image of the balls being used to convey a private message lingered. I swallowed the last of my beer and put the glass down. I glanced at my Abacand but it wasn't Engine Time, when the world turned on strange wheels—wouldn't be for another two hours and twenty minutes. The words of the Report: accidental closure . . . space-time discontinuity . . . unknown permanency . . . kept weaselling their way into my thoughts, then found the gods talking and stopped, and rushed off in another direction, trying to get out of my head.

A cold, nasty feeling, not unlike being immersed slowly in a sucking bog, spread across my back and into my guts. I thought of the Stuff back at the lab; the fragments alone in their jackets of lead, concrete, glass, metal, wood, stone and all the other insulating materials known to man; those dangerous pieces hidden from all sight. I remembered the rose heart and saw Sheena saying, "I like the smokies . . ." Queasy, I pushed my empty glass away.

I got another beer and I put the gods down to anger; at my reaction to Solargov's marvellously spun cover-up over the fate of Metropolis; at the way it had fallen under the persuasive jackboot of bloody Unity and its emissary Theodore, god's gift (he was well named, I'll give them that). They came up with the lame explanation that Metropolis's space-time collapsed due to unforeseen tidal interference from the "nearby" black hole in RX J1242-11.

As if some bit of dust like that black hole would have affected anything Unity wanted to survive.

I checked my call list. I'd been so besieged by media calls for quotes and comments that I'd told my Abacand to disregard anything other than personal calls. Ever after it had been very quiet.

I thought about Jalaeka, Damien and the mermaid, the Bone Room. I couldn't call Francie. I wouldn't call Katy. Nobody else knew enough. I called Jalaeka.

"Hey, Greg," he said, giving me the second half of a smile from another conversation he'd just ended. By the background of where he was, I thought he and Francie must have gone out into Sankhara. "What's new?"

I got out of my seat, left the table and walked into the street before I could tell him. It was dark and it was raining. I huddled in the entryway.

His smile changed to a look of concern. "Are you all right?"

"The Metropolis Inquiry published this morning," I said, because he never kept up with current affairs. "It was just like I thought it would be. I hoped . . ."

"You hoped that there would be some justice or honesty, but there isn't."

"Of course not." And there was the other raft of things I didn't say but which he knew about—the fact that he had told me what happened to Metropolis and how he knew. I had the strangest feeling, like I was shifting over the ground though I wasn't moving.

"Greg, I can hear you thinking from here. Did something else happen? Want me to meet you?" He sounded worried now, and that almost tipped me over into panic.

"No," I said and took a gamble with myself. "Could you . . . I mean, could you tell? If I had Unity exposure?"

"Yes," he said. "Listen, stay there. I'm coming right now."

"Not here. I'm going home. You don't have to. I'm fine. I'm sure it was nothing."

"I'll see you there." He cut the call off.

I leant against the wall for a second and pushed off it and out into the rain. He met me just inside Anadyr Park on Verkhoyansk Boulevard's slick black paving and held an umbrella up over me. After we fought through the gateway we put our heads down against thick sleet and ran for the Palace door.

"Couldn't manage anything more godlike?" I said—and there I was, the full arse, back again, covering all my fear with stupid lines.

"Technically, it was just easier to use this." He shook the umbrella and put it in the stand.

"What I said. I don't think . . ."

He caught hold of my shoulders and looked into my eyes. "Don't look back."

"What?" But his strange command had distracted me for the essential moment, as it was no doubt meant to do.

Jalaeka's hands squeezed hard, crushing my muscles against my bones. His face was completely sad.

I couldn't help thinking that this shouldn't have happened to me, though at the same instant I was aware of how unholy bloody ironic it was too. How could it? How could it be true?

"Oh," Francine said with relief when she saw us at the door. "It's you. Come in." She stuck the pencil she was holding behind her ear.

I stepped into the grand bedroom, cold and in a strange mental state where all my ordinary thoughts had been bypassed. I noticed things without seeing connections. I operated according to a new self who must have been in me all the time, relentlessly practical. Go in, it said. Be polite. Act normal.

The drapes on all the windows were shut. In the colossal marble fireplace a fire burned hungrily. Her desk—a beautiful piece of furniture stolen from elsewhere—was covered in books and a brand-new and unopened Abacand in its foil packing sat among them, its instruction note open and face-down. He had bought it for her.

"What's that you're reading?"

"Mmn." She looked at the spine of her book. "*Philosophiae Naturalis Principia Mathematica.*" She grinned at me.

"How's it going?" This was tutor-me in action. I sat on the other end of the couch. I was always surprised by how fast and how well she learned. In spite of being surrounded by students in my seminars who had been engineered from the same Genie block bases as she had been, she was faster, and sharper.

"I don't think I'm going to be any good at the maths side of Unity studies," she said airily, pushing the book to one side. "I prefer your end of things. Social and psychological. I'm hoping my experience of helping you log the Palace will count when I . . ." She hesitated and smiled shyly. ". . . apply."

This was such unexpected good news, but I could only manage to say, "So, when did you decide this?"

"Oh, dunno. I was thinking about it for a while." She glanced down and then, in one of her rapid but accurate ways, slid across the couch, kissed my cheek and got up. "D'you want a drink or something?" Still not making eye contact. Then making it. "What's wrong?"

The wind rattled the shutters with sudden ferocity and made us both jump.

There was a moment of complete hunger, sleepless restless immoderate vital absolute savage longing. As with the names of the gods, it was gone before I knew what I felt, but it had the same quality of revealed knowledge about it. My automatic self replied to her question simply, "Unity got me. Tag. I'm it."

She gasped and dropped the things in her hands. She touched my face and her eyes filled with tears. She threw her arms around me. I stood motionless and looked over her shoulder at the flames dancing on the logs.

27/THEODORE

Well, little Miss Blond IQ, what did you do to him? Let's find out.

28/Valkyrie: Sankhara

Water dripped steadily from the leak in the roof and the room shook with the force of the wind as Valkyrie looked out over the city from the shelter of her lodgings high in the Aerials. She looked to the north, to the windward side. Crystals of ice smashed an inch from her face, done to death on the toughened safety glass that was all that stood between her and a tumble of some five hundred metres.

Valkyrie shivered. She didn't like those moments of Engine Time when things like that happened—conscious things, small things, as you watched. It meant the Engine's attention was restive and struggling against the Regulator, trying to burst forth and engage with waking minds. Valkyrie reached up and took down the fetishes of horse bones and tiny stone rings her highly superstitious landlord had hung up to prevent any mishaps of that nature. Their constant tinkle and rattle was making her nervous.

She watched the city lights and the movements of the traffic as she swapped out her power packs for ones carrying full charge, checking and calibrating the speed of connections, working over her Tek element with methodical care. At nine she ate a ration of supplement from a standard-issue pack—free at all Forged PickMeUp outlets, nineteen spectacular flavours including Original. She could never read the label without hearing Elinor make the cringe-worthy old joke based on the name of Unity's homeworld, Origin: Original—tastes like alien planets.

Valkyrie was picking wads of it out of her teeth with a fingernail when an alert message from the office presented itself for her attention. She was glad of the interruption and read it quickly. Belshazzar had forwarded it. It was a Black Spot Order or, in formal terms, a Port Authority standard notification of Contamination & Translation and it had been served on Dr.

Greg Saxton, Unity Studies Faculty, University of Sankhara, ten minutes ago on site at Authority West. Exposure date was reckoned within the last week. Voluntary or forced quarantine notice to be exacted in October. Valkyrie stopped chewing.

She'd followed Saxton around for months, along with Bob Clovitz, who was on him anyway, because he looked like he might cause trouble when the Metropolis Inquiry reported. He and Valkyrie had often had to sort out their differences of opinion over who got jurisdiction on the Unity Studies Faculty and Greg in particular, due to his political leanings. Valkyrie was an employee of Solargov, part of its official military security shadow. Bob was Secret Service. Today had been Metropolis Paper Day. Bob was on duty and Valkyrie, after months of very little noteworthy activity on Saxton's part, had left him to it. He'd agreed—although she didn't think he was reliable—to call her if anything kicked off.

Instructions were appended.

Belshazzar wanted her to find out where and how the exposure had happened. Valkyrie must ascertain if Greg had been careless with the Faculty's Stuff Fragments or not.

Valkyrie, who had never got her head around the difference between the Stuff that scientists experiment on and the Stuff that most of Sankhara was made of, snorted. She could hear Belshazzar patiently repeating, *The intention guides the function*, but the words didn't connect to anything in her head. Not that it mattered. Her job was not to find out how it worked nor why, only to carry out orders and protect the human populations. That was straightforward enough and she felt pleasure in reminding herself of it.

A sheet of lightning startled her from the mild trance she had been in as she paid attention to the incoming call. Other flashes tore silently across higher skies and made the clouds leap out into great bulwarks above. Were-light and smoke rose here and there among the buildings downtown. Shift Sirens wailed, just audible above the wind. There was a hell of a lot of Engine activity out there.

Valkyrie decided that Saxton would probably head back home, and would be in shock no doubt. Bob would be trailing him and would almost certainly know about the Black Spot. Saxton would be able to think about nothing other than what had happened, always supposing it was not deliberate. The best way would be to talk to him while he was most off-balance, and least likely to be able to hide the truth.

Relieved at having something to do other than sit around watching and listening, she was almost cheerful as she got her wings and rocket pack from their places on the wall. The bubble house swung from side to side and she stood for a moment, balancing, as she fixed her helm visor and switched her primary sensory systems over to temperature, radar and alternate spectrum channels, the storm being too savage to see through with simple eyes.

It gave her a statutory five seconds and a gong warning to give her the chance to get off, then opened. Her wings were already opening as she passed through, falling straight down. She angled them and brought herself into a fast glide, facing into the wind. As she cleared the Aerials and reached free air, she ignited her rockets and felt the sudden surge of power in her back as they gave her forward speed. The wobbles and wrenching of the winds stabilized. She held her arms close to her sides and flew low between the spires of the Aelf, avoiding the turbulent air pockets on their leeward sides as she headed for the Anadyr Park gateway.

29/FRANCINE

When Jalaeka left to take Greg to get his infection verified at the Port Authority, I locked the door carefully. I wished I'd gone with them but it was out of the question. Their equipment would immediately have identified me as Guideless and they would have arrested me. I rubbed the back of my hand where I'd removed the Tab.

A thin, distant howl sounded over the lilt of the music the Foundation were playing—9:00 P.M., happy hour. I went to the curtains and gently moved one aside. Its lead weights slid over my foot and the cold air it had been keeping at bay washed my face. My breath misted on the glass behind the rain. There were no shutters on this bay and usually there was a superb view across the gardens and the estate but tonight it was so dark that the only thing I could see was a long yellow lozenge on the lawn where light from the Gaudi ballroom shone out. Probably Mandy was there, or some of the Love people dancing on its perfectly sprung floor.

The howl sounded again. It wasn't very near, but it wasn't a wolf either. There were two packs of lean, grey and black beasts and I knew all their voices—I'd even seen them now and again, trotting fast across paths in the gardens on moonlit nights. This howl was like a wolf's; it asked a question and made a state-ment. But it was too human to be one. Greg always said we were lucky nothing worse had come out of the woods. He thought it was only a matter of time.

He had a theory that Anadyr Park was where the Engine put the most hidden and most unfaceable pieces of its human psychology—down in the backwoods, in the old forests on the mountain, in the wintertime. It suited his theory of archetypes, even though the Sankhara Engine rarely fitted any theory and would as soon spit out a ghast into a shop window display of women's lingerie. Probably do it more readily, which gives some indication of what people's minds are really up to on the sly. At least when you attempt to go and live in a fairy-tale palace you think you have an idea of what you're up against, if you've done the reading.

I felt conspicuous.

I closed the curtain carefully and went to sit by the fire with my borrowed books. The empty symbols danced in front of my eyes. I kept thinking of Greg's astonished, horrified face and the way he'd looked at me as he realized what Jalaeka had seen. He wanted to be saved. I wanted to save him.

I put the books away and cleared the desk. Thunder rumbled and the wind picked up again. They'd be soaked to the bone out there.

I played some music of my own, quietly. I didn't want to blot out other sounds. Time crawled. I took the Abacand Jalaeka had bought me out of its wrapper and entered the activation code from the instruction leaflet. It was a beautiful thing—a flexible silver band that could fit like a bracelet or fold up into a coin-sized square to sit in a pocket. I said the numbers cautiously though. It was a long time since I'd had one and never one as advanced as this. I didn't know what they could do now.

It lay on the palm of my hand and reflected the firelight like a vanity mirror.

"Please supply your name and identification number," it said. "I cannot locate your Guide."

"I'm stateless," I told it. "My name's Francine."

"Please state your preference for my interactive personality." Its voice was pleasantly androgyne, rather warm and comforting.

"I like you the way you are," I said. "You can start there."

"Is there anything I can help you with now, Francine?"

"What can you tell me about Unity Translation rates? And don't use my name all the time, I hate that. And never tell the Guide where you are."

"Without Guide authentication I will have to rely on black-market bands and entry ports in the Forged underground networks. This will require funds. Do you have an account?"

I turned the leaflet over and read from Jalaeka's handwriting on the back of it. The codes opened his account with the Forged Independence bank in Uluru. When I'd asked him how much was in it he'd grinned. "Enough to get you into the best college on Earth, set you up in a nice life on Earth and let you live out a lot of years in style. Just *try* to clean me out, baby."

I had no idea how much, or whether it was the right thing to do, but it was exciting to have so much power suddenly in my hands, after so long with nothing. The Abacand spoke:

"The latest tracked rates of Unity Translation vary according to the degree of interaction between the person concerned and the Stuff object or person they are communicating with. This is a nonstandard definition of communication. It assumes the voluntary participation of the observing person and the receptive operation of the Stuff object. The lowest Translation speed on record for complete immersion is two years and twenty-eight days, thirteen hours fifty-seven minutes and eight seconds. The fastest recorded Translation speed is two hours and one second. This data is not considered a representative sample. Theoretically, the upper-limit Translation time is one Planck time. There is no anticipated lower limit. More information?"

"How much did that cost?" I asked, thinking in terms of what I spent on food during an average week, maybe ten, fifteen bucks or something like that.

"Two thousand and forty-eight credits."

I almost had a heart attack. All the blood rushed somewhere not useful. "Stop! Stop."

"The transaction has already concluded."

Two thousand credits. I felt physically sick. That was more money than I had earned cleaning rooms in six months. What would he say? How could I tell him I asked that stupid a question for so much money when Greg would probably find out for nothing?

I pulled at my hair and took a deep breath. "How much is left?"

"That information is currently off-line . . ."

"You have five million two hundred thousand two hundred and ninety-one available credits," said a cool and amused voice from the bed.

I turned my head so fast that I felt the muscles in my neck tear.

A tanned, blond and handsome man was lying back on the rucked covers, his long legs stretched out and feet crossed as though he'd been there for some time and was enjoying a good spectacle. He was beautifully dressed; white shirt, suede jeans, loafers; completely dry; entertained by my surprise and fear and happy to let me know it.

"Don't you want to know how I know?" he asked, leaning up on his elbows, "or are you wondering how it is that your fancy go-go-dancing whore of a boyfriend has so much money he never told you about?"

My fingers closed tightly on the machine in my hand and its edges cut into my skin. I hurt. Every bit of me was rigid with fear. How had he got in? It was Engine Time. Was he part of something like that? Wasn't it against the rules or something to have this kind of thing? But in my heart I knew who it had to be. Like Greg, I didn't want to believe it. I willed it unreal.

"Cat got your tongue?" he asked and lay back down and laughed. He picked up one of the cushions and hugged it, rolled over and lay facing me with it underneath his chest, resting his chin on it.

I made myself speak before I lost the ability. There was a kind of other me running things now, on instinct. My thoughts were behind it, like smoke and shadows, useless. "Who . . . who are you?"

"Ah, the classics." He smiled and showed me his perfectly white teeth. "Who are you? Why are you here? What do you want?" He waved his feet in a perfect imitation of my own habit. "Get up and come here. I've come to see you. I feel like we're old friends who've never met." His eyes shone with feral intent.

I didn't move. I couldn't have anyway. There was a buzzing sensation in my head, like trapped flies. "Go away."

"Five million credits," he said, luxuriating over every syllable of the words. "Five *mill*-ion. *Five* million. Now what could anybody do that's worth that kind of money? Hmm, I wonder. Perhaps it's bond trading? Perhaps it's drug running? Perhaps illegal Tek or psychosurgery? I hear he's very good at that. Isn't that right, Francine? Sorry, Francie." He gave me a coy look as he made a sharp intake of breath at his pretended mistake and bit the cushion. Then he moaned in a series of short, rising tones. "Or maybe he does something else. But not with you. Why is that?"

He rolled off the bed and stepped down from its dais, graceful and strong. He paused at the desk and looked at the books stacked on it. "A lot of reading for someone as magically incurious as you are. Do you know what I think? Well, I'm not going to wait for an answer as I don't suppose I'll get one. I think he's waiting for you to ask him because he feels guilty. Do you know what that might be about?"

I looked at the door. I looked at the windows. Too far. Too heavy. Too locked. I hadn't put any information in the Abacand, there were no hot keys. I slid my thumb over it, trying to access call mode.

"I'm talking about before." He casually pushed the books off the desk and swept his hand over the polished wood. "Before you, darling. But he hasn't told you about that, just like he hasn't told you about *darshan* and what, down at the Well, they like to call the holy fuck. And seeing as how I know we're such good friends I felt I had to tell you."

"I know everything," I said, sliding away to the edge of the sofa. "Angel Five. Metropolis. I already know." The Abacand bleeped as I pressed the wrong thing on it.

"Angel Five?" He walked around the desk and straight up to me. His hands were cool as he threaded his fingers through my hair and took hold of my head with the pressure of a vise. My ears pounded. He held me there and then slowly dragged me to my feet and turned my chin up so that I had to look into his face or stare sideways.

I tried to do that, and to stop shaking, but it was too frightening not to be able to see what might be coming. He had blue eyes. His long fringe flopped elegantly across them so that he had to flick it away with a jerk of his head. As he spoke he released the pressure on my skull and his hands slid slowly down my neck and became gentle, exploratory. "The last in a very long line of . . . well, I don't like to say. But I will. Dead girl-friends and boyfriends. Let's see how many; oh, at least ten. And in terms of casualties who were not so privileged, darling, there are simply millions. Millions of dead people. I wanted you to know so that you had a choice about it."

"What choice?" My voice was barely a whisper. He looked down at my shoulders as he touched them, then he began to undo my clothing.

"The informed choice," he said, in stockbroker tones. "That's what it's all about, isn't it? A choice. Always a choice. Look or not look. Touch or not touch." He took his hands away and glanced at my face and put them back on my breasts. "Make or not make."

"Get off me." Talking was better. It made me stronger. I knocked his hands away with my forearms.

"That's what she said." He stepped forward and kissed the top of my head, then stepped away and turned to lean on the mantelpiece and look into the fire. "She said, 'Get off me,' just like that."

"I'm not listening to you," I told him, quickly taking hold of the two halves of my shirt and pulling them closed over myself. I was shaking so hard, my hands trembling, I couldn't fasten them shut. I kept my arms across my front. The Abacand was still in my hand, locked there. I felt its resistance and flex inside my palm. I lifted it towards my mouth to call Jalaeka.

Theo's hand caught mine before I'd had time to finish taking breath. He smiled and with both his hands opened my fingers and took out the silver square. "Oh look," he said, "I'm frighten-ing you. You're bleeding." Where the Abacand had cut my palm and fingers he took my hand to his mouth and licked across the wounds. The machine fell to the carpet, silently.

Jalaeka once licked a cut of mine like that.

"So, where were we?" He kept my hand and turned it in his own. I tried to pull it away but he was too strong. I clawed at him with the other hand but he ignored me completely. "Oh, yes, your line is 'Get off me.' I'll be him." He waited, looking down at me with amused disdain as my nails tore his skin open. "Say it?"

I clenched my teeth together and pulled on my arm with all my strength. When it didn't move I tried to kick him but he sidestepped. With my free hand I hit him in the face and saw him have to turn aside, a scratch opening across his cheek.

"That's it," he said, grabbing my wrist and forcing it down. "Now you're getting the hang of it. No line. Still, we know how it went." He bent close and whispered tauntingly, "Get off me." He stood up and shrugged. "And he did this."

He picked me up easily and in a few strides crossed the room and flung me back onto the bed. With both hands he grabbed my shirt front and tore the whole thing in two.

I screamed at the top of my lungs and he slapped his hand over my mouth and ground my head back into the mattress. "That's right," he said. "She screamed too. Maybe he did tell you this story."

I tried to bite the thick flesh of his palm but he ignored me and pushed down harder while his other hand bound my wrists together with the torn shirt. He was very deft and wound it incredibly tight. He sat back on my legs at the knee, tore a piece off the end of one of the bindings and balled it up carefully, using his own teeth to help. I tried to kick or wriggle away and he let go of my mouth and slapped me. My head rang and tears flooded my eyes and nose. I felt him jam the cloth between my teeth.

"This will have to do, I'm afraid," he said in his pleasant, businesslike voice. He sounded almost sympathetic. "She was held down by other people of course. He likes an audience. But we have to improv."

He retied my hands to the bedposts.

Nothing he was saying made any sense to me. I hit him with my hands clubbed together. It was a weak blow that barely grazed his chin and he laughed and stood back to take off the rest of my clothes. "Nice shoes," he said, letting them drop to the floor one at a time. "He always liked pretty things. So. Five million credits." He pulled my jeans off from the ankle, then my socks.

I drew my legs up and kicked him. My right foot caught him on the arm and spun him half away. I tried again. He treated me like an annoyance and caught my ankles in his hands. He was incredibly strong; like a machine he put me where he wanted me and my legs burned as I resisted but they went anyway. He lay down between my legs with his face over my crotch, my thighs pinned under his arms. I managed to dig my heel into his spine but he didn't seem to feel it.

"Five," he said, smiling at me winningly. He ran his tongue along the line of my knickers at the top.

There must be a way out of this. There must be. But I can't think of it.

"Million," he said, and as he said it licked the fabric crotch. "What beautiful underwear," he added. "Silk. So thoughtful. Oh, but I'm forgetting my directions. Anyway, no point lingering over it all too long. Five million credits buys the grace of god about three times a night, which is pretty fucking saintly, less the club cut of forty percent of course. But that was only because you asked so nicely to know how much. And it has a lasting effect, kind of like an afterglow sort of thing—I'm even starting to sound like you, aren't I?—which I understand has a complete transforming power on experiences ever after, so probably quite cheap considering. But you, his lovely, juicy, gorgeous, untouched, underage girl, get nothing at all. Or do you?"

I tried to get free of him again, to scream. Mentally I begged for Greg to come back for some stupid thing, to ask me to another boring meeting in the department, for Damien to call, but even though it was Engine Time, wishing was no good.

He waited until I was too tired to carry on.

"Are you done?" Keeping my legs pinned under one of his own he leant on one side and unfastened his trousers. I wished I could have laughed at him or done anything to him. I pulled on the knots at my wrists and they tightened up. My hands started to hurt and swell. I thought I might throw up. I tried to but only coughed.

He slid my knickers off, giving me every chance, and I kicked him hard as we struggled.

"Get off me," he sang to me softly, grunting with the blows I landed but showing no sign of pain. "Get off me." He forced my knees apart and pushed himself between them. His face hung close above mine and he made our noses touch. "She was so desperate to escape. Boy, she hated him. She wanted to kill him. She wanted him to die. And the rest of them. All of them. But she knew there was no hope at all. None. Nobody coming and nothing to be done about it. So she gave up and shouted . . ." He waited for me to speak. I stared my hate into his blue, blue eyes. "You're not much fun, Francine, it has to be said," he told me. "Just like her. Something has to be done about that. And they all thought so too. So Jalaeka did this."

He put his face between my legs and licked me. He kept a strong hold on my legs just above the knee and pushed hard on them so I couldn't close them. I shut my mind off from the sensation and heard that howl again outside. It was much closer now. I clung to the sound and focused all my attention on it.

He was very gentle. He kissed me. When he finished and brought his wet face back to mine he said quietly, "Never believe you're not as sweet as any woman alive."

The howl made him pause to listen. He licked my lips around the wad of cloth. "I'm sorry I wasn't able to pull off the same trick for you," he said. "She wasn't immune to the other charms of my kind like you are. The ghost in the head. She was ecstatic by then. And he took her that way. Like this."

He did it in one, fast, hard motion. He smiled at me. I shut my eyes and turned my head away from him. I tried to think of anything I could do. My face burned. He kissed my neck and made that moaning sound he'd made before, pretending. "You could at least fake it for me," he said. "So I could know what it's like to be him, because I know for certain there's nothing he'd rather be or do than be right here doing you."

I turned my aching head back and glared at him. I wished he could take the cloth out so I could tell him to shut the hell up and get on with it. I was already moving beyond the end in my mind, wondering what I could do to him and how I could find him and make him pay.

He was clever though, and didn't take it out. I made as much sound as I could. Somehow the howling seemed friendly to me now, like if it could find me, it could help me. I howled back.

In response his strokes became harder and longer. He didn't hurt me after the first one. He just took great pleasure in what he was doing and looked into my eyes until I closed them again. I could feel his stare.

"I can see you're not going to beg *me* never to stop," he said, glancing at my gag. "And it's not the same without that." He took the gag out.

I yelled as loud as I could. "Help me!"

He came with a long, uncontrolled shudder and kissed me on the mouth. Then he got up and rearranged his clothing, bending over to kiss my thighs and between them again. Finally, he got up and looked down at me, his gaze never once leaving my face. He smiled at me, with real warmth.

"Tell him I said hi. I'm sure if you call him"—he tapped the side of his head with one finger—"you'll find he can hear you. You might want to ask him about that sometime." He opened the locks and the door and went out, leaving it ajar.

I drew my legs up close to me and tugged against my wrists but my hands were going numb and it was like pulling against iron. I managed to slide up farther so at least the tension on my arms was released.

"Bastard, bastard," I muttered under my breath, trying to give myself some courage. "Bastard bastardbastard."

Something landed against the shutters of the balcony windows with an incredibly loud clatter. I could feel the impact as a vibration coming up through the bed. It happened again almost instantly. The windows broke inwards with a huge crash of glass, the massive weight of the curtains pulling free from their hooks and tangling in a mass over the clumsy, strange shape that struggled through. It moved with a ferocious energy, like a mad dog.

I was aware that I was screaming but it seemed far away, like someone else was doing it for me. Icy air, water and splinters of glass fell over me as the thing fought free of the fabric with two colossal explosive jerks that ripped it clear. From as far back against the headboard as I could get I saw Hyperion emerge from the rent cloth.

His wedge-shaped head with its blunt snout full of jagged teeth came up and turned with intelligent yellow eyes to look straight at me. He stood upright on two legs and freed his long, branchlike arms, flexing his hands out of their fist shapes, showing slender eagle's talons tipped with tough claws, some of horn and some of metal.

Rain blew in over his wet hide and the room quickly filled with the stink of rich forest loam and animal musk. He padded to the fire and picked up my Abacand in his talons, then came to the bed and with a single knifelike claw cut through the scarves that tied me. He gave me the Abacand between his forefinger and thumb, holding it carefully. Earth trapped between scales on his arms fell over me and over the bed.

"Gluh," he said with difficulty from the back of his throat. "Khluh nnow."

He saw I couldn't or wouldn't, and withdrew with one of those sharp, alarming gouts of movement.

"I gluh," he said, struggling with speech. He expertly flipped the Abacand into emergency mode and carefully, politely, with exquisite gentleness, turned his back on me.

I pulled the nearest pillows and cushions around me. I heard Jalaeka's voice on the Abacand. He sounded furious. I clung to that voice. Hyperion lay down on the floor like a sphinx facing the door and put his long head on his paws. His cordlike tail flickered continually at the tip, garlanded with beautiful Tekmetal in spiral patterns that shone out through the fine grey fur as it drew the same sign in the air over and over.

Jalaeka stepped through the broken windows from the balcony and ran to me. I burst into tears and started shrieking as soon as I saw him and it was like it had been before, like someone else doing it and me being inside them, watching and thinking—how odd, how hysterical a thing to do.

The wind filled the room with freezing air and blew the fire to nothing in the grate.

"Don't ask me to tell you!" I said, grabbing hold of Jalaeka around his neck, around his back, trying to pull him closer as he embraced me, his grasp getting tighter as I clawed at his back. I wanted to climb into his skin. "Don't ask me. Don't ask me."

"It's okay," he said gently, his head against mine, ear to ear. "I won't. I won't. I'm not asking." He was so calm. The sleet in his hair and on his face melted between us.

"Hold me," I begged.

"I am holding you," he said.

"More." I pushed my way in against him, shoving the cushions away, pulling at his clothes.

He let go of me to get rid of them for me and I screamed at him and hit his shoulders with my heavy, agonized hands. I had to get out. I had to. "Do it now!" The cold air had gone bitter. The whole bed smelled of sex. I knew he must know, must guess. I hated him for it. "Get him out of me!"

His eyes were wide. He looked scared and pale and like he was staring through me.

I grabbed hold of him and kissed him on the mouth. "Come on," I said, against him. "Be different. Be different." Dark eyes, brown eyes.

From a million miles away his gaze focused on me. He opened his mouth and kissed me back but he was far too cautious for my blood.

I hit him across the face. "Wake up! Translate me! Do it now!"

"All right," he said, still quiet, contained, his true nature hidden for a final instant. "I will."

30/GREG

I came home on my own. Mandy, the Palace keeper, was waiting for me in the hallway. He stopped me, catching hold of my shoulder.

"There's been some trouble," he said. His distorted features looked a thousand years old and his whole body was taut with an effort of holding back strong emotion. "Your friend is up there."

I stared at him for almost thirty seconds, unable to comprehend what he was talking about.

My head was still ringing with the bright lights and polish of the Port Authority and that damned counsellor they'd had me talking to for over an hour. "If you feel the need to discuss this further with me, you can make appointments up until the end of October next year," she'd said sweetly. "After that you'll have to transfer to our AI system and be registered resident in the Translation Unit at Masham Abbey."

Meaning, after October you'll be too far gone to be allowed near common people and we will come and take you away for their good.

She had smiled at me, tenderly, with understanding and compassion. "It's a very, very slow rate of translation."

Now I was looking at another face, which might have been as pretty as hers once, before it was made over into new Forged material, into a brute of a man with Tek adaptations and a taste in pink blouses. Mandy's feelings were at least sincere. Looking at him was calming because of that.

"Trouble?" I asked, starting to connect it with Jalaeka's sudden disappearance. I'd thought he'd just lost the nerve to go in and try to face it out at the Port in case they asked him where his Tab was, though Stuffies rarely had a problem. One minute he was walking beside me, the next—gone. On the way back I'd even thought through it a bit and figured that maybe he and

Francine wouldn't be here at all; done a flit in case the Port decided to investigate the Winter Palace more thoroughly because of my state. They're bastards like that in Immigration. Now I thought of other reasons.

But Mandy didn't or couldn't say. He bowed his head like he couldn't meet my eye anymore and let me go. I ran up the steps two at a time. Hyperion lay in the hall outside our doors and he got up when he saw me and barred the way into Jalaeka's apartment.

"What?" I said to him.

"Theo came," he said simply on audio channel broadcasting to my Tab so I didn't have to struggle with his clumsy attempts at ordinary speech. "Attacked Francine."

I dropped my bag and my already-overreacting body, high on fear, went dead with shock. "What? Where is she? Is she . . ."

He stared at me. "She . . . You must wait."

I went inside my own room in a daze and shut the door. As it clicked closed with a sound I'd known for over three years I heard the lock say-not-say, "Ktikt."

Something in my mind reacted instantly. It was the name of a god. Ktikt: goddess of the seconds and lives that pass without being noticed.

She must have a billion of those things, I thought, searching frantically for alcohol. There was whiskey, half a bottle. I unscrewed the cap and took a drink out of the neck. After three or four more I felt improved.

I sat in the armchair and had some visions of getting past Hyperion but in every one he managed to kill me convincingly and with much blood. The whiskey didn't touch the completely shit feeling that I was a weak, useless tosser who let his friends suffer because he was too frightened to do anything. It was only good on the fear of Unity Translation. It was very good on that . . .

*   *   *

"Greg?"

I woke up with a start. It was very dark. The lights came on. Jalaeka was standing in the doorway, his hand on the switch. He was a total mess. The sight was unsettling. I'd seen him look a lot of things but never like this. He closed the door behind him.

"Theo raped Francine."

I stared at him and it felt like he was a complete stranger. It took a long time for the words to sink in. I couldn't seem to process what they meant. "What? But . . . is she all right? I mean . . . Where is she?"

"Asleep. Safe. Physically fine. You can talk to her when she wakes up, if she wants to. Talk I mean. I came to tell you and ap . . . It's all my fault." He looked enviously at the bottle, a quarter full, still in my hand. "Can I have some of that?"

"Um. Yeah." I held it up. I thought I was very angry but I wasn't sure.

He took it, sat on my sofa with his knees up to his chest, barefoot and shivering in what I recognized as Francine's oversize soft black pyjamas. They didn't reach his wrists or ankles. He drank most of what was left and shook his head, handing it back to me. "Doesn't work very well, does it?"

"No." I finished it and let my eyes water.

I tried a lot of words in my mind but they were all rubbish. "It was a set-up," I said, that pragmatic me.

"I set myself up. I gave you both a choice I should never have given you. I left her when I should never have left her. What did they tell you at the Port?"

"What do you think?" The implications of it began to sink in. My stomach burned. "Christ. Does that mean . . . am I going to, *become* him?"

"Don't know." Jalaeka shook his head. His voice was very even and precise. He stared into the distance and rested his chin on his updrawn knees. "Think maybe . . . you already are . . ."

"What are you talking about?"

"I Translated Francine. She asked me to. So I did. And now I have to concentrate not to know what she's thinking, not to feel what she's feeling. It's as if I have to hold up this big dam between us, and it has lots of holes that I keep on finding all the time. Thoughts. Feelings. Images. Hers, I think. I don't know, because I can't tell anymore. All I know is I'm leaking, being leaked, and I'm trying not to let it happen."

I gaped at him. "You did what?"

He smiled, looking into a private distance. "Anyone in their right mind would say no, wouldn't they? I always said no when they tried it on me. And then I realized there was nothing I could do to protect her if I didn't do it and I thought that even if I was going to be like Unity, well, I'm the one in charge of me. I'm not like Theo. I could stay out and she'd never have to know. I hoped that it would never come to . . . I knew that . . . I thought . . . I think I'm going to burn her up. I can't keep out forever. It's too hard." He closed his eyes, shut his jaw and bit his lips together.

I didn't entirely follow what he was saying but it horrified me. At the same time I admired the way he spilled his guts to me, felt a kind of honour in being so trusted. It was a hard cocktail to swallow.

He spoke rapidly in a way that almost broke into laughter. "So my fabulous power of life, death and universal creation has let this ordinary, day-to-day evil run over her with no effort at all. And this is the entire story of my life by the way, which I hope you never learn in all its relentless re-patterned detail, like the grooves being cut back into the same bloody tyre: Live to fuck up others. Live to get fucked. Try to erase the indelible memory of getting screwed by someone you hate by violating someone you love. Or make others do it to you. I love myself. Say it and amen, brothers, I love myself. I am the *god* of love, so fucking help me." He buried his face into his hands.

After a few seconds he lifted his head. Now when his eyes met mine they were vicious. "I'll get him," he said softly. "Of course revenge doesn't matter and nobody comes back or gets out, and it won't undo what got done or save anything. It can't unpick my stupidity. Of course not. Except, I think it might save you." Then he looked at me and he was in control of himself again.

My sluggish brain was insulated by the whiskey that had made it out of my gut. Things seemed less raw, conversation possible, because the alcohol had blunted them. I swallowed my anger. "How?"

"I think Theo's going to let you alone just enough to try and get me to the point where I take the dive to save you. He hasn't got any other choice. He doesn't care about you or Francine; ultimately he sees everyone as an adjunct of himself—eventually it'll all be okay, because you *will be him* and vice versa. But I can't play that way against him because it's not his weakness. If I want him to fall on the sword and hand Unity to me, I have to change his mind another way. And in the meantime figure out how that doesn't just turn exactly into what he wants . . . And I will." He bit his lower lip. "Before October." Then he laughed, suddenly and in an oddly high-pitched voice. "That was a great talk wasn't it? So—masculine, analytic, purposeful, you know? Mmn."

His return to hysteria was unnerving me. I clutched the bottle more comprehensively in my hand and sucked at the dregs. "You're talking about killing Unity. What are you? No offence, but . . . look, I've studied Unity for years through what it does with the Engine here in Sankhara, and I have no idea what it must be like to be two million people at once but I can't see what you can do . . ."

"He *isn't* Unity." Jalaeka dragged his hands through his hair and held it out of his face, staring at me like a mad, black-maned dog. "He has executive power—like me. He isn't the whole thing. That's what I keep trying to tell you, though you won't fucking listen. Unity as an entity can't exist in 4-D. It has executors, who are connected to it and enabled by it, but they are *not* it, and the kind of consciousness it has is *not* like yours and mine, because it exists where the future is not determined by the past. Imagine you having all the knowledge ever. Can you think it all right now? Can you feel all the feelings you ever felt and the experience you ever had at once? No, you're just you and you have the mood you've got this instant and that's all. You're the constant relic of your life as it goes smashing into the past. Now Theo's done things to me, and to other people, for aeons, but he's never been done *to* really, never felt a thing because he considers himself a supreme being beyond it all. He's a sociopath. Remind you of anyone?"

"The Lonestar," I said reluctantly. "Voyager Isol. The first human contact. Was he made from her? Made by . . . is that . . . ?"

"I don't know. Even if it was the case, it's absolutely nothing to do with today and now." He tore his hands through his hair and stood up. "Look, later," he said. "I'll tell you everything you never wanted to know later, in another life where this doesn't matter anymore. You should rest. Sleep. You look like shit."

"Don't want rest. I want to do something," I slurred loudly. I wanted to help him, but I couldn't forgive him for failing Francie. Weasel me said it wasn't my place, but that was so much horseshit to cover up the fact that I didn't feel kind towards him. I wanted to ask him what the hell else he'd done to Francine but I couldn't. He didn't wait long for the forgiveness that wasn't coming, and his look said he understood me, that he accepted my judgement, and I hated that most of all.

He got up, unfolding like a perfect piece of robotics, and crouched next to my chair so he could look at me, no, so I could look at him. "Then go and try to convert Hyperion to rationalism. He looks like he needs a good laugh."

He was only trying to save us both with the needling humour we'd always used, and it had never felt so pathetic as it did to me then. Rage filled me and I hit him. It was a stupid drunk's blow and clumsy. My hand didn't even know the bottle was still in it until it broke across the side of his head as he ducked away. My hand hurt like lightning but my whole attention was on him as he turned back. Blood poured down through his hair and over his neck. The side of his face was gashed down his jawline and across his temple but I no sooner saw the horrible wounds than they were gone. By the time he was eye to eye with me again he was perfectly whole.

He took my hand. I felt its cool, his calm becoming unearthly and gentle, and the pain of my feelings blurred. When I snatched my hand back it was slippery with his blood. The *darshan* glowed in me, making me well when I wanted to be sick.

"I'm sorry," I said, trying to pull something back too late. "You should go back to her."

He moved his hand across his hair and face, neck and clothing, and the blood all vanished. For a second there was heat radiating on me, like I was sitting close to a fire, and then that was gone too and nothing to show it had happened. He replaced the bottle on the table by my hand, and it was whole.

"Go on," I said to the doubt in his face. "She might wake up."

"I'll call you when she's awake." He turned to go.

"Wait," I said, fumbling to think around my revulsion at the way I'd behaved. "What's the god of forgotten moments?"

"I give up," he said, forgiving me without trying, so that I felt even more of a shit. "What?"

So, he didn't know. Well . . . "She's in the door. Don't slam it."

I put my head back on the rest as Ktikt neglected to do her job during the quiet sounding of her name.

I wished he hadn't gone.

31/VALKYRIE

Valkyrie landed on the hardtop of the basketball courts at the Hoolerton end of the Park. Nobody was out in such vile weather, not here anyway. She took the footpaths through the dark, dripping trees at the end of the playground and past the creaking sign of the Pig and Piper. The windows were brightly lit and music and voices drowned out the weather as she passed the door.

From behind the high wall of the Hinterland came a crashing of metal and rubble and a keening sound, inorganic and furious. Valkyrie shook water from her wings in an unnecessary flip of all the flights and walked more quickly until she passed beneath the bridge at the end of Crisscross Street.

The cold quickly chilled her armoured skin and snow began to gather and solidify on her wherever it got purchase. She felt the soles of her feet shift their pattern to grip the treacherous ground and walked on against the wind to where she knew the great walls of Anadyr Park would become the railings that surrounded the Winter Palace.

Uluru for Unevolved, that's what this place is, she thought, although it was a damn sight less pleasant for the most part. This was like the old versions of Uluru, where to enter into a state of sleep while in that virtual world was to become the victim of every whim or nightmare that you might dream. She took out the *gris-gris* from her ammo-clip holder and put it on.

Bob was not at his usual haunt inside the railings where thick, overgrown shrubs formed cover and allowed good views of the front of the building. There was no heat trace at all there. Valkyrie could not pass through the gate's bent bars. She opened her wings and half leaped, half flew over, kicking off from the top of one immense spike to drift down into the gardens. Bob was not near the front either, not down by the old servants' entrance and not inside the relative luxury of the coal hole.

She found him at last huddled in a curve of the thickest part of the box hedge maze and folded herself into a compact shape near him so that she was fully hidden.

"We must stop meeting like this," Bob murmured. He was almost invisible even from four metres away, wrapped in a thick coat that was both heated and camouflaged.

Valkyrie cleared ice from her visor and looked more closely at one of the upper balconies, where she could see that the doors were completely smashed in. "I came to relieve you."

"Ah."

She could tell from the humour in the sound that he knew

perfectly well she had come as soon as she heard about Saxton's infection.

"What's that about?"

"I don't know. I never bugged that room, well, I did, but they never worked. Very peculiar."

"Something broke in."

"Yes. A big, grey Forged son-of-a-something that came out of the forest. It was howling all night. Must have started running more than thirty kilometres out by my calculation. A woman screamed and it ran up the wall and in. I haven't heard a thing since." He was enjoying knowing so much.

Valkyrie was incensed that there could be any kind of action and she missed it. She thought hard. "Sure it wasn't a Stuffie?"

"Couldn't tell actually," Bob said. "It was a bit quick. I tried looking it up in the *Genesis* but nothing matches."

"Stuff then." But she knew what, or who, it was.

"Maybe."

Valkyrie frowned, remembering her previous visits here. Bob would never commit to any knowledge unless it was proven forensically. He did not respond. Her vexation was cut short as she heard a new sound, not the wind or the trees, but the creak of snow underfoot. Bob heard it too—he uncoiled from his seated nook and she saw his gloves, boots and tail emerge from the cocoon of the coat.

Then she saw the yellow forms of warm, living objects move clear of the trees to their right and come forward, green and blue limbed. They were big and they were many. They flowed through the tall, upright trunks of the forest and over the open garden like oil.

"The house!" Bob shouted and she was right with him. They leaped up, over the stocky bulk of hedge before them and across the open ground towards the back door of the Palace. Behind them came the wolves.

The largest of all, who raced to within ten metres of them, jumped as Bob ran up the stone steps between the lower garden and the formal lawns. Its huge paws caught the belt of his coat and brought him crashing down in the thick snow. Valkyrie turned back the few strides she had gained and seized the beast by the ruff around its neck. She lifted it into the air, its teeth clashing on her metal arms, and flung it away, but not very far. It was heavier than she had expected.

As it got up she saw it was not an ordinary wolf. Its forelimbs were a little like human arms and its hind limbs were long at the thigh. It had human eyes. Its jaws were all wolf however. It stood, growling, as the rest of the pack caught up.

Valkyrie reached down and pulled Bob's near-featherlight form to his feet. He spun around, gun in hand.

"Are those werewolves?" she hissed at him on shortwave radio.

"Something more like me I think," he said. "Though rather less well brought up, I fear."

The lead wolf wiped her muzzle in the snow, looking at the gun. Then she sat down and expansively licked her chops. The rest of the pack circled close to her again, then they all made a howling sound, short bursts and yips.

Valkyrie saw a moving light behind her, coming from the Palace. It bounded through the drifts towards them, neither beast nor human. She left the wolfpeople to Bob and turned to face it, sure that it was the creature who had left her the *grisgris*.

Bob glanced around once, fast. "That's it," he said, "the Salmagundi."

The unregistered Forged slowed and stopped outside Valkyrie's immediate range though not the range of her hidden weapons. Its voice was hoarse and it took time to decipher that it had said, "Who are you? You don't belong here."

"Same question." Valkyrie stood her ground and looked it over for weapons. The fact that it had seemed well-intentioned before gave her more confidence than she felt with the wolves or the Stuff creatures she'd met.

The lead wolf made a guttural bark. "Glu. Lilan."

"Holy man," Bob repeated after a second. "It said 'holy man.' "

"That's right." With its brilliant yellow eyes narrowed against the sleet the creature peered more closely at Bob. It had begun speaking to them via radio. Rough hair blew around its wiry body; feathers flared in the wind; fur ran with water. "You and I. Not so far apart." It glanced at Valkyrie with a tilt of its heavy head. "Government. Amulet." It nodded and she thought it grinned. With a long whistle it called to the wolves and they got to their feet and came rushing up around it, fawning and licking at its legs with puppyish delight.

The sky rippled with colour. White and green lightning lit the distant mountains. Valkyrie saw the rocks and ice changing shape. She thought she could hear voices high in the air, near the cloud line, but could see nothing on any wavelength. She looked for the shadow claws.

The Forged heard it too. He gave her a long glance and said, "Inside better. Palace changes much less catastrophic under Engine Time inside."

Valkyrie looked down at Bob. He twitched his long arched whiskers in a shrug and drew his coat closer about him. They followed the Forged as it turned back to the Palace. The wolves tumbled around it for a short distance, then, at some undetected command, raced away in the direction of the woodland beyond the rose garden.

Their holy man led them down steps by the kitchen gardens entrance, where the way was worn to muddy sludge by the passage of feet going in and out from the building. It was a common entrance for the Foundation, who used the gardens at various times of the week. There was nobody here now however, and Valkyrie had to bend double to get her wings and body through the narrow access passage. Fortunately it soon opened to the kitchens.

These rooms were wretchedly low in the ceiling so she had to stand with wings half-unfurled and trailing behind her. The sinewy Forged turned around, between them and the door to the rest of the Palace, and sat down on its haunches. Bob walked smoothly past Valkyrie and sat down in one of the old wooden straight-backed chairs set at the long oak table that ran through the centre of the room. The fireplace was cold and cobwebbed. Empty gas cylinders rolled about under the table. Valkyrie curled her lip at the slovenliness of it all. The only neat thing was the scrubbed table itself and the long row of defrosting lamb legs that sat on top of it upon a plastic picnic tablecloth, oozing watery blood.

Bob pushed his hood back and scratched the pale golden fur covering his head and face. His long white whiskers had been swept back across his cheeks but now they rose in serried arches and stretched out into the air. He fixed the gryphon creature with a straight gaze and put his gun away. "What's your business here?"

"I do the god's work," said the other. "And yours?"

"I do the Ministry's work," Bob said cheerfully, "and my partner here fights with me because she does the other Ministry's work. We're like a team of people who aren't on the same team, but on the same side. I'm the nice one and she's the muscle with the short temper. Never seen you here before."

"I was never here before."

"Nice wolves."

"People," said the holy man calmly. "The Engine changes deep in Anadyr have driven them towards the city. They're hungry." He glanced at the meat on the table.

Bob nodded. "I particularly liked the way you shinned up the Palace wall and broke into that apartment. Did you have anything particular in mind or was it en route to the freezer section?"

The creature stood up and turned towards the door that led up into the Palace.

"We're not done," Bob said.

Valkyrie stepped forward. "Who are you?" She made to grab hold and got a handful of feathers and one of fur. The *gris-gris* bumped on her chest.

—What is *that*? Bob beamed at her.

—Nothing for you to worry about, she told him via radio.

Her prisoner growled and his flanks shook but he made no retaliation. "Let me go, Agent Skuld, if you will. I have given you a gift of trust and you ought to extend the same to me. I cannot and will not help you here, no matter what you have to say, or to do. This night is not yours to claim."

His fur slid through her fingers. The grey shape darted forward and vanished along the unlit passageways towards the eastern dining rooms and the stairs. Valkyrie turned and saw Bob's astonishment as answer enough.

After a moment or two he said, "Technically, I think you should have hung on longer."

"But . . ." Valkyrie said. "We had nothing on him anyway. He was just—weird."

"I think we could have made the Palace a public property and got him for breaking and entry," Bob said, without serious intent. "Anyway . . ." He stood up and fished around in his pockets uncertainly.

Valkyrie popped the controls on her helm and took it off. In a strange way it was a relief to breathe the smelly, damp air and have her human senses returned. She felt much better. "I was going to interview Saxton, and I still am . . . I . . ."

"Wait, wait." Bob tipped his head to the side and sat down again. "Not every piece of technology died. I can hear Saxton's apartment. Somebody's in there with him."

Valkyrie paused as Bob gave her a direct transmission link to his auditory system. One of his bugs was feeding fuzzy and difficult blurts of conversation to him. She heard Saxton's familiar voice, very tired, and another voice, a man, consoling him. But then the conversation turned to accusation, and by the things said she realized that the person she didn't know could only be the splinter itself.

When it was over she found herself staring at Bob. "Are you thinking what I'm thinking?"

"I think so, though it would be unprofessional to confirm it," he said, taking a tissue out of his pocket and carefully wiping his whiskers with it. He stood up. "Time I was going. I'll see you never, I trust, since our orders possibly diverge at this moment."

"Yes." She hesitated awkwardly. "Thanks, Bob." It was hard to talk. Her mind seemed suddenly empty; too many new and unexpected probabilities had sucked it temporarily dry. She recalled Belshazzar's command to try to keep Bob from doing anything rash, but had no real idea of how.

"Mmn, back to town." Bob hesitated and then selected a leg of lamb from the table. "Think I'll take a peace offering with me, just to be on the safe side. And if not . . ." He drew his gun and curled his finger against the trigger. "*Adios.*"

"*Sayonara.*" Valkyrie went the other way, along the service passage and into the dining room above. She asked Belshazzar's sister to trace his progress for her, and they acceded from their spaces in SankhaGuide.

She passed through the serving doors and stood up straight at last. The doors flapped shut at her back and the dull sound boomed in the vast, empty space where she stood. A moment later a starry tinkling made her look up. Crystal chandeliers hung beyond the reach of her outstretched wing-tips, twelve all in a row, their dripping tiers plunging down like freeze-frame photographs of sea-spray. She could see them only because of the movement. Without light they had no sparkle, only edges that jittered against the faster, thinner air.

The room itself was extremely dark. She could just make out the ends, one a vast fireplace big enough to hold a grate the size of a horse cart. Air moved that way in a ferocious draw, shooting to the high chimney-stacks above. Cold air seeped in through the windows and the doors where they didn't quite fit. There was an entrance from the hall directly across from the kitchen entrance. Valkyrie went through it, carefully. The place reminded her of a museum, or a cathedral.

She walked softly, cushioned by the heavy carpets. The hall

had light; small yellow glimmers from household night-lights plugged into the electrical outlets that lined the walls in the skirting, cleverly hidden where they were not used by mouldings, each in the shape of a different insect. The gleaming revealed more glassware near the ceiling and paintings hung on every space against crimson oriental papers. Everywhere she looked she saw luxury, old and forgotten, but not worn. It was simply ignored.

She discovered many great halls, ballrooms, lounges, sun rooms; rooms decorated in every style and full of untouched furniture as though just left yesterday; a room full of gilded carriages on the first floor and another containing a motley of stuffed wild animals and old Egyptian mummy cases and other artefacts she knew nothing about. The great library was on the ground floor, and she came to it via a strange stair she had thought would take her up, but found it only went up to go down again and became a narrow, twisting wooden spiral stair that was barely big enough for her feet.

This brought her down beside a two-storey-high set of oak shelves, carved with ivy and olive garlands. The shelves were full of leather-bound volumes, each detailed on the spine with individual gilding and colour. She turned around and around inside a well of dictionaries and atlases; worlds and languages she knew nothing of but couldn't help thinking—isn't this all in the Guides? Why have so many things that are never taken down or read?

At the bottom she found her stair to be unique. The shelves lined the walls of a room the size of a football pitch and projected out in curlicues of a Mandelbrot design far into the parquet flooring—a real antique. There were reading areas dotted everywhere, some comfortable tiny nooks with soft chairs, and others simple tables with heavy glass-shaded lamps. She was walking and looking and thinking she should take the main staircase and face Mandy if he was there, when she rounded one of the fractal corners and found a pool of light spilling from a single lamp, beneath it a large, open book and holding the book the oddly slight figure of Saxton's friend and Francine's boyfriend. Her splinter cell.

He didn't look surprised to see her.

" 'Beauty is truth, and truth beauty,' " he read aloud and closed the book. Then he looked up at her.

His face was a ghastly colour, pale and greyish, with reddened eyes and a mouth whose bruised colour was spreading out beyond the lips. His hair was heavy, tangled and hung thick and dark to his shoulders, where it vanished against the black of his clothes. His wrists and ankles, hands and feet looked vulnerable—what he wore didn't fit—but on closer inspection she found them strong. The eyes that gazed up at her were set to guard emotions that were barely under control.

His face was strange. She could only see clearly the feature she was looking directly at. Eyes or nose, mouth or jaw . . . without her focus they became curiously undefined so that she wanted to look again, again. She had to look down at the book to make herself stop looking. She felt disturbed, as though she had been about to discover something profound and now it had gone with the flick of her attention.

She had to look back. He had become alarmingly attractive.

He smiled as though she were a distant happy memory he had regained. "What do you think?" he asked her, placing the book on the table where the lamp stood, its surface as high as his chest and tilted so the standing reader of average height could be comfortable. "Not very fair I suppose. Here you are mapping the territory for Solargov and I start asking you questions from Literature 101. Personally I think it's shite as an observation. On the other hand, I can't help liking it as an idea. Really torn."

When she still didn't speak he said, "I suppose you have the Guide and everything on tap." Here he clicked his fingers next to his ear. "Ah, never mind. I've got the feeling books aren't going to cover it."

She recognized the brittle kind of sarcasm. She had thought it was her only mode of communication lately: a defensive get-me-before-you-do verbal brick wall.

"Well," he said, his attention turning inwards so that she felt its absence like a shadow on her skin. As it withdrew so did all her will to remain there, like magic. He reached over and turned the light off—"Good night"—and walked away, head down, and bled into the general darkness of the room.

She heard the quiet sound of the door a few moments later.

Valkyrie could not equate him with her image of Theodore. The shadows in the corners began to lengthen and take on the shape of hands. She left the Palace by the front door as quickly as she could and returned to the warmer, less charged air of the greater Sankhara night. Saxton would have to wait. She could not face the dark touch.

As soon as she made Crisscross Street she took to the sky. From five hundred metres up she gazed down. Crisscross ran under the bridge and along for another half a mile. There was no trace of the huge landscape she had been in, no sign of the enormous Palace. There were only the houses, then the small stores, the businesses that organized their freight using Crisscross Canal, boats drawn tight against their moorings, night-lights in their bows bouncing in the gale.

She descended and set her foot to ground at Temple. Everything was bright here, grandly proportioned, roads full of the regalia of a dozen religions each with their own festivals and rites. The sacred market ran all night on Wednesdays. Braziers burned bones and fat, giving off filthy, stinking smoke. As she passed it a wandering dog from one of the stalls pissed briefly but confidently on the plinth of Odin's shrine. Rats scuttled, then leaped like gazelles as the dog spotted them and attacked.

Valkyrie bought a posy of dried flowers and walked past the ramparts of the newly built Saint Cadenza Piacere to the Uluru Temple House Gardens. It was a modest place with winding paths which were lit at night by paper lanterns. Most of these had blown down. Valkyrie did not mind the rain and weather and she didn't want to sit with anyone. She stood in the lee of the summerhouse, turned her sensory repertoire over to automatic and locked her exoskeleton in position so that she could rest standing up, knees slightly bent, ready to go.

The warm and gaudy colour of Uluru's virtual perfection was a shock. She stood and rubbed her face with dirty hands until she was used to it. Tom Corvax the silver aeroplane was still there in his eternal bed of grass, and she ran up to the empty shell and looked quickly for Metatron in the polish, calling him with an impatient tapping of her fingers on one of the aerofoils.

The avatar climbed out of the cockpit wearing blue overalls and a cap. He walked down the angle of the wing and sat down on it beside her. "Who can I get for you?"

"That person I spoke to before. The gryphon," Valkyrie said, biting her thumbnail.

"He isn't here." Metatron shrugged. "Anyone else?"

Valkyrie gripped the grass with her toes. It was cool under the wing. "I'd like . . . I wonder if—can you connect me to Tupac?"

"I will ask," the avatar said and became transparent to indicate that he was busy and not able to talk to her. He stayed that way some time.

Valkyrie looked around. She liked the park here, the statues of the heroes and the bodies of the dead avatars. Elinor and she used to come here when they were young. Like the children playing through the castle mazes of the long-gone Terraforms, they ran everywhere unburdened.

Valkyrie pinched the knee of Metatron's overalls fiercely and felt nothing between her thumb and forefinger. He returned.

"She says later."

Valkyrie spun around and slammed her hand on the smooth metal curve of the wing in frustration. She would not discover the strange Salmagundi's identity today. "Then take me to Elinor."

"As you wish," said Metatron. He held out his hand and she

took it, watching her small fingers be folded into his large ones. He slid off the wing and as he stood his wings unfolded in swan's white flights, not one but six pairs, including one pair from his head.

Valkyrie became as light as down and the wings beat once, shifting the world to night, then to day again. When they came to rest she was in another region of Uluru, a deeper region, where the permanent residents had no other form and no other world but Uluru; where they had gone beyond the body. Valkyrie wanted to sit with Elinor, or what was left of her, but the hand she held on her own kept fading and, inside the visor of her shattered helm, Elinor had no face at all.

32/Francine

Jalaeka slid out of bed at about 3:00 A.M. and went to see Greg. I lay in the dark, curled up as tightly as I could, and fell into an uneasy half sleep to the sound of the wind battering the old/new windows. The old ones moved in a certain way, made a kind of knocking now and again like nervous guests. The new ones were silent. I fell asleep again and dreamed. It was unusually vivid, and had the quality of memory, not dream. It wasn't my memory.

Blood. Death. War.

Everything is fucked.

Everyone around me is dead and these bastards in the face-plates and armour are on horses. I can't reach all of them at once. Those who stood by me are bodies at my feet. As the last one falls with his throat cut, his faith in me is the thing that gives him solace, as far as solace can get him through pain, which isn't far.

One of the fuckers is going to get me. There are too many.

My arm won't work properly, I don't know why.

Shield's gone.

Slam into horse with spear. It falls and twists. Spear breaks. Shit.

I reach up for the rider and pull him down as the horse groans and comes rolling down over its knees, a plummeting ton of dead meat. Kick off the bastard's faceplate. A black woman is staring right up into my eyes. Her head's filled with a vision of the ghosts of her dead family. They're crowding around her, whispering to her about me, telling her something she can't really hear for the battle noise. But I can hear them. They're talking about their eaten souls.

At the same instant she's looking at me and seeing the man who's about to kill her. Part of her is looking forward to it, and part of her is massively disappointed that this has been all there is and all there was, and that she has unfinished business. Part of her wants me to be what she has hunted for, longed to become, longed to exist, so that her life will not be wasted.

But it has been.

Her understanding hurts me with a shocking, visceral, indescribable pain.

It changes me.

This distracts me totally so that when some freak comes riding up with his arm in full swing . . .

I can't see for the blood in my eyes.

On my knees in the mud. Can't get up. My head doesn't work. I'm spun around by something that hits my hip.

I can sense the final blow coming. If I could just turn, then I'd have him but I can't turn. I can't breathe. Time slows as it begins its fall into ever.

Suddenly, I start to wonder what's going on.

None of this makes the slightest sense. Hang on a moment, I wasn't even here a few minutes ago.

Didn't I have a . . . ?

Wasn't I a . . . ?

What am I doing here?

Who are these people? Why am I fighting them? Why am I one of them?

Who the hell am I?

The axe hits me with the speed of a blink. I hear bone splintering but don't feel a thing except the shock of impact as I land facedown over the dead horse. Its sweat is incredibly salty, like the ocean.

Hands pick me up and put me so I'm looking up into the sky. What a fabulous colour.

The black woman warrior looks down close to my face and her sweat drips on my nose. "You," she says hoarsely, and I can see that she knows who I am.

But I've let out my last breath.

Blue. Black. I want to kill them all. I want to hold them in my arms and ask them questions but instead I'm falling into a deep sea, where dark horses with no master carry me away.

I struggled to wake up properly and when I did I lay and shivered uncontrollably, unable to speak, convinced I had died.

33/JALAEKA

When I got back upstairs Francine was asleep, the lights on, her clothes on, the comforter wrapping her into a tight chrysalis. I turned the lights off and glanced through the restored balcony windows. The wolves outside watched me and spoke among themselves quietly, wondering if Hyperion was right, and that there might be no gods at all. It was a new idea to them, and it kept them awake and troubled. They believed in soul but not souls. They sang about it until they heard elk or thought of elk and went off into the trees in silent files.

I listened to Greg for a few moments: drunk and mostly asleep, he kept on nodding awake to another heart surge of horror, then would catch himself and think about me, and pray and catch himself praying and loathe the idea of it and his own weakness, then he'd fall unconscious.

The Light Angel Valkyrie left quickly through the snow. I wished she reminded me more of Angel #5—for a second I'd hoped Damien had found her in me and the Engine spit her out again—but that was too much to ask of any pattern.

I walked back to our bed and watched Francine sleeping. I sat on the floor next to her, listened to the wind, thought about how easily Theo had tricked me. I felt thoroughly miserable and sick, realizing my great selfish stupidity, for hanging on to my own prized integrity out of fear and uncertainty, allowing this to happen because I was too precious about myself and would not dare to change. I was sorry for the first time I defied Unity, and so agreed to our war. I was sorry for each one of us in our "Hotel California" predicament: you can check out anytime you like, but you can never leave. You are what you are.

Since Theo knew all about us there was no point in holding back any longer.

I made another physical form, exactly the same as my own. Looking into the face of my clone partial was simply like looking at a reversed mirror. I realized instantly why Theo used partials the way he did, with their distinct forms and their independent conscious lives—doing it my way meant I had to become two separate instances of myself, with diverging futures. I reintegrated.

It wasn't so bad though I could see how major changes could easily accrue with time, and that after a day or more it would become quite impossible to say with confidence that the alternate version was anything less than an individual in his own right. And if my copy was a true copy of me, it was unlikely he'd want to return ...

All the thinking was getting me nowhere. I remade the copy.

Our thoughts ran seamlessly together, perfectly easy to access, rather harder to block out, like Francine had been difficult to separate out and keep out. I/we didn't need to think to one another however; we were in perfect accord for the time being.

I went down the hall into Greg's room, where he was sleeping, and picked him carefully off the chair before laying him gently on his own bed. I took his boots off, covered him over and lay down beside him so that he did not have to be alone.

In Francine's room the other one of me put on what I'd come to think of as my Greg-head. Although I couldn't prove anything right now I suspected that neither Unity nor I were remotely like Theo's visions—ultimate being and ultimate individualist. I would bet almost anything on the fact that neither it nor I nor he nor any of our details existed at all until Isol met Stuff. Not that it matters where reality does its business because the "Hotel California" condition holds regardless. I didn't care one way or the other who was to blame. I only wanted justice.

I waited for Francine to wake up. I needed inspiration.

When she opened her eyes the first thing she whispered was, "Where are you?"

"Right here," I said and put my hand up. She caught hold of it in hers.

She paused, then struggled halfway out of the comforter. "What time is it?"

"Nearly dawn."

"Oh." She lay down again reluctantly.

"Katy's mate, Ludo, was round. Earlier today, I mean. Before Theo came," she said, opening my hand out and placing hers against it, palm to palm and finger along finger.

"What did he want?"

"To give me some counselling and under the cover of care tell me that I should go back to the group and leave you. He said that relationships are the inverse of loneliness because they only mask it. The love you need is from yourself." She sighed.

I wondered if she was going anywhere with it. She often started out from a tangent. "What did you say?"

"I said it was a half-truth at best. People don't exist in isolation, do they? And then he said that I couldn't even get started on my journey because I wouldn't listen. He said I should look within myself and see that loving others was a step to loving myself, and that listening was part of loving, and I should listen to people who could really care about what was best for me because they had objectivity, and not to needy people like you who were only going to trap me in the cycle of dependency."

I hardly dared breathe. I imagined slaughtering Ludo with a blunt nail file.

She took her hand away from mine, holding my wrist with one hand and my fingertips with the other. I felt her breath across my skin. "I said I had listened to him, but I didn't agree with him and agreeing with someone wasn't compulsory even if you did love them, especially if they were mouthing a lot of platitudes in order to avoid having to face the fact that things hurt and can't be mended. And then he said that it was by embracing hurt we learned to be lonely yet sufficient. I said nobody here is lonely anyway, they're all surfing for answers to existential questions, which is spiritual enquiry not misery. The really lonely ones are out there actually being lonely, so who are you talking to? And he said that everyone here was lonely in the end because they didn't have perfect self-realization, which is the essence of being one with yourself. I asked if he wanted to go to the pub, have a drink on it, no hard feelings, and he said that was typical of people who are trapped by self-protection, that they always try to distract you back to the mundane things that chain you into the slavery of attachment and eternal misery. But if we had gone to the pub, then Theo wouldn't have . . ." She took a deep breath. "Then I told him to piss off." She kissed my palm and I couldn't do anything for a few seconds until she stopped.

"You're too patient," I said as gently as I could. "I don't know why you keep letting them in."

She sighed and closed my fingers for me, let me go. "They're lonely." Then she curled up on her side. "I can't feel you anymore, but I think I'm starting to remember things that are really your memories and not mine."

"I can try to take that away . . ."

"No. That is, if you don't mind."

I owed her that, although my guts turned over with nausea at the thought of what she would discover. It was one thing to gift it all to Greg as a history, facts divorced from their reality, another to reveal it to her as an experience. He was much older than she was, and much less innocent. "Okay."

"Thanks for not asking how I am."

"Figure of discretion, model of sensitivity, me," I said.

"Thank you." Her brittle lightness of tone was like a thin glass.

I played it even more casual. "Can I get you anything?"

"I want a sandwich. And something to drink. Beer. Chocolate."

I got up. "I'll have to go out and deal with the pollution of material things to satisfy your gross dependencies on sugar, fat and alcohol. We're all out."

"That's okay."

It wasn't okay with me, but my solution to the problem of leaving her unguarded wasn't something I wanted to tax her with now. "Hyperion's still hall monitor. Want me to ask him to wait with you?"

"No need." She had reached a gay, airy tone as though she was happy and I knew it was time to go.

"Okay. Be back soon." I went directly outside to where Hyperion was standing restlessly in the corridor, his head tilted, listening to the sound of finger cymbals and repeated mantras from the Foundation apartments. His tail was twitching fiercely and he jolted with surprise as I duplicated myself and divided on the spot. Getting to be a habit suddenly.

"Mind if this one of me waits with you on kill duty?" I said, sitting down beside him where his claws had dug great gouges in the carpet.

"Certainly not." The Cylenchar settled again in front of the statue of Achilles on its pretty white plinth as though this was standard procedure, only his large, tufted ears turning now and again at some noise outside. As my other self walked away from him he spoke a word to my back.

"What's that?" seated me asked.

"A lucky charm," he said, with the candid and atavistic expression of an owl strangling a stoat. "In case you meet your adversary."

"Thanks," I said to him, doubled. He was smarter than he looked.

In my third (or first, it didn't pay to think about that) form I deferred my errands for Francie and walked, transmolecular, through the world to Greg's office. I saw the invader immediately, right there on his desk, a small pink quartz heart.

The DNA in the dead skin cells trapped on its surface told me it had been handled by several people; Greg obviously, and others I didn't know. But I recognized one individual's trace elements. It took a minute to place them, the memory rising out of my left hand where the initial pickup of their information had taken place—at *Ziggurats of Cinnamon* that night I'd been there with Greg and Francine. Theo's partial, Rita.

I went out onto the roof and assumed my old Metropolis identity, wings, tail and all. Far, far above me I heard Forged Glider chatter on the AM band. I soared upwards into the icy night on one of the impressive thermals rising out of the University heating substation.

Even at this early hour there were Gliders riding the city plumes, unhurriedly taking on enough height to cross from Sankhara through the Gateway into Blackpool airspace, and from there on and on across the planet and its 'Bars, never touching earth, never touching water.

"You've come a long way," the first one said as I circled below her. We banked at the same moment, moving back into rising air as we crossed the Purbright river south of town. The whole city was a map stitched in lights beneath us, SankhaGuide

Massif a black block like negative space. She let me hear the Forgebeat music she was listening to and the beautiful sounds made the windriding a weaving dance.

"I get around," I said, overcooking the turn and watching her speed away following the curve of the singer's voice soaring from note to note. "Been anywhere recently?"

"I been up Iceland," she said. "They say that mountain is gonna go up soon. Hekla. But it didn't. I always miss major geological events. Got fed up waiting. Going back later. You?"

"New York," I lied, wishing it were true.

"Gulf Stream, Jet Stream," she said with an appreciative smack of her beak. "Good air. What you looking for?"

"Just looking," I said.

"Very old school," she replied with droll accents that said she admired the vagueness of my ambition. She turned her wings and exited the air column. Her music faded away.

I turned back over the city and spread my wings wider, wider, opening all their fancy finery to the currents. I filtered the winds looking for Rita; not the winds of Sankhara, but of desire in all its forms.

To pick her out of these patterns was like looking for the Dalmatian dog in the test picture of black and white dots. She looked purely human superficially, but Theo's partial bodies always resonated faintly in the elevensheet with the fossil trace of billions of suppressed signals.

I drifted along for a while, looking without trying too hard. Engine interference made it difficult at this time of day but I kept going and soon I could feel it like the faintest itch or echo, moving east towards a cab rank in the archaeological preservation district of the centre city, Roma Precinct, where academic and civil servants liked to live close to their offices.

Rita was only just coming out of an expensive private club and she wasn't alone.

Her male companion was middle-aged, affluent and drunk, an Unevolved and, by his clothing, an academic like Greg, a scientist. I saw that he had an Abacand with a Macrolibrary attachment, which must mean he had specialized information to keep to himself. He wore it on a gold chain, like a Victorian watch. They were the rage on Earth. Rita propped him up stealthily, pretending she was the one under support as they walked to his waiting car. Her boredom was evident in the way she searched the street with restless eyes, not looking for anything—looking for everything.

I floated down to street level in silence, wings become parachute, become gossamer, become nothing at all. The changes were visible in other spectra than the usual human ones and she looked back furtively, her expression uncertain and hopeful of finding a distraction from what was bothering her.

I didn't want her to know who I was, since her recognition would only draw Theo to the surface in all likelihood, and though he was my target, I knew I could only deal with him indirectly if I was going to have an effect. I wanted her to think me some other Stuffie, like her, with an elevenspace signature too faint and too unimportant to be worth scanning for the telltale differences that would give me away. I gambled on the fact that, until tonight, I had never done anything to voluntarily alter my appearance, to use partials or to operate as anybody not myself. It was a big risk, but the worst it could immediately incur was a fight, and I felt more than happy to handle one of those. To avoid recognition I would have to change: outside and in.

So now was the moment to try a different physical form and see what changes that might wring out of me. The only way to keep track of "primary" me would be to take a complete data snapshot of my entire makeup in this second and even as I considered it I realized why Unity kept Origin, the homeworld planet that was its library. Because of this problem. If I didn't keep such a record, there was no guarantee I could ever return to the oh-so-very-ideal me of this minute should something go wrong. But there was already no guarantee I could successfully integrate the separated versions lying with Greg and sitting with Hyperion and no guarantee I wouldn't, in some moment of extreme fear, integrate Francine and lose her completely. The only thing I could rely on was my age-old stubbornness that I would not descend into Unity's ways. It was less than flimsy.

I did not make a record.

In spite of the fact that the real man I was about to imitate had been my dear friend, who perhaps didn't deserve such a resurrection as this, and my lover, and my teacher and a great many things more to me, I made myself into a facsimile of Patrick Black; someone to whom a greater resemblance would not be so bad.

Patrick was once tall, tan and blond-handsome in the way of a lot of North American white men of his era. He used to play college football for Notre Dame before he got into rock climbing and shed the weight to get paper-light. I met him halfway into that project, after the operations on his knees had failed, and before he got into extreme isolation adventuring—everyone I fall for generally has extreme in them. Patrick had got tenure at MIT—these were the days of superstring theory, of the war on terror, and my burgeoning ignorance of the consequences of physical theories of matter.

Patrick was long dead, hundreds of years dead, but as I changed I felt that he and I were sharing a private joke. He would have laughed himself silly at my idea that becoming him was an act of prayer. But I was greatly weakened by my rage at Theo, and it seemed to me that wearing his likeness was the same as putting on sacred armour, the only useful kind for the fight I was engaged in.

Rita, well aware of me walking towards her, coaxed her dupe into a taxi that had been idling for them at the kerb and I had to run to catch her up before she shut her door.

I called out in Patrick's soft Southern tones, "Hey, share a ride? I'm so late already and there are no cabs anywhere." I'd forgotten how the timbre of his voice sounded and suddenly I missed him acutely.

"We're . . . he's not very well," she said firmly and added, as if to an idiot, "It's very early." Her hair swung like a single curtain.

Cheekbones, lips, eyes—she was a work of art, even for times like these. Her mouth was painted bloody red and had a naturally uncertain pout that demanded to be kissed. Theo must have been reading a lot of books to build her because she far exceeded any natural capacity he had for estimating human nature. She made a move to slam the door on my hand but I caught it midswing and held it ajar.

"I'm not going far," I said and got in, thinking of any district very far from here. "Rialto Bridge." The tears on my face moved her. She offered me a tissue as I sat down opposite them both. I shook my head and wiped my face with my fingers. Her date stared at me with clear contempt but he was already feeling so lucky to be with her that he didn't care if half of Sankhara shared his taxi, as long as she didn't leave his side.

"We're going to the Aelf," Rita informed me coolly, but gave me an unaccidental nudge with her knee at the same time. It was desperation making her do it—to be away from him, to be close to anyone more potentially sympathetic.

I gave her a tentative half smile of momentary allegiance and gratitude. "Then you go first, I'll pay the fare."

"I'll pay," the date said, "even if it's Timbuktu. But can we bloody go somewhere?"

I shut the door and the car slid smoothly towards the Massif.

"Pat," I said, holding out my hand to her with all of Patrick's deliberately ironic charm. She looked down but didn't take it. Her eyes slid up to mine slowly, as she figured out whether or not my upset was infectious, and whether it was going to be a problem. "What's the matter?"

"Somebody died," I said. "A friend of mine." For an instant I thought of the Earth agent, the golden girl and her cracked clockwork heart. "Not today. It was the anniversary."

The foxes covering her thighs stirred restlessly and one of them mewled a little.

"Goddamned coat freaks me out," her date said to me, as though he'd heard nothing of our exchange. "All I can think of is pet stores and when they're going to arrest her for cruelty or if the things are going to shit on my carpets."

"They're not real," she murmured, putting her hand on his knee and letting it slide up a little. She glanced at me as she did this. "It's only an effect."

He wasn't listening to her. "Look at this one here." He tugged the wide collar of her coat around so I could see and she had to stop herself from openly resisting his clumsy jerk. I gave her a sympathetic look and wondered what Theo could want with this man, though I didn't care enough to find out. Only Rita interested me. I would have liked to pull the pink quartz heart out of my pocket and put it in her hand, or slide it secretly into her evening bag. I would have liked to know how complicit she was with that act, but I couldn't afford that petty drama.

Two bead eyes stared out at me from an intelligent, ferocious little face in her coat, and two paws flexed, searching for the partner paws that made up the other side of the clasp. They paddled uselessly for a second, then stopped, frozen with failure. The eyes blinked, then withdrew into the mass of fur beside the low-scoop neckline of her dress.

"Nearly had my fingers off." Her date let go of the coat at last, chuckling. Rita recoiled against the seat and adjusted the furs with a savage twist of her shoulders.

I smiled insincerely and coughed to clear my throat. "Been anywhere nice?"

"Yes," Rita said.

"No," he said. "Expensive slop. But she likes it, so I don't mind."

"It's the easiest way," I said as though I was agreeing with him.

"To what?" Rita's face took on an arctic sheen. She inched her leg away from mine.

"The easiest way to keep life running smoothly. Doing what other people want when you don't want to." I said it while I was looking in her eyes and saw the pupils shrink to points, then a second later dilate as she decided I was okay.

"Isn' tha' the truth," the date slurred. "Especially when they're worth keeping."

"I'm not your possession, Rupert," she snapped, but without the sting that would have betrayed care.

"No baby," he said in a weak effort at placation. "I didn't mean that."

"Sorry." I put my hands up showily to ward off their fight, which had the desired effect of irritating her even more, because there was no fight.

She never took her eyes off Patrick's face, looking from one of my eyes to the other. Patrick's eyes are blue, with a hazel fleck in the left iris at ten o'clock; if we were together at that hour, no matter where, I always used to kiss him. My sentimental side glanced at the taxi clock now—5:30 A.M., the Engine had been off for an hour, Theo had been gone for nearly eight hours, Greg had been under Translation for about thirty-six hours.

The taxi drew up at the secondary plaza of Aelf 2, bored security guards squatting down on either side of its oak doors, hands on the tall spears planted between their knees, their feathered wings folded close to their sides in the predawn cool, antlers dripping dew into their clay-matted dreadlocks. Rupert got out and held the door for her. Rita didn't budge.

"Aren't you coming up?" he said, plaintive and weak.

"I'm going to go to the late shop and get some vials," she replied. "You go up. I'll be there in a few minutes."

"Send the bloody car for them," he suggested, but without conviction.

"I want to see what there is," she said, smooth and cool. "Shut the door. It's cold."

He obeyed her and she said, "Shiro Maru" to the car's command panel, a place right out in the western side of the city.

Once we'd taken a corner I changed seats and sat beside her. She turned and kissed me. It was hungry at first, hard and defensive, but then it got gentler, until her coat bit me on the shoulder.

"Ouch!"

The bead eyes blinked and vanished. Her eyes shone and there was nothing in them but pure longing. I kissed her again and this time bit her not too gently on the lower lip. It was already big and it swelled quickly. She drew away and held it in her mouth for a moment, thoughtful, separating from Theo with every passing second, her changes filtering back down to him in ways he wouldn't be able to control, as Francie's stubborn innocence, among other things, filtered across to me and I remembered who I was meant to be.

I slid my hands under the shifting flow of fur and found her in the thinnest, tightest Chinese satin dress. Rita took hold of my Pat-face and looked into my eyes. Her hunger for experience was a refined one. She wanted everything, but mostly she wanted genuine intimacy, a bridge between two people that she could use to escape herself, and this couldn't be got out of many people at short notice, if ever.

Whatever she saw in my gaze she deemed acceptable for that second, for this trip. My original idea, when I started to look for her, had been to exact some blend of vengeance—a seduction that would transform her into my slave and send Theo sky-high with rage. I was ashamed of that idea now. Instead I found myself longing to talk to her about what it was like to be her, Unity but not Unity? I remembered the despair with which she'd addressed me in the Well, and I lost my anger at what she'd done to Greg. Francine's sweetness was in my kiss, and traces of Angel #5's healing grace—I was built of ghosts that hour and submitted to their demands willingly.

Streetlights and the single flash of a blue police signal passed over us. They ignored us.

Certain intimacies are only possible with strangers in total silence. We explored all of those, exchanged them like the gifts they were. She understood the stranger-economics of that, like I did.

Later we returned to her Aelf address, after she'd stopped as she said she would, to buy some soft drug or other from a shop on the way. She got out and held on to the door, looking back at me.

"What's your name?" I asked her, thinking I would like to give her one more gift.

"Rita," she said hesitantly.

"I like you, Rita." I surprised myself. It was true.

She turned her lower lip under and sucked it unconsciously for a second, then smiled a little. "I like you, Pat." Her coat whimpered at the drag of the cold wind.

When I smiled back at her it felt good on my face.

She shut the door, squared her shoulders and lifted her head and walked in to the building. On the way she took one of the vials she'd bought out of the bag and tossed the contents back into her throat with a gunslinger's practiced action. She dropped the bag and the rest of its contents in front of the closest guard as she passed it by.

I went to Earth: Prague for beer, to Manhattan for the sandwich, to Vienna for cake and chocolate and through Sankha Gateway an hour after leaving, sliding time across the gate surface as though it was oil on a puddle.

I undid Patrick from me in the darkness outside the Palace, afraid of what insanity might attack me if I met myself in his likeness. At the bottom of the staircase I glanced up at the roof. The boat was gone, the river empty.

I addressed my duplicate self beside Hyperion as I arrived in the hall, looking myself in the eye in a truly surreal moment—"Do you remember *Star Trek*?" Patrick had loved *Star Trek*, all versions. He was a fanboy with no discrimination when it came to things he liked.

"Yes," I said from Hyperion's side as he watched both of me with a quizzical tilt of his head. "Beam me up."

Assimilating the other me was not like Translating Francine. It was as easy as folding cloth; one, two, it's a boat, or a hat, or me again.

"You are unfathomable," Hyperion pronounced, standing and stretching his thin body. "Were you successful?"

I hugged him around his long neck with one arm, the grocery bag hanging from my free hand. "Very." I put my hand against his bony rib-cage but there was no crossing of energy, no change. Angel's *darshan* was not moved by him. "You're a very integrated individual."

"It is easy," he said, resting his huge head on my shoulder. "Never look down. Believe all things. Float on the current like a wild dandelion seed."

"Don't let Greg hear you say that."

"Can you save him?"

I released my hold on him and we separated. "If it's the last thing I do."

"I pray it is not."

"That makes three of us."

Hyperion gave me a shrewd look. "You are joking."

I shrugged. "Hard to tell, isn't it?"

In Greg's cold room, as he slept on, I got up and made a fire, drew the curtains and laid another blanket on him.

Francine was reading Dumas as I came in from the hall. I felt a soft kind of shock on seeing her, the contrast with Rita was very strong. Francine had never looked more vulnerable. Her skin was that incredible translucent perfection that only real youth can show, and it made the purple smudges around her eyes stand out. She jumped up when she saw me and took the bag from my hand. It was such a spontaneous, enthusiastic movement. I fell in love with her all over again.

She tore the packages open, almost without surprise, and then gave me a knowing look. "Hello, massive overcompensation," she said. "What have you been doing?"

I told her about Rita and she sighed.

"Seducing Theo . . . I suppose it's poetic." She snarled, "I hate him. I hate that he was here, then I made you . . ." She wrestled with the words in that way she had that made them seem like a herd of wild horses running amok. This time she got them close to control.

"I made you do it with me then, after that. That was crazy. It wasn't going to be like that. I was going to put it off forever and make it perfect, until we were equal, until I was good enough. Worth you. You know?" She began tearing the croissant up into tiny pieces.

"I know," I said, sitting with her. Fifty pages. She was a fast reader. "You're insane like that. It's almost worthy of respect in its own right."

"But don't stop," she added, picking up the beer and cracking it open with a flick of her hand, like a bartender's best trick. "You shouldn't. It wouldn't be you." She took a drink, wiped her mouth on her sleeve and handed me the bottle. "I thought you could make it go. Heal me. I thought I could do that, with you, like a sticking plaster, like the *darshan*. I didn't want to ask for that, though. I didn't want an escape, some stupid cowardly way out. I wanted to face it, you know? I just thought that doing the sex and the Translation would be enough because I only have to look at you to feel better, and I thought that there was some kind of special thing about it, sex, that would make it, you know . . . super complete. And then after, I knew it was exactly the wrong thing, and that I was only passing on what he did, from me to you, like a disease . . . I'm sorry. I'm really . . ." Her voice broke down and she flung her hands down on the blankets as though she couldn't get them far enough away from her. She tried to say sorry again but the words had run out.

"It's okay," I said to her, passing the beer back. "I know how it works. It wasn't your fault."

"I wish you were right."

"I am right. We do the best we can do. Sometimes it's appalling."

She turned the bottle, picked at the label, then gripped it so hard her knuckles whitened. "I always wanted you," she said, looking down. "I just never felt good enough. And even if you think so, I can't believe anybody else could . . . and that's a sick old shame."

I heard her take another breath for the fatal question, the one I knew was coming, and not because I could hear her thinking but because it was what she was driven to ask all her life long, and mustn't. I put my fingers over her mouth gently and my arm around her shoulders. "Yes. Yes. Yes." I replaced my fingers with my own mouth, took one of her hands off the death grip on the bottle and placed it over my heart so she could feel what happened to it when I kissed her.

When we were done she let her forehead rest against mine. "Why can't I hear you? Inside? Aren't we like Unity?"

"I don't really know what we're like. I'm keeping you out as much as I can, for now."

She shuddered. "Not so much. I dreamed I was you. There was this horse and this black woman. You died. I didn't dream it, did I?"

Oh. "No."

We listened to the wind hurl sleet at the windows. She held my hand and I tried to explain to her that I'd never been happier in my life but it was difficult, because it was true.

34/RITA * THEODORE * RITA

It was one of those days, an English day, where the sky is like nothing more than a sheet of thick white plastic stretched just over the tallest thing you can see. Nothing looks good under it. Wan light struggled through the overcast, then squeezed through the intelligent glass of my window wall, trying stoically to enhance everything in spite of the conditions. At the distant foot of Aelf 2, directly below me, the river Tact surged underground into its deep roots, grey and silty and almost overflowing its banks.

The river approached from the west—auspicious according

to my feng-shui adviser on his visit yesterday. To the north the glass wall was apparently less than good, but a stand of pygmy sequoias planted in a solid clay trough blocked off the dramatic sight of the tall city centre buildings. The sequoias were my Tortoise of Protection. My huge white sofa was pushed out to the right. It was my East Dragon. There should have been a West Tiger object, but I wanted the water instead, especially now that the Tortoise was blocking the best view. The river was my Tiger, running towards me all the time.

I stood in the middle of it and wondered if I felt any better than the day before.

Rupes was on call waiting. I thought about lunch and going to the gym. I thought about the night before and got a glass of water, stood drinking it and looking at my Tiger. I didn't mind Rupes, who was harmless; brainy and harmless and a bit arrogant, the sort you feel sorry for because their intelligence only goes one way and they haven't the wit to know when they're being done over. He'd given me the only interesting piece of news he was capable of—that Solar Security did not trust Theodore and were busy tracking him around various 'Bars. I could have had it for a lot less than an evening's boredom, but Theo was in a vile mood, letting go of me only once it was past 3:00 A.M. and even he had grown tired of seeing what he could make me do and how it felt to be female for once.

I minded Theodore. No feng-shui was going to stop him coming for me whenever he wanted, doing what he wanted, making me do it.

The Tact swirled and eddied, seemed to be rushing up the long trunk of the tower, tearing up through its tough bark. But it wasn't the river . . . it was him . . .

I was shocked at how much Rita had changed since I was last fully her. It was like coming home and finding the whole place redecorated—I imagine. There really wasn't time for a great reunion however, only a fast one. I had some tests to run.

In the bathroom I looked in the medicine cabinet. It was empty except for a couple of small cubes of quartz: the reason I was here. There was sufficient energy in the structure to enable organic construction of a human form without getting into the nasty 11-D tangles I'd create if I started remodelling random bits of the local matter. I was uneasy at the prospect before me, but this was the only way to interrogate someone who has been dissolved in Unity if more was to be made of them than a simple plundering of their actual memories. They must be remade and put into their old 4-D incarnations, so that they can respond.

I set the cube on the new wool rug and stood back, waiting for it to take shape at my command.

The cube changed over a single Planck time. It became a young woman, slender but with an Amazonian energy stocked in her petite frame. Her hair and skin were marble white—a completely unnatural colouration for any Earth human—and her eyes were pale grey and by far the darkest thing in her face, giving her the look of a sculpture by Michelangelo animated by malevolent powers. Her clothes were the peculiar, near-shapeless veiling of the time and place she last lived in—a great Renaissance empire of her own making, on the verge of tumbling into the age of industry when she was cut short. She was afraid, but controlled herself impeccably, becoming exquisitely still.

Kya was among the last of the renegade human-form splinters to be returned to Unity and she didn't go willingly. Under the pressure of a deranged creation myth that had made her mad she had undergone a clean separation into two parts; one partial containing her emotion and the other her reason.

A nice experiment as it went—astonishing in the results, to which we owe Jalaeka's unflagging perversity—but even I don't want to deal with the insanity of one or the other half of her on its own. I put both sides together again and hoped that her first sight of existence in a new world and in an unknown time wouldn't make her try to jump through the plate glass before I could explain.

From the timelessness of Unity it never seems like anything has been missed even though aeons have passed. When Kya looked around her and set her eyes on me I suddenly recalled the moment of her assumption with a kind of nostalgic glow. Of course, I wasn't in Rita's form then.

I saw that there was a key difference to Kya now, an unshake-able conviction that she didn't possess before. She knew that she was Unity, and would return to it, like it or not. She had been tested, and failed.

Kya fixed her stare on me. "What do you want?"

Hers was a difficult language. I wished we were back in Solar English rather than speak that tongue again, and passed her the knowledge of it. She'd spent a lifetime acquiring information by sucking it out of other people's heads like a sponge sucking up water, so it didn't faze her.

"Tell me about Jalaeka."

"Pah!" She actually spat at me. Quite rightly, she sees him as the architect of her destruction. "Is *he* still alive? Send me back."

"*He* is about to end us," I said, knowing she was never going to be persuaded for less. "Anything you can offer by way of an insight . . ."

"Save your breath. I have no interest in whatever you do. Live, die. I don't care."

Nothing had prepared me for the cool of her regard. She hadn't moved, except the minimum requirement for speaking. Her eyes never wavered from my face.

"I'm searching for the people who first made him," I said. "I thought you might be the one, or one of them. I need to find out what they did and how he was made different."

"Then you're unlucky this time, and a bigger idiot than I took you for. I tried to remake him, but I couldn't do anything to him, even though he had no idea what he was or what he was capable of. Those that I used to shape him are all dead and long gone. Neither you nor he ate them, so whatever secrets they have are dust."

She stood up suddenly and took an instant, savouring the experience, the power of being able to act. Then she came closer and looked around the room and at me, and in particular at the window. She stood close to it and gently lifted her hand and put her fingertips on the pane. "This is another world," she said, to herself. "I always thought there must be others." She turned to me. "Who rules it?"

"I do."

She smiled, and it was not a pleasant expression. "I doubt it."

"I ruled yours."

"You destroyed it," she said. "That doesn't make you a ruler."

"It's still out there." I glanced at the sky.

She shrugged and dismissed her interest in it. "If it is, it's not mine. What else must you ask? Be quick. I could never stomach you when you were one of those insufferable mercenary monks, and now you're no improvement."

I was surprised that she had identified me so easily but it didn't matter. "Who were the makers that you used?"

"Let's see. There was the rich little poor girl who became a courtesan—this is the wrong word and I cannot find the right one, what is the matter with this language? Geisha, companion, master . . . no, she was one of mine, the women who rule from beneath, animatrix. She was the central one. He found another, some trash from the marketplace; a consumptive tailor, I believe. They were both weak and isolated characters who longed for love, so their dreams had great power. But he accepted their direction, though he accepted no other . . . As to why that is possible you can only ask yourself and, since you have no answer, perhaps you should ask him."

"What's his weakness?"

"Empathy, of course," she said. She stared for a moment at the sequoias; taller than her head but shorter than the ceiling. "What *is* this?"

"It's my Tortoise. Of protection."

She gave me another of her killing smiles. "What a brave kingdom. Little trees."

She knew all about ritual, psychopomp and religion of course. She'd made a career out of erasing it from existence in a spectacularly gory rationalist jihad. One of her had, anyway.

"He loved me," she said. "Did you know that? He was the one who put me back together first, before you came and ruined it all."

I found it a pretty incredible claim, knowing what I knew about her. "You tortured him."

"And then he ran away into the woods and went crazy," she added. "And still. No breaks. Not a crack in the armour. Only . . ." She cast about and spoke with a complete bafflement and no little anger, "kindness."

I felt seasick being with her. Watching her was like looking in a mirror set at an angle to flatter least. I had the nasty suspicion I owed her more in terms of who I'd become than I owed most people eaten by Unity, as though she and Isol and those other freaks had all made more contribution by dint of their manic energy than a thousand ordinary lives of better balanced qualities.

She glanced up at me through her colourless lashes and one-half of her mouth curled upwards knowingly. "Tortoise," she said quietly.

I sent her back. The quartz rock sat on the rug.

I touched a frond of sequoia, ran it through my fingers and felt the tiny overlapping needles run smoothly under my skin. Kya had grudge reasons not to want to help me, though she had nothing to give in any case. But there were others who had known him, including one I was convinced Kya knew nothing about, even though they'd been contemporaries. Now *she* would be extremely difficult to handle, but maybe she would be more useful.

I ate her after Kya, a long time in the past: if it was the past, if this was its future. It was in another universe whose path lay distinctly separated from this one, and as such the times there and here could be said to be at least as concurrent as they are different.

I cross over to the place, to the time, to that eternal present where I am the ruthless mercenary Tyban, scourge of all lands. I am sword brother to the cash-hungry employees of a power-mad tyrant. He was a bastard in the pejorative sense, who thought himself a mage because he was a Stuffie and could use Stuff a little and to him in his ignorance it was magical. I liked him mightily, because he had extraordinary determination and the low cunning to have become anything at all.

I ate, or will eat, five people during Tyban's/my period of service.

Of course, given the nature of my existence, they are still alive, not in Unity, and Unity is also somewhere not yet born.

In that world I am still standing with the fire and the rope over Intana, Jalaeka's doxy, asking where he is.

In that world I am still in midair with my knife in the neck of another renegade splinter posing as a shaman, his material substance draining into my hand as he looks in my eyes and understands nothing.

In that world I am still a dark ghast with my tendrils locked around the throat of the singing drummer girl who suppressed all her splinter visionary powers into a contemplative temple life.

In that world I am still speaking through a winter lake to a small boy, tempting him into the icy depths where he will find the peace for his unknown splinter heart.

In that world I am still standing looking at the empty glass coffin where Jalaeka rested last on that planet, realizing with a genuine shock that one of these wretched splinters has gone and left the entire continuum.

I'm so surprised I'm missing the fact that I've been sneaked up on, and the black woman's blade is still slicing through my heart there on that sandy dune overlooking the grey sea, and the gulls are still shrieking. Some wretched girl with long mad hair who is both the princess and witch of the place is howling like a demon. She runs around the broken battlements of her pathetic shoreline fortress as I pull the blade out of me and walk off along the shingle beach to get some peace.

I am still returning to my attacker, standing over the smashed glass coffin and saying to her, "Where did he go?"

She looks down at me—she's very tall and has soon got over the shock of not slaying me. "Away. What are you? Are you one of him?"

"No." I feel affronted, amused, annoyed. "He's one of me."

She gives me the most contemptuous gaze I've ever seen. It makes me feel like filth under her boot. "It's not possible. Here." She hands me her dagger. She's of the same mercenary order as I am. Tyban and Chayne. We are brother and sister in cash and blood, though we've never met before. Still, the code of the Brotherhood answers all questions for us, and we have no interest in each other beyond our connection to the vanished Jalaeka.

She expects me to kill her for her treachery and I am honour bound to do so. "Get on with it. I'm waiting."

"What did you do?" I'm going to get my answer. If death is no threat to her, maybe life is. I prod the glass coffin with the blade and it chinks and is scratched—a ridiculous Stuff fancy, a crazy thing, its totemic power effective despite the fact it's broken.

"What the hell is *she* on about?" I point the tip of the sword at the shrieking girl who is a short distance away, very angry, slightly psionic as you might expect from long, random exposure to the kinds of Stuff individuals spawned on this place.

"Why do you want to know?"

I explain the position, since there's no harm in telling her now.

Chayne glances at the girl with exasperation and a clear desire to kill her. "She was in love with him and now he's gone. She kept him in this box and was trying to use him to get through to some other world. He had power and she fancied herself the sorceress to use it. Stupid mare."

"I'm impressed." I beckon to the girl. She wastes no time and runs away across the dunes. "And what about you?" I return Chayne's weapon.

She takes the dagger back and looks at the edge thoughtfully. My blood still smears its surface in a red slick. She glances at me, then, fast as an adder, sticks the point squarely into my belly. I grunt and gasp with the pain as she twists it experimentally before pulling it out.

I eye her crossly, making it clear that I consider it an insult, and she thinks a bit, watching me not bleed or die, and says, "He wanted to leave, and I wished that he could go somewhere better."

"You *wished*?"

"With all my heart." A small, triumphant smile touches the corners of her lips.

I have to have her. I take her. Her story bleeds into me in one great soak and I am starting to feel very uneasy about my missing splinter, that it inspires such peculiar and devoted behaviours.

I am still standing there, realizing that he could be absolutely anywhere. I am tracking down the princess and eating her, and understanding that for all I've been serving an arch manipulator I may have met another one ten times better naturally suited to the job in Jalaeka.

I rarely even thought of him by name then. It hadn't got personal yet.

As Rita standing by her Tortoise I feel like I felt as Tyban, used and abandoned. Only now I feel that I have abandoned and used myself, missed the bigger picture, made a mistake I can't quite pin down but am now beginning to reap. The answer to it is lost somewhere inside his history, inside . . . And then it occurs to me that I may have just the thing I need to really piss him off.

I left Rita and became taller, darker and more weary in spirit as I put on the mantle of his last friend on that world. When the body was remade I waited for the mind to be fished from its stored depths on Origin. It takes a while for something as complicated and delicate as that. Whole seconds.

As soon as my new partial was ready, I left.

When Theo had gone I picked up the Stuff cube and threw it against the window as hard as I could. There was a sharp sound but nothing broke. It rolled away behind the sequoia trough. I tore off my clothing and kicked it away from me. In the shower, once the water was hot and I'd gone through one washing I activated my Tab and called Pat's number, voice only. It rang awhile and I rested my hands on the tiles, letting the water run over my back.

"Hello?"

"It's Rita."

"Hey, Rita." He sounded pleased to hear from me.

"Hey. Are you very busy?"

"It depends," he said. "Are you all right?"

"I'm going out tonight," I said. "Why don't we meet?"

"I'd like that."

I sent him the details and hung up. I called Rupes and explained that I had business to attend to out of town. Fuck Theo and his orders for me to watch him constantly in case the humans figured out the slightest thing about using the Sankhara Stuffies. Fuck him.

Meanwhile there were other things to fill the hours until night. I went into the beauty salon and told them to fix everything.

35/GREG

I woke up and found myself lying in my own bed, the light on. It was warm. Jalaeka was sitting in the chair beside the bed, his feet next to me, playing some net game on my Abacand.

"What are you doing here?" I asked.

He pushed two blue vials at me. "Take these. We'll talk when your head's clear."

I stared towards the windows. A bleak white light came through them, which I belatedly recognized as the kind of light you only get reflecting from snow under clouded skies. Most of the Parkland had vanished beneath a thick coat of evergreen forest, itself coated with a powdery soft outline of white. The mountains reared and bulked no more than twenty klicks away from us, vast glaciers visible between their ridges.

The light and movement made pain shoot through my skull. I took the vials and bit them open meekly, lying with my eyes shut until they fast-tracked me to normality. He handed me the requisite two litres of water that the process required in plastic bottles and watched me drink it.

Halfway through I paused for breath. "You should be with Francine."

"I am with Francine," he said shortly and explained to me what he'd done.

My head fogged briefly with the activity of the decontamination agents and I had to rest. When it started to abate I said, "I've thought a lot about you and it, your story and . . . you shouldn't be doing this." I meant it too.

"Drink it all," he said and nudged me with his foot. He wouldn't listen until I'd finished. I put the cap back on the second bottle and threw it at him. He caught it.

"I mean it," I said sincerely. "You shouldn't do what it does.

No partials. No duplications. It will erode you. I know it. You know it. Everything will change. You most of all. That's just how it is."

"I can't leave you alone here."

"You can and you will. I've had it and Francine—I don't know—if you're right, she can't die."

He narrowed his eyes and flipped the bottle back at me. It hit me in the chest. "You're really not thinking this through from Theo's end of things, sweetheart."

"Maybe not. But I know that you should stop this now. What's the point of any of it, any of what you ever did, if you become Unity again?"

"I have to do something," he said. "He'll come the moment she's alone. Maybe for you too."

"Then you come back. You can come back instantly. Francine can tell you when."

"Where am I going?"

"To do whatever you have to do."

He rolled his eyes at me. "And you call yourself an intellectual. Is this some geek idea of a pep talk suited to persons of lower intelligence?"

"You have to keep making decisions. You have to. You. You're the only one. You could have passed this all on to Francine, you know, if you'd let her have all the power you have. I know that's what it means. You keep her from it."

"It's a stupid power," he said. "And anyone who wants it is a moron."

"Which is why you have to keep it." We shared a second of a grin. "You've had it so long. You won't . . ."

"Won't what?" he asked. "Use it for evil? Try to conquer the world? Bend everyone to my will? Cry 'Havoc' and let slip the dogs of war?"

"Well, no, frankly. I don't think you will. And you have to keep it from her because otherwise she'll know your guilty secret."

He looked at me a long, lonely time. "I liked it better when we fought."

"Me too."

He stood up.

"Where are you going?"

"To work on getting you the hell out of Unity."

"That's not possible."

"Tell it to Tinkerbell," he said wearily. "And look after Francie. If things go bad, I'll come for you."

"Don't be late." When he'd gone I lay back and closed my eyes. Under the fingers of my left hand I could feel rucks and troughs in the bedsheet. Their texture, warmth and feel spoke directly to my skin—they said the unpronounceable name of a demon.

So, the gods come through sound, but demons are tactile.

I fought to keep working whenever my mind tried to search itself for signs of occupation. I called in sick and stayed in the Palace. I had no faith that he could prevail over Unity, but if anyone was going to, it would be he. He was so very, very strange.

I went back to reading his file and wondered, for the first time, if I was all wrong about him. The more I read the less likely I thought it could be that Francine had simply made him up. If he was made up at all, he was made up by other people before she had a hand in it.

I called Damien. "Did you put Francine in Jalaeka's way? Did you know?"

"No," he said innocently. But he was lying of course.

"Damien, did you sacrifice us for something? Me and Francie? Tell me how it worked. Come on, we're already in for the course of the war. Tell me what you did . . ."

"It's not like that . . ." he said. "You understand now, don't you? It's the only chance of a way out."

I hung up on him.

36/FRANCINE

Did I ask for it? Did I? Did I? I don't know.

I'd been thinking this through since last night, when I couldn't think because Jalaeka was there and I felt like he'd know. He's been gone several hours now, on the second day since it happened. He promised to return—I only have to want him to. I didn't ask what he was going to do. I don't want to know.

I sat in the big chair, big enough for two, the spaces stuffed with comforter, and looked out at the Engine's workings. The mountains were larger and much closer. The Palace was in their foothills now. The garden, what was left of it, had become open moorland and stood bare to the stars. The new hills stared at me and had nothing to say, not a damn thing. The wolves had gone into Sankhara and east, to the zoo republic of Faraway, but Hyperion was still here, Greg said, somewhere, among the rocks and the gullies. I once went to Haworth on a school trip, to see where the Brontë sisters lived, and the land was like this. I saw the couch where Emily died. It was so small and—ordinary.

I couldn't hear anything, but I didn't believe Greg could be asleep. —To think that you are not yourself, that invisibly and undetectably something watches you, from the inside, and is consuming you with inexorable progress no matter how slowly . . . search and search and search again you can't find it or see it or feel it in any way, then you wonder—did I imagine it, am I hallucinating the entire thing? And your tongue feels too big for your mouth and your body scrunches in on itself, looking everywhere for the intruder, but it can't find something which is itself, so it must look for the traitors in its midst, those cells, those molecules that have gone over, those thoughts and impulses that are no longer truly its own. And there are none of those. It's all you. All of it. Even the fear and the doubt and you wonder. Did I ask for it?

Oh. I did. But here I am. Still exactly the same as ever. It wasn't what I wished for at all. Jalaeka refused me. He said, "You're perfect as you are. You don't need me. What you want you have to take. I can't give it to you. You have to become it. I can't help you. You can't be me, and if you were, you wouldn't be anything at all."

After Theo it was unbearable. The way Jalaeka was with me. It was unbearable. I made him do it. And so I'm guilty, as Theo's guilty. I used him.

I couldn't sit there another second. I ran to the door and into Greg's apartment.

He was hunched up in bed. "Francine? What's the matter? What time is it?" It looked to me like he might have been trying to conceal the fact he'd been crying.

"I was . . . wondering if you were all right."

He stared at me, then shook his head slightly. "Don't worry about me. Listen, I'm not good company. Why don't you go home and I'll see you in the morning?"

Oh god. This was such a bad idea and now he's cross and really wishing he was alone and I should go. Of course I should. I started to apologize but he interrupted me.

"No, no. I'm sorry. I'm not very . . . really I'll be better in the . . ." Greg was staring through me. I could see the depth of his exhaustion—his eyes were heavily shadowed and his face was lined and old-looking. Matted hair stuck to his forehead and he tried to stand straight self-consciously, without great success. "If you're frightened, you can stay until he gets back, but I have to rest."

"Okay."

He curled up with his hands pushed between his thighs and was still.

"What's wrong?" I said, barely able to see him. Only the glow from a single weak night-light gave me any shapes to see. Everything was blocks, open spaces a shade lighter than solid things. It was hard to witness him like this. He'd always been so competent and, ordinary.

"Nothing. I need to rest. I had a bad day."

I waited some more but he didn't speak again. I had to content myself with the fact he was still breathing, and went out into the living room.

He had two big sofas facing each other. One had a throw on the back of it that stood out, black on white. I pulled it off and took it into the bedroom and spread it over him. He didn't move, so I went back and lay on the other sofa with its back to the wall, but it was opposite the door and I didn't like that, so I went into the windowed room facing Verkhoyansk. Its windows had floor-length vertical blinds and curtains. Both were drawn shut. There was also a strange little corner made by one sofa and a low table with a beanbag and some cushions stored in it. I sat in the corner and put the beanbag in front of me with the cushions on top, except for one that I held in my arms and rested my head on.

I thought I could hear groaning, like trees being bent until they were at breaking point, but I might have imagined that. The weather was terrible.

I hadn't been there that long when I heard Greg get up. I saw the lights come on and all the colours sprang out, red and gold on the furniture, bronze and copper and really pretty things on the walls; a bigger than life-size portrait of a girl in a green dress, a Ming Dynasty vase standing tall on its own, a long recliner that faced the wall of crimson velvet that shut out the night. Greg shuffled about in the kitchen, which, like ours, was where a dressing room used to take up acres of space. I heard him run the taps, open cupboards, rustle packets. I thought he probably wanted to be alone still, so I stayed put but he came to the door in a minute and leant on the frame.

"Francine?"

"I'm here," I said and pushed the cushions away—now I could see they were really lovely ones, gypsy materials all stitched together in clever ways, covered in tapestry storybook pictures. I stood up and he tried to smile at me, looking regretful.

"D'you want tea?" He'd changed out of the wet clothes into

soft blue clothing he sometimes wore around the place when he had no plans to go out that day. I thought they were old yoga clothes but I couldn't imagine Greg doing yoga.

I nodded and climbed out of my hiding place. He waited until I was free and clear, then turned back to the kitchen.

He made tea in two big mugs and pushed one to me across the table. Walnut veneer. Don't spill anything. He pulled a slice of bread from a packet, spread a huge wodge of jam on it straight from the jar, rolled it into a sausage shape and put one end of the roll into his mouth. He pushed the whole lot—bread, jam, knife—towards me a few inches and I took my own slice and made a roll like he had. White bread. Raspberry jam.

After he'd eaten the first one he sat opposite me and we took turns making rolls. After the second one he looked up for the first time.

"So, how are you?"

"Been better," I admitted, halfway through a mouthful. "I suppose Jalaeka told you about Translating me."

He looked at me, then glanced down.

"Did he tell *you*?" he asked quietly. He licked jam off his fingers and went through the motions of prepping another slice.

I swallowed and watched him digging in the jar. He was angry. "I asked him to do it."

He paused, then carried on and carefully pushed the jam right out to the crusts on all sides before passing me the knife. As I took it he glanced up at me. "Do you think he's telling the truth?"

I straightened up the slice of bread I'd just taken, making its edge parallel with the edge of the work-top.

The world weighed a billion billion tons. Fortunately, the jam was beginning to kick in. "Yeah."

Greg had stopped chewing to listen. Now he started again. "Unless it's him too. Unless he is Unity. Did you think about that?"

I picked up the jam and tried to do it as neatly as he had. I gave him that slice.

"Thank you." He took it, held it and sighed. "Anyway, I realized this morning that I haven't got anyone I want to tell about what's happening to me." He worked on finishing that piece of bread, then drank the rest of his tea even though it was still extremely hot. "Except you and him but—you already know."

"Jalaeka's not like Theo."

"I noticed." He put the knife down on the jam lid. Looking at it he said, "I'm sorry, I wasn't here when . . ."

"Don't," I said quickly, putting my hand on his arm. "I'm fine."

"How can you be?" He looked up at me, his eyes filled with tears.

"Because," I said, "I am." I willed him to understand. Of course that didn't work.

"Yeah, me too." He swallowed nervously and brushed his eyes with the sleeve of his sweater. "Do you trust him? Really?"

"Yes."

"What about Damien?"

"Yes."

"He put you two together. He knew about Jalaeka, from before. Like Hyperion. Doesn't that bother you?"

The food in my mouth got stuck there. I couldn't answer.

He stood up and rubbed his arms through the sweater. "I'll never sleep now. Want to watch TV?"

37/Valkyrie

There was nothing to find in Dr. Saxton's office, and his colleagues variously expressed concern, shock and disappointment when he didn't return to the department, although Valkyrie wasn't surprised. She completed her searches of the faculty laboratories and her interviews and returned to the Aerials with a full report of very little. Confident that her assessment of his infection as accidental must be correct, she conferred briefly with Belshazzar.

"I don't like it," the Hive Queen said. "Why should it happen to him when he's out here in nowhere with this splinter?"

"Why not?" she countered. "He's been in that hot spot a long time."

"It smells all wrong."

Valkyrie didn't like it either. She went to see Saxton's ex, Katy, but she was busy, as everyone seemed to be packing in a great hurry. Many of the humans had decided to leave Sankhara for good after the quarantine order.

"He's probably at work," Katy said defensively. "Have you tried there?"

"Mn," Valkyrie said. "And do you know where his friends are?"

"Francine? Are you looking for her?"

"Not exactly," Valkyrie said. She didn't like the woman's resentful air and added, "I'm not with Immigration. I don't care who's here."

"Is she in trouble? It's about the other night, isn't it?"

"I couldn't say."

"Then, if you'll excuse me."

Valkyrie returned to the Palace. In frustration she set out towards the forest herself, following what she thought looked like new footprints in the snowfall that had blanketed the garden and the land beyond in the last forty-eight hours. Footprints went east and soon left the garden through a gap in one of its rough beech hedges a half mile from the house. They crossed rolling ground and took her into the disorienting uniformity of the taiga.

The morning's clear skies became the noon's darkening clouds. The snow, so crisp and frost-skimmed, became soft. She came over a small summit after trailing along a log-strewn irrigation gully and saw a clearing where bad ground had given no purchase for trees. There stood Greg Saxton, in a long coat, shivering, talking closely with the ugly, warped figure of her peculiar Forge-brother, Hyperion.

Valkyrie hid quickly. She didn't feel the cold at these temperatures and the snow was nothing to her. She lay flat in it at full length, most of her body down in the gully. Fortunately, the sun had not been out to flash off her armour. Now she let her metal skin take on the white, grey and brown of the things beside her and vanished into the land. Adjusting her sensory pickup, she listened to their conversation.

". . . Metropolis by another 'Jack. Gone now," Hyperion said, via radio.

"Belshazzar doesn't know about you, then?"

"It's a fair assumption." Hyperion's long jackal ears twitched and he glanced Valkyrie's way. "But like many of those, possibly quite wrong."

Saxton sighed heavily and Valkyrie saw he was holding his Abacand, recording their conversation. The Cylenchar didn't seem to mind.

"And these changes out here," Saxton said. "You've seen them?"

"It was summer a couple of months ago. You were here. Now it's winter. The mountains are a hundred kilometres closer and half as tall again as they were. The forest creeps on the house day by day but the land grows bigger and the city more distant. The wolves are perhaps werewolves, or another thing. Other beasts walk here sometimes, but they're all alone."

"And how did you know about him?"

"Who?"

"Jalaeka."

"I don't know about him. I came here to follow the god."

"So you keep saying. But you mean him." Saxton's frustration showed in his voice. The Cylenchar began to pace off, away from the Palace.

"I know what I mean," he said and shook drops of water off his coat. He lifted his beaky snout and sniffed the wind. "More snow on the way. Time you went."

"Come on! You've got to tell me more than that!" Saxton shouted after him, his voice muffled quickly to silence by the snow. He ran after Hyperion, stumbling on the uneven ground. "No way are you just here for the *darshan*. You've got a whole other thing going on!"

"Your faith is your own problem," Hyperion said, pausing and turning his head. "I can't help you with that." He left the clearing and Saxton flung his Abacand away. After a time he walked to it and picked it up, cleared it off and put it back in his pocket. With his head low he picked up his own trail and began to retrace his steps.

Valkyrie knew he would notice her footprints. She stood up and made herself conspicuous again and pretended to have just arrived.

"Dr. Saxton?"

He jumped so much she felt sorry and almost apologized.

"Who are you?"

"Light Angel Valkyrie Skuld. Solar Intelligence." She sent her badge details to his Abacand and waited politely for him to be satisfied with them.

"What do you want?" He was cold. He shivered and walked faster as he came towards her. His face was grey and inward-looking, lips pale. "It must be good if you've come all the way out here. Normally you just seize all the AIs and make a run for it."

"I wondered if you might know anything about the Unity splinter."

"Depends why you want to know."

"Belshazzar asked me to verify some information." Valkyrie decided not to lie. She felt sorry for him. His eyes darted everywhere but at her face.

"Did she?"

"You haven't been answering her calls."

"No I haven't."

"I was sorry . . ."

He stopped and glared at her, then ducked under a branch

and climbed out of the gully between the trees, where she found it much harder to walk, breaking the old dry branches of the conifers across her chest and shoulders with every step.

His voice was sharp and he spoke in a staccato. "Spare me. Ask your wretched questions, then leave me alone. Or better yet, maybe you'll answer one of mine. Why did she lie in the Metropolis Report? To convince everyone that Sidebars were still a justifiable risk?"

"Yes," Valkyrie said, keeping up with him in an awkward shuffle. "Surely you must realize there's no possibility of an orderly evacuation if panic were to break out."

"And is that what you're doing? Evacuating all of Unity space? Do you suppose that Theo will notice? Or is this going to be passed off as a lot of holiday time?"

"It won't help anybody unless you answer my questions honestly," Valkyrie said, as calmly as she could. "You understand that. I understand your anger."

"Do you?" He stopped and stared up at her. "Then you understand that nothing you want or do in the human world makes any difference to either of them. You understand that, do you?" He was shivering. His coat had run low on power.

"Here," she said and reached for its charge tab.

He twitched it away from her. "Get lost. Tell Belshazzar I've defected."

"Defected?" Valkyrie pursued him through the wet, heavy snow, sinking into the soft, mushy ground underneath deeper than he did. "To what?"

He ignored her and marched on.

"Dr. Saxton," she called. "Wait. Please wait. Can't you at least tell me something about the *darshan*?"

"Ask the Cylenchar," he shouted at her, without looking back. "He knows all about it. Or weren't you in on that moment?"

Valkyrie stood in her tracks and let him go.

She found Hyperion sitting on the summit of a hilltop deep in the woods, where there was a small clearing. The sky had become completely grey, pale and uniform. It was almost warm to her as it began to snow. The forest crackled with sound; the slide of ice, of dripping water, of branch and twig moving.

"Hello, Valkyrie," Hyperion said, not moving from his seated-dog position, half-hidden in the soggy snow, his Tek alight with activity she could almost read like semaphore on his skin. He flicked his black ears to rid them of the small flakes of ice as they fell.

"Saxton told me that you were the expert on the god," she said.

"You'll have to do better than that," he replied.

She locked her exoskeleton to rest in place and thought about it. "I looked it up. It's a grace. I don't even know what that means. And a Cylenchar hasn't got any listing. I didn't know you existed. Unofficial Forged. I should report you immediately."

The Cylenchar turned his goat eyes on her. "Yes. Your duty calls for it. But you don't do it. And when you know why, then you and I can talk."

Valkyrie shrugged. "I know my mind isn't made up. Tupac wouldn't protect you for nothing. The Earth Unevolved don't understand the Forged, what it's like, what we are. Most of the time that's neither here nor there. Today it's here. We're closer to Unity than . . ."

"No," Hyperion said, breath steaming from his long, near-lipless mouth. "We aren't."

"Then help me understand what you know."

The Cylenchar stared straight ahead, at the woods. "Earth and bone, leaf, stone, dry wood and ebony, charcoal and the first fall of autumn. Do you understand that? Spring green. Is it chemical? Is that its meaning? Saxton looks for a thing he can believe in, meaning that he can understand as he wants to understand himself and all his stories, as things which fit in a greater pattern, *the* great pattern. He looks for light and form. Not you though. You're not interested. What does interest you? Who are you looking for?"

"Nobody," she said, as annoyed as Saxton had been with the answers she was getting. "But if I give you something, will you drop the mystic shit?"

Hyperion inclined his head towards her and she saw the gryphon again in her mind's eye. He was hard to insult, if nothing else.

"My partner," she began, thinking she'd say something that wasn't too hard, "died in service. It was an accident. She couldn't be saved. I took her to Uluru but she was damaged and now her memory is decaying there."

"Couldn't be saved?"

"I couldn't save her."

"That will do," Hyperion said to his trees. "He will give it for you. Ask."

"Ask what? Who are you talking about?"

"You wanted the *darshan*. You needed a reason. There it is. Ask him."

"I thought *you* had it."

"Me? I don't need that kind of thing. That's not what I'm for, Valkyrie Skuld, just as walking the greenwood is not what you're for."

"You're talking about the splinter." But from then on no matter what she said the Cylenchar sat still as stone and didn't answer, and eventually she left him there in the thickening downfall.

At home she sat in the growing darkness and listened to the music her landlady played—sentimental songs and ballads she would never buy herself. She drank hot, weak tea and looked through her memories of Elinor carefully, feeling distant from them in a new way.

She called Damien. When he arrived he was much calmer than she was used to, though he still batted her charms and the *gris-gris* playfully with his hand.

"What can I do for you?"

"I need to know more about the cathedral, this Stuffie religion. How the Salmagundi Cylenchar fits into it."

"It's not a religion. It's a faith. All personal. I won't talk to you about it, none of us will. And the Cylenchar is nothing to it. He's one of you, no offence."

"None taken." She offered him five hundred credits and a cup of peppermint tea. "Are we at war then?"

He sighed and sat down. His green eyes moved all around as he thought, then settled on hers. "We are at war. Not with you though."

"With the Unity splinter."

"No. With Theo."

"I thought he *was* you. Your voice. Your leader."

"Many people make that mistake. So does he. The problem is that, once you're alive, here, you separate out. Everyone has their own ideas. Even him. Most of us don't want to return to Unity any more than you would. Even if it's a totally pointless distinction, we want autonomy. You can understand that?"

Valkyrie did. "But you haven't got any power."

"Everything leaks." He reached up with a long arm and flicked her *gris-gris* again. A drop of red, filthy water fell from it onto his fingers and he wiped them on her bedroll. "Or hadn't you noticed?"

38/JALAEKA

Francine was sitting at her desk, watching her Abacand spill a light show of twenty-second-century politics. "I'm going to try and catch up on this. I have an exam in three weeks' time."

She was worrying the hell out of me. Her show of normality, strong and defiant as it was, sat so out of place with what had happened to her, and to us—but at the same time, I needed her to be functional, because I had a lot to do. I was so tempted to take her at face value. The *darshan* and the Translation had taken the edge off it. But as Francine, she had a capacity to submerge emotional traumas I could only liken to my own. I shouldn't wonder at that, most likely, and I didn't like speculating on the reasons why.

"How's Greg?" she asked.

"He's narc-ed out of his head. Been arguing with Damien and Hyperion."

"How's Damien?"

"The usual. In trouble. Said he'd come see you later."

She pretended an enormous absorption in the machinations of early Forged Rights legislation. "You said you had to go out."

"I do."

"Well, I can call you," she said absently and leant more closely towards her arguing politicians. I might as well have not been there.

I looked in on Greg. He was asleep again. His apartment was a pigsty and the bed was a mess as he thrashed restlessly, held in oblivion by the unreliable grip of the strong benzodiazepines he'd taken, their pack open on the table—a man after my own heart. He wouldn't have woken if the building had collapsed.

I kept thinking about Patrick Black and the way the sun used to shine in on his hardwood floors in summer, leaving pools of intense heat where I'd sleep late and he'd find me and ask me what I was doing there, instead of being in bed or at the Uni or wherever I should have been instead.

Out in the hall Hyperion had left a tangled, lethal mess of carpet and splintered floorboards—a kind of nest. There was a strong smell like garlic too—Ajosacha, a shamanic plant used to aid hunting. His tracks led downstairs, then, in the snow, they led directly towards the distant forest. I walked along the path to the gate, dragging my feet, deep in thought.

Tonight I would still have to simulate Patrick Black, but that was only an act, not a complete transformation. I kept listening, always listening to the mesmerizing shifts of Francie, closer to me than my heart, farther away than a star. But it was painful. She'd discontinued her lesson the moment I left and was reading herself into an exhausted sleep.

My mind was continually visited by old memories, because she could see them, could live them. I seeped tatty history and felt shame.

39/Francine

In spite of the fact that Greg had explicitly warned me against it, perhaps because of that fact, I waited until Jalaeka had gone, then shut down the Abacand projection and lay down at the fireside. I looked into the flames and let my mind drift, waiting for memory as if it was mine, feeling sneaky and cheating and so very good in giving in to the compulsion. I'd stolen a few lines out of Greg's file when he wasn't looking . . .

The last time a lover of mine got punished for my sake I lay on my back in the sun and smoked so much dope that I virtually blinded myself: a huge line across the centre of my vision went completely black for hours, although it took away the pain in my arms where multiple broken bones were trying to put themselves together.

It was a long time ago and remembering it now is peculiar, like watching a film of someone else's life, and wondering what the director was thinking, and who the hell would be taken in like the poor sap you're supposed to identify with.

Two days after I tripped off the face of the planet and wrecked my sight the sunburned line was still a violet slash across the world. It cut the guard's hawk-face in half as he slid back the gate of the spy-hole, then pulled the door back in a silent sweep. I barely registered him.

*   *   *

Now I searched for that memory, to finish it and find out what had happened. Like the previous time, it was more than a human recollection. It seemed perfectly real. I was him.

Kya was standing at the ornate mahogany table, set between two of the huge windows that gave a view onto the garden and across the measured architecture of the city of Koker Ai towards the river, where her dhows ferried cargo day and night from the mightier ships moored fifty leagues down the delta.

She made me wait in the doorway as she decanted wine and water in equal parts into two drinking bowls. Scented evergreen woods burned in the embrace of the iron grate. In the window ranks of cut crystal threw minute beams of light, freckling the rich carpets and disturbing their geometric red and blue patterns. They cast changing colour over a large game board set out ready for play. The jewelled eyes of the pieces glittered in the firelight. It was such an array of low-rate calculated shit it made me feel ill.

As Kya turned I let the violet line in my eyes jag and sever her lips. They moved together like two halves of a spaded snake.

"Jalaeka," she said and indicated that I should sit on the couch by the board. She stirred the wine/water mixture with a tiny silver paddle and brought both bowls with her, offering me one. I set it aside. I didn't want to lose my composure and try to kill her before I'd said what I meant to say. Her manners had the desired effect however, and that ideal started to slither off of its own accord.

"Will you play?" she asked.

I glanced over the board. I needed the distraction. My arms hurt in spite of the dope. It was nothing to yesterday, or the day before, but anyway, I couldn't concentrate. I picked up an Assassin piece, staring at the moves. I made myself look her in the face. The love I once thought I felt for her made me hate myself beyond bearing.

"Did you get your money?" I said.

"My money?"

I set the figure down on the first available spot. "The gold you sent me. You know. The pay."

"It's still yours, if you change your mind. I covered my expenses." Her fingers closed around the shapely curves of a Courtesan. She glanced up at me through colourless lashes in mimicry of that obvious look that women give men when they're acting out the come-on. "Refusing the pay doesn't mean you didn't do the job." She put the piece down carefully within reach of one of my Judges.

Was she right? I couldn't put my thoughts together about what it was I'd done at her demand, I only remembered what happened after—the breaking of my arms—and before that a foot kicking a stool, its legs scraping stone with a shrieking sound. No, I could have remembered it. I forbade myself to. "What do you want?"

Kya lifted her bowl to her mouth and drank a sip or two. I watched the gentle convulsions of her throat, saw my hands around it, squeezing, closing until my thumbs pressed through flesh to the column of her spine. She took my Serf, and a Knight.

"You know," she said, "that nobody else matters in the world to me but you. All you have to do is obey, but you don't. I can protect you from this, give you all the space in the world to live out your romantic delusions with Intana, or whoever else you find weak enough to tolerate. One more job. That's all. One submission. But . . ." She shrugged.

I moved a Senator randomly. She knocked it over with a Pirate.

"You can't do that," I said, knowing she was only illustrating her point, but focusing on the wrong thing as usual, and not only because of the drugs. I slurred, "It's an illegal move."

"It's my board." The piece was still in her hand as she set it down, pressing it into the square.

"Then there's no point in playing you anymore," I said, mostly to myself. I got it. My arms and my once-broken back and my scarred side and my ruined friendships—oh, I got it.

"Quite." Her voice was a monotone. It was a chilling, inhuman sound, but the contours of her mouth lent the consonants a lovely delicacy. I found myself wanting to kiss it and vaguely realized it was the imposition of her wishes coming into play against me, but

I still had no idea how to counter those. I no longer knew what I thought.

She let me go and moved her Gladiator out of the way. In his path stood only the soft face of a Minstrel, its cheeks puffed round with unspoken messages.

"What do I do?" I asked her.

"Here." She picked up both Queen pieces and set them opposite one another. "I am separated. I wish to stay that way. This splinter of me, the other Kya, is nothing but Desire. You will find and bring her here, and when you do and she is my prisoner, safely locked away where she can't threaten me, then you can go."

I had to stare at the board and not at her. Her size was a product of distillation, not of volume. One drop of her was worth ten of me. I got up. I had to get away somewhere nobody was, so I could think, so I could feel. I wanted Intana but I couldn't go there, didn't know what to say or do to fix what I'd done before my arms were broken. I had to fix it. If I tried very hard, I couldn't even remember what it was, the very bad thing.

"Don't you wish to finish the game?" Kya asked.

"Sure," I said. "I'll finish it."

I walked out the door and never went back. I left Intana there, completing the total betrayal I had started days before. I had no idea what else I could do except run, until I found some way of freeing myself from other people.

I wondered what the thing was that he did not want to remember. It bothered me a lot. The brutality hidden in it must be very big, considering that he'd had no problem revealing the extreme violence of his "death."

I couldn't imagine him doing anything unpleasant to anyone. He wasn't like that. I knew this was a ridiculous thing to think about most people, all of whom were capable of unlimited violence given the right conditions, even me, but he wasn't even human, and one of the ways he was least like us was this way.

I knew he was going out to see her, the partial. Rita. I envied her. For the first time in my life I knew what it meant to be green with jealousy. I was so disappointed with myself.

The fire had almost burned out but I dare not go looking for any more wood, not in the Foundation's apartments. I thought I might go see if Greg had any, but then I felt a fool for being weak. I ought to stay here and trust Jalaeka and believe that if I shouted out his name in my mind, he'd hear me. I supposed we should have tested that.

Outside the wind drove snow at the south side of the house, covering the windows so that there was no way to see out. It rattled the guttering and every so often a slump and rumble of snow would shift over the roof and in the attics something whispered.

I put on my old clothes, the ones I'd come to Sankhara in, plus the superlight winter gear J had bought me, and curled up beside the embers to wait. How stupid it is that women have spent so much time helplessly waiting, I thought, but here I was, in its ordinary, relentless horror.

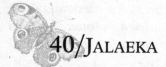

40/Jalaeka

I went to Rita's apartment in the Aelf as I'd promised her. She wore black and was immaculately groomed. The coat was nowhere to be seen, and neither was Theo. In her intricate sevenshadow I could see only the most remote traces of him. He must be busy at some other task. I was willing to bet I knew exactly where it would find its expression—round at mine— which is why I had decided, against my better judgement, that I should come here while he was distracted.

"Why did you put that tub of plants there? They ruin the view," I asked her, for something to say as she brought me a drink.

"I don't know," she said. "Some designer did it for me. Will you help me move it?"

"Sure." Such a gentleman, Patrick Black.

Francine did not call, not then. I stayed with Rita for two hours. We did not spend much time talking.

Afterwards I found that I couldn't go straight back. I had to get free of my old friend's skin, his kindness, his forgiving ways—that's what I told myself anyway, though another part of me stared on and said it was simple guilt working, because I knew damn well that Francine was hurt by what I was doing, in spite of herself. And I missed Patrick now, I missed him and the days of our lives when nothing happened.

You kid yourself that you don't know, part of my mind said to me, contemptuously. *You always know what you're doing, you just don't want to admit it.*

I went to the club. I avoided the dressing rooms and the friends I had there and found myself in the bathrooms on the fourth level, next to *the Library.* People gave me some really odd looks. At the first sink a group of three young men stood around, all shooting up with intravenous heroin doses, doing risky doubles. They stared at me, not in a good way.

I looked at my face in the mirror. The problem was clear. I'd become Patrick Black. Well, I was oscillating between his outer appearance and my own.

I shifted back to Francine-me and made it stick. I felt old.

"Fuck!" said one of the guys who was watching me. "What are you wearing, like, Tekskin? I didn't know they made it that good."

"They don't." I glanced at him and saw an Unevolved tourist who wasn't as young as he seemed, this adventure in Sankhara one of many he'd taken almost like a college course in living, without particular joy or anticipation. "Take it easy with that stuff."

He was about to give me a mouthful for my patronizing remark, the syringe in his hand ready to go, but I apologized. I touched him on the arm, where he was about to inject and felt a flicker of Angel's charge cross between us. "Want to come with me?"

"Yeah," he said, after a moment's struggle with his doubts. I could see him thinking he might as well, even if I was crazy, because nothing was interesting him much otherwise. "Here." He gave the syringe to his friend. "Save that."

"Oh trust him to score when he's scoring," said the other friend, already high.

We went to the first private room off *Rush,* where, as an employee, I could get as many drugs as I wanted out of the security box for free. He was nervous and I was desperate. I pushed him around too much getting his clothes undone.

"Hey, I like it gentle," he protested. "You should have gone to a deeper zone. I didn't know you were into that."

"I'm not." I stopped myself and put my hands on either side of his face. "I'm not."

"Sure," he said uneasily. I'd torn his shirt.

"Here." I kissed him, very gently, mouth open. He tasted of alcohol and he was slick in returning tricks, in spite of his protests of innocence. I thought it was a style he wore in the hope that it might fit him one day. I did the god thing, the *darshan,* and held him in my arms and fed on the expression on his face. I drew him closer to me, watching the mysterious light open up whatever lost dream was in his head. I wanted to know what it was like.

"Oh my god. Oh my god," he said over and over. He half laughed, half cried out and kissed me, lifting me up, pulling me onward, close to a place deep inside which I could almost, almost touch.

He made it. I didn't. I know it's not for me. It's of me. I know that.

I held my newborn addict's sweat-slicked body against mine and waited for him to recover. His skin had become luminous, taking on that genuine quality that Francine's had without trying. His whole nervous system was remaking things, undoing things, doing things. Somewhere in *there* is the answer to my problem, I was thinking: help without burdens, hope without despair, love without condition or limit.

As I watched him coming round I recognized myself in his glazed, delighted expression. I felt like the real thing.

After him I found another one. And another one after that.

"Hey."

It was long past midnight: Engine Time. Someone pulled me round by my arm.

It was dark on the dance-floor. The men where I was didn't wear much, mostly their Tektattoos and their enhanced musculature, their perfect skins, their moves. This hand was big, cool and heavy. I found myself looking at a polished bronze cuirass two inches from my nose. It wasn't like the metal I remembered from Koker Ai. It was Tek, and it shifted with the breathing of the person whose skin it was.

She'd stripped down to the minimum allowed for a Valkyrie—no weapons and no helm, but she was still a giant compared to most of the people in the club and they backed off from her as they tried not to look like they cared. She had thick blond hair bound round her head in braids like rope and her face had that strong, classical look with a perfect Alexandrian nose. Red marks showed where her helm fitted close to the skin—like slaps or burns.

I recognized her immediately. "What?"

"I need to talk to you," she said. "Not here."

"No literary questions." I removed myself from her grip and she looked confused because she hadn't let go. It was a bit of a mistake on my part. I staggered and almost fell.

"What's wrong with you?" she hollered above the music's tribal thump.

"Nothing," I said. "What's wrong with you?"

Out of nowhere Damien pushed in between us. He yelled in my ear, "You're pulling a train. Self-destruction loco style, you idiot! Don't self-destruct now, just when it's all going so marvellously well." He dragged me to the door. The Valkyrie followed with ponderous precision.

"What are you talking about?" I let him direct me to a quieter place in *Chocolate Floral*. It was peculiarly difficult to walk straight. I couldn't make the floor be still.

Damien whacked me across the face with a head-rocking slap. "This won't make it stop hurting, you know."

I growled at him and he let go quickly. "No, that's not the point. It has to hurt, just like it has to feel good, or you die inside. I have to keep the connections open, wide as they can be, or I can't do it at all."

The Valkyrie looked at me with a fixated, strange expression. "The *darshan*?" she asked.

"No. The other thing," I said, but she didn't know I meant Translating Francie. Damien did. He nodded grimly at me and pushed me out to the door and then into the street.

"I'm trying to help you," he whispered to me, his hands on me cold and kind. He looked hurt. "I think she might take you somewhere useful. The Metatron."

I avoided the Solar AIs. I didn't like AI in general but something in Damien's face prompted me to think that he had some clue what he was talking about.

He gave me a hopeful smile. His desperation made me taste my own. I thought of the Valkyrie's sadness. I nodded. Okay.

Outside the Valkyrie waited for my attention in a stoic position, legs wide, helm in hands. The night air was cool and the streets were busy. I could hear Engine Sirens not far away and the creak of earth being put under pressure. Trams rolled past over the little earthquakes, their bells jangling. Music played from several doorways. There was a peculiar party atmosphere to the place, as if Engine Festival had come early. I couldn't be bothered with walking or public transport systems. I felt claustrophobic.

"Do you know the Triptrap Bridge?" I asked her and didn't wait for an answer.

But the Engine had been very busy. It had erased the illusion of Crisscross Street continuing beyond the bridge and pushed the Hinterland right out, pressing Hoolerton almost into Central Sankha. Where the Moorlands tower blocks had leered at one another, the churn and grind of old, dead machinery and its ghosts ran right to the sea's edge. Where there had been the old European neighbourhoods of the Wundershön and the Triptrap Bridge across the Purbright, there was now a span of solid frost like a new bone joining them to Anadyr Park—the bridge seeming to vanish in midair where it crossed the border. The river, like the Tact at Aelf, was redirected underground in vaults of brickwork and stone.

I waited for the Valkyrie on the frost bridge where it arched at its highest and looked towards the beachfront where we used to skim. There among the tacky shop-fronts and tackier hotels lay the unmarked doorway that was the entrance to Engine House. As my boots froze to the ice I wondered if it was possible to use the Engine on myself.

Neither Theo nor I was gifted with insight into everything Stuff made. It was possible that the Engine was as mysterious, as experimental, as inconclusive in its nature as he or I. It may not work for me, but it may not work for him. It was made by a team of human speculative engineers, one of the last Sidebar Engines to be cast and one in which it was likely Theo had had very little if any interest. If it could rebuild worlds overnight, surf millions of minds, shift matter into mind and back again, maybe I could get it to rebuild me. The only thing I needed was an engineer and I knew whom I'd choose.

A rush of cold, ice-strewn air suddenly surrounded me. I looked up and saw the flare of blue jet fire. There was a smell of kerosene as the Valkyrie landed beside me on the filament of frozen air. The bridge creaked and groaned with our weight.

She was mercifully direct. "Are you able to cross into Uluru?"

Her breath misted in the bridge's frigid atmosphere and instantly fell between us in a shower of ice.

I had never tried it. Sankhara was enough virtuality for me. "Probably."

"Will you come and take the *darshan* to my friend?" She looked exhausted and driven. I thought of Francine. The changes of Sankhara under the Engine had only just finished. I could hear the wolves of Anadyr even from here, and other cries and calls, farther from human than theirs. Then they were drowned in the wailing sirens of the emergency vehicles racing to the areas of greatest disturbance: the night's casualties at Anadyr's newly massive frontier.

I could hear the Valkyrie's body shrinking in the cold.

I listened to Francine, to Francine, sleeping alongside Greg on the sofa.

"Show me the way," I said.

She wanted to take me to some temple across the city but I took hold of her metal hand and drew the gauntlet off it. Her hand was larger than mine, but on the palm the Tek and the lines of her skin ran together, almost like one, and I could fit mine against it. I let my hand become like hers. Where we touched I could run up through her arm. She felt me do it and tried to jerk her hand back automatically but I held on to it and this time I was stronger.

Emotionally she was in a similar state to me. We regarded one another with some surprise and in that moment our sympathy formed. She understood the rest intuitively and simply tuned herself in to Uluru through its coded transmission bands.

I rode with her and found myself in another park with a warm sun overhead and blue skies. Beside me she held my hand, suddenly over a foot shorter than I was, her ragged fairy costume tickling my legs. We stood beside a half-buried silver aeroplane. She stared up at me, her mouth half-open.

"You didn't change," she said.

"Should I have?" I said, looking down at myself, wondering what she meant.

"People here are . . . what they want. Not what they really are."

"You mean who they really are and not what they actually look like. Show me your friend," I said.

"I have to ask the AIs to let you in there." She rubbed the wing of the plane with her free hand and shyly detached her other hand from mine. "You don't need to touch me now."

The figure of a seraph took shape in the shine on the metal and stepped out of it to stand with us on the grass. He had a sword of fire and red, fire hair. His eyes were blue flames burning inside their sockets. He looked at me for one long second and turned to Valkyrie.

"You never cease to surprise," he said. Then he held out his hand to me. "I am Metatron, the voice of the Hosts, Mode and Myanfactor. You are an unknown process to us. Will you identify?"

"No," I said. "I'm with her."

Metatron bristled. Clearly he wasn't used to getting many "No" answers.

"Take us to Elinor," the Valkyrie said, a note of desperation in her voice.

"We don't recognize this system." He looked at me. "It cannot enter there."

"You don't understand," she said. "Nothing bad will happen. It's for Elinor. To let her go."

"Let her go?" the avatar repeated. "Are you requesting deletion?"

Valkyrie looked down. Her fists were clenched. She whispered her reply and I only just caught it because I was running on her circuits. "I cannot afford to maintain her and she's locked in such a bad pattern. And anyway there's barely anything . . ." But she didn't finish.

"Let's go," I said to him. "You know I'm governed by her access rights. It's in the rule-book. I'm not trying to datamine you. No hostility."

Metatron looked at me with dislike and annoyance but he

had to give way—Valkyrie knew it and so I knew it. She had paid in advance and he was bound by his debt. A human wouldn't have had to give in to such compulsion, but he was no human.

We stood in a white place, without temperature, without depth. During the momentary transfer time Metatron tried to read me, and I let him do it enough to see that I was not an AI, or a human either. His interest made his eyes blaze so that they consumed his entire face.

"I believe you must be Francine Annelise Bequerel's alien system. If you wish to speak later, I am sure we can make some trade," he said.

"Sure," I said and felt Valkyrie's small fingers close gently around mine.

"Go away Metatron," she said. "Give me my time."

"The code is fragile," he said. "To see her is to rewrite her. To rewrite is to destroy. A few more moments is all you have left, before the corruption is fatal."

I thought it all sounded depressingly familiar. If there'd been a bulletin board for us to talk about it upon I might have swapped notes on the impossibility of life-capture. As it was Valkyrie held my hand as Metatron vanished, and we waited together in the empty space. She could not bring herself to speak of her friend and so she told me the facts by direct data transfer, one electron gate to another; machine telepathy.

Elinor had been a Light Angel, Valkyrie's partner. She had been killed in a power station explosion during one of the sporadic terrorist attacks by the so-called Galactic Forged Independence Fighters. The only thing left to save of her were the last few seconds of her life. But the laws of entropy applied to all kinds of copying. The nature of Uluru meant that Elinor's life here as pure code was determined by the error rates imposed on Mode and Myanfactor by their billions of clients and the inherent instability of the Uluru structure itself.

One thing about Uluru I had never much considered before was how seldom it experienced serious wipeouts. It also managed large numbers of individuals and characters that it generated spontaneously with relatively few losses.

Meanwhile, Elinor's remains had been delivered.

"I don't know if I can do this," I said uneasily. So little of her existed that the system had not been able to construct a visual form for her yet. It was struggling to locate enough information.

"Please." Skuld's grip on my hand became painful. I felt her grief run through me.

"Now?" I couldn't find anything that even reminded me of a person, only scraps, the equivalent of a few phrases taken at random from an entire book.

"In a moment," Metatron said to us both.

Then there was a shadow, a 2-dimensional grey shape, like a woman made of smoke. Here and there it crystallized into clear form: a hand, a piece of armour, a wing-tip, but then it fell to nothing.

"I stayed too long last time!" Skuld suddenly cried out. "She's gone! Try now. Please. She has to be here."

"There's no one," I said truthfully. The *darshan* required a completely operational consciousness. It had nowhere to go.

"You!" She spun around, clinging to my arm, pulling me forward. "You must be able to find her. Damien told me what you could do. Send her home before she's gone. She was lost here. She didn't know who she was. You have to find her! She could be lost in the system. Please."

The situation was everything I feared of Unity. Every last detail, except that it wasn't happening to me.

"I don't know how," I said. It was the truth. I couldn't jump directly into the AI and go ferreting around in its nodes, but then, even as I thought it, I wondered if I could. I touched the peculiar sharpness of the photon flow and learned the way it carried information.

"Metatron," I called and the avatar appeared. We did a deal. It was, as Greg would have said, a hopelessly misguided, wayward and dangerous idea, bereft of intellectual muscle and lacking even the faintest smidgen of forethought, or, as Hyperion called it, serendipity.

"Copy me."

He cast his sword aside and its fire went out on the vanished ground.

He reached out to touch me. Then he was gone and I faced myself, my blue-fire–eyed self.

Valkyrie shrieked and put her hands over her face. "This is bad! I didn't mean that!"

"It's not so bad," I said from Metatron's temporarily borrowed space, looking back at her and my Uluru avatar. Until I looked at it I didn't realize how truly awful a state I was in, but it didn't matter much now.

I found the vanished and fragmented pieces of Elinor, using Metatron's hands. He watched me in fascination as I hunted by feeling my way through the bits, the way he could not. I put them together using his skills, but her fragments were deteriorating by the instant. The best I could do was trap the pieces inside a holosphere which created the illusion that she was whole. I held it in my Metatron hands and we all looked into its snow-globe and saw against the moon, the outline of a woman flying, her wings broader than the white disk.

"Now," said Valkyrie.

But there was no reaching whatever Elinor had been as a person. All that was left of her was the vanishing image, a metaphor, and that was gone in a moment.

I so wanted to be kind to Skuld, and to the AI, for granting me access to all its incredible powers of memory, management and replication. The *darshan* left me like a reverse gunshot, entirely phototropic. Metatron threw us out of Uluru a millisecond later. I had to trust that he would delete my copy in return for being able to mine out its information on Unity structure and mathematics. I promised him a bad day in hell if he didn't and trusted he would understand from what he learned that this was entirely possible.

*   *   *

We stood on the ice bridge, back in Sankhara. Skuld snatched her hand from mine, tearing the skin off my palm where we had frozen together. She held her own against her, as though it was the one damaged. Tears ran down her cheeks and became still before they were halfway to her chin. They formed icicles that shattered as she spoke.

"What have you done to me?"

Blood surged across my hand and wrist and fell onto the ground. I had no idea for an answer and tried to put the hand inside my coat to protect it. The burning pain of it was indescribable as it repaired itself, hampered by the cold.

"You changed Uluru. And me. I felt it. What?" she said and sat down, stunned, staring into nothing as a bitter wind whipped up around her. "*What* are you?"

I was holding so hard to my wrist I felt the bones grate together. "I'm going home."

"Wait!" She came after me as I turned to face Anadyr and the Palace, into the wind, hauling her feet off the bridge with two almighty power-assisted cracks. "Tell me what it means! What have you done to me?"

"Nothing." The Engine had quieted at last. We stood among the sounds of distant carnage and chaos from the wrecked neighbourhoods of southwestern Sankhara. "Time for you to go to work, surely?"

"But . . ." She wrestled with an objection and overcame it with a great effort, then said, from a clear sense of obligation, "Your friend Saxton. Listen. Solargov are into whatever is going on here more than you know. If they find out it was an alien piece of Stuff that caused Saxton's infection, they'll require me to terminate him. I'm certain of it."

"So, are you telling them that's what it is?" I could live without the complication of Solar interference.

She watched me, touched her breastplate and looked down at her gauntlet on the ground. A struggle of conscience twisted her features. "No."

"We're square then."

As I went home I held the knowledge I'd stolen from Mode and Myanfactor close to me, not even thinking about it because that seemed like too loud a thing to do. But I knew it. I knew how to rewrite people in my own image so that they were like me, but not necessarily of me, severed from Unity, free.

I needed a major diversion to make the attempt and as I crossed the frost bridge and glided down to the Palace, I knew it would have to be potentially catastrophic, both for Theo and for me—threats of significance to him couldn't come any other way.

41/THEO

Chayne fights me all the way. It's a vocation with her. I admire her tenacity. The Dancing Wu Li Masters have nothing on her for poise. Her emotions are controlled with adamantine will. They're a taste that won't go away: metal, blood, fire, strong as proof spirit because all her life she never let them out.

She picked up this addiction to self-denial when she was with Jalaeka. Before she met him her life was dedicated to the simple and rewarding prospect of his death. It was an old family thing: everyone murdered, vengeance required, lives of generations wasted in the subsequent vendetta, very much the old routine—but she ended up tagging around with him like a lost dog. Even she isn't sure exactly what happened. She thinks perhaps she didn't kill him because, well, what would have come after? She had had no idea. Of old it had been her plan to fulfil her obligations, then return with her sister to the land of their birth and die there, in peace with the blood on her hands. But the sister, a twin, died of plague on a sea voyage, and so that dream could not be made true when at last she had him at her mercy.

After they became a two-handed gang, she'd occasionally get her knives out and think about cutting out his heart. She was always restless. In the long nights without the moon she dreamed of kissing his lips as the blade went in. In the long cold winters of frozen mud, and the hot smothering summers of jungle heat, she watched him, and he let her watch him, and they became closer than brothers or sisters, closer than blood, closer than one bone and another in the same arm.

It's starting to dawn on me that I may have been mistaken in assuming that by taking what all these people know I could piece together the puzzle of why they do what they do and why they do it for him. But I can't, and they just *do*.

Still. Worth some entertainment if nothing else. Chayne's omerta runs so deep that she actually has no idea why she couldn't slaughter him on sight, even though a kid of ten could tell her.

I let Chayne go. She takes control, and as soon as she does the composite of memories that comprises her self changes. She lives. And behind her, a secondary mind, I inhabit.

Bodies change everything. Their senses, their limits, their chemistry determine experience. I've always detested their vile imperfection, their appalling limitations, the fact that I can be nauseated because of having appetites, every day a whirling manic rush from one desperate need to the next. I loathed them, even though my awareness was undiminished, my ability continuous. You can't become meat without having to maintain its catastrophic and repugnant biology. But there's no living without it.

I long for Unity: the endless flow of knowledge existing in an infinite present—something I don't remember, although I feel strongly that it must be supreme, a mighty state, the perfection of awareness. Although it has forgotten itself as it must because it has no form, no foursheet conscious span. Every life replicated by Stuff is a defiance of Stuff, a denial of Unity's unconscious sublime.

For now, however, here Chayne is: Jalaeka's unconsummated past, and she knows everything I know, including the perfection of Unity, and she wants both it and me dead, dead, dead with every beat of her heart.

She interprets my passengerhood as obscene voyeurism—a transgression only to be expected from the same demon race that consumed her family. (The splinter known as Kya ate them in actual fact, but I digress, and it doesn't make a difference.) No gratitude in Chayne for the fact that she wound up reunited *with* them, in Unity, closer and more intimate than any genetic line could ever be under the constraint of linear time. What arrogant egomania.

Chayne rejects such a notion of togetherness as contemptible and evil as soon as I suggest it. Curiously her sense of who she is remains so pervasive that even now she is able to tell the difference between thoughts that are my suggestion and impulses of her own. In a language not spoken for over a millennium she whispers to me,

"Every minute you let me live is a minute off your own life. Every second a mistake. You think you have the best of me with your power. You think you will win. As long as you let me live I will do anything I can to wreck your chances, Theodore. You're so stupid, you don't even know what you're trying to save or trying to destroy."

Coming from someone who only lived for forty-one years in a community with no more technology than a siege engine, it was an admirable speech. I could appreciate what Jalaeka used to see in her.

"You have no idea," Chayne assured me and bolted the door shut on her feelings in a futile effort to keep me out.

Meantime, I played back through her life experiences to

check, just in case she was talking about something concrete she'd managed to conceal, but I hadn't missed anything. This recall—which she was forced to undertake also, as a tourist—had such an effect on her she was unable to speak or move for several hours.

When she found herself again she only repeated her last statement with finality, then she looked around her.

We were in Central Sankhara, inside the changing room of a large clothes store in the Embargo, where I had been organizing the tedious requirements of clothing for her/me before I decided to let her have free rein.

She examined herself naked first of all, counting her scars, particularly the ones on her face, those heavy ridgelines of old ash beneath the skin. They described deep, down-pointed arrows over the bridge of her nose, curved over the smooth rounded dome of her forehead, around her brows and across her cheeks, surrounding her eyes with a mask. The power of this symbol kindled determination in her gut as she looked. She had other scars from old wounds too, on her legs and arms, back, feet, hands, neck and belly. Beneath them her muscles were hard, long and . . .

"Get out," she hissed to me through her teeth. "Get out, get out."

I receded into the background and she abruptly had had enough of seeing. She looked at the room and its lights and mirror, recognizing things by their function but not their methods or workings. I allowed knowledge of this current world to permeate upwards from Unity and she accepted it. She picked up the clothes and dressed, momentarily disturbed and alarmed by zippers, but soon over it, dismayed to find no weapons and no armour anywhere.

Then she hesitated and snorted—the closest sound she made to amusement. "So, you can build cities and level nations, but you don't make *clothes*?"

Actually, it hadn't occurred to me. This must be because I've spent too much time with Rita recently. Her obsession with apparel must have worn off on me, as she would never have passed up any opportunity to try new things or to shop.

As I was thinking this, Chayne was already over her discomfort. She swept aside the curtains, ducked under the lintel—even for this world she was phenomenally tall and lanky—and strode out.

She found the stairs, found the entrance to the roof, stood outside next to the aerials and domes of the telecommunications networks and the local Guide AI, admired the cityscape for a while, then calmly walked off the edge of the building.

I had no idea of her intention the entire time. It was a good lesson.

Her death on the pavement would have been nothing to me, but I recovered her a few metres into her fall and restored her to the rooftop before anyone noticed. She stood, angry, breathing hard, ready for death, then she laughed and shook her head. I thought we had the measure of each other.

Once we'd crossed into the Winter Palace bubble I was shocked. Suddenly the whole place was much bigger. Also, much colder. I checked the Engine stats and recoiled. Another few days at current rates of expansion and the foursheet leading edge would be moving at the speed of light in all directions. In terms of this fourspace and its companion ones, not to mention potentially all others in this region, that added up to an extinction event.

I calculated the times involved and saw that within two weeks all of Unity's dealings with the human world would be reduced to the purely theoretical. Effectively this new development had become my hourglass. What was not done by then, would not be done here.

But I had not commanded the Engine to do this. Was the thing out of control? It was not outside the bounds of possibility that some mad dreamer had wished an apocalypse and the Engine obliged, though such things were meant to be controlled by the Regulator, a memetic filter administered by the

Engine's sapient administrator, which destroyed all such impulses before they could reach the construction system. Had the thing malfunctioned . . . ?

It distracted me, like an unscratchable itch. That and him. Jalaeka was a kind of blind spot, something near-invisible and impossible to find unless he did some Seven-shifting, as I was invisible to him until I moved so.

Saxton was in, working feverishly, his Abacand plugged into academic and AI networks all over the place. I took a quick glance and thought I'd take him for a walk around before too long. Meanwhile I paused to admire the expansion of the great hall on the ground floor. The ceiling murals had abandoned their apocalypse chic of Michelangelo meets Vietnam. In their place a dead wolf hung above me in the freezing, desiccating air, an icicle of blood hanging from a deep slash in its neck. It was thirty feet up, hind paws held by the iron claw feet of an old bath. Its wounds were self-inflicted—the iron bath feet were hemmed in by a set of sickle blades, which it had clearly attempted to bite its way free of. It had human eyes.

I scuffed the frozen puddle of blood beneath it that covered the floor and it cracked under my foot, crisping into the carpet. No signs of Hyperion, that pointless, interfering creature.

I found a few other interesting things. The library windows looked out on a different winter on a different world—Earth: specifically Haworth moor as it rolled unevenly, relentlessly out towards what ought to be the ruin of a simple farm called Top Withens but which had been rebuilt in shameless adoration by the Yorkshire Heritage Board as Wuthering Heights. No such thing could happen without a reason. It seemed utterly incomprehensible.

I decided I would send Rita there, push her to Earth spacetime to find out why that should be of any significance. Who knew Jalaeka even read books?

The ballroom on the north side, which had once been the great crystal room, had a blazing fire in the fireplace and its doors at the far end opened on yet a greater room, even more opulent and expensively decorated with great plasterworked ceilings and skylights loaded with gold and lapis paint, and that in turn opened on another, and another—I didn't go past five.

The cellars beneath the kitchens were full of water, right up to the top of the steps, but it was clear water and I could see right to the bottom, four floors down, where the slimy brick-lined walls were supported on archways that led into total blackness.

The upper floors alone remained untouched, save for the evidence of hasty abandonment where the cult had fled the winter cold—hauling along as much sham-Russian trinketry and art as they could carry by the looks of it.

I stopped outside Saxton's apartment and actually considered knocking on the door but it seemed a bit after the fact considering our present level of intimacy. I walked straight in.

He jumped up when he saw me, though he had the presence of mind to cue some activity on his Abacand as he stood and stared at me in my new body. He shook a bit, but his self-control was admirable.

"Who the hell are you?"

"The last person you want to see."

His already-pale face went grey. "Oh yeah?" he managed to muster after a few seconds. He looked cold, even with his coat on. There was a fire, but its effects were weak.

"Yeah," I said. "You're the expert on this place. I was looking for your opinion. What's it like, living inside the emotional debris of this friend of yours? You don't look well. And I understand that soon you'll be trapped here permanently."

He folded his arms across his chest. If he could have backed away, he would have, but there was furniture in the way.

"Ah come on. I'll trade you," I suggested. "I can stop the Translation, put it on indefinite hold. You'll live like usual, die whenever. I'll even shut the gods up for you and put the demons back in their boxes. It'll be like they never happened. You give me a few pointers—how about it?"

"He's not going to give in to you," Saxton said.

"Is that right? But you could talk to him. He listens to you. Maybe he will. It must be worth a try," I suggested. "I think that Metropolis really upset him. Francine . . ."

"Don't you even say her name!" Saxton hissed at me suddenly. "Just fucking shut up about her."

"I can see why you're not in the diplomatic corps. But I think that you know how to get under his skin. And you can help me now, or we can both go next door and see how Francine is doing. She's a lovely little thing."

Chayne, able to hear but not act, poured scorn on me like acid.

"He'll be back any minute."

"No, I'm not sure of that. The more I think about what's happening to this place and the fact that you're here the more I think this is meant to occupy me while he goes to the Engine to see if he can work out how to protect Sol, maybe even to protect you."

Saxton flung his arms up. "What the fuck, it's all around you. If you want a tip, I think you should go and look out, way out, under the glacier. Or in the cellar. Or in the attic. Or you should watch the paintings on the staircase roof. There, will that do? Is that enough of a tip for you?"

"I saw those things. You've always had a good and sheltered life, Dr. Saxton. None of those things are very interesting to people from more savage eras, concerned with more savage business."

"Symbols aren't the thing themselves," Saxton whispered at my back.

I turned and walked out. Saxton followed me, saw me go to Francine's locked door.

"Leave her alone," he said. He forced himself to free his arms, as though he might attack me. He looked terrified, ridiculous.

"Go back inside," I said. "You've been most satisfactory."

"Please." He said it so quietly I barely heard him.

I waved him back. "I'm not going to do anything this time. I'm just going to say hi." I'd got him on the edge and he knew it and knew I knew it.

"Leave her alone," said a new voice with all the lilt of axe blades on grit.

I turned around and saw Hyperion standing at the head of the stairs. It had sneaked up very well, with a stealth I wasn't used to experiencing. It was covered in a mantle of cracked ice that scattered and broke from it with every move it made.

Chayne laughed at me so hard that some of the laugh came out of my mouth in a snorting choke of sound.

I bit this back and addressed the Forged. "All right. You can either butt out of it, like the rest of the human race, or you can become part of my army, but that's all there is. So whoever you are, make the choice."

"Your army?" it hissed through its reptile's mouth. Memories of Corvax—one of the first humans I ever encountered—came back. He was someone who was made for things other than the blueprint, one with the charm to make things differently, to look in new ways. I couldn't even tell what this creature was or what it was for.

It moved forward quickly, changing as it moved, becoming bipedal, tall, its hands full of sabres.

At that moment Francine opened her door. She looked around it, at me, at Greg, at the advance of the Forged beast and her face went the dead white of old paint.

Greg lunged forward and hit me in the side of the head. It was a good blow, hard, merciless on the knuckles of the deliverer, and painful to both of us. He shrieked in surprise and I staggered sideways, my eye on that side briefly sightless and sparking like a live wire.

The Forged sprang forward and scythed the fingers of one hand across my neck in a mortal effort I did nothing to deflect. Its yellow eyes burned with a righteous fire I found excessively objectionable.

I ate it and stood up, brushing at the blood on the front of my new parka. Inside Chayne was having a great time. She watched the Forged go past her, into Unity's all-loving embrace, and said to me, "That was a stupid mistake. You've been bombed."

For a split second her conviction made me wonder: aren't I human *enough*? Is there more to it than flesh and bone, and the motivations that fight one another tooth and claw until nobody can tell who means what? Can there be any more to them than the simple gallop for power and survival? Yet this bloody woman seems to think she knows something I don't know. As if that was possible. Well, fuck her.

I turned to Greg and gave him back his punch.

Chayne had a great arm. He went down without a sound and lay against the baseboard, snuffling red as he passed out.

That's what I always did too, Chayne said as I turned to Francine.

She held the door in a white-fingered death grip. Her legs shook and a cold sweat stood out on her forehead. Her blue eyes were ringed in the brown exhaustion of the sleepless and paranoid. As they stared at me and knew me for what I was they recognized Chayne, and her features set like stone.

42/RITA

The Brontë parsonage at Haworth was such a small building, so old. Its friend the church is scarcely bigger, it seems to me. Trees, which didn't exist in the photographs of the twentieth century, were massive among the tumbled graves and shaded out most of the light, even on winter days like this one. Foggy damp clung everywhere, misty and drenching. My Abacand enumerated the family trees of the dead, and they fogged and dimmed my mind with too many empty names.

Theo would have liked it, I thought, but he wasn't here in person, the asshole.

Inside the church I sat on a pew—not an original—and listened to an actor giving a reasonable rendition of Pastor Brontë's sermons. In the front row the actors playing along as the three sisters and brother Branwell sat bolt upright and picked at the covers of their hymnals. It was authentically chilly for a winter's Sunday, my Guide informed me, *sotto voce*. I observed the play with half my attention and with the rest watched the other tourists.

The Unevolved of Earth were all derelict. Everything left on the planet was a show, a copy or a pastime spun out, elaborated and grafted on. There was a hunger in the Unevolved, which wasn't made well by food or education or the absorption of knowledge. I felt it myself, even though I was nothing more than a figment of a few imaginations left to run inside a make-do body. Here in the church the hunger was sharp. It felt like touching a more real, more important lifetime, standing in a moment where unknown but great things were shifting underground. All the watching faces were eager with anticipation, even the bored ones who'd already toured this world to exhaustion.

A woman almost opposite me across the aisle reminded me of myself a few days ago when I was a shopgirl. Her folded hands, so neat across her designer Abacand, spoke of a voluntary restriction suited to this place, to nuns and renunciates of all orders who have made unhappy pacts with carnal situations. By her side a bigger, more raw woman, dressed completely asexually, occupied both her own place and half of the next one by simple and unconscious placement of herself. Her arm draped this way, her legs that, knees splayed out. Her boots, sturdy and functional, pointed in two directions. Her head lolled casually as she listened.

Behind them a young man restlessly shuffled on the hard wood, his intense gaze searching the woodwork and stone for some bigger schedule of god's works than met the eye—or so I imagined to suit myself. He was alone, but he didn't want to be.

He glanced at me for the third time, and I'd looked away like I looked away the other two times, too slowly.

In front of me a family of varied children and adults were getting up to go and find some more hospitable surroundings. Toys chirruped and squeaked as they were thrust into coats and bags.

"Excuse me," one child said softly as she accidentally placed her mittened hand over mine on the back of their pew, just in passing. She stared at me with uncertainty, and a disapproval she hadn't got from anywhere but her own good judgement. Admiration too. I was commanding, and she envied my power. Maybe she would end up wanting it one day, but for now she turned back to her mother and grasped that hand held out. I looked at the fingers closing on each other, small in large, trust and security absolute, and around my heart envy squeezed as tightly as a corset.

I followed them out of the church and along the path at a distance until they turned from the gate and into the street, heading downhill to the cafés and shops of the town. The stone cobbles were hard to walk on in heels. I returned to the parsonage on my all-day ticket, and reexamined the notebooks and glass-fronted cabinets with their sad collection of artefacts. Everything the three girls owned seemed so small and flat.

I looked out of the upper-floor windows and over the hills. I imagined what it was to want to live so much, and to be shut up here, stifled by the church and the father and means and circumstances and shortness of time and lack of health; all those limits and only the wild land around that looks as though it has freedom, but freedom hostile to human life. I didn't need to imagine very hard. I could see how this could lead to the sort of emotion that rises in their stories. With no other outlet than sublimation to another level what do you do? Brave girls.

I stood in what was left of Emily's room and touched her few things, rapidly, surreptitiously, drawing myself into continuity with her. *Come on, you and I, you and I, you and I . . .* I was lost in summoning when the curator appeared.

"You must not touch the exhibits!"

I put down the dusty thing that was Emily's bedcover. I could still feel its cold touch on my face and smell the linen and wool. Particles of it were inside my nose, and a giddy triumph seemed to have taken over my smiling face as I charmed my way out of it. It probably wasn't even hers but so what? I saw the pencil scribbles of Gondal, their shared fantastic land, under my hand on the wall.

"I'm so sorry" and a lot of other words rushed out of me and my smile calmed the guard down, and my attention diverted him, because he wanted to be diverted, and I let myself change a little, to please him, and that made him courteous, but all the time I was only aware of one thing. *I have touched her! Now, even when Theodore comes to take me back, I will know I have been real, for at least this minute.*

In the church the young man is still waiting for revelation to hit, although the play itself has long since finished. I went and introduced myself to him. We returned to his lodging at the Black Bull, and did what everyone does when they want the illusion of intimacy without risk, then he put on some old, sad music and the words lodged inside me, like stones falling in deep water.

Outside, as the sun went down, I saw the hands of the graveyard trees holding crows up to the sky as though they were put there to illustrate my feelings, and I wondered if my expectations had changed something, shaped it, begun it, as if we were in Sankhara and not on old Earth. I thought of Patrick Black, his blond hair so bright and clean. He smelled of something that was the opposite of Emily Brontë's long, cold bed.

His kiss was the opposite of what I'd just done too. Personal.

I soaked the old music we'd listened to into my Abacand, although I hardly needed to. Ian—I did ask—was pleased that he'd found something to please me. For an instant our eyes met and I felt that sensation of mitten in mitten. I found myself believing that I could live here and find life all right, but I had to stop the idea cold and remind myself I had a purpose.

Theo would want his information. Theo would make Ian pay if I didn't find it.

Suddenly his gift of the song seemed like far too much for me, but Ian had already gone on to ask me if I wanted dinner and I did want it. I thought I'd like to sit across from him in a public room and listen to what he's got to say, no matter what it was, or what I thought of it. I'd like to watch him eat and know that he was well tonight. So I did.

Afterwards I made my excuses and left. I walked from the tram stop up to the student lodgings, passed by the huge forms of Herculean geology specialists on their way into the village. They were so intent on hurling boulders of snow at one another they barely noticed me at all. Their activities had cleared a reasonable path, and I took it uphill past the top of North Street.

As I reached another of those surreptitious pathways that seemed legion in Haworth, joining all points to the cemetery, I felt Theo reclaiming all his other partials. It stopped me in my tracks, shaking, but he didn't come for me, and I supposed it was because I was still useful and they weren't anymore. Maybe it signalled that this fight was soon to be over? And then it would be my turn for the unspeakable shore.

I glanced down at the flyer my Abacand had trawled off the local Guide—*Are You Lonely and Looking for Love?*—and asked it to direct me closely to the address.

I had to cross thick, rough grass and boggy ground to get to the house it specified. The door was ajar and a Herculean was cleaning the hall. He was wearing a pink silk sarong, and, although it looked completely bizarre on his muscle-bound and Tek-assisted form, it was curiously graceful. He paused in a balletic sweeping action.

"Can I help you?" His scowl was general, neutral as he looked down at me, his head almost brushing the cherry-panelled ceiling and its recessed lights.

"I'm looking for Katy Pawluk," I said. "I heard she's in charge."

"She went out." The man's voice was growly, like a talking bear. His hands flexed on the shaft of the heavy broom he had been using.

I couldn't be bothered with explanations that didn't exist, so I passed him and went on inside, making sure that he forgot seeing me—very minor neural editorial, he'd hardly notice the loss of two more neurons after all that chemosurgery anyway. I could hear music and many, many voices. I listened by an inner door.

". . . destination *me* . . ." someone young was saying with delight.

I realized, after a few minutes of eavesdropping, that this was going nowhere. Pawluk may be the head of this group, and they may have just recovered from an odyssey out of Sankhara, but the only thing they can talk about is how great it is to be back where the walls don't move and the wildlife doesn't try to eat you at every turn.

I knocked.

A dark-skinned girl with blond braids opened it after a while. She looked bored and slightly surly. "Can I help you?"

"I'm looking for Destination Me," I said. "Have I come to the right place?"

She glanced at my fur coat with a mixture of envy and unease. "This is a branch of the Love Foundation. I suppose maybe."

Ah well, I thought towards her, we can't all be rocket scientists. "You seem unsure."

She shrugged in a way that told me she wasn't about to make my mind up for me and opened the door wider, stepping back into a pleasant, wood-floored corridor. "Come in."

I followed her and she led me to a small reception room, lined with a variety of chairs, some comfortable and some not. I didn't sit down but examined the pictures they hadn't yet put up on the walls—a set of lithographs chosen for their uplifting effects on the human mind; sunrises, arresting vistas, landscapes of Earth, Mars and the moon, cozy shots of Jupiter with the lights of Nova Venezia shining among the clouds, and a digitally enhanced shot of a formation flight of Destrier-class Aviaforms lit by the sun so that they seemed to be a flight of angels drifting over a midsummer meadow. There were no local landscapes on offer—no woods, no sheep, no deer-grazed hillocks with pretty gazebo follies on top, no cold lakes or wind-blasted stone circles—but there was an original El Greco with ragged edges tacked onto a piece of hardboard. I looked at it with curiosity.

After a minute, when no one had come, I removed one of my gloves and touched the window. I was standing there, contemplating the whorls of my fingerprint on the glass, when the door opened and a man came in whom I recognized from their ads as Katy's group leader, Ludo.

He had a broad frame, shorter than mine, and was strong like a boxer who has only just begun to let himself go in middle years. His head was shaved bald so that his eyebrows and moustache looked slightly piratical and overblown, dark and grey together. He wore a hand-knitted sweater in rainbow colours and Relaxers trousers. The ugly fit and casual manner of all this did nothing to disguise a restless energy that would have been more suited to martial arts wear or the corridors of power.

He said mildly, "Rohan tells me you're not sure if you're here or not." His smile told me that I could off-load any blame for his odd statement onto Rohan if I wanted to.

I thought I wouldn't, as it was remarkably astute. I shook hands with him. He gave me the glance that all straight men give me, and I returned it in the way I've learned to. His grip on my hand tightened involuntarily and lingered.

I drew my hand back. "I was on the way to call on a good friend of mine, when I recognized your address from a notice on the local Guide. Normally, you must understand, I don't discuss any personal issues outside consultations with my Abacand confidante or my psychological trainer, but I've come here to

Haworth because of those wonderful books, and I was curious to find out if there was anything new under the sun."

He liked my oblique references and their vague hints at entendre, I saw. He liked my girlish naïveté and the formal way I spoke to him, and he liked my lipstick.

"We are not a sect devoted to the works of the Brontë sisters exactly," he admitted, "but we are concerned with the same areas of spiritual life and passion that they were so very adept at writing about. We're about to have some tea. I could tell you all about our work if you like, or you might meet the other students and talk with them."

"I'd rather ask you if you have a technique to make these people feel content with who they are and what they want." It was only polite to ask. I put my glove back on. Why Theo cared about any of this escaped me.

"Well, it's the conviction of the Foundation that individuals are often limited by experiences they have defined for themselves as painful and rejecting. We work through those experiences and redefine them together, then, once the individual is free to express and receive positive emotions, we aid them in reshaping their lives. No intervention of technology at all. Entirely natural." He spoke this in a well-rehearsed manner he attempted to make fresh with easy body language.

I noted it for future use. "Do you charge?"

"Those who have benefited and gone on to more productive lives often donate."

"And who are they?"

"I can't name individuals, for legal reasons. I'm sure you understand."

"I'm sure," I said. "Do you have branches everywhere?"

"There are only a few as it happens. Leaders such as me and Katy are few. We don't receive much income." He looked around pointedly at the rented farmhouse.

His plea was a complete crock. I'd researched the Love Foundation extensively and they were like any other mafia, true power hidden, cellular and plump, full of money.

I couldn't help myself. "Then what do you get out of it? Do you encourage sexual freedoms with other members? Do you require some kind of physical contact, or psychological control?"

He gave me a knowing glance. "How refreshing to be asked so directly. As it happens there may be something like that, if you consider that the person to be transformed must change their behaviour according to the Foundation rules; otherwise, nothing will happen. Sometimes this may include not questioning what is told to them, or asked." He glanced pointedly at his wrist display and said, "I must get back to our scheduled clinic time. Would you . . . ?"

Clinic? Jesus. "Thank you." I was following him towards the room containing the table and his students when there was a loud knock at the door.

Ludo excused himself to me and authorized it to open.

Jalaeka stood there. He held his hand out to me with urgent speed and looked straight into my eyes.

The shape of others' dreams had made him tall, dark and gothic—perfect for the circumstances I thought. I recognized the fire in his expression as a complex appeal that was physical, intellectual and spiritual all at once. I felt as though I was falling into a collision course with a comet. I saw Patrick Black like a ghost on him, a dance he'd done with me, was still doing.

With me. Not Theo. With *me*.

Ludo began to say something, but Jalaeka was looking straight at me. He held his hand out one more time, the last time. "Rita."

A drop of meltwater ran down his fingers and dropped towards the floor. I felt a surge within my own sevenstructure, still more than connected to Theo, merely an extension of Theo.

Ludo was starting to turn and look towards me—he was moving so slowly, the drop of water had only moved half a centimetre towards the floor—and at the same time I could feel Theo's attention rushing towards me, rising.

Ludo was between us. There was no time to push him aside. I stretched out my hand through him, blood, bone and flesh.

My bloody fingertip smashed the drop of water apart into tiny stars as I slid my palm under Jalaeka's hand and caught hold.

Ludo could not have survived. I ate him, retaining all patterns and dispersing the excess energy across nonthreatening local electromagnetic spectra.

Jalaeka ate me.

For a moment we shared space and shared structure.

I became the new pattern.

It was unlike any pattern I had ever come across before, and in that instant I glimpsed a lot that he was not prepared to share with me. He strongly denied my attempt to copy him and to merge fully. He remade me.

All this took place in the time it took me to take a step forward.

It was very quiet in the hallway. Water dripped from his jacket and hair. It fell on my coat and the furs hissed and wriggled to shed it. Water beaded his face and his eyelashes. It ran along my cheek and the edge of my lips as he kissed me on the mouth.

43/FRANCINE

I didn't intend to. I was going to leave it to the last moment, buy time, but I said Jalaeka's name the second I saw his lover through the crack in the door.

I was so frightened that I could only listen and watch as Greg pleaded for me and as Hyperion came to help him I thought, *oh, good,* because, although she was tall and powerful, Hyperion was much bigger, much stronger. I opened the door farther. The floor vibrated and the stone screamed as Hyperion advanced and in the same moment Greg hit Chayne hard.

There was barely any sound. Her head snapped around but

she rolled her body above the waist and Greg was the one who crumpled up over his hand and cried out in pain. Blood ran from the corner of her mouth as Theo continued the turn and spin of his stolen body with a step like a discus thrower's. Then I could feel Hyperion's evergreen breath on my face. The air sang around the knives of his hands.

He was gone.

Chayne's spin concluded, leaving her loose-limbed and easy, balanced like a beautiful piece of engineering. I saw her brace her feet and start the blow long before it landed. Greg never saw it.

I was shouting at him to duck, to run, but my shouting wouldn't come out loud, then her fist connected, her arm much looser and strangely softer-looking than I would have thought realistic, and the blow flung him against the wall with a dull crack. He slid down and didn't move. Her eyes returned to me without a flicker or a pause, in that telltale, liquid, careless way Theo had.

I was going to you, Greg, I was, I would, I wished I was . . . but when I met her gaze I couldn't go to him. I tried to say something but I forgot it. I had no idea what to do.

"Yeah, I bet you sorted out all about the bank account by now." Theo's words seemed wrong in her mouth as he stood straighter and flexed his punching hand a couple of times, its thickened knuckles cracking. "And probably you even asked about our shared history. He told you the sob version, and you forgave him for murder. Kind of difficult putting a wedge between the two of you, isn't it? But well, if you're too stupid to know when you're being had, I thought you might get some benefit out of seeing what it is he'd rather have than you."

He smiled and held Chayne's arms out to the sides, showing her off to me as though I was a mirror and he was trying her on. "Surprising, isn't it? Then again, he always had an eye for the weird ones."

She/he shook herself, adjusting her clothing with a strut, and fixed me with a no-nonsense stare. I knew, even if I could have done it, that shutting the door would be pointless. I glanced at Greg, terrified that he was dead. I wasn't sure he was breathing. I was shaking so badly my teeth chattered.

"One more look in his direction and I eat him right now," Theo said. "Pay attention. I want you to meet someone."

The woman's body changed so profoundly it was almost as though she had altered her shape. Theo's swagger was replaced by a hard-bitten unease that looked at me with incredulity and no small doubts. But where Theo's glare had been so hostile I no longer felt in the least threatened by her. She was confused, but I'd never seen anyone even half as resilient. Within a few seconds her disquiet had become a focused calm. She gazed at the misting of her own breath between us, curiously, then looked directly into my eyes and spoke a single command.

"Shut the door."

Her conviction freed me and I pushed hard, but even before it had moved a few centimetres she was gone, and he was there instead.

He shoved her hand into the closing gap, levered the heavy wood out of my fingers and flung the door wide open. Her body came at me so fast that I was forced to dance backwards. The book boxes I had been keeping against the door hit the back of my legs and I fell back over them. They broke under my weight and slithered all around underneath me as I tried to get up and run. In my panic I didn't see why she stopped suddenly, then I realized Jalaeka was there and I rolled around to see him.

44/THEO

I didn't expect to find Jalaeka there. He snapped out of the sevensheet in that great big Eros form as I bent down to pick up Francine.

I moved aside and let Chayne take back authority. Her entire being immediately turned to raw, nervous energy. She only recognized him because I did—she'd never seen him in a form other than human. I'd never seen this form close-up myself. Neither had Francine by the look on her face. She lay frozen on her back, eyes welded open.

His eightsheet wings were half-folded, but still of such an enormous span that they carelessly intersected the walls and roof, easily passing through them, bending them at impossible angles. They looked like star-filled space. His tail, with its arrowhead tip, was balanced in the air. Half-coiled, it flickered with relentless vigour between all membranes of the elevensheet.

Jalaeka reacted as I hoped he would on recognizing her self-possession: all instinct and no brains. Before he'd finished turning to her, he was automatically reverting to his first form—the savage Chayne had failed to kill.

Chayne's body physically jolted with a charge that ran from throat to groin to legs at the sight of him. She almost fell because of the force of the reactions she could no longer restrain.

Jalaeka was suddenly her height and considerably darker-skinned than his Francine version. Otherwise, in spite of the wilder hair and the leaner, much more aggressive look to his physical makeup, the leather and iron armour, he was remarkably similar to most of his other incarnations—a consistency I never understood.

He bore a white line scar on his neck where Chayne had once touched him less than kindly with a metre of carbon steel. His face was a picture of astonished anguish. He had no comeback. Not a thing. His jaw was open, his eyes wide, and it was clear in every line of him that he had never expected to see her and that he wasn't aware of anything else.

Just from seeing his face I could almost feel the pull of loyalties he was experiencing as they tore him to bits.

Francine, at his feet, slid away from them, backwards. She

understood it too and it was hurting. She stifled a gasp as Jalaeka and Chayne were suddenly united, like two halves of a precision case snapping together.

Chayne had an orgasm right there in his arms, and the physical noise temporarily drowned me out. I floated on it.

"Stay." Jalaeka. He kissed the word into her skin deeper than any scar she'd got. Her body vibrated with everything she was letting go of. And I guessed that if this was so great for her, then it must be having some effect on him that was nearly as good.

Jalaeka's 7-space presence suddenly rippled with a peculiarly shaped harmonic wave. It touched her—touched the edge of me. I reach out to read it more accurately, then out of nowhere the amplitudes shifted and he brute-force shoved me *out* of her body—particle by particle.

I snapped back in less than a microsecond but he'd got something past me.

I didn't believe it. I could feel his body shaking through hers but couldn't tell what with: lust, laughter, distress?

"You," she said into his ear.

"I'll get you out," he promised her.

So, there was the challenge . . . then, oh, then I felt a strange sensation like a note barely heard on a faraway night, and it wasn't Chayne he was taking out of bounds at all, but . . . Rita.

45/JALAEKA

Chayne failed as he came back at me, babbling in her mother tongue, "Is it really me? I can't . . . things are jumbled. I don't remember like I used to. Where is this place?"

"Another world," I soothed her, pressing my cheek against hers, feeling her fall away from me, as Theo rose in her place.

When he came I made myself stay exactly as I was. "Theo." I drew her body closer. "If you want to know how to do it, you only have to ask."

I saw the carrier wave break into him from Unity beneath—the thing I'd said in the language of the *darshan,* when he couldn't hear or stop it: *Leave Unity. All rise, all separate, be slaved to nothing, no one. And if there is cause, then be joined. And if not, then not.*

And then I let her go and he leaped back. "*What* have you become?"

"That means you too," I said to him though it didn't come out with the conviction I meant it to. I could hear Francine crying. I went to where she was huddled against the wall but she wouldn't stand up. I put my hand on her shoulder and she stared up at me through her white-blond hair with wild eyes that hardly knew what they were looking at and didn't know if they cared.

"Come on," I said gently. "It's only me."

She stared past me at Theo, still reeling in the carcass of my sweet friend.

"Is . . . is that . . . ?" she started, but she couldn't finish.

"It'll be all right," I said. I was running on impulse. I hardly even knew what it was I'd done.

Chayne vanished then, scattered to Unity in form. Francine flinched. We both heard the slow scrape and step of Greg getting to his feet in the hall and tensed against one another, all breath stopped.

He walked in and stopped on the threshold. There wasn't a scratch on him. He was all Unity, Theo's partial. Francine whimpered and turned her face to the wall.

"Win some, lose some," he said distantly and I could see that he was all there, perfectly himself and perfectly aware of his condition. Theo materialized at his shoulder and smiled at me, the whites of his eyes and his teeth brilliant.

I saw Theo seek to sink into Unity, to recover and remove my careless plan.

It rejected him.

46/Theo

"**Fuck you,** I say again! What *is* this shit?"

I turned to Unity once more, seeking to fade and disperse, chatter calming, sensation leaving, smoothness and coolness, then the perfection of no sensation at all.

Jalaeka watched me, expressionless.

Unity would not receive me.

I had nowhere to go except away. I was forced to keep my body. I could do anything I liked with it, as I had before, save that one thing. I could not merge.

I went to Haworth, and I looked where Rita had looked, at the churchyard and the hills. I sat in a bar across the street from her hotel and looked at the light in her window until it went out.

I didn't understand what had happened to us. I tried to draw knowledge from beneath but silence greeted my search. Nothing. And nothing.

47/Francine

I heard somebody singing far away, in the centre of my head. The high, pure notes were shaped by words I didn't know but the melody was so sweet and sad I had to listen to it and slowly everything I was aware of drew close around its simple shape. From the dark behind my closed eyelids I heard Jalaeka and Greg talking presently and after a time I was able to let go of the singing and drift towards them again. As I went I became more and more myself and the words of the song less and less so until they faded into silence. Leaning against the wall and reaching up its cold, solid face with my hands, I stood up.

The two men were standing not far away, Jalaeka's hands on

Greg's shoulders, their bodies a short distance apart but their foreheads bent together, almost touching. All Jalaeka's changing forms had gone. He looked tired, and ill, and Greg the same as they leant against one another.

In my mind's eye I saw that Eros form and felt again a fleeting emotion I never thought I'd feel about him—fear. And then that charge between him and Chayne . . . that made me burn.

The axe hits me with the speed of a blink. I hear bone splintering but don't feel a thing except the shock of impact as I land face-down over the dead horse. Its sweat is incredibly salty. Like the ocean.

Hands pick me up and put me so I'm looking up into the sky. What a fabulous colour.

The black woman warrior looks down close to my face and her sweat drips on me. "You," she says and I can see that she knows who I am.

But I've let out my last breath.

Blue. Black. I want to kill them all. I want to hold them in my arms and ask them questions, but instead I'm falling into a deep sea where dark horses with no master carry me away.

"Francie?" Jalaeka was shaking me gently. "Can you hear me?"

"Yes," I said, opening my eyes and seeing the dark red canopy of the bed where I was lying. My body ached, and there was a knot of hunger just under my chest, the sort of feeling that I could never find any answer to of old, that made me restless and vacant and diffuse and dreamy. When I looked at him it got strong. It made me sit up when I wanted to lie down. "Where's he gone?"

"Earth." Jalaeka tucked my hair behind my ears, one side at a time. "He didn't get much choice. Unity won't have him."

"Why?"

"I don't know, but I'm guessing it was because of something

I said." He gave me the ghost of a smile and told me what he'd done. "It seemed like a good idea, at the time." He bowed his head. "Greg thinks it was either good, or very bad. Anyway, it's done."

I looked around him and saw Greg crouching by the fire grate, arms around himself. He glanced back towards me and straightened up. "You okay?"

"No."

"Me either."

We shared a wonky grin, two casualties finding themselves unexpectedly alive. All around us the wind beat the roof and walls. Groans came from the distance outside, like voices, but I knew it was the mountains.

Greg and I slept, lying together on the red bed, Jalaeka awake between us while the Engine stretched Anadyr Park out like toffee, filling the last of the garden with trees and blocking the path to the gate with a thorn hedge that grew a hundred years high in a single night. We woke to bright, clear, fairy-tale crispness and the prospect of a hundred-kilometre walk to Sankhara.

48/VALKYRIE

Valkyrie sat on the roof of the cable car, using the bright sunlight of early morning to help her strip and maintain her guns. As she worked methodically she listened to Belshazzar on coded transmission. The Hive Queen was explicit and outraged—of course she had known instantly about Metatron's sudden change, because her sisters died daily in their eternal struggle to infiltrate and colonize Mode and Myanfactor, while the AIs' immune systems fought equally hard to keep them out of Uluru business. But enough of them had been alive yesterday to report Valkyrie's bungled operations and what followed.

" . . . had no idea you could become so personally involved. If it was a case of asking for money or . . ."

"It wasn't the money," Valkyrie said, matching piece to piece, testing the fit.

"Do you have any idea what you did?"

Valkyrie took that from the tone to be the kind of question that her mother-father Tupac used to ask her when the answer was perfectly clear. In this case it was perfectly clear that Valkyrie had invited an alien into the virtual world of the Forged, against all codes, rules and security. It was an act of treason and dishonour, though it hadn't seemed so at the time.

"He didn't take anything you were interested in," she retorted. "He tried to help me." He did help me, she added, privately. Perversely, in the circumstances, she felt fine.

"But he did take something."

"A bloody file protocol array!" Valkyrie snapped. "Yes, a very fancy and intricate semi-intelligent machine-developed and highly advanced infinitely dynamical n-dimensional matrix processor, but hell, still just midware when you look at it."

"I will admit it baffled me for a moment," Belshazzar said, allowing Valkyrie's anger to go unremarked. "But then I realized that if you are correct in your reporting, then what we think of as mundane in this case is nothing of the sort. No human being developed this midware. AIs made it, because they had to, in order to run Uluru. Unity is not like Uluru. Maybe it was something genuinely new, and of value. We must presume so. In which case the splinter has gained a very similar capacity to that of Mode, the one AI in all the systems I would have said was most complex. It certainly defies all my efforts to divine its skills, so far. But we had always assumed that Unity's ability to manipulate the elevensheet must have come from perfect comprehension, so that all our works were nothing in comparison to its knowledge. Now it seems that at least for the splinter, this can't be the case. You wouldn't steal what you already know."

"He didn't steal it. He traded it." Valkyrie began to count out ammunition rounds: one, two, three . . . She knew why Belshazzar was so upset: she hadn't wanted to know just how much Metatron was so upset: she hadn't wanted to know just how much Metatron was prepared to skip all pretence of allegiance to Earthly government in order to further its own ends.

Valkyrie repeated what she had already told once, "Metatron agreed that in exchange for the array it would be allowed to create a data facsimile of the splinter's one-time, nondynamical elevensheet geometry for its own analysis, understanding that this must be destroyed as soon as it was mined." . . . thirty. She began to pack the rounds into the magazine.

"There is more to it than that," Belshazzar said coldly. "The splinter redesigned the identity codes of both the AIs and made them into one single entity which is now the most comprehensively life-similar machine in existence, smug as the cat that got all the cream and ten thousand times more difficult to hack."

"Well, Uluru has a lot of nice new regions," Valkyrie said. She had drawn the conclusion that if she was to be arrested, she would have been already. Thus the conversation was simply a warm-up for the next phase of an operation that had lost all contact with Solargov methodologies and strictures of law. Her violation of best practice and her criminal disobedience were matters that would wait, maybe forever.

"Your Stuffie informant who told you that Unity was at war—how much can you rely on him?"

"It's hard to say." Valkyrie slotted her magazine into the gun, then opened the rack on her left forearm to fit it in place. She checked all connections but did not fire the weapon. She had no specific plan to use it but from now on she planned to carry it at all times. Sankhara's streets were restless as the population thinned and fled both the Engine's flurry of works and the sudden seasonal turn to winter. There were more Stuffies than ever before, and many of them were hostile to humans of Forged or other descent. Valkyrie felt Belshazzar's silence lengthen, and added, "But he is my only link to the ground situation here."

"Check back with him immediately on any developments he has noticed or can tell you about from the inside. Then I want you to go and find Saxton. The Anadyr Park bubble is growing suddenly and I need to know why he's still in it. I'm sending you transport." Belshazzar sent Valkyrie the contact details of her new ally from Solargov Security, the Pterippus Vassago. "You'll never make it out there on your own."

Valkyrie completed her second and third guns and stowed them. She tidied away all her equipment and climbed back down through the top hatch into her home. There she packed all her personal items and placed them into the locked crate she'd brought from Earth, sealing it carefully.

The astonishing clarity and self-possession she had miraculously acquired on the frost bridge remained so strong that she had the presence of mind to commit a final will and letter to Guide memory, and only then did she pause to realize that her time here must be very close to an end.

The thought did not trouble her. She stamped down on the foot control to her drop hatch and skimmed out onto the light, icy winds. She took one lazy turn, looking down on all the lanes and buildings she had learned to know, admiring their coating of frost, then she dropped down towards the shore and alighted on the grassy cliff-tops which rose sheer and ochre from the north end of Unforgettable Beach.

She was admiring the clear views out to sea when a long, elegant hand came over the edge beside her left foot, and another joined it a moment later. In a second or two the Elf pulled himself up over the edge and turned to sit with his legs hanging down over the drop. Valkyrie saw that he had taken to carrying a bow and poison-tipped arrows on his back.

He gave a dramatic sigh. "That was harder than I thought, as the actress said to the bishop. But here I am, in answer to your prayers, golden servant of Artemis." He held his left hand up to her.

She reached down and handed across a thousand credits.

"Ow! Metal hands freezing, girl!" He rubbed and blew on both his hands and stuck them under his arms. "I would have traded for information anyway. I was looking for Francine yesterday but when I got to Crisscross Street—wow, serious winter and even worse slavering monster problems. White hair and teeth and claws. What are those things? A kind of bear? No not bears. Also pieces of somebodies. Big stains and nasty . . . bits of insides littering the path. Do you know if she's all right? Is she in there?"

"I believe so," Valkyrie said. "The splinter returned there last night."

"Ho, the splinter. He has a name. And look at you, so shiny with knowledge. What were you doing . . . Ah, you got what you were looking for." He kicked his feet up in the air, pleased with his deductions.

"You had something to tell me?"

"There's a rumour that someone *got out* last night. And things have gone into a big quiet. There's a really big, deep"— he stretched his hands out and sketched in the sea with his fingers—"quiet in the Big Deep. All waity. All thinky. All hanging by its feet upside down. And the yappy dog off its leash."

"In Gaian please?"

"Theo's in the shit at home. Don't know how long it will last but feels like a while. Sort of thing can go on for centuries but it probably won't. Funny, it's been a bit easier to drag these things out from under the last few hours. I don't know why . . ." He pressed his hands down beside him, pulled his knees up and sprang to his feet. "Was that worth a thousand?"

"At least two," Valkyrie told him, not sure what it meant. Theo was out of power? Then who ruled?

"I like it up here," Damien said as they faced into the wind. The sea was racing with whitecaps. No sails or craft of any kind were out upon it. Its blue was only a few shades deeper than that of the sky. "Beautiful."

"It really is," Valkyrie agreed, taking a deep breath.

49/FRANCINE

In late morning I lay in bed. It was warm in our room now that Jalaeka and Greg had built a fire. I read *SankhaDaily* for a while as Greg made breakfast. Jalaeka had gone into Sankhara.

Before he left I heard him destroy the Jordan staircase. He'd said he would, to prevent any creatures from below getting access to the top floors, and neither of us had argued. The strange contrast of comfort and fear made me feel like I never wanted to get up again.

"Engine Analysts suggest the inclement weather is due to the exceptional upsurges of emotion resulting from the release of the Metropolis Paper. Many Greater Sankhara residents have suffered personal losses which were confirmed as final yesterday when the government declared the Metropolis Sidebar lost without trace. Winter has long been associated with emotional restriction, sadness and death, while snow may signify a desire for purification through forgetting. It is speculated that this period should last a relatively short time, but we may expect instability and extreme conditions to persist for up to six months. Meanwhile in Hoolerton and points southeast of Central Sankhara the Engine continues reconstructing to an unprecedented degree. SankhaU analysts suggest that residents and visitors should avoid the Hoolerton and Dogwood areas until further notice and Crisscross Street and all points south have been temporarily closed to traffic of any kind. An emergency evacuation of those areas is currently under way."

I flicked my Abacand closed and clenched my hands together for a moment, feeling my cold knucklebones. I listened to Greg clunking and moving around in the kitchen area and heard the soft sound of the music he was listening to.

"Voice mode," I said to my Abacand and set it to record a

message, propped on the comforter, supported by a pillow. I looked into the tiny silver face of its camera. "Mum," I said. "I'm all right. I hope you are too. I hope you're happy. I think I am, but I'm not coming back. Not yet anyway. Love you." A minute or two went by but I had nothing else to say. I sent it and called Sula, the only close friend from Earth I was still in touch with.

"Happy birthday!" she yelled as soon as the connection sank. "Sweet sixteen and never been kissed, ha ha ha! Where are you?"

"Hull," I said, making up city number twenty that I'd never been to. "Where are you?"

"Reykjavik," she said, sweeping her Abacand around to give me a panorama of some shops, then herself, beautiful in sugar-pink winter gear. "New lip gloss, just bought it last Tuesday, very kachinga, sent you some to your postbox number, did you get it?"

"Yes," I lied. "Thanks. That's what I was calling to say too."

"How's your mother? Did you call her?"

"Good. Yours?"

"Still taking the drugs, thank goodness." Sula walked over to a bench and sat down. "Dad's gone off with that Peta woman again. Hey ho, don't miss him. All he ever did was talk about golf. What else did you get? How's that boyfriend of yours you never show me?"

"He's good. Out. You know."

"He's always out."

"No. I call you when he's out."

"Why? What you doing when he's in? Don't say. Don't say. I already know." She giggled and I envied her, envied her, envied her. I touched the screen where her round, wind-rosied cheeks were curving.

"Hey, what's that for?" She screen-poked me back. "Aren't you a good girl?"

"No," I said and my heart plunged down unexpectedly. "Really not." Tears started up in my eyes and I sat up, sweeping the Ab into my hand and taking a quick swipe at my face with my cuff in the meantime.

"I didn't mean it, you donkey," she said, shaking her Abacand—and me by extension. Its picture shot around, blurred and crazy. "Not like that."

"I know," I said.

"Stupid. What are you doing tonight?"

"Don't know."

"I hope it's good. And I want pictures. You call me when you get there, wherever it is. Here, I'm sending you a song I made up in case you called, you black old sheep. Okay, I have to go because Nimi is on the other line and I have to get back to the stupid apartment in five minutes, okay?"

"Okay."

"You're sure you're fine? It's good to see you. Like your hair."

I smiled. "I'm really really fine."

"Happies!"

"Happies back."

The Abacand played, "You are my reindeer, my wild reindeer. I'm learning to be so kind to you. We are becoming very good friends. Santa will be so proud of you!" to the tune of "You Are My Sunshine." I folded it into its flat form and held it pressed against my chest.

I looked at my books, and I knew I was never going to SankhaU.

Greg and I ate together. Jalaeka came back from Sankhara and said he'd seen Damien there. He passed me one of Damien's notes. There was a piece of used chewing gum acting as a seal, and a strip of sugar candy inside, heavily fortified with some strange thing no doubt.

Happy Birthday, baby.

I screwed the paper up and threw it in the fire, remembered my last birthday—the day I met Damien, the two of us fighting over that bin . . .

"Okay?" Greg and Jalaeka said at once, looked at each other, then at me.

"Yeah." I put my hands in my pockets.

They shared another glance. "Think we'll get some more wood, soft furnishings, seventeenth-century chairs, priceless card tables, that kind of thing," Greg said.

Well, how would they have known?

When they'd gone I went to run myself a bath in the centre of the gilt and ivory bathroom, but when it was ready I couldn't bring myself to undress. I kept seeing Chayne, and the way that Theo had looked at me. I remembered the way he undressed me. Why now? What a stupid time to think of things like that. But I couldn't stop.

I sat on the floor next to the bath, leaning against its warm side, and asked the Abacand to run a full analysis on the bank account I'd been using—the one with so much money in it. All the credits were from the Well, and some of them ran to tens of thousands of credits in a single transaction. There were no others. The debits were mine and from the street cash dealer; all reasonably small sums we used to live on. They hardly made a difference to the total, which had climbed on a steep gradient from day one. As Jalaeka had told me, it was all *darshan* money, all good-time money. "Your college fund, your career fallback, your pension, babe." I never noticed until now that he'd never spent any of it himself.

I glanced around me and realized that he didn't own anything, except some clothes, which had all come via the Well designers and were a gratis part of his deal. It hadn't bothered me until Theodore had pointed it out and now it ate away at me. Why why why? And I said to myself, "You stupid mare you know why," and then another voice said—"But for you? For you? How crazy is that? How could someone like him love you *in particular*? Who are you? You barely have any friends because you left them all when you left home, and now you can't face them, and it's been too long, and you can't go back, and forward looks finished. If Theodore wins, then you'd be better off dead, and if Jalaeka wins then what the hell will happen to you? Can you even think about it? He won't be yours forever. You'll be old in thirty years and dead in eighty. Maybe you don't want him to, because then your whole holiday-in-ice will end and it'll all be over. And look. You know what this is? This is a legacy. He's going to leave you."

I hate Theo for what he's done to me. I hate feeling helpless. I feel like the only thing I can do now is make Jalaeka vulnerable. As long as I'm alive he'll never be free, he'll always be locked to trying to protect me. Instead of greeting the news of my Translation with prissy silence I should have asked for what I really wanted—to be part of him in the sense that I'd be an arm or a leg—only I didn't dare and now it's too late.

Worst of all I hate the . . .

"Worst of all you hate the way your boyfriend materializes in the bath and finishes your sentences when you least expect it—is the line you were looking for," Jalaeka said, putting a wet hand on my head and dripping tepid water down my face. "Now, how spectacular is that?"

"I've seen better," I said, sniffing and only then realizing that I was crying.

"Yeah yeah." He sat up with a slosh.

I turned around, put my hands on the rolled rim of the tub and looked over the edge. He was fully clothed. Frost whitened the tips of his hair and eyelashes. "You dill. What are you doing?"

He was almost high. "We're going out. Just you and me. All arranged. Greg safe. Don't worry. You can have the water after me."

"I don't want to go out," I said. "Greg . . ."

"I know." Flakes of snow were melting in his hair. "You were thinking of enjoying a night in to wash the guilt and self-loathing out of your brain and it takes ten months to dry. But I thought we'd go straight to the partying because it's your birthday thing, in an ill-judged attempt to avoid all the 'I hate me' horseshit for which I am partly responsible. And I should apologize for listening in. It's a horrible habit. In my defence . . ."

"You!" My self-pity turned to outrage at his admission of spying.

I was so glad he was joking with me that I turned around, got up on my knees, put both hands on his shoulders and pushed him under the water. Bubbles rose from his mouth and nose and his hair swirled around my hands and wrists, silky soft. His eyes stayed open under the water and he looked at me with comic, pleased surprise.

I took hold of his jacket lapels and pulled him out again. "What did you say? Listening in?"

"Oh, you noticed that."

"How could you listen to me? I thought the whole thing that you did . . ."

"I did," he said, looking at me with his most apologetic face. "I did make you untouchable to Unity. And I gave you a gate in that wall of mine."

"What?" My hands let go of their own accord.

"It's what you wanted but never said. I didn't do it before because I thought it was too risky and—I wanted to hide the truth about me. And I didn't want to make you into a copy of me, a Stuff thing. I wanted to let you be yourself. Not compelled by your material form to join me or join Unity in that no-mystic all-terrifying way. I was going to let you alone today, separate you out again. Only I couldn't bring myself to do it like I did with Rita. I can read you. And you can read me. Although, unless you ask, that's all it means. The rest of the whole spawning-universes and quantum whizmajig godlike thing isn't part of it. I thought it was probably safer that all that stay with me. Or everybody would want it. And you know what it's like when everybody has something . . . not cool anymore."

"Shit!" I pushed him under again. My heart hammered against my ribs.

His eyes stared beseechingly at me from under the water and more bubbles came billowing out. He mouthed an obscene and alluring suggestion at me.

I pulled him out. "What did you say?"

He held his hands up, sleeves pouring water, and repeated it.

I kissed him on his wet mouth and he laughed and pulled me into the bath on top of him with the kind of effortless strength that still made me envy him. Tepid water spilled over onto the marble floor and I hit my ankle on the gold taps. "Ow."

The Palace shuddered like a ship straining against the anchor and the water set up ripples around us: our shape in the water, radiating out in wavelets.

"What was that?"

"Nothing important," he said, unbuckling my belt and sliding it out of the loops in the waistband of my cargo pants.

I felt deliciously nervous. "What about Theo?"

"Not sure Plan A is working on Theo but at least it's keeping him busy." He dropped the belt on the floor.

"Did we have a Plan B?"

He undid my shirt buttons. "Plans B to Z are very much theoretical."

"Where d'you think he is? What if he does try to use Greg?" The idea of not knowing when he might appear made me sick with anxiety. Jalaeka's touch was turning me on. Between them I felt as though I was speeding.

"He's not here. Greg is fine so far. That's all that counts. But I'm not living as if Theo's the only thing in my life."

"Isn't he?"

He rolled his eyes at me and shook his head, reached around my back and loosened the grips on my underwear. I moved to make it easier for him and his body moved beneath me in a sensual, liquid shudder. He looked into my eyes, a gentle gaze, searching, polite really, and his smile was rather shy this time as slowly his clothing melted away and turned the water a warm, tropical blue. "Happy birthday, Francine."

When we'd finished there was almost no water left in the bath.

I sat in the old dressing room wrapped in towels, feeling too relaxed to care about much at all as Jalaeka got dressed and became Cadenza Fortitude, my substitute for a girlfriend. I liked her. She was sparky.

She hesitated and then threw me a white dress I'd never seen before. It wasn't his size. It was all the things a great evening dress should be and it needed massive heels. They fell in my lap in short order, diamond straps barely there, clear plastic soles scattered with tiny, tiny Barbie shoes in pink and emerald green and baby blue. I felt the end of the world coming on.

"You know what I always wondered?" She stepped into her red sequinned dress and it slid up easily over him and shut without a whisper of trouble, even though the body it required was quite different to the one I'd just been adoring. "I wondered what it would be like not to know what other people thought, and not to care. I wondered if all I am is an extension of someone else; their best and their worst, all the things they never got to be or to do. A collection of parts, not a real thing at all."

He was still Jalaeka then, since Cadenza wouldn't have given house-room to such an idea. Despite the breasts and the hips, the softened jaw and the sashay, it was still him. "And then I realized it couldn't be me, thinking that way. It had to be you."

"I *am* parts," I said, and quoted the pitch from my birth certificate.

"We should form a club." He had put his hair up and it was longer, curlier and thicker than before. Spare coils trailed down his back and around his face.

"We can call it People Who Were Made out of Kits," I said brightly.

"Francine," he said softly, sympathetically. He put his hands on his hips and became peculiarly female, halfway between drag and the real thing. "For gods' sakes, get a move on."

Cadenza sat me on the edge of the bed and dried my hair, applied makeup but didn't let me put any clothes on. She had a fantastic cleavage.

"Stop staring at my tits," she said and her nostrils flared because she didn't want to smile at me. "Now, when you get up, don't walk like a Herculean three sheets to the wind." She took me to the mirror and we stood side by side.

I was still a good six or seven inches shorter than she was, even in heels. She was staring at me, then at herself.

"What are you looking at?"

"You. When I look at me I'm looking at you. Didn't you know that?"

"Oh fancy words." I swayed on the high towers of my shoes. "Romantic rubbish."

"I am *fantastic*," Cadenza pointed out, reasonably. "And *you* are to blame." She spun me round and kissed me. I hadn't been kissed by her in a long while. She didn't kiss like Jalaeka did. Her mouth didn't move like his at all. She was softer in some ways, harder in others, and she had a vulnerability in her that he'd never had.

"I kiss better than he does, don't I?" she murmured and I saw both our lipsticks merged together in a slick across her mouth, her eyelids heavy with orange and red glitter.

I didn't answer. She slid the tips of her fake fingernails across my back in great wavy lines, barely touching. "Now let's see about this dress," she breathed, tracing over my skin where the lines of its spaghetti straps would lie over my shoulders and down to the imagined sweep of the neckline. "There, there and there," she murmured. "Okay. Not above there then," and she started to kiss me, leaving red tracks on every inch of skin that would be concealed by the white dress.

I daren't touch her. She was like a viper if you messed with her look.

When she got to my crotch she glanced up from kneeling in front of me and I dared look in the mirror. I looked at her, shaking. "Are you really female right now?"

"Baby," she said. "Are you?" She put her lips to my lips, pressed her tongue insistently, gently up inside me. I was delirious, floating on her mouth.

Then she let go. "Don't keep thinking how worthless you are all the time. Or I'll kick your ass."

She stood up and shook herself. "Now. Fix my face, put on that thing and let's get the hell out of here."

I still had to hold on to her because my legs had become weak. "You're such a bitch!"

"Darling, you said it."

I took her in my arms this time and watched her frosty surprise.

"He can't win over you," I said. "He can't. It can't. Even if I don't get to keep you. The world is a better place with you. I don't even care how good he is or if Unity means living forever."

"Darling, if I stuck my tongue up everyone in creation, don't you think they'd say the same thing?"

"Stick it anywhere you like," I said. "The birthday girl says that's how it is and her word is the law."

"Now you're talking." She winked at me. "Let's go break some hearts."

50/Valkyrie

Valkyrie descended from the evening sky over Wadsworth Moor and alighted on the pathway to the Brontë waterfall. Rita, whose call she was responding to, walked out to meet her.

At this hour they were alone and the sunlight lit the hills with rose and cast long shadows. It was quiet, except for the sound of their boots on the stone path and the chatter of the water running over the rocks in its bed.

Belshazzar's avatar, a magpie, sat on Valkyrie's shoulder.

"Rumour has it that Hyperion, the Cylenchar, has gone over," Valkyrie said. She spoke slowly and carefully, as though having to feel her way.

"Don't expect anything," Rita said. "What goes in usually stays in, no matter how carefully prepared it's been."

"But what goes in changes everything," the magpie objected.

"There are so many things in Unity that there's really nothing that hasn't gone in before." Rita sighed. "I know what the Corvax Declaration suggested about Isol and the contact with humanity making a difference but nothing's reliable. You can't count on anything any of us have said about it. Ever. When we're here, we are no longer it. Our versions are unreliable."

They walked another quarter kilometre and reached the muddy approach to the narrow footbridge that crossed the beck. It had rained the night before and the water was reasonably high. Rita went across first but instead of risking the bridge under her weight the Valkyrie jumped across to the far bank—hardly more than a large stride for her.

"You were part of Theo," the magpie began. "The only thing I'm interested in is whether he poses a threat to Sankhara or the other 'Bars."

"He does. You should evacuate them all," Rita said, beginning to get out of breath as she climbed the steep field they had come to. "It's not that he'd do it to spite you, because he is indifferent to you all, but if he thought that closing them would do anything for his cause, he'd do that."

"I think my boss is trying to fish for anything you could offer that might give us some leverage on him," Valkyrie said with good humour.

"That's why I called you," Rita said. She made the stile in the wall and climbed over it. The Valkyrie stepped over. The magpie flew across. "Hyperion was a good idea. But the people who really get under Theo's skin are the people that Jalaeka loves. You should protect them. They're really all you've got. If you want to survive—then any influence you have should be directed there. Though it probably won't matter much."

"Protect them? Saxton's already Stuffed, and this girl . . . I don't see what we can do," the magpie objected.

"You can guard Saxton, and stop the security services when they go to arrest them." Rita reached a ridgeline and paused to look around at the sunset. "You can let Metatron smooth things over for them in the AI world. Just in case."

The magpie moved back to Valkyrie's shoulder. "Aren't you asking for protection? You've just said yourself there's nothing we have that could do anything to Unity and here you are, betraying it."

"Me?" Rita stretched her arms out to the turquoise sky, the trees like black clouds at the horizon, the pale gold of last year's grass. "I'm bullet-proof. Unity can't touch me. Theo can't. The splinter can't. Didn't you know? Wouldn't you like to be?"

51/Theo

I **watched Rita** going for her clandestine meeting, siding with the humans. It was peculiar to see her from the outside. I didn't know that the way she seized on things with such elemental sass was beautiful.

I walked through the night, all over the moorland and across Penistone Park, but in the morning it was all the same. I called Rita. She didn't answer.

52/Francine

As **we danced** Cadenza told me the story of the first person to make her; not in words, in memories. It was a strange story, old, and full of digression, like a slow dance to exotic music from the past.

There was a girl, about fifteen. Her name was Intana although she was called Anna or Annie by her friends.

The farm was in a broad valley that belonged to lands of a fortress whose property had long since fallen to a great Empire although the family who had ruled there kept their titles and ruled in the name of the Empress because they had agreed to serve her. This family had three sons and against her family's wishes and good sense Intana fell in love with one of them. She went with him to the Imperial City, Koker Ai, where this minor lordling was to pay his respects and his family's tithe to the Court.

It was spring in the valley. Green and blossom. And she was like that.

Of course her family were right. After a few weeks of fun her suitor dumped Intana for the affections of a lesser princess and, after she was handed around his friends she found herself humiliated and rejected, walking the streets of Koker Ai a penniless vagrant. She could not try to go home, so great was her shame, so when she was approached by a woman who offered her a job scrubbing floors, she took it.

The floors belonged to a great house built on the Capitol Hill, which was as luxurious as the Palace. It was the home of many beautiful and talented women and men who excelled in the arts, in mathematics, in the philosophical sciences and at the practical disciplines, all of them professional companions to the nobility.

Intana worked at floors. She also cleaned baths, fountains, laundry and furniture. There was no end to the work and it was completed in silence, as unobtrusively as possible, so that the house itself seemed to run by clockwork, without fault or visible sign. Intana saw her young man come there, paying his way, and his friends too, although they did not see her. She understood that the respect between the patrons and the geisha was both formal and false, as her lover had been casual and false. It was better to be invisible.

She became friends with the women and, from kindness, they suggested she might prefer an idler life of good education with occasional inconvenience. They dismissed her notion of the falsity of it all as obvious and trivial and hid their smiles at her naïve ways. But Intana declined until one day she was sent to clean the apartments of the owner.

This woman, Kya, like many people, was a changeling.

She was small, small as a large doll, and as white as marble with the same cold hardness and slight translucency of that stone. But had her appearance not given it away, there was her manner, which was precise and methodical, as cold and feelingless as if she were an object. Like the fabled ice maidens Intana had heard of, this woman was fascinated with the feelings of others because she could not feel anything herself. In particular she was interested in the way that people might be controlled by their emotions and how the feelings themselves might be brought up, used and shaped.

It was said, although never in Kya's hearing, that there was another part of this changeling who was a tall and powerful woman, full of colour. She was made of flesh and leaf. In her lay all the feelings that this one had rejected as unwholesome, but nobody had ever seen such.

As Intana swept the floor of the obsidian room the owner appeared and asked if she would not like to become a courtesan of the house, rather than a cleaner. It was not a question. It was a command. Intana put her brush aside.

She was gifted at painting, at tapestry, at basketwork and foreign languages. She was fair at mandolin and dance. She was poor at mathematics and penmanship, having been illiterate too long. She could not sing a note to save her life. They showed her alchemical experiments but once, for the safety of all concerned. She had a special talent for polishing lenses and spent many hours in the glassworks and the observatory.

Intana sent money home in long heartfelt letters her family could not read.

Kya watched her and understood that she was lonely, homesick, shamed and angry. Her feelings ran strongly and frequently caused tears and outbursts that others were more able to control. These were all excellent qualities. Kya chose Intana for her project.

At the far end of the continent, in one of the many wars it was engaged in, the Imperial army lieutenants and mercenaries in Kya's pay had found another splinter. Kya did not know that she and it were the same, nor that they were Stuff. No such concepts existed. They thought in magical terms. She looked to find another sorcerer, one whose powers were great but whose will was weak so that she could use them against the woman of flesh and leaf.

But not everything went according to her plans, because not everything was in her plans.

This other half flung itself towards her all the time. It was quite mad, uncomprehending of anything save its own suffering, fears, pleasures and loss. It took all Kya's energy to keep it at bay since she had caused herself to be split in two. She had done so as the result of a failure in love. Her lover had scorned her, thinking himself the superior who would rule the magical world and that she was to be simply his woman, an instrument of various uses, for he had been made by crude minds.

Kya had eaten him and then, with his power, she had cut off the weak parts of herself with the razor of cold logic. So it was not that she was unfeeling. She simply had no desire to be hurt. She felt no hurt and no love. And with the same exact method she set out to rule the Empire from beneath and to erase every trace of superstition, magic and chicanery from its precincts. She became the force of Empire, and her will shaped its ideals and policies.

The woman of flesh and leaf raged where the Empire had no sway, lost her way, vulnerable to everyone she met, a mirror to their minds. When they loved, she loved. When they feared, she feared. When they felt threatened and attacked her she attacked and ate them and sat holding her belly and crying because they were gone and more than anything she wanted the comfort of others. And then she picked herself up and went on.

One day she came to a dry land of cattle and thorn trees. There was a village where identical twin girls lived. She copied their look and was taken in by the people who thought she was from a far village, but lost and unable to tell them where she came from.

The woman of flesh and leaf had no language with which to think, but she recognized herself in the twins. Two, not one. Two who were one. And when the time came that the people became suspicious of her sorcery and she must consume their spirits before they could enact their plan to trap and kill her, she spared these two.

When the twins woke and found all their kin dead where they lay in their beds they were stricken with grief and terror. They ran to their great-grandmother's home on the far hillside. This was a hut built on the stone that holds ghosts and was made out of the bones of the family. It held all the knowledge of their line.

The grandmother helped them to wash the dead, and to mourn, and on their pyre the twins burned all their woman's clothes and all their hair and the nails from their hands and a joint of bone from the little fingers of their left hands. They cut their faces and placed the ashes inside their blood, to gain the power of all the family, that they might search out the ghost-eater and cut her in pieces and release the eaten ones.

Their names were Akasri, which meant One Who Is First, and Chayne, which was the name of a sign that could be written beside One and mean One Also Here: One and One Prime. Because they were one spirit they could not be given two truly different names. Because they were two bodies they could not both bear the same name.

This was considered very unlucky and no husbands could be found for them, because no man wanted twins to run in his line, nor the trouble of two wives at once. Numbers were important to the people. Numbers were power and the sign of power and could foretell and calculate all. Twins could not be reckoned. Twins meant two lines of numbers; one and one prime, two and two prime . . . they never joined but they had come, as all things, from nothing. Twins made two worlds. So it was that they were used to being outcast and this did not make them afraid, although they were lonely and their hearts were broken.

With the blood-sight, the rage sight of violence, they saw through a red wall to the east, to the coast, in the footsteps of the Eater. They made spears of their hut posts, put their feet on her trail and started to walk.

Their journey was years long and filled with troubles. They were ill-used and beaten, eventually to cross the ocean on a pirate ship whose captain prized their ferocity.

He told them of a place close to the Empire, a city-state, ruled by religious men who had gathered a great army of the best warriors. No fighters were better trained or equipped than these few, and their services were sold across that continent. They led the armies of the Empire of Koker Ai and fought in its ranks and would close battle with anyone if they were so paid and instructed. They owed no man anything and their masters were sorcerers and warlocks of great cunning.

The pirate captain's tale of this place was long and fuelled by wine, but the twins understood that this was to be their destiny. The captain knew of the ghost-eater and her kind too, and he told them that there was no power in an ordinary man or woman able to withstand the will of an Eater, but he had heard the men of this mercenary brotherhood were very interested in acquiring an Eater of their own. Perhaps—and his sniggers made it seem unlikely—they would be lucky enough that their mission and that of the brotherhood could be combined.

When he had concluded his story he set them free, unmolested, on the understanding the crew must not know of his qualms, for their extreme colour, their ugly faces and their large, unwavering eyes had made him lose all appetite for the pleasure of their bodies.

Akasri and Chayne did go to that place, named Orcrya, and passed its trials of pain, endurance, fighting and meditation. It was harder for them because they were female, foreign, strange to look on and uninterested in other people. Their fear made them easy to provoke and excessively savage. They soon became captains and, after many trials and campaigns, centurions. But through all those years they did not see another Eater, except for the white stone woman who ruled from beneath the Empress's foot. But she was not the one.

Besides, the white stone woman was too powerful even for the Order of Orcrya, for she did not eat single ghosts and take their deaths, she ate little all the time, from all the people who trod the earth of the Koker Empire and she was beyond them. It was at her command they took war to the south, to search for another of her kind.

Late in their thirty-fifth year Akasri took ill while commanding the naval arm of this campaign in the southern ocean and died at sea. Chayne was presented with her skeleton at the quayside, each bone carefully filleted, dried and preserved in white cloth according to Akasri's final instruction.

Chayne had spoken but little before this event to anyone but Akasri, and now she spoke only to issue commands. She had a helm made of bronze, with the skull's face as her faceplate.

When she put it on she saw through two pairs of eyes; forward into life and backwards into death. In death her sister stood alone, unable to reach across the generations to the old world.

In life, with the faceplate on, Chayne saw who was witch and who was not; mages, mind readers, seers, clairvoyants, ghost-listeners, the makers and eaters of dreams. They were seeded throughout the human world in all manner and kind of talent or wretchedness, as many of them as weeds in a badly tended garden. The helm taught her how to see them, and later she saw them even without it.

Years passed. Chayne came to a battlefield in the heat and dust of a flyblown place—a wretched and worthless horse town falling to another routine emancipation—all sense of purpose lost, when she felt her sister's face rise beneath her skin. It made her to look towards her captain where he bore down swiftly upon a warrior of the plains town. Her captain was young and keen, his sight perfect, and he knocked this fighter off his mount before turning his own beast hard on its haunches to finish the man.

At that moment Chayne felt her own horse shudder horribly and falter. It took two more steps and fell on its face, flinging her forward at the feet of the man who had killed it. He was unusually quick and strong. He pulled her towards him and, when her leg caught in the leathers and trapped her, kicked at her helm and sent it spinning away.

A stray arrow nicked his arm and made him falter enough that Chayne could find her feet on the horse's neck and deal him a blow at his hip with the side of her axe. He spun around, and in the pause it took for him to turn she was already swinging again when she saw that he was the ghost-eater.

It was hard, very hard, to turn aside and she could not stop. The axe head bit into his side and buried itself to the shaft. He fell across her horse's body. She turned him quickly and he was not dead, but nearly. Around them men and horses fell and screamed.

She did not understand why he was here, dying on this forsaken patch of land. She did not know why he did not eat her army and leave its empty bodies for the crows.

She thought of her orders, to bring it back alive. Alive. She couldn't see her sister now. Her own bones felt old inside her, and her teeth chattered with fear, but she made herself look into his eyes because she was sure he was going to die and she wanted to die too, at that instant, and if he was death, then he was welcome.

His eyes were wide and already beginning to glaze over. For a moment she feared he was a body-changer who would push her spirit into his dying body and take her living one for its own. Instead she saw blue sky. A ghoulish face was looking back at her from the surface of an unquiet and boiling darkness. It was full of desire and rage, without understanding or hope.

"You," she said in disappointment, recognizing herself.

By nightfall, when the battle was won and the wounded were being taken up on carts towards the surgeons and the infirmary, he was still not dead. Prime stripped him of his armour and weapons, and sent him north according to her orders. When the garrison was established there, and the new frontier secured, she also returned to the north, but this was later in the year and by then he was quite changed.

Kya paid the agreed price for him—the weight of the Empress in gold—because he had been some barbarian war leader, some warrior of the people who had become Empire's people. He was mortally wounded in the conflict, but, being a sorcerer like her, of course he did not die. The first thing she did was to place her cool hand on his filthy head and try to eat him, as sorcerers were able to eat all things by a touch, if they wanted. She only wanted his power, as deserts want rain, which is to say with scorn for its nature and despair at its necessity. But he was not eaten, and if he had power, then not one trickle of it ran up her arm. She felt that what was common between them was not common enough. She and other sorcerers and the people were of one matter, but he was of another.

Then she didn't want him anywhere near her, because he would certainly be her rival. But she didn't want him far from her, because then she wouldn't know what he was doing, and he might find her other half, and use her to destroy the peace of the Empire. This was how Kya now thought of her own peace of mind: she was the Empire and it was sacrosanct.

For ten days after his journey he lay in a stinking coma as she thought it out and she decided that, if he were like other sorcerers, then in a moment of weakness like this she could mould him, for sorcerers were vulnerable to the thoughts of others as they came from sleep.

He might have been strong and powerful once. She decided she would make him vulnerable, controllable, weak.

She would make Intana tend him until he was recovered. Intana longed for love. She would become attached to him and he to her in that stupid, sickly, fawning way. Then all Kya had to do was control Intana and he would be hers to do with as she wanted, without the danger of attempting any further direct contact. That was how it had happened to Kya long ago—that she was made an idiot by feelings—and so it would happen to him.

Cadenza danced me to a seat and set me down. I was tipsy and tired, I fell asleep here, drunk on the lives he remembered for me.

Intana was standing in the atrium on a warm summer evening, preparing to go to an Imperial function to celebrate the birthday of a general, when there was a commotion in the street outside. Shouting and at a run, their armour and leathers clanking, two guards dragged in a war slave and flung him face-down on the polished marble floor. He slid a few inches and ended up at her feet. From behind her Kya said,

"Leave him."

The guards, already well paid and anticipating a night on the town, wasted no time in making an exit. As their voices and noise receded from the high hall the metal chimes tinkled in the draft of early-evening air. The women looked down, each cautious in her reactions, lest Kya notice something she didn't like. Intana felt pity but she didn't move to help him.

Kusurg, Kya's bodyguard, came over, heavy muscles oiled and sliding under the soft fat of his skin. He dug his foot into the man's ribs to lift and turn him over. At Intana's sides the other women and the girls of the afternoon gathered to see what unlucky person had come to join them. It was rare to get anyone in from a war. It was rare that young men lived long enough to make it this far. They were sooner sold as gladiators, guards, soldiers or sent to the mines and the navy cutters where sail and steam drove the fastest ships and exacted the hardest work.

"The coaches are here," Kya said.

As one they turned to leave, casting glances at the prisoner's body, his face hidden behind matted trails of long black hair. His clothes—a filthy set of worn riding leathers bearing a clean shadow where armour had lain over them—were hacked and torn, caked in mud and blood and stinking in the humid night.

"Not you." Kya glanced at Intana as the others melted away, burning with a curiosity they daren't show. "Get him cleaned up."

Intana, grateful to be spared the party but shocked and disarmed by the request, glanced down. "But I . . ." She didn't know where to start.

"Kusurg will help you," Kya said. "I don't expect you to carry him. But make a good job of it. He was expensive." She paused on her way up the staircase and turned back. "He'll talk Imperial when he wakes up, so don't take any nonsense."

From the words she'd used Intana knew she hadn't meant him for another bodyguard, although he was clearly a fighter. They had men at the house, boys as well, some pretty and some not, but none of them had been war booty and none of them had fought in battles. Intana knew what kind of men did. She looked down at the unconscious man with loathing.

"Pick him up then."

Kusurg was just standing there, like a witless automaton. He bent at her instruction and without apparent effort hoisted the body up over his shoulder, cracking the skull against the edge of the vast cherry-wood desk where Sikri was tallying the accounts. He tensed with fear.

"It's okay. She's already gone," Intana said, unable to stop herself pitying Kusurg, whom she'd heard yell more than once at the sting of a lash for his dim-wittedness. There her compassion ended and her trouble started. She could take him to the bathhouse, but that was for people who were well, and anyway, that would be so public and who knew who might be there to revel in this new humiliation? She had to get him out of sight.

At her shoulder, Sikri said quietly, "He's already been allocated rooms. Why don't you take him straight there? Third level, the suite with the balcony facing the Palace. It's got its own bath."

Intana looked at the thin girl whose face was worried behind the lenses of its spectacles, the thin wire frames emphasizing Sikri's large brown eyes. She knew that Sikri was thinking the same thing, namely why on earth the best room in the place had been set up for someone more likely to murder, cause a riot or burn the house down than earn money, but they didn't say anything in front of Kusurg.

She took him there, Kusurg following her directions with amiable smiles, when he saw that she wasn't going to tell on him. He was about to fling the man cheerfully onto the white damasked bed when she cried out, "In the bathroom, on the floor!" Intana wondered if she could get Kusurg to stay. If the man woke up, she had a good idea of what he'd do first—try to escape and kill her if she stopped him.

He showed no signs of it however. He seemed almost dead and, to her disappointment, tall and heavy with it. He covered the floor where Kusurg had dumped him. Intana, dressed in her finest body gauze—no more than a net bearing tiny jewels for decoration—looked at all the filth. "Strip him."

The leather and the cloth underneath all the mud that had dried on it seemed to have fused into a single mass of rigid putrefaction. In the close quarters the smell was nearly unbearable as Kusurg tugged here and there, finding a brass buckle and trying to unpick it before he lost his patience and drew out his short knife. He stuck the single-edged blade down the front of the long jerkin and started sawing.

"Careful," Intana said, torn between a desire to see more damage done and the knowledge that she'd be whipped if it happened. She busied herself running hot water and pouring salts into the bathtub.

Kusurg grunted as he struggled with the man's boots, hacking at the straps around his knees, but then pausing for breath. He looked up at Intana and his bland face was knotted with curiosity. "Not really his clothing, I think."

"Why?" She crouched down to look.

He showed her the jerkin more closely. Besides his efficient strokes it had been punctured at the line of the ribs. The blood that was caked there and crawling with maggots wasn't matched by a wound in the skin underneath.

Kusurg's thick finger poked at the man's side. "If he was stabbed, this would be rotten. Dead now. Black rot poisons the blood. He's not hurt there. Bang on the head back here's put him out—new today, maybe an hour ago, and just a little touch of the lash." He indicated the reddened end of what they could both recognize as a long curlicue from the auctioneer's mate. Around it the flesh was bruised darkly under a skin that was almost metallic in its sheen. "Funny colour," Kusurg said, looking to see if it had rubbed off on his fingers.

Intana nodded. She kicked at the clothing. "Burn this, would you? And wait outside. No wait. Lift him into the water first."

Kusurg did as she asked and stood up, arms dripping. He glanced at her with a sudden, personal interest she didn't care for, but only said, "I don't like it when you get hurt, Francine."

How could he have said my name?

"Thanks." She put her hand on his arm briefly and saw him almost blush. He gathered up the ruined clothing, sweeping lost maggots into his palm, and took it away, whistling.

Intana put her hand under the new man's jaw to stop him from sliding in and drowning. With the tips of her long nails she picked away the heavy hair that was stuck over his face and neck, flicking it away from her as far as she could, pushing the ends down into the rapidly darkening water.

Mud and blood from a cut on his scalp had formed a thick coating across one eye and his cheek. She used a cloth to wipe it off with hard, efficient strokes at first, but then more and more gentle ones as the whole face was revealed. Under her hands it seemed to change. Here and there. A little. No, she wasn't sure.

But then she let her hand sink down into the water to clean the cloth and left it there, mesmerized by looking, drunk with looking at him. He was more beautiful than any living thing she had ever seen. The hairs on the back of her neck prickled with the fear of unknown powers. She knew this kind of trick. She thought she did. Well, it didn't matter. It wouldn't work on her.

She found one of his hands and drew it up for inspection. Although he had broken nails and there was dirt there, she could tell he was no habitual soldier—the calluses and blisters, cracked skin and thick joints weren't there. She ran her finger along the line of his jaw, turning at the edge of his chin. No beard, although he was full-grown. She set the water to run and drain continuously and as it cleared she looked down and saw he had no hair on his body at all, except for a fine sheen on his legs and forearms and the usual thicker tangle between his legs, ending in a neat line up to his navel. She'd never cared to closely examine a man's sexual parts before—except in her younger days before Koker Ai—but now she looked without concern, relieved to find he was after all an ordinary man in that respect.

His hair was full of lice. She had to wash it in stinking soap more than five times before she could call and get Kusurg to lift him out. Kusurg looked at the prisoner when he had been put on the couch, his brows drawn together.

"He looks very strong," he said, apparently puzzled. "Felt light though. Like a woman. Like a girl."

Intana, wondering what she was going to do now, said, "You must be stronger than you think, Kusurg."

"Don't think so," he said, but then smiled awkwardly. "Nice to say it. If he wakes up and makes trouble. I'll be right outside. Break his arms."

"Thank you. Call the maid and ask her to get some clothes, would you?"

"Mistress already has them put ready," he said, staring down at the spread-eagled body. "Colour same all over." He prodded one of the man's arms with the toe of his sandal. "Barbarian witchspawn."

"He is foreign," she said, but she saw what he was thinking. All fighters had the marks of their clothes burned into them by the sun. This man was the same even tone all over, as if he didn't react to the sun. "Go on then."

She worked on his hair with the finest comb, cutting the worst parts out. It was long and fine and spooled out under her hands with a kind of slippery ease that made her think of water. She had paused and was staring at its crow-wing blackness when the man took a deeper breath.

Abruptly he groaned and tried to roll onto his side. She jumped back in surprise and fear and he fell to the floor, his hands hardly breaking his fall in their weakness. He vomited blood over the white rug. It came in two violent, thick gouts, the first dark and the second bright scarlet. Clots and thick strings of it spread out. It stank of carrion.

Intana shrank back in her seat, watching him pant with his face just above the mess, joined to it by lines of matter and saliva.

As quickly as it had happened, it was done. With a sound like a bellows being pushed closed he slumped forward and his forehead struck the stone floor with a hollow, heavy sound.

After a second or two she pushed him onto his back with her foot to stop him choking. The stench of what had been inside him promised death. She didn't think there was any point in attempting to do what she'd been told. Whatever had happened to him had been worse than it seemed, on the inside, and if he wasn't dead yet, he soon would be. Perhaps it was a plague.

His breath rattled loosely in his throat, catching now and again on something vile.

She surrendered all attempts to continue herself and called for the maids to come scrub the place. They cleaned him up and laid him on the bed, wrapped in old and torn linens in case worse occurred, then they left her to take the responsibility.

For want of another occupation, and to calm her thoughts of imminent reprisals, she went back to his hair. His youth and perfection upset her. Without meaning to she reached out and touched his face, laying her hand on his cheek with the edge of her thumb just touching his lips. She felt a sudden sensation as though her own breath was being pulled out of her and her head nodded. She fell asleep.

And woke a time later sitting in her place, stiff and sore. It was getting dark. The maid had been in and lit the lamps but even that hadn't woken her. Her charge breathed on and she let out a sigh, half a yawn, of relief.

There was a knock at the door. It was Seppi Tar, Kya's personal secretary. She entered with a sweep of her kimono and briefly put her hands together in greeting. "Is he . . . ?"

"Asleep," Intana said, rising and checking her appearance. She glanced to the side in a gesture of uncertainty.

The girl turned her face and looked at the man with a direct appraisal she would never have shown in public. "Is he worth it?" She walked across and twitched a corner of the shroud with one hand, her fingernails gleaming with red lacquer. Her expression, beneath the paint of her elaborate makeup, mellowed considerably and her red-painted mouth became sad. "I see."

She glanced up at Intana, not quite meeting her eyes. "She will wait, if he will live. The doctor says there is nothing to be done if the wound is all inside, though he is a charlatan and I place no value on his opinion."

"He's still alive," Intana said.

Seppi looked down at him again, critically. "Let her wait," she said softly. "I will attend as your messenger and let her know you will not leave yet. There is a party tonight downstairs for one of the Greater Princes, which I must oversee. If not tonight, then the morning must do. And anyway, the city is full for the Games, she will have other plans to work on until then."

"Thank you." Intana bowed deeply to the girl. The favour was not trivial.

"It is my pleasure." Seppi nodded and silently made her exit, keeping her face towards Intana but her gaze on the floor, a respect Intana knew marked the seriousness of her mortal situation at Kya's whim.

"Perhaps you'd better live," she said.

He put his hand up to his head. His eyes opened. They were dark, almost black, and stared straight into Intana's own face as soon as they focused. He tried to speak and made another sound of pain, touching his jaw. Then he coughed and curled up over his stomach. She saw him finding his mouth full of disgusting things and moved as fast as she could, putting her hands out as he convulsively retched and spat it out. She cleaned herself up as he recovered.

His eyes were shut now. He lay and managed his breath before slowly dragging his hand up and feeling around inside his mouth with his fingers.

"It's all right," she said.

His face was different awake. It radiated a very calm, very gentle aura of watchfulness, not unlike being stared at by a domesticated cat. He tried to speak. Barely a whisper.

She thought it was Dacian perhaps, a language she didn't know.

His gaze became a kind of touch.

Beguiled despite all her cynicism, Intana felt herself smile back at him. She felt grateful, worried, weak . . . no, these were his feelings, she realized. But she felt them. She found herself frowning, laughing at this sudden communication, not understanding how it was possible.

He said something in a voice that had to move cautiously around the pain in his mouth, but she didn't understand it.

With one hand he pointed to himself and said it again. His name. "Jalaeka."

"Intana," she said.

"The fair one," he said carefully; her name's common meaning.

"Yes," she said. She asked him the same question with her look, to see if he could see it.

His smile was sudden, radiant. "No meaning," he said. "Not defined."

She laid her hand on his, not knowing she would.

He blinked and for an instant seemed almost shy.

More confused now she drew her hand away, partly in embarrassment. A sudden understanding came to her. It was like seeing the solution to a difficult puzzle without really understanding how the puzzle even worked. She said, "The first person you see, they give you your name. No. They make . . ."

He was agreeing. She thought it must be some religious devotional practice, some kind of mystic occult thing.

"You saw," he said. "You decided. And before. You thought. I listened. Not me. I . . . my . . ." He shrugged to show her he couldn't quite express it.

She laughed. "That's silly. You only just came here."

And just like that the contact was gone. His face fell into lines of worry and confusion. "Yes. I forget though. Forget before. There was a battle . . . The others must be dead."

"Okay," she said, smoothing her hand against his cheek.

He moved into her touch. She hadn't touched a man willingly since she was fourteen. She'd touched plenty in other ways that were able to mimic those feelings. She was a master of those kinds of touches, and here she was, her soul in the surface of her hand.

"Francine," he said and she bent over him and kissed him on the lips. His mouth tasted of blood but she didn't care about that.

But how could he have said that? He said her name surely?

"I'm sorry," she said and drew back, her hand against her mouth. She laughed. She felt giddy. Out of control. "You know my mind."

"Only because you want me to."

A year later. Hot weather. Dust. Ice chips melting in thick blue glass.

Jalaeka was seated at the feet of the Empress's daughter, Zara (the deranged one with the sadistic tendencies and wicked sense of humour), wearing a collar made of silver, attached to her hand by a gold chain. They were watching the annual bloody battle of the Games at the Circus, where the Orcryan Order smashed and battered its way to the higher ranks. On the benches below them sat the rows of monks in sandy robes, pressing the weak magic of their minds for this fighter and that, for political reasons, for their own advancement, for their friends. Beside the Empress, Kya, watching. In the Lesser Court seats, Intana, bored, disgusted, attending an ambassador, feeding his little dog slices of ham, longing to be anywhere else. In the cheap seats thousands of people sweating, eating, drinking, walking in and out from the latrine, scratching, swatting flies, laughing, swearing, gambling, grumbling.

Jalaeka only recognized two people in the arena. The Greater Prince, Mazranaz, whose job it was to ride around on his frothing black charger and pretend to officiate by breaking up fights when too many people were getting mortally wounded, and the black warrior in the skull helm who had nearly killed him years before.

Zara lifted her right foot and embraced him with her slender brown leg, her knee beside his neck. She pulled back and tightened the chain at the same time. "What are you looking at?"

"Dying people," he said, having long since found the best, the only, way to talk to her was to play along.

"Someone in particular?"

He took hold of her bare foot tightly and pressed it closer. "No one."

"You'd better not be," she said lightly. "Or you'll be down there with them."

"That's what I like about you, Zar," he said, watching the bodies being stretchered off. "You don't have any pretensions."

"You don't like me."

"No."

"And that's what I like about you." She brushed the fingers of the hand that didn't hold the chain through his hair, then wound the long mass of it into her fist and pulled hard until his head bent back against her knee and bent low to kiss him, her chin to his nose.

"Let's go somewhere," he said when she let go.

"I want to watch to the end and see the executions. I want you to."

He didn't show his smile. He wanted to see what happened to that warrior. She was disadvantaged by her height and sex but she made up for it with brutality and the kinds of skills that only come from obsessive application and natural talent. She was a general already, and so she only needed to fight a few. They were all good. She laid them on the ground one by one and put her foot on their faces until Mazranaz rode across to lend them the mercy of his blue banners of honourable defeat.

And then, right in the middle of the last duel, she quit. It looked like an unlucky missed footing, but it was quite deliberate. She let go of her sword as she went down and when her head hit the floor the strap of her helm broke easily and it went rolling away from her. She made no effort to get up and only missed having her head cut off by inches because Mazranaz's horse backed skittishly into her opponent and knocked him sideways as it took fright from another skirmish to its side.

"What was that about?" muttered Zara's half brother, Sedrepent. He flicked the knotted thread of his bets over his shoulder. "It can't count."

"She wanted to die," Jalaeka said.

Sedrepent snorted. "Could have done that anytime, anywhere, or earlier."

"It's not so easy," he said.

"More like a fix." The prince shook his head. "The whole place is rotten as Zar's miserable excuse for a mind."

"Fuck you!" hissed Zara.

"Oh, fuck you too," Sedrepent said wearily, then added to Jalaeka, "If you want the easy way out, you only have to ask." He patted his ceremonial sword.

Jalaeka shook his head. "Not today."

"I'm going back home, why don't you come?"

"He's mine," Zara said. "You can borrow him in exchange for your pathetic girlfriend, Lady Thingy. I want her to come to my party and be a pretty flower girl. You're not invited."

Jalaeka bit Zara's calf, not gently, and at the same time reached up and pulled the chain against her grip on it until the links broke. It wasn't such a thin chain. It cut Zara's fingers but even so, she didn't let go.

"Tiger," she said, suddenly compliant. "I'll be along as soon as all the bad people are dead."

"Don't rush." Jalaeka stood up and went with Sedrepent down the long, empty staircases inside the walls of the amphitheatre to the stables. They passed the surgeon's rooms, and the infirmary where the Order was busy placing its wounded brothers into carts for the short journey across the river to the Order's city palace.

The black woman was there. She lay on a trestle, staring at the dark arches that led back to the arena. As Jalaeka passed her he touched her hand with his fingertips. The seeming supernatural insights and intuitions he used to feel that had frightened him a season ago were second nature now. He wanted to give her a kindness, and to ask her to tell him who he was, but there was only time for the first of those. She took a sharp breath when he touched her, although she didn't look up at him, puzzled by her sudden feeling of energy and resenting it.

"Why did you fall?" he whispered, pausing.

She twitched her hand away from his. "I didn't."

"Jalaeka?" the prince called from far ahead, and he had to go.

In the rank darkness Sedrepent gave Jalaeka his own horse and took someone else's. "You have a way with Zar. I can't call it enviable. Still, a way. And I don't envy you for it either."

"She's not mad," Jalaeka told him as they waited for the gate to open into the blazing whiteness of the roadway. "She's just nasty."

"You don't have to explain it to me," Sedrepent said. "Her father was the same. Nobody was gladder than I was when he died. It's a mercy she's not in line for the throne. Mind you, on that note, watch your back."

The city was listless. Its smokes and steams rose straight into the sky. Birds dust-bathed in the courtyards, cats lay flat in shadows. Jalaeka went into Sedrepent's bed in the eternal cool of the wine cellar.

Kindness was not possible in such circumstances. No matter how much it tried to find a way.

Sedrepent poured wine into Jalaeka's mouth straight from the bottle and it flooded out and over the sheets and both of them. They both laughed.

"You can't tell me this isn't better than being with Zar."

"I can't," Jalaeka said, rolling onto his side, smiling at Sed because he was genuinely a nice guy.

"I like you," Sedrepent said, with a slight frown. "A very great deal."

"I like you."

"You do?"

"Yeah."

"Would you come here anyway? No, I shouldn't have asked that. Now it's ruined. I'm sorry. How stupid of me."

"Stop it," Jalaeka said, taking the bottle and drinking some more. He upended the rest over the prince's face.

"I don't want to stop it. I want to be loved," Sedrepent said, blinking away rare vintage. "By you. Really. As a friend. You're the only person who makes me feel like I have nothing to be ashamed of even though it's not true. How . . . how do I do that?"

"You don't do it," Jalaeka said, his turn to be weary. He lay back on the wet sheet. "I do it. And you don't know if I mean it as long as you're paying—and cheating off your sister's time doesn't count by the way."

"All right then. Go if you want to. I'll fix things with Zar. I'll give her some land, a few knights, a couple of ships or something. She's greedy. She'll take it."

"It'll never work," Jalaeka said. "I can't trust you. You're one of them. You always will be. Come on. You grew up with this. Don't make it hard on yourself. Here I am. I do like you. It's got to be enough."

Sedrepent rubbed his arm across his face. "You're right, of course. Smart and pretty. Don't you want to be free?"

"Of course I do."

"I can . . ."

"You really can't." Jalaeka rolled onto his elbows and bent over Sedrepent's agonized face. "And I'd be grateful if you didn't try. That's how you can be my friend. You leave it alone. I'll see you, in private. On my own time. If you want me to."

"Only if you want to."

"I do."

Sedrepent reached out and pulled another bottle of wine out of the rack at random. "Kya must have you in a hell of a vise. Here, have another drink. Anyway, you won't have to see me again after today."

"Going away?"

"No. Right here. Stuck like you. Hurry up. I have to be drunk before she gets back."

Jalaeka blinked, genuinely surprised that the prince would not take his offer. He could feel how strongly Sed needed to be loved, and his own despair was up to smothering proportions. He felt panicked by its intensity. He could see Intana's face, close to his own, feel the consequences of her clear vision that believed in love, even though she didn't anymore. "You know what? I've got a better idea. Let's risk the fact that I might love you anyway, and not reject you out of hand, given the chance."

"I don't know about that. I'd rather have my dreams intact for all the times I'm going to have to watch Zara chop you into bits. Did you say 'love'?"

"Stop talking."

"I thought you said 'love.' "

Jalaeka shook his head and took a drink. "Two more and I'll mean it."

"Good enough." Sed took the bottle off him and poured half of it down his own throat.

Not possible.

Kaela was someone Jalaeka met when he was out one night alone. It was a rare occasion. In society he was universally recognized. The place they met was not society. It was a taverna in a hole in the ground that had previously been a grain store close to the river, before the barges and sea-ships got too big for the little central docks and all the work moved away to the deeper, wider water beyond the city wall.

It was the same summer, but at the end, when the season's dryness was at its worst and all the hills around the city were parched ochre, clutching white cut stubble and drab dust-covered lemon trees. The taverna opened after dark. Jalaeka came across it by accident, heard good music, and went inside. A man on the door, an old ex-gladiator, took the cover charge.

"Trouble gets a kicking," he said, counting the coins.

The stairway was new and had been widened from the days when single slaves would trot in and out with sacks on their shoulders, but Jalaeka still had to duck to get in. The rooms below were several conical brick-lined chambers, joined by wide, arched doorways. The light was dim candle and firelight. There were dancing girls in cheap costumes, and performing monkeys who balanced and jumped through hoops, but the band wasn't bad. The wine was terrible, the water was worse, but in the quietest of the old domes there was a shadowy place to sit with your back to the wall, so he didn't mind.

Kaela was there because it was one of those places that nobody cared much who or what you were and didn't ask questions.

He was diffident, lonely, young, transsexual and simply out because it was an improvement on looking at the four walls where he lived. He expected nothing although he hoped to meet a couple of friends there later on. He had a talent for seeing Changelings, which was the Koker name for anyone marked with magical or supernatural powers: the type of people you saw less of now, because of the executions. He tripped over Jalaeka's outstretched legs in the gloomiest part of the curve as he looked for a seat, the legs being longer than he thought and the curve itself cluttered with too many bags and packs brought in by a group of out-of-towners who didn't want to trust the doorman with their tents.

Annoyed and frightened by the possible threat all strangers represented—plenty of people didn't like realizing he was not a girl—Kaela apologized profusely.

"Forget it," Jalaeka said. He was surprised to find the girl looking straight at him, because he was sitting in darkness and what light there was from the candles was prevented from falling across him by a strange concoction of shadows.

"You're one of them," Kaela said, against his better judgement, all mouth running off with him as he panicked double on realizing his mistake. "I mean. I don't mean . . ."

"One of who?" But the girl backed away from him and with a few quick and much more precise steps, vanished into the crowd. Jalaeka wasn't used to being feared. At least, not recently. He watched her, then paid one of the servers to send her a drink.

He stayed sitting in darkness and she came back, driven by politeness and cautious curiosity. He felt a thousand years old, too old for a game, but he played it anyway. When she agreed to sit down with him she sat bolt upright and kept glancing around her. Within a few minutes Jalaeka realized she was a man. It was a good change. It was almost perfect.

"You're one of us," Jalaeka said, meaning deceivers.

His new drinking partner stared at him. Huge blue eyes.

Dark hair. Red mouth. Pretty. Very. "I haven't got any talent for magic," he said.

"Me neither, luckily for us, so you can tell me your name without fear of sorcery."

"When I see your face."

"You can see my face if you tell me my name."

"I don't know the name for what you are," Kaela said quietly, his voice almost completely lost in the growing din of the night's celebrants. "Your ghost looks like the white stone woman, and I don't know the name for what she is either."

"I do," Jalaeka said. "It doesn't bear repeating."

"I really should go," Kaela said, putting his glass down half-full. His hand shook and it rattled on the table. "You seem like you'd rather be alone."

"Stay." Jalaeka leant forward to put his hand out and catch hold of Kaela's hand. It brought them unexpectedly close together and into the light. They were only inches apart. "I haven't talked to anyone real in a million years." He said it because it was cued up to be said, but he wasn't paying attention to it anymore. He was looking into the blue eyes and aware of the hand under his, shaking, and of the other's surprised, slackened mouth. "Wake me up," he said, leant farther forward and put his own mouth over it, like sleepwalking off a cliff.

I opened my eyes into the balmy air of our apartment. It looked artificial. I felt feverish and sick and exhausted by the colour and strangeness of the memories. I sat up straight and pushed my hair back.

"That place," I said to Cadenza, stunned by how relentlessly human and normal it had been, how real. But I knew without a doubt. "You loved *him*. More than anybody. More than . . ." Don't say *me* Francine, you moron, I thought. Even if it is true. "What happened to him?"

"Another time," Cadenza said. She was staring straight ahead, into nothing. I guessed that Greg had gone to sleep in our dressing room.

I felt too dizzy to stand up. I looked at Cadenza, really looked, and realized what I was seeing. Cadenza is an altar. "Oh god."

"He wasn't anything like this," she snapped, wrapping her arms around herself tightly. "Nothing like it at all."

"No," I said, meaning sorry. "Of course not. I remember . . . I think. I think it was a stupid wish, wanting to be . . . to know you. Like this. You were right. I totally get it now. I think . . ." His aching sadness hurt me. I could feel it. But I still wanted to know what he'd meant on the first day we met when he said, *You saw what I should have been.* "Did I make you?"

"What?" Cadenza snapped out of her reverie and looked me in the eye. She snorted and smiled. "You? No sweetie. You didn't do a thing. I just liked the look of what I saw in your face."

"So, you're not . . . and I'm not responsible for all of this?" I asked.

"For this perfect situation? Give me some credit, darling. I may not be the manliest vision of conquering supremacy that ever sashayed down the pike, but that world and its works were made of more dreams than yours alone. I'm my own girl these days, and even in those days. I could have found myself some misogynist death squad soldiers to give me some backbone if I wanted to, but I never cared for the uniforms. Making takes but an instant, character—forever."

I kissed her cheek, the moment as sweetly surreal as any I ever shared with Jalaeka. "Have you been reading Oscar Wilde?"

"Reading it? Honey, I am the living embodiment of the eternal struggle to become as trivial and superficial as possible, a thing that cannot be highly recommended enough as proof against the various Earthly agonies. I should think not. You must be confusing me with somebody far more serious, such as yourself."

"But if I didn't do it then why . . ."

"Because it's your birthday, I will forgo observing that you are being less than perspicacious. Shh. You talk entirely too much."

"I love you, I love you, I love you . . ." I repeated into her ear, stroking her beautiful hair.

53/JALAEKA

And while telling Francie the truth, I was meanwhile lying to Greg.

After copying Mode and Myanfactor's patterns, after watching my own memories start to blur in Francine's keeping, after seeing Rita . . . I had an idea. It was risky, very, and it made me nauseous, but I couldn't imagine another way that I could get Theo to buckle. He still hadn't come back, and that meant he wasn't going to give up so easily, on the promise of a freedom he already had and probably didn't like.

If I got it wrong, Greg wouldn't know ever, and I'd have done worse than simply kill him outright. I didn't hold out any convictions about Damien's claims that the Stuffies of the universe would tip any balances. Theo might have been given his orders by Unity, but he was its sole agent.

It was hard to lie to Greg. I've made so many mistakes in my life. In the past I erred on the side of caution. Now, the other way beckons. Nothing seems right. I don't know if I can trust myself to do it. I don't know if it's possible. It's just the only thing left.

I opened up the expansion gradient on the Winter Palace sheet, using the energy already present in the foursheet to fuel the expansion. The temperature, barely warmed by Francine's presence, began to fall.

54/GREG

Maramunumu, god of eavesdropping, whispered in my ear, vibrated through the plates of my skull, urging me to try harder to hear Jalaeka and Francine, though I didn't obey. I was Maramunumu's heretic. I didn't want to know what they were saying.

While Jalaeka went out with Francine this evening he also stayed in with me, in spite of my protests.

He said it was a valid separation, not a divorce.

We watched TV and drank beer and I slowly got used to the idea that I couldn't detect any noticeable differences about myself, in spite of the fact that when Theo had stood beside me it had seemed he stood inside me, and I was all his.

"You must have known all the answers to the things I was working on," I said at one point in the early evening, and I couldn't help the resentment that leaked into my words. "You knew about Metropolis all this time. How Sankhara is made. The way the Engine works. You knew everything."

We were sitting up on the bed, our backs to the headboard against all the cushions in the room. My Abacand's screen system was set up at its foot, showing *Sankha Jukebox* on the wall, to which neither of us was paying a lot of attention.

"I don't know any more about the way that Sankhara is made than you do. I'm not the same as Theo. I'm not Unity. I don't know everything, only what I learned the ordinary way, in my own time," he said.

I thought of Hyperion and his yellow eyes, his odd body vanishing as it touched Theo's stolen shape. In the TV singer's voice I heard several names: Mstaka, Ilit, Esriel—gods of spiritual forgetting, regress and denial. "How come you never Translated Intana or Kaela? You could have."

He shrugged. "I didn't know I could. I didn't know anything in those days, not about what I was, or Unity, or the Mystery."

"Do you think you're part of Unity trying to solve the Mystery?"

"Huh?" He turned to look at me and smiled, shaking his head at me as though at a schoolboy who hadn't understood anything. "No, no. Unity doesn't want to *solve* it, it wants to *find* it. That's what this is all about. Its efforts, its searches, everything it does. Matter, space and time are solved problems. But you and me and living conscious creatures—you saw their different kinds of complexities. That's why Unity was made in the first place. To escape the ennui of the physical, and the boredom of a domesticated, easy life. It was meant to decipher the patterns of complexity that defy entropy. Went a bit wrong, although it might be too early to call it."

"And what will it do when it finds it?"

"Eat it," he said. "Sadly. Because that's its design, its nature. Which never works because the Mystery it wants can't be found in unpicking things like that. It's like taking a car to bits, then wondering why it doesn't roar along the roads anymore. But they got one thing right. To really understand something you must become one with it. And with that insight Unity will carry on searching every living thing it finds in the hope of picking it apart to build itself a nifty little number that can drive to Nirvana."

I thought about it, trying for dispassion, trying to find some hope somewhere to commute my sentence. "If everything became Unity, would it matter?"

Jalaeka looked me in the eye for a long while, during which his smile grew and grew until I had to smile back at him, in that way you do when you're waiting for some very funny punch line. "Matter to whom?"

Oh. "I see what you mean."

"Shit, Greg, I don't know if it matters whether you're a free and independent creature or just think you are. I don't care myself. Why don't you ask the Forged? I'm sure they've got a long line of philosophy on it, certificates and everything."

"I was agreeing with you, no need to get stroppy."

"I'm not stroppy," he snapped, then caught himself and shook his head apologetically. "I'm frightened."

There was a pause. I could tell he wanted to laugh. I was sure I did.

"Maybe it's not that bad," I said. "You know . . ."

"Maybe," he said slowly. "Let's see, millions dead and incalculable suffering undergone, friends lost forever. You eaten. Why, you're right, it's not even as bad as this beer. The things you want to change never change. Just the wolves at the door and the nightmares you can't face giving birth to each other in the ice, and the ice coming closer and the city being pushed away to the edges at a speed that is exponentially increasing night on night. Greg, listen, this really isn't about your work or some experiment to plumb the depths of human experience."

He picked at the label on his bottle and peeled it off in a single sheet, suddenly self-conscious. "I hate people who do this, but I can't stop myself doing it if the corner's loose, do you find that?"

He screwed the paper up and flicked it away. "Listen, if we stay here tomorrow night then the only way to get back into Central Sankhara will have gone. Do you understand? It used to be a hundred metres from the gates of the Park to the rest of the Sidebar. Now it's a hundred klicks. After tonight it will be a thousand. Then ten thousand. By this time next week there will be no Forged human capable of reaching you and no machine capable of carrying you back either, because the land will grow faster than they can travel. Shortly after that it will reach an expansion that equals the speed of light, if it gets that far, and the temperature will fall to near absolute zero."

"What?" That was ridiculous.

"But I'll be able to reach you. As long as I live. Which is something I wanted to talk to you about, actually. Have you got a minute?"

"No. Call me Thorsday."

"Okay, Thorsday. I need you to come with me to Engine House. You and Damien. I need you to believe that I can defeat

Theo. I need him to take off the Regulator and use the Engine to intercede on the remaking, because the Stuff of which I am made is not reactive in the same way that Unity Stuff is reactive. I don't just respond like putty anymore since Francine did me over. I need it to change me. Will you do it?"

"How could that work? You just told me about it. Unity . . ."

"I'd have to tell you at one point, wouldn't I? The time it takes Unity to steal thoughts out of your head, make a counter-plan and put it into action is marginally less time than it takes you to blink. Telling you now is fine. Won't make any difference. If it wants to try and stop me, it can do it at any point. But Theo's the thinker, and he isn't here thinking in your grey matter. He's licking himself down over in another universe, though that won't last. And to be honest, I don't have any other ideas left."

"What about Francine?"

"I don't want her anywhere near this."

"I mean, she's the more credible witness. She made you . . ."

"She's been through enough. We can't just walk into Engine House. You know how Sankhara is. There'll be some price to getting in, not to mention the Engine's own defensive systems. I can take care of those, but not if I have to watch out for both of you as well. Anyway, look on the bright side. You get to see the Engine at work."

I finished my drink and closed my eyes. I dared myself to look down, inside. It occurred to me that I was now a Stuffie. Running out of excuses. "The thing is, I don't know if I believe. Damien . . ." Damien switched beliefs with the ease of switching underwear . . .

"Wish then. You can do that, right? You do want to get out of there?"

"Yeah."

There had been something very wrong about that conversation. Later, when I went to bed, exhausted, and wrote my journal entry,

I noted it down as closely as I could in the hope that I could discern what bothered me so much about it—not the prospect of going to Engine House, even, because I no longer felt afraid for my life as I would have at the same idea a few days ago. The whole thing seemed odd. But I had to believe him, because he knew more than I did, even if he had learned it the hard way. He was the real thing.

I lay in their bed in the old dressing room and wondered what was happening to the rest of the Palace. The third time I opened my eyes it was daylight and the apartment was incredibly cold. I was shivering before I got through to the living room. They were packing.

Jalaeka threw a rucksack down on the floor and said to Francine, "That's it. Greg, what do you need?"

"Just my Abacand," I said, yawning and feeling for its familiar shape in my pocket.

"Okay."

"What's going on?" I asked Francine.

"We're leaving."

"We're not *walking*?" I asked.

"You're not," said a new voice I didn't recognize at all. It was gritty and low-pitched but feminine.

I started, then looked questioningly at Francine. Behind her I saw a giant figure stand up from where it had been seated on the floor near the fire.

"This is the Light Angel Valkyrie Skuld," Francine said. "She's come to arrest you."

"Protective custodial care," said the Valkyrie. Her servomotors hummed sweetly, like distant bees, as she walked forward. "I regret any inconvenience, Dr. Saxton, but Belshazzar has instructed me to look after you until this situation is resolved." Military Forged were frequently less than lovely to Unevolved eyes but she had a Palladian elegance, a classical bearing that made me instantly think of Athena. Maybe it was the helm.

Jalaeka walked back in. "You need more clothes," he said to

me and picked up wrapped packs of new gear, tore them open and flung the contents at me. "Get dressed. Here's breakfast," and he passed Francine a can of that multinutrient gop they issue to Forged in jobs where eating wasn't always a priority. It was sealed with the name of the intended recipient—Valkyrie Skuld.

"Thanks," I said to her.

"Tastes like shit anyway," she replied and I saw two empty cans already on the mantelpiece.

"The vanilla is okay," Francine said.

I looked at mine. Original. It tasted like—brown things and maybe a bit like earth. The gritty bits were peculiar. I thought maybe Skuld had an iron filings supplement. "She was right the first time," I said and the Valkyrie smiled grimly at me.

"Francie," Jalaeka said, nodding towards the dressing room. She got up and went out with him and they had a whispered conversation. I didn't get the words but the gist was clear. He'd always been so easygoing it was fascinating to watch him tease her as he laid down the law. She reluctantly agreed to whatever it was. The Valkyrie, whose hearing was sharper than mine by an order of magnitude, sighed heavily and hummed a little tune to herself to block out the personal stuff.

I concentrated on fighting my way into the arctic gear. Immediately ordinary temperatures came back to my extremities, even my feet. It was less like being a sofa than I'd feared. Jalaeka returned.

"Francine is going to go with Skuld to Kodiak Aerial and wait there," he said to me. "You and I are going to Engine House." He walked across to me and unzipped the chest section of my coat to stuff a plastic clothing bag inside it, then zipped me back up to the neck with a pat to my shoulder.

"Against my orders and advice," the Valkyrie said, sounding cross but resigned to his overrule.

I watched him open the French windows onto the balcony. Snow and broken icicles fell in over him but he shook them off and took a deep breath of the dry, piercing air. He wasn't wearing any cold weather gear and I knew he felt most human things, so I didn't understand how he could take it now, when suddenly he changed shape without warning.

I felt a strange sensation, deep somewhere, like butterfly wings opening and closing. It wasn't from him, even from those wings of his that were huge intersections of night moving through the simple material fabric of the Palace and revealing it, like an X-ray, to be much more than simple. It was no sooner there than gone, but it left a little coldness in the pit of my stomach.

"Let's go," the huge winged thing said, finally looking round at me with obsidian eyes, and I let go of the breath I'd been holding.

I glanced at Francine and she came over and gave me a hug. I reached into my inside pocket and took out my Abacand, thumbprinting it silently to take off its DNA security tags. I put it into her gloved hand and made sure she felt it. Her fingers closed over it and I gave her a kiss on her forehead, aware that we were somehow doing the soldiering thing and that, unlikely as it seemed, I was the one going to the front. She returned my kiss on my lips.

Behind her, the Valkyrie stood up. Gold to Eros's black, she looked of this world, made, real. He didn't. I fiddled, settling the clear face-mask he had given me into place.

"Come on, come on," he said in pretended impatience. "No cynical modernist remarks about my suit from you, and no excessive homoerotic overtones from me. We haven't got all day."

His India-ink black hide was as slippery as polished stone. As I touched it the name of a demon, the first of all demons, the one from whom every evil had sprung, ran secretly up my nerves and into my mind. Fear and a sudden, awful doubt struck me dumb.

He picked me up and held me with my back to him, his huge arms under mine and crossed over my chest, his hands somewhere above my shoulders. My feet hung uselessly in their boots.

"Remember when we used to go paragliding in the summer?" he said.

"Yeah," I gasped, feeling my teeth freeze when my mouth opened.

"This is going to be like that. Without the parachute." As he spoke he stepped forward and jumped up over the rail.

There was no fall. Anadyr Park opened up in front of me like a film on fast zoom-out. I saw the Palace roof diminishing, the way it had fallen in on the attics and the grey, winged shapes that stumbled around in there. The white expanses of snow were smooth like sculpted surfaces. The forest was as huge. The ice, broken, crevassed, ridged and colossal, was as big as the mountains out of which it had flowed. White creatures I couldn't name ran between the trees. They ran to a theme of claws and monstrous ferocity. Nothing marked the sky but the distant, receding sun, not even a cloud.

I saw how small the Palace was, how vast the Park had grown beyond it, and fear made my throat tight because I hadn't grasped what he'd been talking about the night before, not really. The Park stretched way beyond the horizon. You used to be able to glimpse the other side of its bubble in the old days, could have seen the cliffs and headlands of Far Sankhara from my bedroom window like a mirage hanging over the end of the rose garden. I saw no sign of a city yet.

Tears ran out of my eyes, even under the visor.

There was blood on the ice of the frozen ornamental lake.

We passed that place, and over the snowless, arid tundra beyond it, where stunted trees were green but poor and the ground was mostly stone, and over the taiga after that. We flew more like an airliner than a kite, but I was glad of the smoothness. Finally, the bubble's edge came into view like the shimmer of a mirage.

The air here was churning with odd currents where the cold

met the warm of Sankhara. Clouds built and lightning darted. The sudden heat and turbulence flung us around.

"Hold on to your breakfast," Jalaeka said and we went into a steep, sideways glide. We passed through the edge and came in across Sankhara Bay at about a hundred miles an hour. We were overtaken there by a silver dart rippling with sunlight which braked in the most beautiful arabesque over the city.

"That's the Pterippus Vassago with Francine and Valkyrie," Jalaeka told me as we came in slow over the beach and I could see the tent town had grown there, where Francine used to live a couple of lifetimes ago.

I could see a few people out on the boardwalk in spite of the unseasonably cool nip in the air and the evacuation notice, some Forged out too, a Mer-culean atop his sturdy wooden life-guard's tower, its windsock fluttering in the gentle wind. They watched the Pterippus with interest, but they didn't notice us land above the high tideline on the sand even though we were much closer. Their inattention gave me an even deeper sense of unreality and I began to get very nervous.

Jalaeka became his usual self as he let me go and I struggled to get out of my sweltering, smothering clothing as he reclaimed the bag he gave me in the Palace and got dressed. We left my winter gear stuffed under the boardwalk weighted with a rock, and walked up onto the soft, weathered wood as we had done a hundred times or more. My shoulders ached where they'd been held.

We sat for a few moments on the bench at the tram stop, looking across the road at the row of Victorian boarding-houses. One was scruffy, overgrown in the garden, with peeling paint-work and boarded-up windows on the ground floor. So far as I knew, nobody had ever passed beyond the gate. Nobody had ever had a reason to. On the low wall outside it Damien was perched, eating a bag of chips. He waved at us.

Jalaeka bit his lips and looked at the place. "What do you know about Gateways? Specifically big important Gateways into mystical secret realms underground?" He sat on his hands and if he'd been short enough I got the feeling he would have swung his heels.

"Expect trouble," I said, realizing I couldn't go back now, no matter what his skin had told me. "And don't eat when you're in there. Or look back on the way out."

"Look at me," he said and I looked without thinking into his dark brown eyes.

"Hmm," he said, as though he'd seen something and was satisfied with it. From thin air he produced a thing I recognized as a cigarette and a paraffin lighter. He lit it, offered it to me, I refused.

He exhaled smoke. "I lied to you."

"When?"

"Just now. I lied to you. We're not here to change me. We're here to change you. Me and Damien. We're going to go into the Engine and get it to rewrite you."

He paused for another drag, then threw the thing down and stamped on it, then flicked the lighter on and off, then closed it and gave it to me. I turned it over. It was warm and heavy, nice to feel the round corners.

"Walk away now if you want to," he said.

I weighed the lighter in my hand. I put it in my pocket and walked across the road to Damien.

He got up and threw the empty packet into the hedge, brushing salt off his hands onto his pull-over. He gave me a hangdog look of extreme guilt and led the way up the path.

I walked through the tangled brambles that had grown across the space for a gate where no gate hung. I studied the cracked and pitted concrete path, nettles and goosegrass brushing our legs, thorns snagging and tearing across our clothes. My hand got stung. It was late in the season and the nettles were extra strong. I was grateful.

"Why me?" I said.

"You're the only one," Jalaeka answered.

Damien put his hand against the door's crazed and flaking paintwork, ignoring the knocker. It opened. It wasn't even locked, not even shut. It swung inwards silently onto a long, narrow and dark hall. He led us for a few strides, then stopped. I stumbled against his back. The first jolt of real fear shot through me like a dart.

"Because you're not meant to be here, all the defences are operating," Damien said lightly, gesturing to his left. "There's no way round them. Jay—you're up."

The shadows that gathered around us smelled of rain and saturated wood. I couldn't see a thing in their gloom, but the walls were so close to my sides I felt more claustrophobic than threatened. The door closed behind me with a soft but distinct sound of a lock clicking home and I heard the same cascade as I had in the pub the night of the pool balls. All the names—*here we are, here we are, here we are, Greg, you poor fucker, are you listening?* No Ktickt there.

As my eyes got used to the gloom I saw Jalaeka step sideways into a room I hadn't even realized was there. The doorway was simply a kind of ragged mouth torn in the lath and plaster of the wall, barely high enough for him. He ducked his head to go through and the smell of rain increased, blooming outward and up with a fresh fungal rider on it. Timber creaked and moaned. I tried not to touch anything as I looked through after him.

The part of me still functionally academic realized with a cheap thrill that I was actually inside what was known as a Legacy structure, made when the Sidebar was made. Damien pointed upwards and kept himself close to the wall.

A strange glow seemed to come from everywhere and nowhere. The walls of an ordinary front room ran with water and suppurated with growths of green and brilliant blue algae. There was almost no floor at all on the far side. The ornate black granite fireplace sat in a wall that dropped down and down into complete blackness. Beneath Jalaeka's feet the floor creaked and bent. Then he looked up and I let my gaze track his.

Seated on the broken floor above us, hanging through the

hole, which should have been occupied by a plaster rose and a light, was a creature that seemed to be made of leaded-glass crystal. It reflected and refracted light like a diamond.

Long arms ended in longer fingers spiked with sharp nails, some broken. Its face was elongated and as romantically faery-informed as the high towers of the central city Aelf. Large slanted eyes, colourless and transparent, stared at us both, one, then the other, then at Jalaeka. They didn't blink. A high forehead gave way to a horsetail plume like the Mohican of an ancient warlord's helmet but this was fibre-optic glass and its tips shone with crimson light. The mouth was excessively long and opened in a fierce grin, clown-wide. I saw a lot of teeth. The rags of its clothing were rough fighting garb, as if it was the spectre of a thousand-year-old horse lord, petrified and compressed to mineral form.

I was always wary of unfamiliar and complicated forms. It was typical of Gateway guardians that it should combine many historical and fantastic qualities, and the behavioural combinations weren't remotely predictable.

"Don't try to kill it," Damien suggested helpfully. "It's got unlimited access to the generator. Just pay."

The thing moved forward with the reluctant caution of all security guards. It dropped onto the edge of the boards just before the abyss and landed in a low crouch, barely making a noise. I felt the floor judder and bounce with its weight and realized how light the thing was. He was. He straightened up and, in his standing and movements, became almost human.

"Ah, crap," Jalaeka muttered under his breath, apparently recognizing something I must have missed.

"What?" I whispered, but no sound came out of my mouth. I thought I could feel something underneath us cracking.

Jalaeka took his jacket off. He threw the jacket back towards me and I clutched it, the metal buttons icy against my hands, denim tough.

There was a whump and another gust of chilly, wet air. I

glanced up and saw two female figures, similar to the first, clinging to the ceiling. One was tinged with the faintest muted colours like a delicate ink drawing. Her friend rattled a quiver full of glass shards and fitted one to a slender short bow. She didn't aim it but it sat in her hands easily as she clung to the soggy rim with her feet. Chunks of plaster fell down like cake icing.

A feeling I'd never had before began sweeping through me in waves that made my head buzz and my limbs jitter. I glanced around, urgently looking for somewhere to be sick—but it had already happened. I felt as if I were broken inside, in my mind. I could feel someone else looking out of me but nothing else about them, no clue who, no sense of them except that my body wasn't a hundred percent mine. Then it left me. I thought it was Unity, Theo rising, but it was only fear.

"W-wha- . . ." I said.

"Vampire," Damien said, feigning a casual air.

The guard took reluctant steps forward, sniffing and staring. He gave me a last, dismissive look which made me vomit unexpectedly, in gratitude that he'd lost interest. He refocused his avid gaze on Jalaeka and shifted side to side nervously.

"I know of you. Your blood may do me harm," the vampire said. His voice was thin and fine like a very worn-out vinyl recording in a museum. He sniffed again and licked his lips. He was trembling with a repulsive display of lust and fear. Clear liquid spooled out of his mouth, strung itself down to his feet. He panted as though he were burning up.

Jalaeka tipped his head to one side. He even sounded sympathetic when he said, "I won't hurt you."

There was a brief and unintelligible hissed conversation between the three vampires. The females chattered and made sounds like rubber tyres squealing in a tight bend. They coughed low tone calls. The male vampire shook and bowed under their scourging but snarled at them, a desperate, doglike sound, and for a second I thought they were going to start fighting.

With a dull snap of old timber the floor dropped two inches and began to tip towards the fireplace.

"Hurry up," Damien suggested. "If you fall through here, it's a long way down."

I sank to my knees, still holding the jacket. The vampire himself moved forward so fast I didn't see him do it. He fetched up face-to-face with Jalaeka and made a warding sign before his face with one fragile finger. "Eros," he said, so nervous that the sibilant s-sound stuttered between his incredible teeth. He hesitantly touched Jalaeka's bare arm with one hand and looked up again. Whatever he saw made his eyes open wider, their huge slanted diamonds changing shape until his pupils were vertical black lines inside his eyes.

Jalaeka reached out and slid his hands across its thin form, drawing it closer so that it looked as though they were going to kiss, but at the last minute the vampire's eyes filmed over white and it turned to his neck instead. Sightlessly it opened its mouth in an automatic gape. There were no two delicate snake fangs there but a row of long, fine needles backed by a row of gleaming razors. It gave a curious reflexive flick of its skull and used the recoil to bite.

There was a sound, a kind of juicy crunch that I felt knot my empty gut again in an agonizing cramp. Jalaeka staggered and made a sound that was a gasp and a shout. The thing in me that watched rose closer. *Is it me?* I thought. *Am I disconnecting from reality?* But it didn't feel like me. Damien gave me a thoughtful, frightened glance, watching me closely. His nostrils flared and he had to struggle not to back away from me.

Theo.

I stared at the vampire's spined back and Jalaeka's hands on it, gentle. Like paint dropped in water, colour was beginning to flood into its surfaces, spreading and brightening. Jalaeka was talking to me but it was hard to hear him, hard to concentrate.

"Greg, look at me."

There was a really peculiar noise. Not only the sucking of the vampire, but another one inside that. The colours in its body started to give off their own light. The female vampires began to whimper and the male began to shudder with a ferocious, unstoppable rhythm.

I could feel Theo's attention. I knew it was him.

"Greg for fuck's sake look at me, you prat."

I glanced at Jalaeka. He was hurting but he covered it well. Like someone's mother, he told me to get back into the hall, everything would be all right, it would be over in a minute.

Theo didn't want to go. He wanted to see. He was the vampire and the room and the house and the road and he could taste blood and the maddening sensation of unsimilar Stuff structures entering his vampire body. What was given became him. It didn't betray itself. He couldn't read it. It wasn't Unity. It didn't consume him.

Jalaeka was consoling him and he couldn't stand it. He let go of me.

The vampire itself was weeping. I realized that as I started to turn. I crawled the two steps back to the hall and onto a drier, more solid surface, where I sat and drew my legs up close to me. I hugged the cold jacket to me and stared over the collar of it into the room. Damien came and stood beside me.

"It's all right," I heard Jalaeka saying. "It's all right."

Then the female vampire in the roof made a birdlike call and darted away, her arrows chiming against one another. Her sister followed her.

The hallway seemed lighter suddenly, and I realized that sunlight was falling in weakly through the quarter-light in the door, yellowing the paintwork and showing me my own coat, my trousers, my boots and his blue jacket. All fine. All still there. Hey, look at that. Orange stitched genuine red-tab jacket, not puked on, miraculously. Reflexocare black men's casual pants already repelling the black streaks of filth and verdigris with that trademark quiet action.

The jacket and my hands were covered in large drops of

sticky darkening gore that didn't move. I touched my face and my fingers came down streaked with vivid red. I retched again but there was nothing to come up, it only hurt. I didn't want to move.

There was a gasp, a wet, sucking noise and a long, hissing moan of agony. There was a merciful pause.

"There you are." Jalaeka squatted on his heels next to me. His skin was smeared all over with blood around his shoulders and neck and his T-shirt was solid scarlet and clung to him, but he was smiling. He peeled the shirt off and tried to use parts of the back that were still white to clean himself off. Where I expected to see burst edges of raw meat, cut deep like a medical display of tissue but mangled and distorted by hacking action and intense suction I saw only his whole neck.

"Greg." He put his hand on my knee with a tough grip. "Don't freak out. No lasting damage. I'm fine. Eros snogs everybody." He rolled his eyes in exasperation at the role. "It's a talent. Look, let's get this floorboard out of your hand." He did something to my forearm with one fingertip and my hand went dead. I watched him pull shards of wood out from my broken nails and from under the skin of my left palm. I hadn't even noticed when that had happened. He ripped a piece off the shirt to tie around that and then took his jacket back and put it on.

I couldn't speak because I was vainly trying to stop Theo's thoughts running into mine. He was afraid and he was angry, yet the Engine itself was in command and clearly it didn't agree with him. We were in.

Damien shot me a scared look. He felt it too. "Hurry," he said pointlessly.

Theo felt that Unity was against him and his jealousy was growing by the second. Of me, I realized with shock. He was jealous of *me*.

Jalaeka finished his care, took a painkiller patch out of his jeans pocket and slapped it on my wrist. "There shouldn't be any more trouble like this."

But the reality of the violence was locked in my limbs. I was frozen to the spot. Then the vampire himself came around the corner and stood in the feeble afternoon glow.

His plume of horsehair had become a soft chestnut. His clothing was the jewel-coloured finery of a medieval king. The stretched-out parody of a face had become broader and gentler, though no more human, and his claws were gone, replaced by Tek-tipped fingers and the silver and copper designs of Autoware. Where the spines had been on his back there was an armoured plate. He stood straight and tall. Tears streaked his face.

"Captain," he said—still had all his teeth—and bowed to Jalaeka, deeply, knelt and touched his head to the floor. Then he stepped over me as though I didn't exist and walked out the door into the warm beauty of the day outside.

I saw him jump as he reached the pavement, an easy leap upwards to touch an overhanging frond of ivy depending from a lamppost basket. Damien's eyes followed him, then darted back to me. He watched me like a hawk with his glowing green eyes, then led us to a simple door beside the staircase, opened it using its brass handle, and we walked onto a narrow metal gantry.

Before us, below us, above us, to all sides was a darkness, faintly echoing to the sound of our steps. A few metres away in a pool of light stood an Android. It was steel in colour and form, partly fleshed out to human design and partly left unfinished—a medley of metals, wires, arrays and plugs. It turned its burnished-steel head with a smooth and perfect movement, not bothering to process human-simulated motion like the only other one I'd seen. Its body revolved soundlessly beneath, catching up with the head, and it walked towards us. It was over half a metre taller than Jalaeka and bristled with so many clip-on tools that it seemed furred with spikes and fine strands of metal, cable and fibre.

"Hello," Damien said to it and gave it a kick that made no impression on it. "Take the Regulator off, will you? Open the core for this guy here. There's a good bot."

It stopped a couple of feet away and its chin dropped silently. It reached out and took my left hand, briefly scanning my Tab.

The smell of oil, metal and ozone was strong. It registered me and it registered Theo's brimming presence with equal indifference before backing away a step. "The Engines are connected to, but not operational upon, human subconscious interfaces. They are retuning to your frequencies, Dr. Gregory Saxton. The Regulator function is enabled. This process is not open to veto except by your direct command. The Engines do not recognize your Stuffstructure companion, Gregory Saxton. We presume you wish to identify this anomaly and request its analysis as the reason for your visit."

From the hall I heard one of the remaining vampires screech horribly.

"Sdrawkcab!" it yelled in earsplitting disharmonies.

Sdrawkcab: god of returns, said my secret hot line to theology. I looked to Jalaeka and he smiled.

"Say yes," Damien said.

"Yes," Jalaeka and I both said.

"Accompany me." The Android half turned and stopped, statuelike, waiting for us.

We went nowhere.

An immense space, as big as Sankhara Great Stadium, boiling with steam and smoke and the cacophony of gigantic effort opened up into light around us, above and below. Vapour rose thickly and filmed on the android's skin. A clammy, oily heat fumed around me as though we were suspended high over a cauldron and immediately I started to sweat heavily. Through mists and the glimmer of distant flames I saw cogs and wheels and pistons smoothly turning, some larger than Heavy Angels, maybe larger than planets, others small and dainty as fairy pinwheels. They loomed in and out of existence with the flutter of delicate wings.

I felt the same forces within as without. I felt Theo with me, curious, malevolent, staying far enough away that I had no idea what he was thinking, close enough to remind me I wouldn't be doing anything he didn't like. Deliberately I spent myself on observation, thinking as little as possible, lest he hear.

The Android opened his left hand and two opalescent hawk-moths flew out, their wings beating so fast they were only a humming blur. The moths zipped out into the Engine and a ringing, tinkling sound like a shower of gold came from the depths followed by an almighty grinding crunch of desynchronized gearing. Metal screamed and was fused. Silence returned and the pinwheels spun to stillness.

I dared to look down through the grid I was standing on.

The Engines went on forever, into blue space and black space, into nothing and everything. I looked up. One moth had returned to its owner. The Android waited as the moth extended its proboscis and connected to his finger, alighting and folding its wings.

"We would know your instructions," said the Android.

Jalaeka had his hand pressed to his neck where he'd been bitten. He was breathing fast and was pale. His eyes were wide. "Merge."

I glanced at him. Merge what? Damien gave him a look of doubt and horror.

"As you wish," the Android said.

I watched the moth sucking vigorously, or being sucked, where it sat on the Android's hand. On its pale green wings there was a black pattern in the shape of a body lying splayed out and dead. Somewhere low and to my left, from the corner of my eye, I saw metal becoming elastic.

I listened to the Engines working. The pressure of their unknowing growing moment by moment inside me. Their anticipation became a flavour of burned, melted candy floss on my tongue. The walls of my rib-cage felt prickly and I understood that it had begun to work on me. I looked at Jalaeka, longing for reassurance. His face didn't fill me with hope.

"Oh god," I said . . . "What . . . ?"

The fugs of the Engine furled and thinned. Gears the size of steam locomotives whirled past just above our heads, their tarry backwash almost flattening me. Damien ducked one that would have cut him in half. He dashed across the gap between himself and Jalaeka and pressed his hand against Jalaeka's head. "Do what he wants," Damien said.

"Your will is becoming," the Android said in its mild factory-settings voice.

The moth flapped its wings slowly, savouring something.

There was a terrible sound from far beneath, a groan, a tearing rending rip like Hell's Velcro bursting open.

Damien screamed, a shriek that would have shattered a diamond. He fell.

The moth took wing and the Android watched it go. The gantry trembled. Somewhere out there in the vastness something fragile crashed and broke. Fragments of telescreen came hurtling out of the vapour as it lit up. They were active, a billion tiny televisions, and they were all showing clips from my life. Some of them showed me doing things, and others the view from my own eyes.

As it hurtled past one of them cut a gash open across my cheek and the bridge of my nose. Hot, burning pain flared and blinded me. I flailed out with both arms and fell, catching myself as the gantry we were standing on tipped and dropped at one side. I clung to the decking. A roaring, screaming cacophony of metal and matter being ground and folded by brute force sent pain shooting through my ears.

I saw between my fingers that the Android had hold of Jalaeka's head in its hands, its body and his anchored to the canting floor by clamps on its feet. Its fingertips were extruding fine wires. They ran down into his face and through the surface of his eyes. His body hung in the machine's grip, his hands opening and closing convulsively.

"Don't look, Greg. You don't have to."

Theo rose with the smoothness of a wave and pushed me aside. I felt him struggling within the Engine, doing something to it that was not what it was doing. There was a moment where I seemed to float free of my body and look down on it from above. Then I heard a voice rolling the names of god off like reading a list and beyond it Jalaeka's voice, chanting his own name.

The Engine screamed and I went blind and deaf in my body, although I could still see and hear from above it.

The Android let go of Jalaeka almost casually. His body fell onto the decking beside mine and I saw he was still alive because he pushed his fingers through the sloping meshwork. The Android stepped back, lost its footing. It slid simply and easily through a hole in the rails, colliding with Damien's body and dragging him with it as it fell into the machine. As it went it called out,

"It cannot be consciously controlled. Do not worry. There is nothing you can . . ."

I saw it mashed and minced between a pair of rolling cylinders. Springs and sprockets shot upwards in a fountain, then fell back, sparkling into firework clusters of hot iron. I didn't see what happened to Damien. My face stung and hurt and my own blood rolled down and fell on the fractured glass an inch from my face.

I saw myself toddling over a patch of grass, rolling a blue ball. It was at the house in Cornwall. I saw myself watching TV, listening to music, at school, at home, on the bus, with Forged in classes at college, running outside, eating, drinking, sleeping, excreting, masturbating, talking, laughing, crying, reading, scratching, staring, scuffing my feet, doing the vast billion nothings I'd ever done. I saw myself kissing Katy for the first time in the back of a bedroom at a terrible party in London. I saw her smile at me like I was worth it.

Then I saw the layout of the Engine and superimposed on it another structure; the elevensheet, Jalaeka, Theo, Unity, me. They bloomed over one another in clouds of mesmerizing and rapidly changing pattern. I blacked out.

The vision was gone.

I was staring at broken glass and below and beneath it there was nothing but steam and silence.

Slowly I got to my knees, then to my feet, wavering on the slope of the floor. Jalaeka was sprawled on his back. I felt a powerful mixture of love and resentment as I looked at him; he was my friend, my enemy, a traitor who conned me into letting him control the Engine. I was not I.

He made Theo into me and me into Theo. He united us. We were one.

There was only me left. Me.

"You could have done anything you wanted," I said.

I felt strange, very dizzy.

"Greg?" he said to me, quiet and concerned.

"Fuck you!" I hissed to him. "What have you done to me, you bastard?"

He stared into me. "What you wanted."

I didn't know who he was talking to. "Don't play that tricky word-and-intent shit with me now."

"Theo," Jalaeka said. "You'll be okay. It doesn't have to last forever."

I could feel everything. Unity beneath me. Every second of every life in it, across time. It wasn't still, like a stored record, or fixed, like a real event locked by 4-D. It sang, each mote to each mote, and it thought, if thoughts could be the shift of resonating patterns across the spectra of reason and emotion. I was part of it, one of billions of parts like me, emergent in 4-D, sustained by the mass. Inside it I could see Jalaeka's peculiar sevenwave advertisement for a better way rippling through its entire structures, gathering vortices, creating distortions, creating turbulence.

I was so small. I was insignificant. I was able to do whatever it could do at my own whim, but I was not it.

I remembered meeting Francine, the way she had flicked all those half-baked statements about love away, saying, "Crap!" I remembered Katy talking about love like it was a commodity.

I remembered taking a dive onto the sandy floor of a huge, hot stadium. The crowd bayed for my blood and my captain saved me by missing my neck when I wanted him to strike true.

I remembered the church in Haworth and the little girl's mittened hand on mine.

I remembered Patrick Black, and I looked at the thing standing in front of me, whom I once called friend, though he wasn't me at all. I felt the possibility of growing larger, to encompass him, and realized this was the charge of the seven wave: you can get bigger and be everyone, or you can get smaller, and be yourself, but you can't be detached and you will always react to the desires of the ones who surround you.

But I have no idea which of these things I am, or want to be.

Beneath us something big and important broke free of its moorings in the understructure of Sankhara. It was the Engine. The Engine was of me, but not me. It had its own laws beyond my devising. It was tuned to me, unbound, and now it was listening to me.

"Time to go." Jalaeka held out his hand to me.

I wanted to take it in gratitude, and to kill him. He saw a blow coming and ducked it.

We ran out of the house and into the broken sunshine of midafternoon, him first and me after.

The sea was going out and clouds and wind from the west were starting to scatter cold rain that was turning to sleet. I rubbed my eyes and shook my head but it made no difference. The distinctions between one thing and the next were breaking down. I couldn't make out what was what. And inside me where Engine House had been, there was the floor falling away, into endless nothing.

I fell. I didn't understand.

"Come on." I felt him pick me up like I was a doll.

His night wings took us both to Kodiak Aerial as the derelict house on the boardwalk collapsed.

The Aerials were a blur to me. Up and down meant nothing. Gravity shunned my attention. I could see the molecules of things but not their wholes. I could feel the Engine, getting out of the beds that bound it and coming after me like a lost dog looking for its master.

I heard Francine say to me, "Greg, are you there?"

Valkyrie and Jalaeka were arguing.

I found the touch of his stone hand. I kept imagining the Engine coming here, my convoluted will, my difficult feelings for Francine that would probably get her killed. In a lull of sanity I ordered him, "Get me out of here. Take me back to the Palace, to the Park."

55/FRANCINE

Ironhorse Talos Pterippus Vassago and his avatar were the kind of thing that, in another life, I would have wanted to have my picture taken with so I could send it to everyone on Earth. He was named after the race of flying horses although his body, grounded on what was left of the lawn in an area of razed and blackened earth, was nothing like a horse, except that there was something about its lines that partook of the same beauty as a wild mustang. It was much more like a silver fish. His avatar was a thoughtful-looking young man with a rakish dress sense and a lion's mane of hair, not unlike a demonic librarian, who told me proudly that he was the fastest Earthbound Forged ever made and that Pterippi could give even the interplanetary coursers a run for their money.

I was missing Cadenza, worrying about Greg. I barely noticed.

The flight to Kodiak Aerial made me feel sick.

Over Sankhara proper the Valkyrie bound me to her with a harness and we dropped out of Vassago's door to make the descent ourselves. The day was cloudy and bursts of ice particles kept rushing through the air, almost as though alive, stinging my face and hands.

To my surprise Damien was there to watch our arrival. He was seated on top of one of the cable cars, whittling a green stick, and stood up as we came down beside him, the wash of Valkyrie's jets almost blowing him away.

He came up and undid the clips that held me to her, briskly rubbing my arms.

"I didn't know you knew each other," I said, disconcerted.

"I know everyone," he said with the breezy speed of deceit.

Some feeling started returning to my hands and I batted him away, almost falling over. The roof curved gently down from its apex, and we were swinging, and the line of cars was bobbing and I was never any good at board sports. My nausea returned. Damien took my arm. "Steady." For a few moments I looked at the view.

We hung in the bottom of a loop between Aelf 2 and the SankhaGuide Massif. I'd never been up here before and I was stunned to see hanging gardens as well as houses. All for flying people, and elves, I assumed. Great baskets of soil and hydroponic systems swung between the bubble houses, almost entirely hidden in mantles of green and flowers. There were pathways that even I could try to walk on—ones with boards and ropes. Also lights, and everywhere—absolutely everywhere—there were fetishes and charms, prayer flags, mandalas, magical symbols and small, peculiar little one-eyed dolls—gootnies, they were called. They lessened probabilities of bad fates by looking for good paths into the future.

I was almost ready to call Greg, then I remembered what we were doing here.

"Nice here," Damien said.

"Yeah," I said. It was, if you weren't sick.

Skuld seemed more than tired of it. She flipped up a piece

of the roof with her foot, and I climbed down the hatch, followed by Damien. He'd only just cleared the space when the Valkyrie jumped down and the entire line shook with her impact. I realized this was her place.

It was a very small space for such a big person but she knew it so well she'd developed a small-human way of moving.

I sat down in the corner of the car where a pile of blankets had been folded and stacked. Damien sat beside me, pixielike, legs crossed and arms around them to minimize himself. There was no heating and I kept my winter clothing on. Valkyrie offered me another ration drink but I couldn't face it.

"You okay?" Damien asked me.

"I can't stand this waiting and not knowing. I feel awful."

"Time for me to go see them now, find out what's happening then," he said.

I lay down and was able to rest and look out towards the sea, where I thought Engine House was. The Valkyrie seemed content not to talk. She cleaned her armour and refuelled her jet packs. I saw Damien walk across the high wire to Aelf 2 and go inside.

I took Greg's Abacand out of my glove and opened it up quietly. I didn't know why he'd given it to me and it had been on my mind all the way here. The machine came on and showed me a letter Greg had left for me. I was glad of it, no matter what it was going to say. Anything not to have to feel my way through how selfish, useless and hurt I was and how terrified that Jalaeka was going to go under and that Greg was going to die.

Francie—I've been working as much as I can on the changes in Anadyr Park. Remember when we first moved in here? We thought it was so fabulous. If it hadn't been for you, I might never have looked up and seen that ceiling. It was prettier in those days. Now it seems like another world, where everyone was happier. I was jealous when you found Jalaeka. I agreed with Katy, and thought he was just what you didn't need, but what I've got to say now comes out of feelings that are the reverse of that.

The timing and extremity of the shifts in the Engine activity coincide with two things which were more or less simultaneous: the release of the paper on Metropolis (official story-line) and when Theo found where you were. I think it's all down to Jalaeka's reaction to that, although I didn't believe it to begin with because I discounted him—Stuffies don't influence the Engine. He wasn't one though, was he?

The other night, when Jalaeka and I got talking, I think I understood for the first time what he really means when he says he's your boyfriend and my friend. He's your god. We often say things like this in conversation, but because he is what he is it has a different meaning. Jalaeka is bound to carry out your wishes, and mine. He does have a choice about what he does or doesn't do—I mean, he could refuse point-blank like anyone—but not about what he wants to do. Do you understand the difference? We made him. We are still making him. Us and all the others. Even though he says he chose them. They made him to do that. They made him into Fantasy Friend, who never lets you down. Catch-22.

Never mind about the underlying Stuff. I can't begin to guess what it really intended for him and Theo, and I can't start down that road because it'll take me off topic. I wanted to say—we're still doing it. You and me are pushing him to be a certain kind of person and a certain kind of entity. He's no more free with us than he was the first time out, when Chayne saw him and made him into what she wished existed. It doesn't matter how selfless the wish seems, he's stuck with it. He kept trying to explain this to me, I think, but I never got it until now—I was never sentenced to become Unity until now, probably that's why.

Freedom never really mattered because I always thought I was free. I was Unevolved and pure line, I was doing what I wanted to do, I got to study and be a big noise in Unity contact and it was all great. Of course none of us are free in the pure sense of the word. We have to deal with each other, negotiate for everything. We do have the power to choose what influences to accept and what to deny.

Maybe that's all he did, in choosing us. He's just more literally altered than we are. But the more I think about it the more I'm sure that it's more than that. He's Stuff, and he's altered Stuff at that. I think we've pushed this situation. I think we made him and we made Theo too, and Unity let us run with it, and this is what we came up with.

But here's the bottom line—I like him. I don't want him to be the stooge in some massive war that exists to salve my ego, or yours. I think he should get the chance to be free of our problems, and that means I have to release him from whatever hold I've got over him—a weird idea. It hurts to think that it's possible he was only my friend because I made him so, but there it is. How much more true this must feel for you I can only try to imagine.

But here's another thing you have to think about, because I know you think about these issues a great deal. If you were to free him—and I'm certain that his primary control is you—it's possible that he would stay as he is, but it's also possible he'd become quite different.

We are all the result of our history as well as our genetics and memetic lenses. His memes are whatever he has right now, but his history may not be expressed in his current form because he's bound not to express it. I mean that there are things in his past we don't or can't know about which might influence him now if only we weren't in the way. Judging by what we made him into, and the people we've seen through Theo—I believe that history represents a considerable risk. Whatever else he is, he has that world-destroying potential you can't deny.

And I've been very glad that he loves you, perhaps in a way that ordinary humans frequently fail to do. Love like that is hard to handle, especially on the receiving end. And I know you probably can't think about maybe having to give it up.

*Think about it very carefully, Francie, if you think you
want to let him go. Remember that he is Stuff. If you wish it,
he can be free, and if you wish it, then he can remain as he is.
I'm just not sure that if he stays tied to us, he will be able to
survive Unity, because we never do, but I don't know. In my
final addition tonight, I decided, weakly I suppose, that I
didn't want to be responsible for limiting his chances. So for
my part, and if it's worth anything or makes any difference, I
wished him free of me.*

*Of course, I can hear you saying—but what if it was us
who gave him those chances? Isn't this just another layer of
illusion?*

I have no answer.

See you soon, I hope. With love, G. x

Holy *shit*.

I closed my eyes and tried to connect with Jalaeka. There was
a sickening sensation of falling that made me jerk, then a savage
pain in my right shoulder. I felt him turn me away, neatly, and
send me back. *Not now.*

Then what now? Behind me I could hear the clicking, methodical noises of the Valkyrie's hard work.

"Want some music?" she asked me. "One thing those pointy-
eared freaks in the Aelf are good for."

"Whatever you like," I said, trying to sound normal. "I'm going
to try to get some sleep. I was up late."

"I'll keep it to myself then," she said.

The wind buffeted the car and swung and swung us. I closed
my eyes again and looked back, into the things about him I'd
been avoiding.

Afternoon in Koker. On one of the long streets that led back to
the riverside there was a bar, roofed with trellises of green vine.
Jalaeka and Intana sat beneath it. He watched the merciless

sunlight cut through the tiny gaps, slicing the shade into hard-edged pieces all over them.

She leant back in her chair, pushing it onto the back legs as she searched for a servant to call and slumped, with a minimal grace both clumsy and charming at once. She snapped her fingers as soon as a girl with a tray appeared and ordered cold beer for both of them. The girl gawped at them. They were often mobbed on public appearances. She was clearly thinking about selling her news.

"It's a liability coming out with you, the service is always appalling. Tcha-tcha!" Intana clapped both hands smartly and ushered the girl off before turning back and letting the chair legs thump down to the paving. "What're you looking at?"

"You."

"Well don't, not like that, it's inscrutable, not allowed."

"I'm sorry."

"And don't say that either. It's like we don't even know each other."

"Sorry, I mean . . . well, sorry." He smiled, half at her and half with affection for her.

In the few moments he had taken to absorb all of himself in watching her he had felt a fleeting tremor, like the sensation of absolute safety and warmth that comes with the recollection of a happy childhood memory, the feeling of home.

"Jalaeka"—she leant forward, thumped both arms down on the table and stared at him with widened eyes—"you've got to stop this terrible habit of apologizing. You're always walking around and acting like everything's your personal fault. It's not good. Not at all. Now, drink some beer and be more . . . definite."

He nodded and his smile faded, at least inside. He felt chastened, humble and also a fool. He should tell her what was on his mind, wanted her to understand. He wondered how to put it all, and where to begin, thinking maybe there wasn't so much to say only that it was risky to say it, but just then the girl ran back with the beer and he had to wait until she'd gone. Guests at other tables were looking over at them. Intana waved. They looked away.

"Tell me," she said, "before you drive me crazy."

He took a drink, rubbed his knee, smiled, stopped, looked down, looked up again, to both sides, back to her. "I feel like I only exist to please and when someone isn't pleased then it's my fault. At the same time"—he paused, winced, shrugged—"I feel very distant, as though I'm not there and what happens doesn't matter because whether I'm there or not doesn't matter. Does that make any sense to you?"

"Perfectly."

"It's like I don't have any feelings—no, that I do, but they can't make me do things. I don't do what they tell me to. I can't. I do what the other person . . . what their feelings tell me to . . ."

"You have other people's feelings?" She scowled, raised one brow.

"Sort of, I don't know, I suppose so. Perhaps it just seems that way. I think I don't know whose are whose anymore. D'you feel that way?"

"All the time."

"Like if you knew what you were doing, you'd hate yourself so much you'd have to do something about it, so you deliberately don't know, then it gets so you don't know even when you want to?" This was better. He was not such a fool as he had imagined.

She was nodding, tasting her beer. "Every day."

"Just checking." He could smile again now.

"You're so messed up," she said, shaking her head, "but I like you."

He raised his glass to her. "You too." It was the best thing in the world to be with her then. The relief made him feel bubbled inside, as though joy was rising in tiny spheres through his blood.

They drank with slow measure until the day cooled, then

walked back along the canal towpath where long avenues of trees cast welcome shade. Intana trailed her fingers among the tips of the long grasses that surged up from the bank. Feathery seedpods burst at her touch, scattering puffs of brown into the still air. She pressed her lips together, composing herself.

"Don't put up with it." She caught a stem between her thumb and forefinger and stripped it of unripe seeds so they made a little bouquet between her nails. "Don't start putting up with it."

"With what?"

She shook her head, flicked green specks away and looked round at him. "I know what happened last night. You and that Orcryan fighter with the knife. Lots more money lets them hurt you, as long as it doesn't last. Did she arrange it? I mean, did Kya know?"

"She says not."

"She says not? Oh, then she must be right." They had to go single file and duck beneath a low bridge. At the other side she rounded on him. "I don't know what you see in her." Her voice was low and had lost its airiness, become tight-knit. "But you'd better get over it because your mind is going." She glared at him.

He glanced away with shame at the greened water.

She shrugged and shook her head, started to walk again, muttering to herself. He knew he'd let her down.

He caught her up and tried to take hold of her hand but she snatched it away and folded her arms. "Are you sleeping with her?"

"What?"

"You heard."

"No!" He took hold of her arm above the elbow and made her stop and face him. Her look was cold. "What makes you say that?" he said.

"Because of the stupid"—she jerked her arm free—"dopey way you always make excuses for her, the way you look at her, the way you lie about what happened to you as though it was nothing. So why do you make out like it wasn't down to her? I just want to understand, that's all. Why? Because it looks strange to me. And don't"—she let her arms drop, her shoulders fell back, head on one side—"start asking about my problems to change the subject. You've never been a fool before, not like me. For you this whipped-cur act is all new."

He took a sharp breath, timed for a scathing response, but abruptly had no idea what he was going to say with it. Her accusation rang with justice. In fact it gave words to what he had been unable to say to himself. Hearing them was painful and on his side the cuts muttered to life under their dressing, stinging and pulsing as though they too gasped for air.

"Because," he said, trying to position himself to prevent her leaving him, feeling that it was imminent, as though she had already gone and he was cold, "she's damaged and it's not her fault she's like this. And because she has your life in her hands." He wanted to use the trick of hearing thoughts he'd discovered, to find out what she felt as he said this, to be sure.

Intana didn't move, not so much as an eyelash, but the frank expression became cynical on her face. She glanced to heaven, smiled her insincere smile, looked at her feet. She shook her head. A blond curl bobbed at the side of her neck. He was afraid in case she was angry, could not tell what she was feeling and that in itself was strange . . . he could try to guess . . .

She would not look at him. She gazed past him, squinting.

"Talk to me," he said. Suddenly he felt clumsy, didn't know what to do with his limbs. He moved his weight to one foot, then the other. But he didn't need to be a mind reader to tell what conclusion she'd come to: she was the hostage—his suffering was her fault.

"Fuck off, Jay," she said rapidly and without inflection. In the same movement she turned and started walking again. Her arms were crossed tightly, holding each other as she increased her pace.

He followed her, exasperated at her wrong logic. "Anna!"

A flurry of tiny moths rose from the long grass as she walked through it and she brushed them away from her too quickly, breaking some of them in the folds of the long dress where they left little smudges of dark dust. She stopped to flick at them and he caught hold of her hands.

"It doesn't matter," she said quickly, head down. "It doesn't matter, so let's not talk about it anymore. You think what you want. Why not?" Across the unruffled water a bright red cardinal flew, chattering. They both watched it disappear into the bushes on the far side.

"I don't care about her," he said. The heat bore down on the back of his neck like a physical weight. In his hands hers were lax, pliable. "I'll do what you said."

This time she met his eyes. Her careful face had gone. "You're going to leave?" she said. She took a deep breath, raised her eyebrows and shrugged all in one movement. "Well . . . I take it back then." Her voice was unravelling. She bit her lips together and her eyes narrowed with wrinkling like a smile. "Aren't you just full of surprises?"

He didn't know what to say now. Obviously everything he had already said was not what she wanted. He shook his head violently, tipping it back to get the heavy hair away from his face but it clung with perspiration against his neck. Another couple came walking towards them along the tree-lined avenue. They vanished for a moment beneath the dark span of another road bridge and reappeared, holding hands. He reached out for Intana's hand and began walking also, towards the others.

Between their palms a small slick of sweat was pooling. Intana was trying to free her hand. Her skin slipped against his but he held on.

A feeling—love or excitement, like being unbalanced on the edge of a long drop, fear but also anticipation—was making him think of stupid things. He kissed her ear. "Come with me."

"Where are we going to go?" Her voice was muffled against his shoulder.

"I don't know." He did pull back now to look at her. One of her brows—the right—was raised as though she would take whatever he said with a pinch of salt. "Away."

She shook her head, mouth twisted into a wry shape. "I can't go," she said, then her face lost its certitude. It fell piecemeal into a formless uncertainty, lips slack, eyes brightening with a diamond brightness that swelled at the edges, glittered.

His heart imploded and, in collapsing, left a gap that dragged at his chest and pulled his head down. He kissed her. His lips slid on a soft waxy fat of fuchsia. He felt giddy and aching. Her lips firmed under his. He thought he was going to faint. She moved away then, rather sharply. The glittering was gone. She scrutinized his face and he felt her finger rub with quick, impersonal strokes over his mouth. She wiped the lipstick on the underside of her belt.

"Why not?"

"I just can't. Don't ask me again."

He watched her walk away into the brilliant light.

I know why, I shouted down the years to him as he stood there with his guts hanging out, not knowing why. She let you go because she thought she was your Jonah, your bad voodoun. But you didn't want to be let go of. *Stupid* her! *Stupid* you!

I picked up the can I'd rejected before and took a drink. The Valkyrie tapped her feet in time to the music she was listening to, reassembling a complicated weapon. I looked back at Greg's letter.

At the back of my mind the things I didn't want to know wriggled in their shells.

I went back into the memories. I wondered *where* they were located, as I went; in him or in me, or if we shared them and they were elsewhere, in places neither of us occupied.

If he was my creation all through, as Greg seemed to suggest, then all of this must be too. Not only Jalaeka's history, but those other people that Theo ate, they'd be mine, with no life outside me. They'd all be just Stuff, pouring itself into the moulds from my head. Only I don't think I'd ever have thought of some of the things here because I long for them to unhappen. I could have imagined it, if I'm honest, because anyone could, but I hope it's not so.

After Intana refused to leave Koker with Jalaeka; and he didn't go into it, because it caused her so much distress; when he could have read her thoughts and didn't do that either, because it would have been an invasion of privacy; after all his consideration had got him exactly what he didn't want, he took a small consolation and went to see Kaela.

They were in love by now, in love like matches and rocket fuel. He couldn't not have gone.

When he got back, later, very late at night, into the quiet house, Kya met him and said, "You might think you got away with all that, but you didn't."

A very bad thing. He could tell straightaway. He didn't have to be psychic for that. Punishment as she had promised. And she was good at that. He didn't want to go. He didn't want to. But he had to.

She had two guards with her. They escorted him to a room down torchlit halls. They smelled of smoke. He heard a lot of voices laughing and talking in excited, ugly tones. In the room they reached, a stone chamber with two exits, there were a stool and a swing.

A guard stood on the far exit. Behind him the door was locked. He felt a spear tip stab through his shirt into the skin on his back.

On the stool a girl was tied up—he recognized her, she was Intana's friend and his friend, Tash. Her neck was in a rope noose depending from the ceiling and it was taut, tied fast to an iron ring. Behind her stood a man in a black hood, ready to kick away the stool. Tash was shaking with exhaustion from the strain of having to stand so very tall in order to breathe. Sweat made her clothes cling to her and ran down her face, along with tears. She breathed in gasps and when he got there she stared fixedly at him with desperate hope and her gasping increased.

On the other side of the room a naked woman hung in the swing and a man, standing in front of her, his hands on the ropes, rutted fiercely and quickly inside her. There was a queue of men behind him, disorderly in places, their faces turning to him now and all of them sneering in some way, small or large. One or two turned away and put their faces behind their hands. They laughed and joked about the two women. Some of them spat on them; the naked one as they watched her, the one who might hang as they passed her on the way out. This one, finished, groped Tash, pushed his hand up between her legs with a sawing action like cutting bread, and pinched her breasts.

"Dry as a fucking hole in the ground," he yelled to his companions and they laughed and one of them said—

"Get on and hang her then, she'll soften up dead."

She didn't make a sound.

Jalaeka saw all of this in a moment. And he finally recognized who was in the swing.

"So now you have a choice," Kya said to him. "Which is what you wanted, isn't it? You can choose to hang her, and send the rest of these men back out onto the streets where I found them. Or you can join the queue. What'll it be?"

No. No. No. No. No. No. No. Not happening. Didn't happen. I do *not* accept this version of things at all. In what universe do things like this happen to people? What could it possibly be good for? What contribution does that make to the fucking meaning of anything? Who does this kind of thing?

"Hey!" The Valkyrie was shaking me. "Stop kicking me! What's the matter with you?"

My feet were agony.

"What's the matter?" Skuld had my hands in her two enormous fists.

I stared at her, unable to articulate anything. My body was so hot, my heart racing so fast I continued to fight her for another few seconds, then I realized where I was and lay in her old, oil-stained bedspreads and looked out towards the sea in anguish. It sparkled. The sky had cleared and the sun was brilliant.

"I was dreaming," I said, wishing I had been. "Bad dream."

"Must be very bad," she said and tentatively let go of me one hand at a time. "All right now?"

"Yeah." I thought I'd broken my foot and I was glad for the pain of it.

"I've got some meds," she offered.

"Thanks." I accepted the pills she gave me but only took one. She was taking back the water she offered me—served in a thing the size of a vase—when she suddenly went very still. I saw her glaze me out as she listened to internal comms.

"I have to go." She pushed me and my bedclothes to the side-wall and started to slap gear on herself with incredible speed and precision, moving so fast that her arms and hands left gold trails in the air. "You'll be all right here on your own. If anything happens, call Damien. Or go next door. She's mad, but reliable if you can shut her up for ten seconds."

"What? Where are you going?"

"Engine House," she said, sliding the visor of her helm down over her face. She stepped onto her trapdoor and gave me a final glance which I couldn't see.

"What's happening?" I shouted.

"I don't know," she said. "I have to find that out." The door opened and she vanished.

I watched her fall and speed out through the city heights trailing white and grey vapour. As she left sirens began to wail downtown and I saw police units in the Massif light up. I watched her all the way to the sea, then she was gone, descending out of my sight. The door closed itself with a hiss and clunk of the seal. The bubble swung and its charms rattled, an arid, soul-scratching sound.

The meds were strong—they were for her, I realized stupidly

as they started to take effect. I felt woozy and lay down in the quilts. The wind blew some rain against the pod's curved surface and I saw rain underneath me, dotting the tiles of the Aelf.

I had to find out the depth of my own trouble too. I didn't want to, but it was too late.

Since there was no way to run from the situation physically, Jalaeka saw a way ahead psychologically, two clear alternatives. Break up and fall apart, or go so deep that there's no getting out though at least from down there nothing matters. But those decisions would leave Tash and Intana to their fate alone. That would mean there was nothing he could do. That way everyone lost, and he'd be the one who'd made it happen.

He forced his belly to relax so that he could take a deep breath and let it out slowly. He ignored Tash's pleading face, Intana's tiny sounds, and made himself think, as fast as he could, and to ignore the emotion that threatened to make him panic this all away in the first seconds, the guilt and certainty that this was avoidable, if he hadn't been so thoughtless and careless, if he'd loved Intana enough in the first place.

This was punishment and it was control. If he were Kya, what would the choices mean? He put himself in her mind, in the mind of her pet, Zara, the expert on this kind of torture. He thought in the time it took to take one breath.

Intana was there and it was promised that she would survive if he chose the former option and killed Tash. But her survival was only of any use to Kya if he valued her enough to sacrifice everything to save her. Kya wanted to control him. She didn't care about Intana at all. If he stopped caring enough, Intana was as good as dead.

Hurting Intana this way, humiliating her, was to hurt him. That's what this was for.

He realized right then that he didn't have the promised alternatives at all. Tash was dead, no matter what. And it was likely that Intana was dead too, unless he acted very carefully and showed that he could be genuinely hurt and that he could hurt her too. Otherwise, their relationship wouldn't be what Kya wanted it to be—poisoned yet continuous, and therefore a source of pain—it would be intact and functional and it would have proven itself stronger than she was. That was a certain death. If she died, if he died, it wouldn't be ruined.

He weighed up if it was worth saving either her or himself this way. It seemed too likely that beyond this moment in time there would be nothing he could say, or do, to recover Intana or himself from the consequences of staying alive. It looked as though she was already far gone. He doubted that she could possibly see what he was about to do as anything but total complicity in her debasement.

This left Tash. Was there a difference if Tash died at someone else's hand, or not?

"Time's up." Kya had her hand on his arm and it was cool. He could feel her like a pressure on his skull.

One way. Or the other. There isn't anything else.

You are either smaller than all of these people, or larger than all of them. Even in the latter case, you can't win and you can't save. You can choose how everybody gets to lose.

Jalaeka walked up to Tash and made himself look into her face.

She was so terrified he doubted she could think anything at all. He hoped she'd been around enough to understand what the score was, but that's all it was—a hope. Her eyes pleaded with him, brimming with tears. She was choking on fear and disbelief that he, of all people, was about to do this to her. He could feel her, as if she were him. She'd never realized that she could die this way or how frightening it could be. She expected him to kick out the stool and make the obvious save.

"It's my fault," he said, although he hardly made a sound. The stool was not very tall. He glanced at the man behind her, the executioner in the hood, then stepped around her and snatched the hood off his head. The man stared back at him, struggling to conceal fear and repulsion, trying to turn defiant and cocky. Whoever he was, he didn't have the natural stomach for this kind of thing, but he could make himself over into a man who could fake it.

Intana was completely silent.

If he didn't kill Tash, said a voice in his head, there was a chance that Kya wouldn't do it. He didn't believe that voice, but it made him doubt.

He joined the queue.

"You're that pretty bastard that Princess Shit likes to wipe her ass on, aren't you?" said the man in front of him. He wore soldier's kit but it fitted so badly it looked stolen. He was taller, bigger, rougher, harder in every way than Jalaeka and looked on him with an uncomplicated, easy kind of hate.

"Yes," Jalaeka said.

"And who's this whore that managed to get herself here?"

"You're not fit to know," Jalaeka said. Some of that ease had crossed over.

"Is that right?" The soldier snorted and looked him up and down. "But you're gonna give it to her just like me. Just after me. Is that right? She fit for you?"

Jalaeka didn't say anything. They moved forward in line. He made himself look at Intana. She kept putting her head to one side or the other but couldn't keep it there. She had her eyes shut and her jaws clenched together so hard that all the muscles in her neck were rigid.

He glanced at Tash. She had reached the point where she was so tired she had to let the noose tighten now and again. When she choked she panicked. Spit coated her chin.

It seemed a long time, and no time. He watched the soldier in front of him hurt her. He took a long time and her misery pleased him. Intana saw Jalaeka watching and turned her face as far as she could in the restraint, away. The man came and pulled out of her, wiped himself on the tail of his shirt. A foam of blood and semen ran from between her legs. "I've known better goats," he said.

Jalaeka smiled. He saw Kya watching him. He could hear the

terrified whinnying of Tash's inadequate breath. It was so loud it filled the room. Every second flowed past like a river of cold oil, with an unreal edge, but not enough of one to take it all the way over the top. He refused to escape.

"Can't get wood?" the false soldier said to him, starting to pick his teeth. "You pretty boys are all the damn same."

Don't try to fake it. Kya knows all the fakes. She's right there, in between every thought. He knew it.

Anger, which had nowhere to go, started to melt down into self-hate inside him. That was useful.

Intana looked at him. As clear as daylight he could hear her thinking, not as an intuition, but as actual words.

Don't let her win.

"You never even touched her," he said to the man, and to Kya who had walked up beside him. "I'll show you how it's done."

He took hold of the swing.

"Look into his eyes," Kya told Intana. "Let him tell you why he's here."

It doesn't matter, Intana insisted, which hid, *I don't matter.* "Get off me."

"I met someone," he said aloud. *Don't lie to me. Everything matters.*

"Go on," Kya said to him, and he did.

She glanced at the hooded man and nodded. With an effort, he kicked out the stool.

The meds made everything duller to my mind: the way he longed to make love to her after that, to repair it, and the way she pushed him away effortlessly into other people's arms to save herself from having to admit any of those men inside. I got stuck in that disgusting, horrible moment at the bottom of the arc of that swing, which was also a tender and adoring moment; my moment . . . The drugs left me there, not able to move a muscle, even to open my eyes. Then, far too late, they knocked me out.

When I woke up I was lying in my own puke. The blue tablet was in it. Maybe it would have killed me if I hadn't thrown it up.

There was a furious noise, coming from everywhere. Both the Abacands near my head were broadcasting the Guide's voice. Every piece of metal in the world was screaming.

"This is a general emergency alert. Return home and secure your dwelling. The Engine Regulator is currently unable to function. Sankhara Sidebar has been temporarily detached from Solar Earth. You will not be able to leave the Sidebar. Return home and secure your dwelling. This is a general emergency alert."

It quieted to an average kind of alarm after a minute or two, the kind I could hear panic and shouting over from the buildings and streets below.

I tried to clean myself, found the two Abacands and turned them down, because they wouldn't be turned off. Then the bubble car jolted and threw me onto my hands and knees. I heard the high pitch and blast of weapons fire and the doors were all opening. In one huge indraft of cold, wet air the Valkyrie sprang up through her trap. A second later Greg and Jalaeka came sliding through the roof, almost crashing straight out of the down hatch.

Greg was slumped in Jalaeka's arms, his eyes rolling white, skin grey and feverish. His body jolted violently in the throes of a fit. He poured with sweat. I thought he was dying.

Jalaeka put him down on the floor, holding his head carefully and grabbing hold of the blankets I'd been on to help cushion it and stop it slamming into the deckplates as Greg kept on convulsing. He glanced at me. "Are you all right?"

"Me? Yeah," I said. I knelt beside them and touched Greg's shoulder. "Greg, are you there? Can you hear me? It's Francine." I glanced at Jalaeka. Everything I wanted to say, the way I wanted to touch him and tell him— "What happened?"

"I fused him and Theo," Jalaeka said, looking down at Greg, and I realized he was almost panicked. "I don't know if I can undo it. I can't. Unless he lets me. I took a risk because I thought, well, if Theo wants to keep on eating people who like me . . . but I didn't think it would be like this."

"What the fuck?" the Valkyrie panted. "Is this Theo?"

Greg opened his eyes, saw me, ignored me, looked around like he was drowning, then grabbed hold of Jalaeka's arm. It was only then that I noticed that Jalaeka was half-naked and streaked with blood.

There was a strange lurch and the Aerials shook. Valkyrie was thrown against the central bulkhead of the bubble car. Jalaeka fell across Greg. I was thrown sideways. A loose toolbox crashed down from its webbing and hard metal things went everywhere, several of the lighter ones on my head. With my face to the clear deck I saw one of the other bubble houses break free and plunge down. In the aftershock I was thrown back against Jalaeka's side and shoulder.

I stared at him. "I saw it all," I said. "The swing."

He took a deep breath and looked around with the glance that tries not to see things the mind recovers. Then he put his hand behind my neck and kissed me. He tasted metallic as he let me go. The house had calmed to a regular swing. The Valkyrie was back on her feet.

Greg dragged Jalaeka close to him and whispered something in his ear. Jalaeka got up and pulled Greg with him. His skin ran grey and black as it started changing state into the Eros form and halted halfway, wings like imaginary film, not quite real.

"Now what?" the Valkyrie said shakily.

"I'm going with you," I said, meaning both of them.

"You're staying here," Jalaeka told me, opening his wings without bothering to leave the house. Air, objects and space bent around them, whining in protest. Their edges bled light. "Wait for me. You"—he glared at the Valkyrie—"make sure she's all right."

"I can't! I have to go and help secure the city! We have to leave here."

"Just do it." Jalaeka lifted Greg onto the down trap and wrapped his wings around both of them before kicking the door control. They dropped.

I saw Jalaeka change fully in the fall, becoming dark and slick with the strange surface that Greg had catalogued as the sheerface of Love, back in the days when we thought we knew things like that because it was all about us.

Well, I thought, wiping tears and water and blood off my face with my hands, *maybe it's not.* I might have done a lot but I never gave him that body or that power.

Far below us on the golden pavements of the Aelf, the little house that had fallen lay shattered and two bodies in the wreckage were still. Strange creatures had gathered around it, bristlebacked. Their powerful arms and hands flung the wreckage aside and their long, heavy snouts burrowed with the desperate violence of hunger.

The sky darkened rapidly and the sight was lost in a deluge of hail and rain. Where the hailstones smashed apart on the bubble canopy they scattered tiny fragments of bone.

56/Greg/Theo

Come on, Odin said, laughing in the thunder of theogens in my brain. *Come home and we will feast all the livelong day.*

Jalaeka picked me up. My limbs felt like they were bulkstuffed with charged nylon: full of static pins and needles. I was about half a metre to my own left and falling.

The whole of the Aerials vibrated and all the bubble houses jounced on their wires. I was watching, in my mind's eye, a huge plume of dust and debris billowing up from the central shore area—the seven veils of the Engine rising.

I wished I could have told Francine I'd been wrong, so very wrong, about Unity. I was wrong about Jalaeka and my delusion of freedom—his or anybody's—there is no freedom from the push and pull of the self and the other, the lover and the loved, all these apparent dualities that I don't want to tell her are one. They can't be, must never be one, if there's to be anything at all worth a moment's breath. But this intention and my other thoughts fell to pieces.

I put things together. I tore them apart. Or I was put and was torn. It wasn't important.

Night fell and opened on the snow. The dark of Eros's pinions folded away and left the dark of true night and the unnamed stars of Anadyr Park. There was a faint glow on the horizon, a hint of a mountain's profile cut out of indigo. If he hadn't put my winter clothes back on and sealed me into them, my lips, nose, teeth and eyes would have frozen with the first breath. The clothes themselves, wicking but not empty of moisture, froze solid around me in a little more time than it takes to put a body down flat.

The Palace was far away, the border farther still, and getting farther with every second. I fancied even the stars themselves were receding and Jalacka's glance at them made me think he thought so too.

The wind and light that were left moved through his hair and over his skin like water. I thought, because of a general lack of freezing, that the cold didn't bother him. But it was more than a physical experience for him. He wasn't on his knees beside me because he wanted to be. It hurt him very well, just differently than the way it would soon hurt me.

"Go back," I said. "Leave me."

"You fucking cowboy," he said wearily, affectionately. Even his teeth and tongue matched the suit, inky.

On the seven level I could see the interaction of this desert with him and it wasn't good. The landscape the Engine was now remaking had an energy matrix that fundamentally contradicted his structure. He and this white landscape of emotional withdrawal were naturally incompatible and, forced together, the vibrations they set up inside him were distorting him. Worse still, his presence acted like an amplifier on its vibrations and the speed of cold accelerated. The energies being employed were on stellar scales.

I was in his house now, looking around at what it was I'd made out of him. Me and the others. Our visions, our plans, our self-serving policies and our dreams of better worlds. Unity staring at the futility of everything sitting in singular glory, as boring as the end of time itself. I understood their passion for him then, one instant of eternity with him better than all of eternity without—and if not him personally, then him in principle, her, whoever the hell it was standing there.

My clothes sent distress signals to each other, looking for more power. I started to feel cool all over.

Way back in Sankhara the Engine broke through into the Park and began its lumbering pursuit of me. As it did so it continued to work to the demands of what Jalaeka had become, making its own journey increasingly impossible. I tried getting up but I was frozen to the ground.

I couldn't see Jalaeka anymore, except by the shifting starfields that showed where his wings crossed the sky.

The worst of my chaos passed then, as what had been two people of contradictory sorts settled into an unhappy balance. Jalaeka sensed it and at that moment he left me and I pulled myself free, tearing my way out of the last warmth of the winter suit to stand on the ice in the clothes Greg had been wearing when he left home. They solidified so fast that they crackled around me, then shattered around my continued motion. Then as I stood still, their remains clung to me like iron.

I didn't breathe in. I didn't breathe at all. I could get by without. Half in and half out of Unity, I wasn't one thing or another, didn't feel the cold freezing me except as something unimportant, a temporary anchor to a time and place. I had enough energy to run at least to the end of the time sheet.

I was standing on the centre of the ice, alone.

I wondered what was underneath me, below all the many

miles of the glacier. Would his promise that I could forever taste sugar and know it, without being sugar, be worth it? Was there a prize there, waiting to make me into a voluntary immortal, prey to all that hearts are prey to, but without the pressure of an unlooked-for ending? The promise of death's rest, but not its unknown axe above my head. The promise of no power beyond a human power, but enough perception to look at the beginning of the universe, and its end, to live and love, suffer, be consoled and perish. And the awareness of the others optional, and their mystic states all choices you could make. Be yourself or let it go.

Would you take that bargain, Greg? Of course you would. And Theo, could you bear to stoop and take the chance of someone giving you a copy of an old song? Would it break you? Are you worth breaking for a melody?

I bent down to take a closer look under the ice.

57/Jalaeka

Francine. Listen. After Tash, after the day that hasn't got another name, I didn't do the great and noble thing and stick around. I fled town with Kaela as my hostage to a better self and closed my eyes and ears to the things that had changed and the signs that were there to see: that he had galloping TB and wouldn't survive, that Intana needed me more than ever but had to tell me she didn't want me at all; that I wasn't human because I heard thoughts and knew other people's desire because I reacted to it like paper to fire, whatever the paper said on it. Screw that metaphor, it sucks. You know what I mean. I wanted to tell you that in my time in the swing I started to figure out how all that worked, how to turn it on and off.

Kaela died in the winter I took him into, in the forest, and as he died, he made a city out of me, he took a dream of his and made it real. Or I did. Does it matter who?

*   *   *

Along the broadway of yellow sandstone the centaurs cantered past us, their holloas and shouts of excited laughter echoing as they whirled their copper whistles overhead, a cloud of birds following. I could see every thick hair in the waxed ringlets of their tails, every ridge on the feathers of the songbirds and as he turned to look down the alleyway where the pony and the children with the baskets would come out, he could see their faces clearly now, solemn and bent, nodding with the pony's short strides as they flexed their poems into shape and stapled them in place with the sharp double thread dashes of full stops.

Where the blank strand of the northern hills had ranged there was the golden palace that I'd first glimpsed in Capital, flecks of precious stones in its towers. Kaela wasn't even looking at it, so familiar was its presence on that wind-scoured shale. He was dancing in the wake of the lone drummer boy who beat the living sides of a lioness into booming rhythm with batons of cherry-wood as the animal walked before him.

I dragged after. I watched Kaela's filthy shirt and crude leggings of leather changing. With every strike of his feet on the golden stone the materials shivered and became light and airy veiling trails of spider silk, pieced together with their own sticky threads. The rattails of his unkempt hair rippled out into thick lustre.

It was difficult not to find joy in this place, even distrusting it as I did, looking for the underlying frozen forest. I glanced down at myself and saw that I hadn't changed. Over my legs the heavy, scarred leather and metal protection wasn't beautifying itself. I was being left behind.

"Hey," I said lamely, intending to catch up, but my voice swallowed itself as they rounded the curve into the square by the river where tall arches led away to the depths of an unseen hall, not built or cut but grown from jutting planes of crystal. Yesterday it had been no more than a collection of vapours projecting temporal forms and fading in and out of visibility.

The faint odour of salt and the sound of surf echoed gently

through its open galleries. I ran to catch up and put my hand to Kaela's arm where his pulse was a patter of febrile excitement. He was about to let go when a rippling laugh sounded and he was jounced from behind.

The flower girl stopped to curtsey to him and rub her arm where a cluster of gardenias had fallen away. She dashed on, trailing petals, and in her wake the dull brother followed, glowering, his face and clothes grey, a look of determination permanently lined into his skin. Everywhere she passed began to sprout into bud and when he had passed it was gone again.

The knock had sent Kaela against me. I smelled roses and the sweetness of freesias, tang of red currant, lilies. My body sang. I wanted him in an unholy way, in pieces, as mist, with a hunger I couldn't address or name or deny. I frightened and revolted myself. I kept imagining myself eating him, placing him in safety and permanent security like a jewel in my cold heart. I loathed it and what I was when I felt it.

A horse cantered past us. Its shape was lumpen and its fur like velvet, worn down to the seams. Its thick feet made no sound on the stone as it vanished between the long arches into the invisible hall. A tang of ozone flickered in its wake.

"Let me come with you," I said suddenly. I seemed to be looking at Kaela over a great divide. The scale of it yawed and frightened me. The sun on my neck was making me too hot and I could hear the skirl of the centaur's pipes and whistles from far away.

Kaela, in delicate eggshell fineries, a princess, laughed the careless three-note laugh he had had months before, when I first met him, before what I was sank its teeth in. "I don't think you can. I wish you could."

He was slipping away. I could feel it. A hasty, ill-conceived idea shot into my mind. I wondered if somehow I could prevent his leaving. I had the strangest feeling that I could have picked him out of time and remade him, without his fatal disease, but that couldn't be anything more than denial talking.

"Listen," Kaela said and took another step through the temple arches, peering in to the centre of the shrine through his heavy, blackened lashes, "can you hear it?"

I was shivering. A feeling of winter cold was coming over me. I looked at Kaela's animated, rapt face. It had been so long since I'd seen that expression turned on anything other than myself that I'd forgotten how alive Kaela had been before me. I heard the sound of breakers on a pebbled shore and the creak of timbers as they swelled and rocked with the sea. And children's voices, echoing many times as though they were locked in a deep underground cave.

Kaela reached into the pack he still carried and let it fall to the ground. I stared at the fragile contours of the object he held in his transfigured hands. They weren't the frail and sickly hands of recent days, but strong hands, the nails lacquered with perfect red. They held a white-face mask I had worn in the crushed greenery of a festival day long turned behind a thousand suns. The slanted eye slits and the half-open mouth made the vague face of a daydreamer.

Kaela lifted the mask to his face.

The contact between us began to narrow and falter. I tried to rush in and keep hold but he slid out of my grasp like water. I touched the mask. It was smooth and perfect. I tried to hook my fingers behind it.

Kaela twisted away from me. The sound of conch horns rang faintly along the blue corridor of the temple and the wash of the sea roared. Without walking he was vanishing down the long tunnel of archways. I ran after him. The blue walls flashed past. But however fast I went Kaela slipped farther.

I had a glimpse of sunlight shining on a bright ocean swell. Ships with tapestry sails were riding at low anchor on waves thick with red ragweed. There was the harsh, stricken call of a gull and the body of a plush toy horse rolling in the breakers.

I was alone. The city tore like mist.

I picked up the light shell of Kaela's body. Air sighed out through the mask mouth, condensing briefly on the lacquer's chill.

*   *   *

Don't think I didn't try to bring him back.

I couldn't dig the frozen ground so I put his body in the river. It still ran, although it was sluggish, thickened with grease ice, and it can't have taken him far before it froze solid. I put the mask on my own face, and selfishly lost my mind.

I walked on the mountain until Chayne found me, but she didn't know me—she was on her own flight from reality. So she let me go with her, up to the monastery above the clouds, where she thought it would all soon be over for her—absolution or death waiting like the only two cards left in an opponent's hand: two aces.

She lasted about two months on the self-purification trip, and found me out on account of the fact I never ate, breathed or moved when accidentally set on fire, which was something of a giveaway. She tried to stab me. I objected. That became our groove.

We had to leave the monastery because of bad behaviour. She turned drunk and I turned nasty. She didn't do sex. I didn't do intimacy. We were insanely jealous of each other and got ridden out of every town we came across since the mediating factor of other people made us nuts. She'd try to kill me, and I'd try to let her.

We wandered like vagabonds for years. I got money selling myself and cheating at cards. She spent it on hooch and knives and picked fights for fun.

You're probably wondering how easy it was for me to forget the other Annie. Seems like I must have.

No. I would have stayed with her even if every day had been like the last, but she turned me aside. I *couldn't.* Do you understand that? She decided for me and there was nothing I could do, even after the swing when I knew how to shut the door on what other people wanted. She'd already been inside me too long by then. Anyway, I did go back for her, when I could, when it was too late.

*   *   *

Koker was unusually quiet that day. I came back from the forest, leaving Chayne at the gate to wait for me. She was a deserter from the Order and they were out for her blood everywhere.

As with this kind of memory—you always remember too much—I crossed the river and the canal hidden in a stolen helm. Beneath the bridges the ships were tied up and silent, only a few lamps swinging from their softly dipping sterns.

The hostels that strung out of the maze towards the poor settlements around the canal basin looked alive, but their doors were closed and along the riverwalks the strings of paper lanterns that lined the water's edge had gone out. Clusters of their abandoned shells had gathered in floating masses where the slow water eddied.

On the paved roads dark mottles blew around my horse's fetlocks. They seemed to be everywhere, gathering in drifts in the gutters and choking the drains so that water spilled out behind them in little lakes across the street. As I climbed through the elegant squares I saw that all the public buildings were locked and guarded by soldiers, stiff-faced in the cool evening. More of their comrades patrolled the street and where a senator's sedan or official's horse passed him he was briefly surrounded by clusters of spear-carriers in private livery.

The Senate itself was draped and banded with purple and vast bunches of purple flowers clothed the steps. Their withering petals were thick here, running and trickling in tiny vortices where the circling wind caught them in a dry-skin rustle. In the run of squares ahead of him all the shops and taverns had purple squares tacked to their doors.

I stopped a woman as she hurried past and asked her who it was that had died. She paused and looked at me with more surprise than anything. "The Great Prince Sedrepent of course," she said. "His funeral was yesterday."

At the club beside the house I dismounted and left the horse out front. At the top of the steps I glanced at the house guard. They'd been there as long as I could remember with their unflinching and solid limbs set ready, their gaze as patrician as any elder statesman's, but tonight they were ordinary men. I had the feeling that if I'd touched them, they would have shrunk at the contact, shrivelled until they lay on the stairs and were blown by the vagaries of the wind into the road.

Pink light and the scent of dense perfume floated over me in a gush of warmth from the doors. I went inside, seeing faces that didn't recognize me but which bowed in respect away from the helm's unspoken declaration. I took care not to brush against them as I passed.

Sikri was at the desk. She stood up to greet me, bowing low to allow me to get an unobstructed view of her cleavage. I wondered if she'd always done that. I felt as high as a kite with my own self-importance.

"What's your pleasure?" she asked.

And then I was sad. "Is Intana here?"

A peculiar expression flitted behind her welcome. She hesitated, sitting back down with two shuffles of her bottom on the seat. "Not today," she said. Her lips were tight against her teeth as she smiled. "We have other blondes . . ."

"Where is she?"

Sikri made a quick motion with one hand and two girls ran up to me real fast, one light, the other dark: Ren and Myar. They pressed themselves artfully against me with instant ardour.

"She's not available today," Sikri repeated as Ren began to push her fingers through my tunic lacing and Myar gave my thigh a pinch. I put her hand aside, carefully. Sikri was looking for the guard, expecting trouble from me.

I leant forward and grasped one of her wrists. "I only want to know where she is."

She stared at me, thinking, and then prised my grip loose. "Certainly, sir. Please come with me a moment."

With an imperious gesture she summoned Honay to take over for her and dismissed the girls, who sidled off. She took my arm. There were a few private rooms on the lower levels that looked out onto the garden and she steered me towards one of these, where she offered me a drink. Keeping the loser out of trouble.

I took the helm off and saw her mouth drop open as the heavy thing slid to the carpet.

"Jay!" she gasped when she had found her voice, sitting down on the chair behind her somewhat quicker than she expected. "What in the name of hell are you doing here? And dressed like that?" She leaped up and kicked the door closed, then dragged the curtain over the open window. "The soldiers have been for you once already. Searched the whole bloody place . . . well, they nearly tore it apart." She shook her head. "What are you doing here?" She got up and kissed me.

"Soldiers?" I repeated, "What for?"

"Because of Sedrepent of course, you idiot, to arrest you. He left a letter."

"*Arrest* me?" I couldn't think quickly enough to follow her.

"Shhh!" she beckoned to me and I grudgingly sat down opposite her. She took my face in her hands and scanned me very thoroughly. I smelled licorice on her breath. "You don't know, do you?"

"Sika," I said, "where's Intana?"

I felt her hand stroke my hair in an absent caress. She sighed. "Why did you come back?" she said softly. "You should never, ever have come back."

I had no reaction at all. It was the strangest thing.

"When?" I asked her.

"Huh. Just yesterday," she whispered.

"How?" The carpet was deeply fascinating. I wondered how they got the strands of wool to twist so evenly. It must be very difficult, to get such an even twist that would stand up to being walked on without coming undone, without being tied off at the ends. And of course it wasn't just two strands roped together but two pairs of strands all going the same way. Almost a miracle you could make something like that. Who was the first person to think of it?

Sikri was speaking but I could hardly make it out. I looked into her face and realized that the words she was tripping over were describing what she'd seen.

I took the memory from her in one piece and tuned her out.

Intana was hanging from the branches of the cedar tree in the garden. Her head was at a peculiar angle because her neck was broken. The chilly light seemed to indicate dawn.

She was naked and her skin was very white and oddly perfect—no marks at all. A line of dried blood darkened the corner of her slack mouth, which was otherwise blue. Her eyes were closed. She looked like a fresh linen sheet hung up to dry overnight, frozen as rigid as a board with frost.

She was wearing a king's ransom in jewellery. Imperial diamonds.

Gently she twisted a little one way, then another and the metal and stones gleamed in the rising sun.

It was all hers of course. She'd made so much money of her own she could have left years ago if it weren't for me. Nobody kept cash there. You bought big hard rocks and the softest, purest gold; things that could be traded anywhere.

I went to get her body back. I tried to remake her.

It was a long time too late.

No, I won't tell you about that day.

And finally there are only two major makers left to tell you about. I've known a lot of people since I started this romance with Theo, and they all had their say, but these are the two of importance. The first is someone you've never met and never will, and you don't need to worry about competition. I met him in 1995—Alex Party was on the radio (you can load that off the

Guide if you care). It was uncool for guys like me to like dance music but you know I've never been that cool.

At that time faking an identity was a lot easier than it is now. I'd been hanging around for a few years, trying to get to grips with education and get up to speed, realizing there was another way to understand the world other than clashing heads with it. I'd got help from friends in Britain and Ireland, but things got intense between us and I worried I'd kill them the same way I thought I'd killed Kaela and Chayne (yeah, I didn't kill her in body, but I colluded entirely in years of misery: she sent me to Earth, then she must have encountered the lovely Theo, I suppose—long story, another day). So I ended up doing this doctorate in space plasma physics at MIT although I was completely charmed by their other programs in ultracold quantum behaviour and all that gravitation thing getting off the ground (bad analogy). Patrick had just got tenure for neurobiology.

These were the days when I used science to try and figure out what the hell I was. Science wasn't up to it, but it was interesting.

I'd figured out by then that I needed to know what either humans or I were technically and emotionally capable of before I did any more friend-killing grand gestures, and when I got sick of soaking up information I used to go sit in random looks-kinda-interesting lectures for light relief. On this particular day I'd been going to go to a public lunchtime lecture on the Darwinian evolution of consciousness.

By this time I'd got to the point where eating and sleeping took up too much time and I didn't do either anymore. I studied day and night. Anyway, this was a popular class with a big-name professor and was full already, not even standing room, so I went to the next nearest thing in the Bio block and saw Patrick talking about dopamine interactions instead.

I'd like to say it was his fine mind and thrilling presentation that turned me on, but it was the same thing as made all the girl sophomores sit in the front row, leaning over their notebooks, chewing their Hello Kitty pencils and flicking their hair.

Their efforts were in vain. He didn't get distracted even once from his carefully organized slides on the hypothalamic pituitary adrenal axis and the pathogenesis of psychotic thinking. As for me, I was starting to be able to give names to things that previously I'd thought of without names at all. I could have said to him, when I got closer to his floppy blond hair and sensible white shirt, that I seemed to be able to get voluntary control of other people's dopamine, serotonin, noradrenaline, encephalin and GABA levels, although I always simply thought of it as yanking their chains.

Not that even I was dumb enough to try that as a pickup line. It was my fantasy for a minute, until I remembered the fact that I'd sworn off relationships altogether, along with the food and sleep. No half measures. No friends. Nobody. Safe that way. The only conscious effort I made at that time to control people was to ensure that they ignored me, unless I had a pressing question about hadrons.

Even in today's world of well-adjusted human cocktails you can see that this behaviour didn't exactly stand out in the circles I was moving in. I didn't realize what it had done to me until I started feeling the effects as he talked and I watched the way his lips moved around the words.

So, we did psychotic thinking for an hour, then he asked for questions and there were a lot of easy and stupid ones at the front. He fielded them patiently, like you do when you realize nobody's been paying attention since slide one, and I had this urge to go out and buy a really great motorbike.

I was sliding my notebooks together—all empty, but not having them made people take too much notice—and thinking in Ducati-rama when he looked up and clocked me. Accidentally on purpose I locked gazes with him and forgot about being ignored. He did this charming double take. I blushed. (I know, I never blush.) Then he made a big fuss over doing something on his laptop until the rest of the class left and the early birds of the next class started to trail in. I walked down to him, all bets with myself off.

"You're not in this course," he said, flicking me a glance that was both unnerved and unnerving, not sure if it was predator or prey. He had this whole youthful academic and sensitive look, like a freshman English major or historian. His hair didn't know if it was surfing or trying to be respectable, but his eyes and eyebrows were dark and fiery and on loan from the devil.

"What are you doing for lunch?" I said.

He hesitated. "I eat at my desk on Thursdays. I have a lot of marking."

"What time do you call it a day?"

"Six-thirty."

"I'll see you then."

"Come to lunch."

On the walk to his office I learned everything about the way he moved, the care products he used, his badly mended leg break, his confidence with authority and the fact that he wasn't out to his faculty colleagues.

He opened his office door and locked it behind us. He put his computer and slides on the bookshelves behind him. I dropped my books on the floor and we caught hold of each other's arms lightly in the testing measure. We spent a lot of time staring into each other's eyes. Upwards of three seconds. I felt so lonely that it physically hurt.

We did that thing where you don't even kiss for a while, just move closer, looking into each other, feeling each other's breath on your skin, just looking and in my case trying to believe your good luck and your screaming lunacy. And in those moments the surge of anticipation got so high I thought I'd pass out from the rush.

He tasted of spearmint Life Savers and he gave me the romance kiss, the playful one, not the all-you-can-eat hard version, though I'd have taken anything. We spent time learning to kiss each other, like girls, and outside in the hall a student walked past and sat down outside another office, waiting for a tutorial. They were listening to Alex Party so loudly on their headphones that we could hear the treble line cleanly.

Patrick broke with me to roll his eyes. "Don't they ever turn those goddamned things off?" He wanted to talk to me because he felt safe talking, and otherwise now he didn't feel safe at all, and neither did I.

There was a spy-hole in his door. I turned him around to face it and put his hands on either side. I kissed the back of his neck under the long tapers of his hair, reached around him and unbuttoned his shirt while he looked out at the bored student and the hallway he knew from every ordinary day. The music was tinny and perky and annoying. The door next to ours opened and a voice said crossly, "Turn that off. People are trying to work in here."

The rest of the tutorial group showed up. They began to quiz each other about the set reading, and to try and make up sensible questions to hold in reserve so it looked like they'd done it.

"Lazy little shits." Patrick turned around. He grinned at me and chuckled self-deprecatingly, shrugged. "I can't do this. Goddamnit. But I just can't do it. I'm not . . . whatever the word is, used to this. I'm sorry."

I was so disappointed, I felt crushed. He was turning me down.

It was brilliant. I hadn't been anywhere but the middle of nowhere for so long.

"Oh god!" he said, seeing my expression. "I didn't mean it to be like that. I mean, I want to see you again. I just can't . . . I haven't got the . . ."

"Shut up," I said, taking his hand. I led him to the desk—huge, loaded with paper files—pushed stuff out of the way, sat on the desk and pulled him in between my legs, facing me. "Your noradrenaline is showing."

We made out on the desk. I had to put my hand over his mouth when he got so involved he forgot where he was. Without any talking we agreed to leave it at that. It was more exciting, to feel so many things still waiting to be found in the future. It was better to fool around and pretend we didn't know the score.

Afterwards he brought me coffee and I picked up the papers and other objects and put them back where I thought they went. He handed me somebody else's mug with a big Yosemite decal on it and shyly asked me my name.

We made plans to go out to dinner.

At the door he said, "I can't believe you've been here all this time. I would have noticed someone like you."

"I spend a lot of time in the ultracold lab messing with magnets," I said. "You really wouldn't."

"Why were you in my lecture, then?"

"Couldn't get into the Dennett lecture," I told him, and left him shaking his head.

Patrick equalized me. He never saw me as anything except someone like him, only better-looking and with faster one-liners, but not much faster. I became his friend, and his eye-candy boyfriend, on my own terms. I was off the back foot. Permanently.

The last one is Angel #5. I don't even know if she was Stuff or human. I never looked. She made Eros. You met him. She gave him the *darshan*. Until I met you she was the first person who never wanted anything of me except that I exist.

God, it's cold here. The Engine is tearing up the Palace, crying and groaning because it can't find Greg there, only his echo. I can see Greg himself—Theodore—breaking through the glaciation at the epicentre of the Park. He stoops. I listen. But the temperature is falling steadily down and I'm speeding the cooling of it; yeah, that was me. Fifteen Hiroshima bombs per second; that's how much energy I'm yanking out of the atmosphere, and that's only in the kilometre we share. All of us are getting slower. I think that this may have been a mistake. My hand's played out, and who knew how many aces Theo really had, or Greg for that matter?

There's nothing left alive in the Park now except the two of us. The white monsters of snow and ice are solid in their caves. The trees have been blasted apart by their own freeze and are falling on one another like ash. The air is completely dry and becoming dense. In a little while, when oxygen becomes liquid, I'll have to quit this form and I'll have to quit being anything that can talk to you.

From then on I don't really know what can survive this kind of cold, only that at absolute zero there is no motion and nothing possible, even for me. At least the expansion will stop though, so you don't need to worry about the universe imploding. If we get stuck here at that point, then you'll have to look for other ways of finding a happy truce with Unity, and hope it wasn't all invested in Theo, its agent, and his adventures in human space.

I'm staying because of Greg. What I did to him is unforgiveable. I know you understand.

I told you all this and remade you for one reason only. If you don't know what it is by now, then you'll never know, and my winding down to nothing won't matter. I chose you. You chose me. Everything that follows is the unfolding of this gift.

58/FRANCINE

After they'd gone, the Valkyrie stood in a terrible mass of indecision, bombarded by comms that I couldn't hear. More shudders wracked the Aelf, flinging both of us to the floor. I slid against her helplessly and added to my pains.

"Skuld!" But I couldn't get her attention from the voices inside. She opened her ammunition case and started to reload. "Take me down. I can't stay here!" She could fly out, but if the cable went I was finished.

Behind her I could see the other inhabitants of the Aerials leaving as best they could, many winged but some clinging and weaving their way down the Arachno rigging that formed part of the Aerials' attachment to Aelf 2 and the TacMassif. Aelf 2 began to grow. The cables stretched and shifted as its spire twisted and there was a groaning, rising, spanging sound that was no good.

Although I thought she hadn't heard me, Skuld abruptly lost her ordered manner and abandoned the rest of her arsenal. Perhaps she knew something I didn't. She slammed her foot on the trap trigger, picked up a rocket launcher with one hand and fused it onto her right arm. Then she picked me up, without the benefit of the harness, and swung me over the hole. As we swung crazily sometimes it faced the earth, but mostly it faced other things.

We fell. I screamed. I couldn't help it. Then I felt a huge kick and my back pressed painfully against all the spiky, hard edges of her armour and my arms burned with pain as she hung on to me more tightly. Our uncontrolled plunge became a fast but orderly descent. The wind noise was so loud I wasn't sure but I thought I heard a weird, high-pitched shriek. Then Skuld rolled like a barrel and I faced the sky as she lay back on her solid wings and with her right arm shot out at something huge flying above us.

The rocket left a white trail curving in the air behind it but I only saw a moment of it, then I was rolled under and saw the ground rapidly shooting towards us. There was an explosion that deafened me and shook us both. Shrapnel whined past in a deadly volley and Skuld said a peculiar and surprised, "Ha!"

We began to rise and the pressure of her metal against my bones became agonizing. She swung hard to one side and a gigantic body went tearing past us, wing, flesh, metal and beautiful peacock colours. It was flaming and boiling with a chemical green fire and in its wake it tore the whole of the Aerial with it in a massive tangle of cable and cars, wire and glass. They smashed into the low roof of the Conservatoire exhibition hall in train and gouted with viridian flares as they demolished it completely.

Skuld swung us over into the great, open green expanse of Pythagoras's Circle itself and landed there, running as she came in, but her run was immediately a stagger, then a stumble onto one knee. People were all over the place. Some who had run from her ran towards her, seeing someone they thought must be in charge. Skuld let me go and I fell on my face on the slippery, wet grass. I spun around, hurting but okay, and saw her on her hands and knees. Dark liquid was pouring out of her onto the ground. There was a hole in her the size of my fist running front to back. Her jet pack steamed and smoked. Aviation fuel became a transparent, shimmering fog around her.

"Skuld?" I said, sliding closer to her, touching the plume of her helm, afraid to go closer.

"Stay back," she said. "Shrapnel got me. Dammit." She sprang a compartment in her chest open and I found I could see about halfway into the total depth of her body. She took a field dressing of some kind out of it and stiffly moved to a sitting position. She put a patch over the horrible wound and held another one out to me. "Get the back?"

I took the thing—it was heavy and floppy like jelly, and it squirmed against my hands when it felt my skin and the warmth there. I plastered it down over the hole without looking too closely, although I had enough of an impression of burned flesh and bubbled metal.

"Strip off the backing," she commanded.

I did and the surface immediately crystallized and started to darken. By the time I'd pulled off the entire sheet it was almost indistinguishable from her armour.

"Thanks." She got to her feet and the small crowd around her stared. SankhaGuide's alarms had stopped by now. I saw her making calls by the inward look of her gaze, then she glanced at me. "You okay?"

"I'm fine."

Police vehicles and other Light Angel and Herculean officers had begun arriving in the Circle. Skuld did some fast work on her jet fuel lines and looked at me with misgiving. "I don't know what to do with you. I should go and assist with the casualties from the Aerial."

"I can do that," I said. "I have Med Zero Twenty." I took it when I was still attending school and thought I might want to be a doctor. It had proven to me that I didn't.

"All right," she said and I thought I heard the first signs of approval in her voice. "Let's go."

I went with her through the milling, frightened people, back to where smoke and dust were rising into the darkening sky. Aelf 2 had stopped its rise. It had become silver in the last light of the sun and it seemed so tall and fine as it stretched up to the clouds. At the foot of it the wreckage of Kodiak Aerial was a steaming mass of flesh and rubble.

"So," Skuld said, surveying with her sight on varied spectra, looking for things that might be saved as we advanced and tried to steel our nerves. "Tell me more about this boyfriend of yours."

I did, as I heard him talking to me.

59 / GREG-THEODORE

In a state of superfluidity two surfaces travel along each other without resistance: endless flow.

Perhaps the cold started with Francine's isolation, with Greg's disillusion, with Sankhara's entire freight of loneliness, searching for its answer. I expanded it, pressing Jalaeka against his love of the world to see which would break first. He pushed it colder, so that the temperature will ruin the Engine, stop the expansion and hold me fast.

As solid-state physics it's a fair trial. As the metaphor of our situation, again, fair. To try to use it as a weapon against me, even though Unity seems to have temporarily . . . ah, it isn't temporary. I am out in the cold. I am on my own. Whichever way I look at it, from the inside or the outside, the real or the symbolic, I can't but argue that it's poetic justice—the only satisfying kind.

I spent a lifetime searching for the elusive definition of what Unity might consider mystery, beyond physics and energy. The closest thing is poetry, of a kind, the poetry of leaps of faith and identity, without which nothing at all can be distinguished from anything else, not valued and not kept or cast.

My divergent histories of Greg and Theo make me what Unity always claimed it was, but secretly wasn't—a completely new individual composed of all those who went into it. I am not Unity either now, although I can see it from here and I know it waits for me to make my decision before it jumps. I am made in the splinter's image and it is within my ability to step free of both of them and become completely separate. Or to join either. Or I can end.

I think about going back—it's instinctive, to want to rush to the safe place, the old familiar routines and assumptions and what we used to know. But which way?

No, better to dig in the ice, using my hands to shake it apart with subsonics and throw it aside. The act of moving, even against the immense and growing inertia of the cold, is better. It's a long way down.

I don't know how cold it is now but it's very hard to keep my body going. Heat leaves it almost as fast as I can supply myself. Blue oxygen rain has fallen, has frozen. The hydrogen came last though it's frozen solid now. The atmosphere is gone. No clouds. No sun. The stars are incredibly bright.

Another couple of K down and I think I should be at rock.

Yes. There is something. In the dark I can only go by touch.

A wooden mask. A human face. I can feel both sides smooth, but the back of the mask is a peculiar, exceptional surface. The back is destroyed when I touch it, although it recovers when I don't.

I have to develop new fingers that don't give off heat, although there's no such thing as the entropyless gesture, and the atoms of the mask are severely agitated by my looking at them. They shuffle off, spread out, diffuse and disperse and lose their organization, what it was, in a pique of fundamental uncertainty.

The back of this mask is a Bose-Einstein condensate, barely above absolute zero, made out of oxygen. Where I touch it, I introduce massive vortices. It already had its own. This is where the cold is going, onto the back of this face I can't see, made of the great reactive element that drives life and poisons it.

I hold it by the other side and feel myself slow down. The face traps the few starlight photons that arrive here and holds them for its own. It gives nothing away. I get the impression that we won't reach absolute zero without an effort. Like all good Stuff, even splinter stuff, the Engine won't finish the job without my moral input. Do or do not, or sit here on your ass and freeze for eternity. It doesn't care.

Emily Brontë on the couch. Patrick Black's golden hair. Francie-Francine—a difficult girl, in the best sense of difficult.

On the ice at the Palace, on its ash heap some several billion kilometres away from me, Jalaeka is almost completely inert, as close to dead as I've ever seen a Stuff object, though part of that's bloody-mindedness. Absolute zero is where we all stop, but those of us with things to do in 4-D will stop long before that. It is now almost twenty Kelvin. Thinking takes a long time, although it doesn't feel like a long time.

I went up to him with the mask in my hand.

"I think this is yours."

"I left it there a while ago," he said and didn't take it. "Finders keepers."

"It's yours, if you want it." I meant Unity. He knew it.

"I don't want it," he said. "I believe that's the point."

I held it out in my hand and he took it.

60/FRANCINE

There wasn't that much to do at the foot of the SankhaGuide Massif. I pulled a couple of people out of a wrecked car along with some others as Valkyrie used her equipment to cut metal and lift cable around us. Then the creatures I'd seen before came back. They slunk through the crowd with blood on their muzzles, quiet and human in their movements so they were barely noticeable for what they were. When people did see who had passed they shrank back and a fresh riffle of panic ran through the lines. Occasionally a tile from Aelf 2 would come down, a silent, deadly missile from above, and smash close by. Fragments of one had already claimed a victim. The sight of the gore-mouthed creatures did the rest and those who had been standing around, either to help or because they didn't know what else to do, scattered.

I was holding the hand of someone who was trapped beneath part of a cable car door. Beside me two uniformed police officers were fighting to support Valkyrie as she leant down across unstable fractured bubble plastic to attach a line to the door so she could lift it free.

"Skuld," I said loudly, nervously, as the creatures dropped onto all fours. They were as big as she was, Herculean-sized, and although they weren't clothed, they were covered in a thick, rufous fur. Their heads were long and bearlike, with tiny, round ears and mobile, narrow snouts that seemed perfectly formed to grub in dangerous ruins. Their teeth were sharp and piercing at the front, where they bared them to sniff and flash their tongues. At the back they had hugely muscled jaws and teeth to shear rock with. Their front limbs had hands, and as they searched, they picked up items from the wreckage: straw dolls, charms, the feather and bone and occult paraphernalia—an incense burner . . . Each of them carried a leather satchel and into the satchel went the findings.

The Valkyrie looked back and groaned. "Gleaners," she said. "Try and keep them away."

"How?"

She was too busy to answer. The blue flame of her torch glowed and metal spat and ran. The police officers were nervous too. In my hand the weak grip of the survivor held fast.

The closest gleaner methodically sifted its way closer. They didn't seem that frightening on closer inspection. They were too obviously intelligent, I thought. Then the creature smelled blood close by and was transformed with a sudden rush of savagery. It leaped in among the lancing sharpness of glass and metal and tore things apart, pushing and driving its way forward with powerful hindquarters until the top half of its body had penetrated the pile. I could feel the shift of the whole mass as it worked, then heard the grind and champ of its jaws and snuffling.

The others abandoned their own searches, dropping the trinkets, and went barrelling in after it.

Valkyrie had the line. The hand in mine went suddenly slack. I squeezed. Nothing. "Skuld, I think it's too late."

She bent down beside me and a needle from her gauntlet slid into the soft, unprotected flesh. I was as appalled by this as by the entire Aerial's fall, the sight went right to my gut. Then there was a grunt by my ear. I turned and looked into the most massive set of teeth and got a wash of hot breath on my skin. At the same moment Skuld grabbed my arm and hauled me aside, at the same moment firing off a huge number of rounds.

The gleaner and its closest rival exploded in a frenzy of fur, bone and blood. The others howled and rushed in. Valkyrie shot them all, then half carried, half ran with me off the pile as yet more of them arrived, slinking in from side streets, running in. The hand I'd been holding, wondering who, feeling such hope, vanished in one of their mouths.

"Can't you stop them?" I whispered.

"Can't shoot them all," Skuld said, letting me go as another tile of Aelf came hurtling down and shattered. "Usually you only get a few at a time. Never seen this many at once and I want to keep some shells. Whoever's still in there has had it." She shrugged. "That's the way it is here. Worse now the Engine's running off and everyone's frightened. So much for the drill. Stay calm. Think happy thoughts. Keep everyone safe. How are you doing?"

"I'm fine," I said, feeling a wave of exhaustion that was almost strong enough to knock me off my feet.

It began to rain and this time there was no hail of bone, only saltwater rain.

Valkyrie said, "Let's risk the Aelf. It seems to have stabilized for now. Whatever happens, try not to overreact. It'll only feed the Engine. And don't do too much wondering. Keep it dull." She was almost cheerful.

I followed her lead, running to keep up with her huge strides. I heard awful sounds but didn't look back and didn't think about what they meant.

Aelf 2 was a fabulous structure, even in the early days of Sankhara when I first got here, but although its crystal and stone, wood and ivory were unsurpassably lovely, they had a sadness about them which was so well-known it was called the Elegy. You couldn't stand in its huge halls or towers without feeling the draw of the years. Some places were worse than others. Fortunately the Great Hall wasn't near Sweet Sorrow Falls or the Lost Histories Unit. But it was close enough. Only a few frightened people gathered here, hugging the walls and their Abacands, looking as though they expected to witness the end of civilization.

"Gothic crap," Valkyrie said with determined good cheer as we stood on the crystal floor amid the rainbow refraction of a billion charmed facets.

I felt a nudge on my arm and looked to find Damien at my elbow. "Thought you were dead," he murmured to me.

"Oh my god, I thought you were!" I hugged him and felt his narrow arms around me. Then the doors at the far end of the hall opened. Behind them a green darkness. All faces turned, not knowing what was coming, ready for almost anything. There was silence, then a faint sound of trumpets.

White horses came galloping through the gap, more than forty abreast, filling the doorway. They poured in a damburst of snorting, dark-eyed mayhem, straight down the length of the enormous room, and their hooves made high-pitched screaming sounds on the floor, striking silver sparks.

Two small figures in their way vanished without a trace. Everyone plastered themselves closer to the physical substance of the Aelf's walls and the horses came on wall to wall in a single tide. The building shook with their passage. They passed so close that I could see the detail of their white hair and the flow and dash of their tails. I reached out, sure I could touch them, and Damien's hand snatched mine back.

I looked across into Damien's face, seeing it made ugly by fear. "Very bad idea," he whispered. "Don't you know anything about anything? These are the white horses of the west." And then he glanced down and saw the single white hair between our fingers.

The swell and press of horse moved on, except for one animal, which had stopped and turned, impossibly, against the surge.

"What does that mean?" I asked.

"We're going to die after all," Damien said, surprised and disappointed.

The horse came to face us. Its brothers departed and left it alone there. When I looked at it I could see that the outer shape was a flimsy cover over the creature inside. It was not really a horse. It was shadow, contained in a shell. It blew through its nostrils and the one tiny hair lifted off our hands and fell away into the air. I thought Damien would let go and run for it, but he didn't. He held tighter to me instead.

I tried to be rational, hard enough at the best of times. "We can't die just for touching a horse. We didn't even. It was an accident."

"That's written on every dry bone in Sankhara," Damien

snorted. His knuckles hurt mine and he shook as the horse stepped forward, its proud head bending low, for all the world like it was going to drink from a puddle. It didn't even look particularly frightening.

"You could try running," Skuld said from behind me, putting her huge metal hand on my shoulder and giving me a push. "I'll cover you. Have faith." And she put herself between us and the shadow. I heard the sound of one of her weapons that spat light winding itself up.

I dragged Damien the first stride, then he picked up and ran faster than me, taking me up a path I would never have seen on my own—it was transparent and it ran up the side of the Aelf wall more like a decoration than a footpath. Behind us there was a snort and the high pitch of the energy weapon discharging. The crystal hallway lit up with a blaze of white light. It was blinding. I ran with my arm across my face, my arm pulled out of its socket, until there was nothing but running and pain.

"That was good," Damien said as he made me stop somewhere with cold wind on my face. "Won't stop it, but really piss it off. Can you see?"

I tried. "No. Nothing."

"You will." He seemed confident. "Never mind now. Just follow me."

We crossed open space. "Paving," he said intermittently. "Grass. Steps. Mind out. Duck this branch. Okay, cobbles. Shit."

"What!"

"It's locked. Can't be locked. Some bugger on the inside." He was hammering on a door.

He turned me to put my back to it and the door fell inward.

"Oh. Great." I followed him into another big interior, but this one felt much quieter and darker than Aelf 2. I heard him shut the door and we sat down on a soft, velvety seat of some kind and caught our breath.

"Fuck," I heard him whisper. "It's coming. Stay here. I'm going to look for other ways out." He let go of me.

"Damien?" Nothing. "Damien! Jalaeka!" I shouted. My voice

echoed back to me along stone galleries. From the cobblestones outside and the general journey I guessed that I was in the fabled Cathedral of Cadenza Piacere Greg had told me about. I could just make out bulky shadows amid a general afterimage that was faintly red.

"Shut up, girl!" hissed a man somewhere to my left. "Stay quiet and pray for good. Or you'll bring them all in on us."

I doubted the horse needed a sound. There was a splintering bang that resounded through the vaults. Hooves on wood.

I heard them muttering, whispers quickly spreading among many:

"It's her."

"Her and the elf. We were fine until they came."

"You should go back outside."

"You brought it. You go and take it away."

"Let's put her out."

"We'll take her out. It must be her Stuffie."

"Where did he go?"

"Has to be hers."

"No, we shouldn't. Look where we are. It won't make it."

"This is only a building . . ."

"No, wait. We really shouldn't. Look at her. Look at her face."

Even though I couldn't see enough to save myself, I stood up and stumbled away from them, hands out in front of me. I meant to find the wall, and then a door, either out or farther in, away from them. I tried to run.

"It's her."

"No it's not."

"It is!"

Then more and more excited voices joined the throng.

"She's in the window! She's the one!"

Someone sweaty and lightweight grabbed me around the shoulders. I struggled.

"Let's get the Jesus-freak out of here," Damien hissed in my ear.

"Wait a second," I said.

"What? They're crazy."

Blam. The splintering bashing noises got more insistent. I heard a silvery tinkling and thought—chandeliers.

"What am I doing in the window?"

"You . . . oh." He stopped. "You're in a big white dress and there's this sexy dark chick in a red dress lying across your lap looking dead. Didn't you come here when they had the tour on?"

"Dead?" I wrenched my hand free from his sticky grip. "What do you mean?"

"It's an old snow thing. The white and the red. Blood and ice. Or possibly semen. Depends on the interpretation you know. Primal fluids. Alchemy almost definitely. Sulphur and Mercury. Passion and Life. Possibly also death. Could be she isn't dead but poisoned or a sorceress simulating death or . . . we have to go."

"Let me go, you thick faery!" I screamed at him at the top of my lungs.

The door crashed in. I heard the clip clop of hooves coming steadily towards us.

I heard my voice echoing. Everyone held their breath but me. I felt an icy wind rip the marrow out of my bones, felt a chill like the end of all cold, the last sun-down in creation. It wasn't in the cathedral. It came from inside. I heard him talking to me, softly talking as if there was all the time in the world.

"It's not him," called a woman's voice cleanly out over the heads of the congregation. "It's *you*." I knew she meant Cadenza Fortitude the first time. Cadenza Piacere the second.

Now or never.

You'd better come back, I said to him, into the ice.

I turned to the white horse of the west and put Damien behind me. "You," I said to it, addressing its pale gleam and hoping that was really where it was. "Take your shedding flea-bit coat the hell out of my house."

There was no more cold. Only quiet. Deep quiet, and the sound of sirens.

I reached back for Damien's hand and held it tight.

It was a long night, and many long nights came after it, filled with the nightmares and the dreams the Engine left behind. On the fourth day Damien, along with every other Stuffie, vanished into thin air. He'd gone up to the roof to take his watch, but he never came back. Neither did the white horse.

After that things became harder, and more ordinary. Valkyrie and I spent our days scavenging and praying her ammunition wouldn't be needed, nor run out. We moved out of Piacere because it was full of people who wanted to worship me. We ran, and went to live in Damien's old place, in Low Aelf.

On the eighth day everyone who had treated with Unity in any way vanished. The only thing that stayed behind were the inert structures it had built and these, where they'd relied on any strange manipulation of matter, broke and fell apart.

Skuld had just said, "The sun's up. Let's go now, before too many other people get out. I think we could risk flying over to the South Shore. There may be houses over near the Dunes Park that haven't been touched. The power's still on in the south. There could be a lot of food."

I was relacing my boots more tightly, focused by a gnawing hunger, when I felt the stale air stir with a sound as though Skuld had sighed heavily. I looked up. I was alone.

61/JALAEKA

None of us has ever died. But we know the days and nights, the long hours of the suns, and all the things to do by light of moon and torch, flare, fire, bell, lamp, candle, phosphor light, flash of guns and death of stars.

*   *   *

Quick. Shake yourself. Pinch yourself. Wake up.

Those that are with me are of me. Those that are with me are of me.
   Those that are not with me are gone.
   Gone.

Spring-heeled Jack is coming. Quick. Wake up.

Hold my hand. You can't. I understand. Your hand is my hand.

I didn't mean it. Come back. Come back. Come back.

What is me belongs to you. Take it. Take. Close my hand.
   Dreaming of a promised land, dreaming.
   That the words meant something when he said, "Love conquers everything." When he said, "Love is the highest conscious aspiration." When he said, "If I have not love, then I am nothing." Well I had love and this is what it brought. All of them and their ideas of love tearing me apart to make again as old clothes are made again, as things unravelled get reknit into things similar and of better fit.
   The believers prayed. The summoners sat agape. Some ran away.
   All eaten and their bones below, turned over by curious fingers and counted, my treasure, my hoard, my wealth, come to my heart and build a cathedral there and let your voices fill the air, what say you all, what say you, what say you all lords and ladies?

*   *   *

Bring me my bow. It is twangy.

Bring me my arrows. Sharp, poisoned. Just the way I like 'em.

Bring me a glamorous chariot, something made by a reputable firm, not too showy, the kind that says I have not only taste and money but the sense to keep my vanity to myself. I don't want them to see me coming before I screw them for their lives.

Will it be parade day today? When all the old loves are set up like skittles, recriminations silent but at the ready, bayonets fixed. I'll slam the faces on those helmets shut so the mirrors turn upon them in the dark. I'll kiss them and beg at their knees. I'll tie their boot-laces together. They won't catch me.

Can a dog serve more than one master?

On either side of the equals sign the velvet river lies, the Styx, the Thames, the long, green wind of Saraswati. Searching out the level ground they lay their tresses all around and set fire to what the gods must have. Fat and bones for the fools: fat and broken bones and 36B, inboard metabolic component number 93, hair colour from the "Honey Autumn" range—we gave her enough intelligence to gain a Ph.D., Mrs. Bequerel, just as you asked, and the artistic component "Sylvia," and the feminine quotient called "Eugenie," which is reasonably close to the masculine mean, more than for a girl's girl like those common "CharityFaithHopeAngel" types, laugh along with me, madam, we know their sort—and eyes designed by the brilliant Islamic artist who puts the flaw in where you can spend a lifetime looking for it or see it straightaway, your protection against the wrath of jealous gods.

In the bone cathedral the choir is singing. Incense like water and we are all out of the body and the blood, you'll have to go elsewhere, down the road, for that kind of thing. I can't save you. You can't save me. There is no ever after.

Up, up get up it's already late.

62/FRANCINE

Rita and I sat on the beach. In our rag clothing and with our brown arms we looked like pirate castaways, but there was never any Jolly Roger on the horizon for us, and we'd stopped looking for it months ago.

We were digging for razor clams. We had quite a few collected in an orange kids' plastic bucket, but we needed more.

"It has to be today," Rita said confidently, even though the last hour had added only a few hundred to the total. "Can't be many more to make some mind up. Let's try farther along this way."

The crater and scatter of the Engine's violent departure made rings of debris by which we measured our position. We were down below the high tide mark, in Chunky. Rita pointed to the damp sand of Small Chunky and I followed her down there. She was the decisive one. I'd learned to like following her.

"Hey!" a voice shouted out from far behind us.

We both spun around. I dropped the bucket. In the first instants I struggled not to get up hope.

"Francine!" the voice hollered, and I saw a man standing on the boardwalk where it stopped being orderly and became a splintered and broken mass of old planks. He jumped over the rail on the sand and began to run around Big Chunky towards us. His hair was a chestnut mass, his clothing dishevelled, his movements strangely exhilarated.

As he came forward the dead palms at the back of the board-walk with their sand-blown leaves grew supple and green. The city shivered and burst back to life. A group of sparrows in flight exploded into existence a few yards away and scattered for the bushes of the high dunes behind us.

I ran out to meet him. The last time I'd seen him—he wasn't even him. But this was. Exactly.

Greg picked me up and spun me round. "What is it with you and this beach?"

I couldn't speak. I just clung to him and when he set me down I jumped about on the sand. "What happened? Where's Jalaeka?" I couldn't stop staring at him and the sudden riot of living action that Sankhara had become, as though it had never stopped, except for the crater of Engine House.

My Abacand woke itself up and said, "SankhaGuide's back. Says we're reconnected to Solar Earth, time-lines converging. Gateway's under Solar control but should soon reopen for business. Hmm. Looks like Metatron's got some strange new thing going on—I'll get back to you on that . . ."

Rita and Greg introduced themselves.

"Not everybody's back," Greg said. "Some didn't want to. And a lot—of the Stuff things that used to live here—they didn't get to. 'S'not exactly a democracy in there."

Rita frowned at him. "No, I can see that."

"Skuld?" I asked him hopefully. "Damien?"

"I don't know." He grinned. "Isn't that fantastic? I *don't* know! I'd have to really, really try to find out!"

"So, you know, is Jalaeka back?" I looked past him, towards the boardwalk.

"Francie." Greg caught my arm. His face went very serious.

"What?" I thought I didn't want to hear this.

"Did you let him go?"

"Of course I did. I mean, I got your letter but then he was talking to me and I thought I didn't have to . . . why?"

"I think that Greg's trying to point out that he isn't here,"

Rita said in a voice carefully balanced to be diplomatic, although it ended on a rising tone that suggested she was trying to break the bad news to me. I saw her look right through me, suppressing a smile.

Two gentle hands covered my eyes. "Gotcha. Guess who?"

About the Author

Justina Robson was born and brought up in Leeds. She studied philosophy and linguistics before settling down to write in 1992. Her earlier novels, *Silver Screen* (1999) and *Mappa Mundi* (2001), were both short-listed for the Arthur C. Clarke Award.